Sex, m
Some peo
nothing

Robyn Prescott: Eager to begin anew, her All-American beauty—ash-blond hair, emerald-green eyes, perfect, glowing skin—leads her to an exciting life of riches, love—and danger . . .

Scott Kendall: When the handsome, charismatic head of Wellington Cosmetics selects Robyn to represent his company, it is his one chance to save his father's precious legacy . . .

Georgina Kendall Richards: Replaced by Robyn as Wellington's Fresh and Lovely Girl, tormented by her husband's blatant infidelities, she drowns her pain in liquor, her bitterness growing until she is pushed too far . . .

Beverly Maxwell: Determined to reclaim Scott as her lover, Beverly will go to any length to get Robyn out of his life—forever . . .

Lance Richards: Exploiting his good looks and influence as a top fashion photographer, Lance beds some of the sexiest women in New York—whether they are willing or not . . .

Kristen Adams: Beneath her bubbly, sassy exterior, Kristen longs for love. When she realizes the mistake of giving her heart to Lance Richards, it's too late . . .

Erica Shelton: As the object of one man's obsession, her perfect world turns into a nightmare that results in murder . . .

Once Innocent

Jessica Gregory

POCKET BOOKS
New York London Toronto Sydney Tokyo Singapore

This book is a work of fiction. Names, characters, places and incidents are either the product of the author's imagination or are used fictitiously. Any resemblance to actual events or locales or persons, living or dead, is entirely coincidental.

An *Original* Publication of POCKET BOOKS

POCKET BOOKS, a division of Simon & Schuster Inc.
1230 Avenue of the Americas, New York, NY 10020

ISBN: 0-671-69554-1

First Pocket Books printing July 1991

10 9 8 7 6 5 4 3 2 1

POCKET and colophon are registered trademarks of Simon & Schuster Inc.

Cover photo by Jim Galante Studio

Printed in the U.S.A.

Acknowledgments

Special thanks to my family and friends who took the time to take a look at *Once Innocent* in its various stages. The support and encouragement was much appreciated!

And special thanks to my editor, Gina Centrello, for giving me a chance.

Prologue

New York
February 1990

Robyn Prescott stared into the full-length mirror, pleased with the image of herself. On her face was a mixture of awe and joy. Was that really her in the mirror or was it someone else? She still couldn't believe what she was seeing.

The day she had dreamed of for so long had finally arrived. Today was her wedding day. In a few minutes she would be walking down the aisle into the arms of the man she loved.

Her wedding gown was made of silk satin and silk tulle. The bodice was embroidered with seed pearls, crystal drops, and chalk bugle beads, while the skirt was overlaid with Chantilly lace. The headpiece was a coronet of seed pearls and diamonds from which flowed a twenty-five-foot veil.

Robyn's fingers traced the delicacy of the materials she wore. She still couldn't believe the beauty and extravagance of her gown. She had always envisioned what her wedding gown would look like, but her dreams paled by comparison.

She reached for her bouquet, holding forth an arrangement of miniature pink, white, and yellow roses. Turning again to the mirror, she admired the full effect. Perfect.

Never before had Robyn been so happy. And she owed it all to the man waiting for her outside at the altar of St.

Patrick's Cathedral. When she had finally allowed herself to trust someone again, love had reentered her heart, restoring her faith in an emotion she had long ago abandoned. After all the years of suffering and heartache, she had finally found her happy ending.

The door behind her opened. Robyn turned, expecting to greet yet another well-wisher before the ceremony.

It was a woman dressed in black. On her head was a wide-brimmed hat accompanied by a black veil. A fleeting thought was ushered through Robyn's mind. Wasn't it against tradition to wear black to a wedding? Wasn't it supposed to bring bad luck?

She tried to get a look at the woman's face in the hopes of recognizing her, but the hat and veil masked her features. In addition, the woman kept twisting her face away from Robyn's prying eyes, as though fearful of being recognized.

"Excuse me, but do I know you?" Robyn asked.

"Did you think I'd let your wedding day go by without giving you my best regards?"

The woman's voice was low and harsh. Her tone wasn't what Robyn had expected and she tried to keep a smile on her face as she took a tentative step forward. There was no reason to be rude, but for some reason she didn't like the idea of being alone with this woman.

"That's very sweet, but the ceremony is about to begin. Let's talk after the ceremony?"

"By then it will be too late."

There was something dreadfully familiar about this woman. Robyn's instincts immediately went on alert. She stared at her, searching for some factor of recognition. Something was wrong.

"I'm sorry, but I can't seem to recall your name," Robyn apologized, drawing closer. With each step she took forward the woman drew away, until she was pressed against the door she had come through. "We have met before, haven't we?"

They were standing inches apart and Robyn still couldn't place her. Who was this woman and what did she want on today of all days? Robyn was tempted to pull away both hat and veil, but before she could act, the woman spoke.

"Forgotten me already? After everything we've been through?" Her voice became mangled with hatred. "After everything you've done to me? You took away everything that was rightfully mine! You deserve to die for what you've done to me!"

Suddenly the connection was made, and Robyn's eyes widened in horror. This couldn't be happening. She had been assured that it was all over. She had been promised that she no longer had anything to fear.

The woman reached into her handbag, removed a gun, and slowly twisted a silencer into place. "I believe a gift should have a personal touch, don't you?" She lifted the gun, aiming it at Robyn. "I've had the bullets engraved with your initials."

Robyn's mind scrambled for some means of escape. Outside in the church she could hear the organist begin the wedding march. At the sound of the music Robyn's eyes welled with tears. She was supposed to be out there. She had come so far. She couldn't lose the man she loved.

"I've waited so long for this moment," the woman rasped. "I've hated you from the moment you entered my life. I've always wanted you dead." The gun was leveled at Robyn's heart. "Looks like my wish is about to come true."

Just then there was a knock at the door. The woman turned in surprise, startled by the unexpected interruption. Robyn took advantage of the distraction, throwing her bouquet in the woman's face.

"Help!" Robyn screamed.

"Robyn? My God, what's happening?" a male voice cried in alarm.

As the door opened, Robyn tried to throw herself against it. "Stay out! Call the police!" She couldn't let the man she loved place his life in jeopardy.

Although the woman had been momentarily thrown off guard, she immediately regained her composure. She pulled Robyn away from the door with a vicious yank, savagely shoving her against the wall. Robyn crashed to the floor, desperately trying to get back on her feet.

"I'm not going to fail again," the woman promised with a maniacal laugh, closing in on Robyn. "I really want you to suffer. Killing you might give me some personal satisfaction, but killing the man you love will make the rest of your life a living hell. Watch your lover die!"

The door crashed open and the woman whirled around with her gun, preparing to shoot.

"No!" Robyn screamed in anguish, watching as the woman was tackled to the floor and the first shot went off. Robyn pulled herself off the floor, rushing to come between them. Both figures were still struggling. Robyn fought furiously for the woman's gun, trying to remove it from her grasp.

There came the sound of a second gunshot, and Robyn was thrown back against the wall. As she slumped to the floor she noticed a pool of blood increasing in size. She had been shot. Darkness began to close in. Flooded with memories from the past, Robyn fought to keep her eyes open. She didn't want to remember the past. She wanted to see the man she loved—the man she had intended to marry. She needed to see him one last time. But both his image and voice faded as the darkness grew and she was returned to the past she had tried so hard to escape.

— BOOK ONE —

Chicago
June 1988

1

"Who am I?"

The beautiful young woman stared at her image in the mirror. Shoulder length ash-blond hair framed her face in silky, cascading waves. Emerald-green eyes sprinkled with flecks of gold and fringed with thick, dark lashes sparkled with determination and intensity. Lips, firm and sensual, displayed perfect white teeth whenever she smiled. The smoothness of her skin and the natural blush on her high sculpted cheeks hardly made makeup necessary.

Her long shapely legs, firm breasts, and slim waist always managed to capture men's glances. She was every man's fantasy and every woman's envy. Those passing twenty-one-year-old Robyn Prescott on the street would think she had it all. What more did one need beyond beauty and youth? Yet Robyn Prescott did *not* have it all. Despite her beauty, Robyn was burdened by frustrations and problems she could not easily solve.

"Who am I?" she again demanded of her image, searching her mind for the slightest clue that would unlock her past and restore her lost identity.

Robyn Prescott didn't know who she was or where she

was from. No matter how hard she tried, she couldn't remember a thing.

She had been hit by a car and had been in a coma for six months. The doctors thought she wouldn't make it because of her extensive internal injuries. There had been no witnesses to her accident except the driver of the car that had hit her. He said she had run blindly into the street. Who had she been running from?

Three months ago she had awoken from her coma. The doctors thought she would be able to fill in the blanks. She hadn't. All she had been able to provide was her name and age. Nothing more. The doctors told her to concentrate only on getting well. The amnesia was only temporary. Eventually the pieces would all fall into place.

They didn't.

After regaining consciousness, the police had been contacted about her again. Yet no one was looking for her and she still wasn't listed as missing. It was as if she had never existed.

There were other pieces to the puzzle, but trying to put them together proved meaningless. She had been wearing a tight red leather miniskirt, leopard print bra with beads and fringe, black seamed stockings and stiletto heels. Hardly tasteful attire. Why had she been wearing such an outfit?

As the weeks went by and she still remembered nothing, she became increasingly frantic. Then Dr. Quinn Marler entered the scene. He was a handsome psychiatrist in his late twenties with jet-black hair and dazzling blue eyes. His quick wit and easy smile always put Robyn at ease and made her look forward to their twice-weekly sessions.

Dr. Marler advised her to take one step at a time. He said her amnesia was blocking out a painful past she didn't want to remember. His theory was that something traumatic had happened and her conscious mind was unable to deal with it. The secrets of her past were buried deep within her subconscious. He warned her that the search could prove long, hard, and meaningless. She might never remember her past.

As their sessions continued, Dr. Marler started suggesting that perhaps it would be best if she concentrated on building a new life. They weren't making any progress. There had to be a reason why her mind was so adamantly refusing to let her remember.

Robyn always refused Dr. Marler's suggestion, believing she couldn't go forward with her life until she remembered her past and put it behind her.

Yet recently, late at night and unable to sleep, she began seriously contemplating Dr. Marler's advice. She had been given a second chance when she had come out of her coma. Why was she wasting so much of her time trying to regain a life she couldn't remember? She should be building a new life for herself. She was realistic enough to realize that her current situation wasn't going to get her anywhere.

After her release from the hospital two months earlier, she found a job and an apartment. Both were not the greatest. She was living on the fringes of Hyde Park, too close to the South Side for comfort. Her job at the hospital laundry was exhausting. Long hard hours were spent working in grueling steam while her hands became red and chapped from daily contact with hot water and harsh detergent.

Weekends were lonely. She had no friends. The only important person in her life was Quinn. Even though he had given her his home phone number and insisted she call at any time, she refrained. She wasn't a child who needed to have her hand held because she was afraid of being alone. She wouldn't allow herself to impose on Quinn's kindness. He had already done so much for her.

Her sessions with him were free, and sometimes he gave her checks, knowing she wasn't making much at the laundry. The first time she had tried turning down a check he had been offended.

"Robyn, I have plenty of money. My session fees are ridiculously high, and most of my patients have inconsequential problems. They come to me because it's the *chic* thing to do. Be careful I don't charge you." His blue eyes twinkled with humor. "Seriously, I want to help you however I can."

She grudgingly accepted the first check offered but refused the next. When it came time to pay her monthly rent, she discovered Quinn had already done so. Groceries were delivered to the apartment, miraculously prepaid. And one Saturday Quinn took her clothes shopping, insisting she replace the drab secondhand clothing the hospital had given her.

If the truth had to be known, Robyn liked the attention Quinn was lavishing on her. It was reassuring to know Quinn was hovering in the background, ready to step forward if she needed his assistance. All she had to do was ask. The only problem, she felt, was that she was becoming too dependent on him. Just as she was keeping herself chained to her past, so she was becoming chained to Quinn. Right now they were just friends. Quinn had never indicated that he wanted more than a friendship. She was afraid her feelings for him would change if she wasn't careful. More and more she found herself wondering what Quinn's embrace would feel like. How would it feel to stare into his gorgeous blue eyes as his lips descended on hers? Robyn was afraid she was falling in love, and she was scared. Something inside her refused to let her acknowledge her feelings for him. She *wouldn't* let herself fall in love with him.

It was somehow connected to her past.

She had to leave Chicago and start fresh somewhere else. Thanks to Quinn's assistance and her own weekly paychecks, she had managed to save some money. She had close to three thousand dollars. It would have to do.

"Who am I?" she asked again of her reflection.

"Talking to yourself?"

Robyn turned from the mirror to Quinn, a smile on her face. "Right on time."

"You look lovely today."

Robyn, dressed in an olive shirt dress with padded shoulders, blushed at the compliment. Sitting herself before Quinn's solid oak desk, she tossed her hair over one shoulder, brushing it with her fingers. "Thanks. Ready to begin?"

Quinn settled himself behind his desk, gold pen and pad ready. "You seem quite chipper today. Do you have some good news?"

Robyn thought he looked extremely handsome in his charcoal-gray suit. Onyx cuff links glittered on his shirt cuffs, and his silk tie was a bold splash of color against his white Oxford shirt. She could smell the distinctive scent of his cologne. He had mentioned the name once. Drakkar. She loved the smell of it. His face was freshly shaven, bronzed from a morning on the tennis court. Quinn played on the days they met. At one point he had offered to give her lessons, but she had graciously refused. Dr. Quinn Marler lived in an entirely different world from hers. His was a world of privilege, wealth, and status.

She remembered how awed she'd been the first time she had visited his office. It was decorated with only the best that money could buy. Rich leathers, dark woods, plush carpets, solid brass, and original paintings all combined to give a look of airiness, substance, and taste.

"Tell me your news," Quinn urged, shaking Robyn from her thoughts. "I'm dying of curiousity."

Telling him was going to be even harder than she thought. She avoided his gaze and took a deep breath. "I'm leaving Chicago. Tomorrow."

"A trip sounds wonderful. It'll do you some good to get away. Where are you going? How long will you be gone?" He reached for his appointment book. "Will I have to reschedule you next week?"

"Quinn, you don't understand," she gently interrupted. "I'm leaving Chicago for good."

He was stunned. "You can't be serious."

Robyn slowly nodded her head. "I am."

"Where are you going?" he asked again.

"New York."

"Why New York? Why leave Chicago at all?"

"I have to do this. I have to start a new life, and I can't do it in Chicago. There are too many ghosts and too many things I can't put my finger on."

"Like?" he prodded.

Robyn shifted uncomfortably in her seat. "If I tell you, you'll think I'm being paranoid."

"I won't know unless you tell me."

"Lately I've felt as though someone has been watching me."

"Watching you?"

"On my way to work. On my way home." She shivered. "Sometimes I get phone calls in the middle of the night.

When I pick up, no one answers at the other end. I only hear breathing. Whoever it is hangs up after hearing my voice. It's scaring me, Quinn."

"It's that damned neighborhood you live in. I never should have allowed you to move there. We'll get you a new place."

"Quinn, I can't and won't keep letting you be my crutch," she adamantly insisted. "I've got to make it on my own. Having you around has been wonderful, but I have to learn how to depend on myself. Can't you understand what I'm saying?"

Quinn sighed. "I do. What are you going to do in New York?"

"I don't know. I'll figure it out when I get there."

Quinn leaned forward, asking with concern, "What about your past?"

"What about it?" She lightly tapped the side of her forehead. "It's all in here. It'll all be coming to New York. Like you always said, the littlest thing could set off a flood of memories, or they could stay locked away forever. We'll see what happens."

"You sound pretty determined," Quinn conceded.

"I am."

"Promise to keep in touch?"

Until that moment Robyn hadn't realized how much she would miss him. Quinn had been her rock, and now she was setting herself free. She gave him a brave smile. "We're friends, aren't we? Friends always keep in touch."

Quinn started to say something, but then reached for his checkbook. "Right. Friends. Let me write you a final check."

"Quinn, don't!" she protested. "You've already done enough."

"You're still on home turf, so your guardian angel still has certain rights." He wrote out a check and handed it to her. "This should tide you over for a while."

Robyn read the amount and her eyes widened with disbelief. "Five thousand dollars! I can't accept this."

"You can and you will," Quinn firmly stated, placing the check back in her hand.

Was it her imagination or was he holding onto her hand

longer than necessary? Stop it! she chided herself. You're letting your imagination run away with you.

Quinn draped his arm around her shoulders, leading her to his office door. "You're going to let me take you out to a farewell dinner, aren't you?"

Did she dare? She gave him a quick peck on his cheek before rushing out of his office. "Deal! Pick me up at seven."

Quinn arrived at her apartment promptly at seven, presenting her with a single white rose.

"Have a vase you can put this in?" he asked.

Robyn surveyed her empty apartment. All her belongings were packed. She'd take the rose along since it was too pretty to leave behind.

"Just like you," Quinn replied with a smile. "Listen, why bother coming back after dinner?"

Robyn pointed to her suitcases. "There's the matter of my luggage."

"Why not leave your suitcases in my car? They're going to wind up there anyway."

"They are?"

"Sure. I'm giving you a ride to O'Hare in the morning."

"What if I need something when I'm getting ready for bed?"

"Didn't I tell you? You're spending the night at my place."

Robyn gave him an open stare. "I am?"

"I don't like the idea of you being here alone, especially after what you told me this afternoon. How about it?"

Robyn silently agreed with his suggestion. She didn't want to worry him, but that afternoon she had gotten another phone call. No one had spoken. But whoever it was had been listening. The thought of being alone tonight didn't appeal to her. Spending the night with Quinn conjured up an image of safety. "Thanks for the invite. I accept. Where will I stay?"

"I had the guest room all prepared." Quinn moved around her, picking up her suitcases. "Ready to shake this joint?"

Robyn followed after him without hesitation, shutting off the lights and scurrying from the darkness. "Am I ever."

* * *

They went to Water Tower Place to have dinner at the Ritz Carlton. The grandeur and luxury of the restaurant was intimidating to Robyn, but there wasn't a doubt that Quinn belonged. As they were led to their table he met a variety of familiar faces and stopped to chat for a few seconds. All the people he spoke with were extremely wealthy. The men wore finely tailored suits, while the women were draped in fine silks and jewels. Robyn felt conspicuously out of place in her aquamarine knit dress. Once they were at their table she buried her nose in her menu. The prices were outrageous and every dish sounded extremely complicated. She looked to Quinn for guidance.

"Don't worry," he said. "I'll order." He turned to their waiter, ordering with authority and knowledge.

The dishes were the most delicious Robyn could ever remember having. They started with fresh New Zealand mussels and eggplant slivers with shrimp and scallops. They then sampled an exquisitely tender duckling with ginger cassis and wild mushrooms, roasted with thyme and wild garlic cloves. A fine selection of wines, from white to Burgundy, accompanied each dish. For dessert Quinn ordered frozen chocolate soufflé with burnt almond sauce. Robyn decided to indulge on peach Charlotte with caramel sauce.

Their conversation flowed freely, as it always did, and the privacy of their table intensified the intimacy that had been building between them. Robyn found herself studying Quinn's face, and couldn't help noticing that his hand kept brushing against hers. Deliberate or accidental? The slightest touch of his skin against hers generated tingles. She allowed herself to enjoy the way she was feeling. Tonight was her last night in Chicago; her last time with Quinn. Who knew when she would see him again? There was no harm in creating new memories.

Toward the end of their evening her mind started to wander. She tried to concentrate on Quinn's words and laugh at his jokes, but she kept wondering about what would happen once they returned to his apartment.

She knew the guest room would be waiting. Quinn would never lie to her. But would she be spending the night there? Did she want to? Or would she wind up in Quinn's bed and in his arms, where with each passing minute she found herself more and more longing to be?

All too soon they left the restaurant. Quinn was the perfect gentleman, assisting her into the butter-soft interior of his champagne-colored Porsche. The ride to his apartment on Lake Shore Drive was smooth and quick.

Quinn's apartment revealed a combination of richness and comfort that put her at ease. While admiring his stereo system, Robyn was surprised to discover Quinn had an extensive jazz collection.

"I didn't know you liked jazz," she said.

"There are a lot of things you don't know about me."

Surveying the rest of the apartment, Robyn had to agree. Bookshelves were crammed with thrillers and mysteries. His video collection consisted of a number of black and white classics. There was a personal gym with an impressive selection of weights and barbells. Robyn wondered how well-proportioned Quinn was under his clothes, but chased the thought away, switching to more serious ones.

For the first time she realized she didn't really know Quinn. There was another side to him. Why hadn't she found it before? Had she been too wrapped up in herself, or had he chosen to keep part of himself hidden?

"Would you like a nightcap?" he asked from the bar.

She declined, turning her attention back out the window and on Lake Michigan. The water was so calm this evening. Why wasn't it matching the inner turmoil she was experiencing?

"Lovely view, don't you think?" Quinn slipped behind her, placing his hands on her shoulders. He drew her closer, pressing her against his chest. Quinn buried his lips in her hair before moving them down to her neck. He started kissing her. Robyn started to respond, then Quinn's hands moved down from her shoulders to her breasts. Although she didn't mean to, she moved away from him, pulling herself free from the closeness he was initiating, ignoring her awakened desires and feelings.

Quinn didn't say a word. He only waited. Robyn was torn. She didn't know what to do. Part of her yearned for Quinn's touch; wanted it desperately. But her mind kept screaming at her: *No! Don't do it! Don't trust him! He'll only hurt you!*

Why was she experiencing such a conflicting range of emotions? Why was she so afraid to allow herself to be loved? Did she believe that she wouldn't be able to fit into Quinn's world? Would she always feel as if she didn't belong? Would Quinn tire of her and toss her aside, just like . . .

Robyn racked her brain. There had been a name! A name she had almost remembered—someone from her past. A man who had hurt her. What had he done to her that made her so afraid to trust Quinn? Would she feel this way with any man she started to care about?

She knew Quinn would never hurt her. He wouldn't. Yet she wasn't ready to totally trust someone with her heart. She and Quinn were only friends. There was so much they didn't know about each other, and if she followed her feelings, if she allowed herself to step back into Quinn's arms, there was a strong possibility that she wouldn't be on a plane to New York tomorrow.

She couldn't give up her new start.

"I could stand here all night looking out this window, but if I did, I wouldn't be able to wake up in the morning." She looked at Quinn over her shoulder. "Could you tell me where the guest room is?"

"Last door at the end of the hall. The bed has already been turned down."

Robyn headed toward the hall. "See you in the morning."

"See you in the morning," Quinn wistfully replied.

Robyn's plane was scheduled for departure at ten. She and Quinn had a tender farewell.

"You came into my life as a mystery, and now you're leaving as a mystery. Will I ever learn who the real Robyn Prescott is?"

"Someday," she vowed. "As soon as I find out who she is, I'll make sure you're the first to know."

"I want to apologize for last night," Quinn said. "I shouldn't have made such a move. I'm sorry."

"What's there to be sorry for? You were gentle, warm, and loving. Part of me liked the way you made me feel. Another part of me, the part that's locked into my past, didn't.

Unfortunately, that part is stronger and still has a hold on my life."

"Let me help you, Robyn," Quinn implored, taking her hands in his. "Let me teach you how to love again."

"Learning to love and building a relationship takes trust. Along with my lost memory, it's not something I've been able to easily regain. At least not yet. I'm going to have to learn how to trust again."

"Learn with me."

Robyn didn't know what else to say. She *couldn't* stay in Chicago anymore. "Quinn, I don't want to hurt you. Let me get on with my life in my own way. Maybe there's still a chance for us. Right now I can't give you an answer. I can't tell you what you want to hear."

"You're not coming back," he stated matter-of-factly.

Robyn looked at him in puzzlement. "Why would you say such a thing?"

"You're building a new life, and I'm being left behind."

"Quinn, you'll always be a dear friend."

He brushed a hand across her cheek. "But nothing more."

Robyn took Quinn's hand in hers, giving it a gentle squeeze. She gave him a farewell kiss. "Nothing less," she firmly promised.

Tiffany Hunt was getting ready for work. She slipped into a tight tube of black spandex. The stretchy material snugly hugged her sleek curves and ample bosom. She wore no bra and succeeded in jiggling whenever she walked. Next came the sheer stockings and white anklet socks trimmed with lace. She wore candy-red high heels and a strand of gold around her ankle.

Blond curls were artfully arranged with a selection of bows and ribbons. Cherub cheeks and pouty lips were darkened with the reddest of rouge and lipstick. Her eyes, two narrow slits of coal shining with meanness, were heavily mascaraed.

Tiffany admired her completed handiwork. Totally enticing. She sprayed a rich, musky perfume between her breasts, beneath her wrists and behind her ears. The scent was guaranteed to send male noses twitching. Once they got a look at the package the scent was wafting from, they were hooked. All Tiffany had to do then was bat her eyelashes, crook a finger, whisper a few meaningless bits of conversation, and then name her price.

Tiffany was a very successful prostitute. The only problem was, she hated being such a success.

Tiffany Hunt was living her life on the run. In the past eleven months she had worked in New York, New Orleans, Miami, and Houston, never staying in any city for very long. She used aliases, and kept her ears open for word on the streets.

Vaughn Chandler was after her. She had crossed him. Tiffany was constantly looking over her shoulder, fearing she would come face to face with Vaughn's brutal violence again. He wouldn't stop pursuing her. Not until he found her. Not until he made her pay for her betrayal.

Not until he killed her.

Now she was back home in Chicago, the last place she ought to be, and she was angry. Very angry.

Robyn Prescott was no longer in a coma.

When Tiffany had returned to Chicago last month, the first thing she had done was call Robyn's hospital, hoping to hear the little bitch was dead and buried. She hadn't been prepared to hear Robyn was alive and well, starting a new life. Keeping herself well hidden, Tiffany started watching Robyn. Then came the phone calls. The first time Tiffany heard Robyn's voice, she freaked, smashing the receiver down with such force that she broke the phone.

The unfairness of it all! Here she was living a life in shadow while Robyn got a second chance.

How she hated Robyn Prescott!

Thoughts of Robyn reignited Tiffany's anger. Striding across her motel bedroom, a gaudy room in garish colors and cheap fabrics, she seized her newly installed phone, dialing Robyn's number. She loved hearing the fear in Robyn's voice.

When the ringing stopped, an unfamiliar voice answered. Tiffany cleared her throat. "May I please speak to Robyn?"

"Robyn doesn't live here anymore. I'm the landlord. You interested in an apartment?"

"Where is she?" Tiffany demanded.

"I don't know. She said she was moving out of state."

Tiffany slammed down the receiver in frustration. Robyn couldn't be gone. She couldn't! She hadn't had her revenge!

Tiffany forced herself to remain calm. At the moment the most important thing was keeping herself out of Vaughn's clutches. She had already been careless, spending too much time in Chicago and preoccupying herself with Robyn. She hadn't been watching her back. It was time to move on. Robyn could wait for another day. Even if she crossed paths with Vaughn, she had a bargaining chip. How would Vaughn react to the news that Robyn was no longer in a coma?

Deciding to make a few last dollars before leaving Chicago that day, Tiffany put the finishing touches on her appearance.

"Run, Robyn," she whispered in the motel room silence. "Run as fast as you possibly can. You'll never get away. Never. I know all your darkest secrets, and one day, when you've got it all and you least expect it, I'll make sure those secrets come back to haunt you.

"Oh yes." She laughed gleefully, glossing her lips. "I promise."

— BOOK TWO —

New York
June 1988–
November 1989

2

Robyn stood motionless in the center of Kennedy Airport with crowds of travelers milling around her, realizing she didn't know what her next step should be. She was in a strange city with no place to go. Immediately she started to have regrets. What had she done? Why had she left Chicago? Why had she left Quinn and the one place where she had had at least some sense of security?

The reasons sprang to mind immediately, and with each one Robyn knew she had made the right decision. Not one to brood for long, she walked with a determined stride toward the array of waiting taxis.

Robyn began planning as her taxi headed into Manhattan. The first thing she had to do was find a temporary place to stay, then a job.

"Excuse me," she asked the taxi driver. "Do you know of any hotels with reasonable rates?"

"How reasonable?"

Even though Robyn had an ample supply of cash, she knew her funds wouldn't last forever. She couldn't spend all her money on a hotel room, and had decided on the plane that she would have to stick to a budget. Although she hoped to find a job immediately, she knew it would be some time before she did. Once she found a job, she would be able to settle into an apartment, putting down a security deposit and at least one month's rent. In the meantime she still had to eat and take care of other miscellaneous expenses. She'd have to keep careful count of her dollars.

"I haven't got much money and need to find a job," Robyn alluded, not wanting to give out too many specifics. "Can you recommend anyplace?"

"If you want, I can cruise by a few places and let you take a look. The neighborhoods aren't the greatest, though."

Robyn settled back in her seat. "As long as the price is right, I promise not to be picky."

She felt like she was back at square one as the taxi took off, leaving her on the corner of Twenty-third Street and Eighth Avenue. The neighborhood was hardly desirable, but it was no worse than where she had been living in Chicago.

Robyn choked back her desperation, resolving not to cry. The situation was only temporary. She had to look at things realistically. She couldn't spend all her money on a room she would probably only use a few hours a night. If she settled for a hotel in midtown, all her money would disappear. But if she stayed here, her funds would last longer. Besides, during the day she would be job hunting. She'd be away from this place, and once she found a job, would never have to come back.

Deciding to start as soon as possible, Robyn went to the nearest newsstand and bought copies of all the daily papers. With her suitcases in hand and the newspapers under her arms, she stoically climbed the steps of the hotel.

A musty scent assaulted her nostrils as she entered the darkened lobby. Although it was only two o'clock and the sun still shining, there wasn't a golden ray of sunshine to be found inside the musty lobby. The windows were filthy, caked with years of grime and grease. The rugs were tattered and torn, the furniture chipped and scarred.

She rang the rusted bell on the front desk once. Then twice. No one came. Robyn placed her things on the floor, leaning across the desk gingerly. "Hello? Is anyone here? I'd like to rent a room."

A woman with gray-streaked hair emerged from the back office. She eyed Robyn suspiciously. "Whaddya want?"

"I'd like to rent a room."

"For how long?" the woman demanded.

Robyn was taken aback by the caustic tone. "I don't know. Maybe a month."

"Got anyone with you?"

Robyn shook her head. "I'm alone."

"Ya sure?"

"I'm alone," she repeated.

The woman reached for a key, sliding it across the desk. "Rates are fifteen dollars a night. I expect cash in advance, payable before three, otherwise your stuff goes out on the street." A greedy hand was held out. "First payment, please."

Robyn handed over the twenty-dollar bill she had removed from her purse earlier.

The woman headed toward the back, returning with a five-dollar bill. "What's a girl like you doing in a place like this?" she asked.

"Trying to survive," Robyn answered. "Just trying to survive."

The stairway and corridors were poorly lit and Robyn clutched her suitcases fiercely, heart in her throat as she climbed up the stairs, edging her way around the people in her path. Every time she turned her head, a new pair of eyes was studying her. She ignored them, afraid to make eye contact; afraid the fear she felt would show.

When she reached her room on the fourth floor, she opened the door with a trembling hand, immediately locking it behind her and wedging a chair underneath the doorknob.

I will not cry! she vowed. I will not cry! Carrying her suitcases to the bed, she began transferring garments from suitcase to closet and drawers without thought. Soon, though, the exhaustion from her trip caught up with her. Pushing her suitcases to one side, Robyn collapsed upon the stained bedspread, hugging a pillow to her chest.

Thoughts ran rampant in her mind as sounds filtered through the paper-thin walls. What am I doing here? she asked herself in a moment of anguish. This isn't where I want to be. She hugged the pillow tighter, curling herself into a ball. Why does all this feel so familiar? Why do I feel like there's a connection between the lives around me and the life I used to lead?

Quinn's face floated before her eyes. Robyn remembered passing a phone booth out in the hallway. She was sorely tempted to call Quinn for a pep talk. She fought the urge. She had vowed not to call him until she had settled herself into her new life. Before she could prove to Quinn that she would be able to make it, she would have to prove it to herself.

Sleep started to overcome her. As Robyn struggled to keep her fluttering eyelids open, she asked herself one last question: Am I going to make it?

Nine weeks later Robyn was still at the hotel, discovering that job hunting in New York wasn't as easy as she had imagined. The few secretarial skills she had were useless in an age of word processors. Her high hopes quickly dissipated as she went from one interview to another.

Money was another problem. No matter how little she spent, she found that her funds were quickly diminishing. She still hadn't cashed Quinn's check and was relying solely on her savings. She had wanted to be able to return Quinn's check, yet it looked like she might have to cash it soon. To conserve her resources, Robyn stopped eating in restaurants and started preparing her own meals. She shopped at delis and grocery stores, fixing herself sandwiches and salads. She avoided expensive taxi rides, and even subway fares, by arranging her job interviews within walking distance. Some days she would take the subway down to Wall Street and go from company to company, filling out applications.

Robyn knew she didn't have any skills to offer beyond the basics. But she was determined and willing to learn. She would take any job as long as she was given a chance. Things had to change soon. No matter how wisely she economized, her money wasn't going to last forever.

* * *

Retrieving the newspapers she had tossed on her bed, Robyn began skimming the want ads again. There had to be something. Anything.

As her eyes moved from column to column she noticed it. Those magic words: *No experience necessary.*

She checked the time. Five-thirty. Someone could still be there. Grabbing a quarter, she hurried to the phone in the hallway. Maybe she could get an early-morning appointment.

Robyn deposited her quarter and punched out the number, hopefully waiting for the ringing line to be answered. It was. The voice at the other end was enthusiastic. Without even taking a second to organize her thoughts, Robyn began talking nonstop, extolling those skills she had while at the same time promising to be eager and hardworking.

Robyn got herself an interview. When she hung up, she knew that tomorrow would be her lucky day.

The following morning Robyn hurried out for her interview. She had taken extra care with her appearance, choosing a black and white glen-plaid double-breasted jacket over a long-sleeve cream top with a black and white hound's-tooth skirt and a wide black leather belt. She had splurged on the outfit during her first few weeks in New York, fighting against her reluctance to spend her precious dollars as she had waited in line at Sak's. After all, she had to have something to wear to interviews. The outfit was decidedly the most impressive in her wardrobe.

With her hair coiled on top of her head for a more businesslike look, and a minimal dusting of makeup, Robyn thought she looked like an asset any company would want.

She crossed her fingers as she headed for the subway.

Three hours later she was back on the streets, fighting against the August heat and trying to decide what to do with the rest of her day. The interview had gone horribly. Once again she had been told that she didn't have enough experience. How much experience did one need to be a receptionist? As Robyn contemplated her next move, her stomach growled with hunger. She had been in such a rush that morning that she had skipped breakfast. If her memory served correctly, there was a Houlihan's nearby. Maybe she'd splurge on lunch.

Deciding there was no longer any reason to be so dressed up, Robyn started removing the pins from her hair, shaking free her cascading waves. Immersed with her thoughts and the delights of window shopping, she was unaware of the figure determinedly stalking her. Then, as she was preparing to cross between Thirty-fourth and Sixth Avenue, in front of Macy's, she felt a savage tug on her arm. To her horror, she found her handbag being pulled from her shoulder.

"Stop! Thief!" Robyn pointed at the retreating figure. "Somebody help me! He's stolen my handbag. All my money is in there!"

Robyn watched helplessly as the thief ran away. At first she tried to follow, but found it impossible to squeeze through the crowds. A few people smiled sympathetically, but other than that, no one offered any assistance. The crowds kept milling around her until finally she realized there was nothing more she could do. Emerging from the crowd, she spotted a police officer on the opposite street corner. She ran for his assistance.

"Officer, I need your help. My handbag was just snatched."

"Did you get a good look at the assailant?"

"It happened so fast. There wasn't time to notice anything distinctive about him. He was wearing blue jeans and a white tank top."

"Do you know how many men in New York fit that description?" He shook his head ruefully. "I'm sorry, but your bag is as good as gone. There's nothing more I can do except take down a list of the items that were in it. If we find anything, it will be returned."

"But I had almost five hundred dollars in my wallet and a check I never cashed! I can't wait for the money to be found!"

"The first thing they make off with is the cash. Miss, your money is gone."

"It can't be! All the money I had was in my wallet. Without it, I'm broke. I've been in New York for close to three months. I haven't been able to find a job. If I don't come up with today's payment, I'm going to be evicted from the hotel where I'm staying." A note of hysteria crept into Robyn's voice. The thought of being out on the streets petrified her. "Isn't there any way you can help me?"

"What can I do? Listen, you seem like a nice young woman. Why don't you go back home? New York isn't the place for you." He reached into his wallet and then placed a folded bill in Robyn's hand. "Take this and buy a bus ticket home. I've seen too many girls like you destroyed by New York. It doesn't have the glamour and glitz you're searching for."

Robyn stared numbly at the fifty-dollar bill in her hand. Searching for glamour and glitz? If only he knew the truth! The only thing she was searching for was happiness and a place where she could belong. Nothing more! So far it was blatantly obvious that the only thing New York had to offer was bitter realities. Robyn berated herself for carrying around all her cash, but she hadn't felt safe leaving it hidden in her hotel room. After thanking the officer for his kindness, Robyn decided there was nothing more she could do.

Wrapped in her thoughts, Robyn started walking until she found herself in the heart of Rockefeller Center. Small growls of hunger emanating from her stomach reminded her that she still hadn't eaten. She pulled the fifty-dollar bill from her pocket. Why not have one last meal? Who knew when the next one would be?

Finding a small, yet cozy diner on the corner of Forty-ninth called Earl's, Robyn slid into a booth. Paging through the menu, she was unsure what to order.

"Make up your mind yet?"

Robyn looked up at the waitress waiting to take her order. She was an older woman in her late forties. Closing her menu decisively, Robyn waved her fifty-dollar bill from side to side. "This is all the money I have. After I spend this I'm broke. I haven't got a job, and by the end of the day I probably won't have a place to stay. Bring me the works."

The waitress poked at the dark roots of her bleached hair. "You're kidding me, right? A classy chick like you, broke?" She cracked her gum loudly. "You're just trying to get out of leaving me a tip."

"I'd love to leave you a tip, but I honestly don't know when I'll be eating again."

The waitress slid into the booth. "Are you serious?"

Robyn nodded. "My handbag was snatched. All my money is gone." She picked up the fifty-dollar bill. "A police officer was nice enough to give me this."

The waitress shook her head in amazement. "I'll never say another bad word against New York's finest. Look, don't you have anyone who can help you?"

Quinn's name was on the tip of her tongue. It would be so easy to call and ask for his help. She would have to call him anyway, because his check had been in the stolen wallet. But Robyn didn't want to ask Quinn for his help. Yet with no money and soon no place to stay, what other choice did she have? As she was about to answer, the cook yelled from the kitchen.

"Hey, Ruby! This ain't no social club. Take her order and get back to work."

"In a minute, Earl. The lunch mob won't be in for another twenty minutes." Ruby turned to Robyn. "How desperate are you for work?"

"I'll take anything," Robyn implored.

"How about waitressing?"

"I've never done it before," Robyn began hesitantly, "but that doesn't mean I'm not willing to try." During her job search she had gone to a number of restaurants looking for waitresses. Her lack of experience hadn't opened any doors.

"Then this is your lucky day," Ruby exclaimed. "You're in need of a job and we're in need of a waitress. I'll bet Earl would be willing to give you a shot."

"Do you really think so?" Robyn could feel some of her enthusiasm, along with a spark of hope, returning.

"I don't see why not. Wait here while I go have a word with him."

Robyn fidgeted nervously as Earl scrutinized her from the kitchen. She could see him shaking his head furiously while Ruby kept wildly stamping her feet. Finally Earl threw his hands up in the air and Ruby came racing over.

"You've got the job!"

Robyn jumped from her seat, throwing her arms around the woman. "Thank you! You don't know what this means to me. How did you convince him?"

"It wasn't easy. Earl doesn't think you can handle it, but I told him you looked like a fighter. You'll give him your best, won't you? I put my neck on the line."

"Don't worry, Ruby," Robyn assured her. "I won't let you down. I'll be the best waitress Earl ever had."

"Second best," Ruby corrected. "I'm his best."

Robyn laughed happily. "Whatever you say."

"Be here tomorrow at six. We don't open till seven, but we have to set up. The breakfast rush is usually from seven till ten. After that it's pretty quiet until lunch, which as you can see, is just about starting."

"I better go," Robyn said. "It looks like your hands are going to be full."

"They can simmer a few extra minutes," Ruby proclaimed, ignoring Earl's waving spatula. "Where are you staying?"

Ruby was aghast when Robyn told her. "Oh no! That ends right now! A girl like you doesn't belong down in the dregs." Ruby scrawled an address on her order pad and gave it to Robyn. "My sister Lydia has a boarding house in Greenwich Village. It's clean, affordable, but above all, safe. Go back to your hotel and get your things. I'll give Lydia a call and tell her to expect you."

"Your offer is so generous and thoughtful, but I don't have any money to pay your sister."

"We'll settle accounts later. Run along." Ruby whisked Robyn to the door. "You're keeping me from doing my job."

"I don't know what to say. Thank you, Ruby."

"We'll see if you still feel that way tomorrow afternoon after eight hours on your feet," Ruby teased.

"I knew today was going to be my lucky day!" Robyn exclaimed on her way out. Not only had she found her first job in New York, but her instincts told her she had also found her first friend.

3

Scott Kendall stood outside the boardroom, preparing to enter battle. Beneath his arms were a series of reports, sales figures and demographics. All focused on Wellington Cosmetics.

For as long as Scott could remember, Wellington Cosmetics had been an insignificant portion of his father's empire. Purchased by Michael Kendall in the early sixties, Wellington had never received the full attention of his father's business acumen. Rather, it had become a company whose growth and potential had withered with each passing year. Its only asset had been in providing Michael with an excellent tax write-off.

But Scott intended to change all that. Though he hadn't fully realized it until this morning, today was one of the most important days of his life. It would take some time, but he intended to bring Wellington into the same ranks as Revlon and Lauder.

Taking a deep breath, he opened the door to the boardroom. All eyes focused on him. Each pair had a different look, ranging from curiosity to indifference to hostility.

Scott Kendall was an exceedingly handsome man. Usually his looks were an advantage, especially with females, but not today. With his startling green eyes, tawny streaked hair, chiseled features, and muscular build, the older members of the board saw Scott as nothing more than a hotshot playboy dabbling with a new toy. They didn't credit him with creativity, persistence, or determination, believing that once the challenge of trying to turn Wellington around failed, Scott would discard the company and move on to something else.

It wasn't true. Scott had a plan to salvage Wellington. The

only question was, would he be given a chance to put his plan into effect?

He gave a smile of confidence before taking his place at the head of the table. "Gentlemen, shall we begin?"

With the death of Michael Kendall six months earlier, Scott, his mother Lucille, and sister Georgina had inherited a vast fortune. Before succumbing to the cancer he had fought for two long years, Michael Kendall had gradually liquidated his entire empire. Companies he had founded and board positions he had held were all given over to others at a costly price. All monies received were placed in trust funds, sound stock investments, and prime real estate ventures.

Yet before following this course of action, Michael had spoken to Scott, who had had no objections to his father's plans. Scott didn't feel he had the right nor the experience to take the reins to his father's empire. After all, he was only twenty-five and still fresh out of Harvard Business School. He had plenty of time to carve his own niche in the business world.

The surprise had come with the reading of the will. As expected, trust funds had been established for Scott, Lucille, and Georgina. However, Michael had retained his forty-five percent of controlling interest in Wellington Cosmetics. That controlling interest now belonged to Scott. After the reading of the will, a sealed envelope had been handed to him. It was a last letter from his father. The message had been short and simple: *Make Wellington the cornerstone of your future.* At that moment Scott's loss for his father had intensified and determination had coursed through his blood. Wellington would be the first step as he followed in his father's footsteps.

Scott took a sip of water to clear his suddenly dry throat. For the last hour reports had been skimmed while figures were tossed back and forth. From the general feel of things Scott believed the members of the boardroom were divided regarding the fate of Wellington. Scott felt he had the perfect plan, and now was the time for his pitch.

"Gentlemen, you can see from the reports that Wellington's profits have been consistently declining. For whatever reason, Wellington Cosmetics has never entered the eighties. Founded in the sixties, we've remained rooted there. We need to totally revamp our image. We need to update and glamorize Wellington.

Richard Templeton, business attorney and holder of fifteen percent of the company, spoke up. "How?"

As Scott rose from his chair, his nervousness evaporated in a torrent of creative energy. "Because Wellington has remained rooted in the sixties, there's a market out there that we've failed to grab: the eighteen- to thirty-six-year-old female consumer." He hurried to the other side of the boardroom, holding up a bunch of magazines. "Have any of you flipped through a magazine or turned on the TV recently? We're constantly being assaulted by youth and beauty. Perfect hair. Perfect body. Perfect *makeup.* Wellington hasn't tried to grab any of that."

Arthur Landers, holder of ten percent of the company and speaker of few words, held up a hand. "Your plan?"

"Isn't it obvious? Grab our share!" Scott proclaimed, green eyes blazing. He headed for the presentation he had set up earlier, unveiling it with a flourish. "This is our main priority. Fresh and Lovely cosmetics. Launched by Wellington last year, it was a good concept but badly handled. It was our first attempt in years to try to capture the eighteen- to thirty-six female market. Present plans call for scrapping the entire line. I think we can still salvage it. In fact, I think Fresh and Lovely cosmetics will recoup our overall losses and start bringing us back into the profit margin."

"How?" Arthur Landers demanded.

"The idea behind Fresh and Lovely was perfect. A line of cosmetics aimed at teenagers and young women. Moderately priced, but with quality and selection. Presentation is where we failed. We were out in the market, but no one knew we were there. The problems were endless." Scott held up a hand, counting off. "Packaging was wrong, advertising was misdirected, the stores hardly gave us any shelf space." He stopped counting, turning to Arthur Landers. If anyone stood in his way, it was him. "What's always guaranteed to grab tons of media attention?"

The sudden question threw Landers off guard. He flushed,

and Scott didn't wait for an answer. "A pretty face. And what does the public love more than a pretty face? Glamour. Excitement. Mystery. Can you imagine combining all these elements? It's the answer to our problem. Wellington Cosmetics launches a search for a Fresh and Lovely Girl."

Scott could see he'd aroused curiosity. The sluggish atmosphere had been replaced by intrigue at his words. "Our product has to be identified, and what better way than with a beautiful woman? We launch a contest for the Fresh and Lovely Girl. Entry forms will be found at cosmetics counters and in all the major magazines and newspapers. We'll do radio and television spots. The attention we grab will be bigger than Eileen Ford's Face of the Eighties search. The contest will generate interest and curiosity in Fresh and Lovely cosmetics."

Scott paused for breath. He had spoken almost nonstop. Of course there was more, but the general outline of his plan had been laid out. Now came the crucial part. Decision time.

There was silence in the boardroom. Scott looked from face to face. He could read nothing in the expressions. Reports were being paged and figures jotted. Scott looked from Richard Templeton to Arthur Landers, the only two who had voiced any significant interest while he had spoken. They were the only two he needed.

"Your approach to the situation is innovative," Templeton began, "but have you given any thought to how you'll finance it? Wellington funds would be at your disposal should the board decide to approve your plan, but they're limited."

"As you know, my father left me a substantial trust fund," Scott answered. "I'm willing to use it. I believe Wellington is worth saving. The money I invest will more than double in the long run."

"It might work. I'm willing to keep Wellington alive awhile longer. Arthur?"

Arthur Landers cleared his throat. "Naturally we'll have to go into more detail, but I concur with Richard. However, I'm sure you're aware that Wellington has received an outside offer. The sum being offered is most substantial."

Scott felt his heart drop. Did this mean his plan was being axed?

Landers continued. "Your proposal shows promise, Mr. Kendall. I'd like to see what becomes of it. You show an admirable amount of zeal and fervor. Nothing would please us more than profits. But I must remind you that Wellington is a sinking ship. As the years progress she sinks deeper and deeper. Turning the company around won't be easy. Your progress shall be subject to periodic evaluation by the board. If at any time we feel that the situation is not aimed at our best interest, we shall have the right to put an end to things. Are our guidelines satisfactory?"

Scott answered without hesitation. "Yes."

"Then the project is yours." Arthur Landers held out his hand. "Congratulations."

Scott felt a wave of exultation rip through him. He had won! He returned Landers's handshake with a beaming smile. Richard Templeton approached with the other members of the board, all offering him best wishes. Scott smiled and nodded to all, appearing to be attentive, but his mind was elsewhere, already formulating and planning.

He had a search to begin—the search for a Fresh and Lovely Girl.

4

Sculpted from the very best life had to offer, twenty-five-year-old Beverly Maxwell had grown up in the lap of luxury. Sent to the finest schools, integrated into the international jet set, and wealthy beyond anyone's wildest dreams, Beverly Maxwell had it all. Except for one thing. Despite all her possessions, there was only one thing she craved to make her life complete. There was only one man who she loved and desired to have by her side: Scott Kendall.

Yet he had walked out of her life six months ago.

Beverly still could not understand how she had allowed Scott to get away. She had been totally unprepared when he had broken things off, since she prided herself on her ability to maintain control of any situation. Even after six months she could still remember every last detail of their final meeting.

Returning home from an afternoon of shopping, she had been surprised to find Scott waiting in her Park Avenue duplex. Her many packages from Gucci and Sak's had scattered over the black and white marbled squares of her foyer. "Scott, what are you doing here?" she exclaimed.

He jangled a silver key before her eyes. "I have my own key, remember?"

Beverly was miffed at his sharp retort. If there was one thing she detested, it was surprises. Although she had given Scott a key to her duplex, she felt as though her privacy had been invaded. The key was intended for his use only when she was at home and didn't want the inconvenience of letting him in herself. She hadn't intended on his roaming through her duplex when she wasn't around.

"That wasn't what I meant and you know it." She began gathering her scattered packages. She hated disorder. Satisfied that her packages were all neatly aligned, Beverly carefully removed her mink, hanging it on a padded hanger while checking her image in a gold-edged mirror.

The image staring out at her was cool and austere. Dressed in dove gray by Ungaro, with a double strand of black pearls around her neck and wrists, Beverly Maxwell oozed of wealth. Her rich chestnut-colored hair, taken care of twice a week at Sassoon's, was pulled away from her face and worn, as usual, in a French twist. She preferred the style not only for its elegant simplicity, but also for the way it flattered her patrician features: high cheekbones, arched eyebrows, ice-blue eyes, and a perfectly straight nose. Her complexion was a rich, creamy color never exposed to the sun and startlingly highlighted by the ruby-red lipstick she always wore. Standing tall and regal, she exuded an air of confident elegance that many in New York's social circles tried to imitate but failed to attain.

"How are things at the office? I imagine the paperwork

must be horrendous, but that's the price for taking a vacation."

Scott was at the bar, pouring himself a hefty scotch when Beverly joined him. She wrapped her arms around him. "I haven't even begun to unpack. I wish we were back in St. Thomas, don't you?"

"Not particularly," Scott sullenly answered. He shrugged his shoulders, shaking off her embrace.

The gesture irritated Beverly, but she wouldn't allow it to deter her. Scott's unexpected arrival had put a delicious idea into her head. "Don't you wish we were back on the beach making love?" she purred.

"Making love is the last thing on my mind," Scott snapped. Then his voice became hollow and lifeless. "My father died this morning."

The words of comfort immediately sprang to Beverly's lips. "Darling, I'm so terribly sorry. Is there anything I can do?" Her slight unease disappeared. Knowing how to conduct the situation, her lost reserve returned.

Beverly smiled to herself. Secretly she was pleased by Michael Kendall's death, having taken second place to him for far too long. Ever since his cancer had been diagnosed, he had been the entire focus of Scott's attention. With him finally out of the way, an infinite number of possibilities were now open. Scott had just lost the one person he loved most in his life. Surely his emotional state was vulnerable. With a touch of manipulation, she was sure to attain the long-elusive commitment she had been after: marriage.

Beverly made herself comfortable on a pale green settee. "Come sit next to me, darling," she coaxed, patting the spot next to her. "Have arrangements been made yet?"

"Does it really matter to you, Bev?"

Beverly inwardly cringed. She couldn't stand being called "Bev," and Scott knew it. He was purposely trying to incense her. She chose to ignore the barb, crediting it to his mourning. "Could you please make me a drink?"

Scott sat across from her, placing his feet upon an antique coffee table between them. "You're a most capable woman, Beverly. I trust you can make your own drink," he said sarcastically.

She immediately rose from her seat, pulling Scott's feet to

the floor. "This is a ten-thousand-dollar antique. I won't have you ruining it with your shoes." As she poured herself a Perrier, she discreetly watched Scott from the corner of her eye. "How's your family taking things?"

"Why are you asking me? Why not ask them yourself?" Scott tore off his tie, tossing it to one side. "This is the perfect opportunity to ingratiate yourself."

Beverly decided she would continue to be understanding. "Scott, you're an important part of my life. What affects you affects me. I know you're hurting, and I want to help ease your grief. Won't you talk to me? Don't you know I'm here to listen?"

"When have you ever been there for me when I've really needed you? My father meant the world to me, and you saw him as nothing more than an inconvenience in our relationship."

"I never felt that way." Beverly didn't like the direction things were headed. Scott was in an openly hostile mood, and she was the object of that hostility.

"Really? Then how come I never got Georgina's phone call when we were in St. Thomas?"

"What phone call? I don't know what you're talking about."

"My sister called our hotel. She left an urgent message for me to call New York. At one point they didn't think my father would last the night. I never got that message."

"And you're accusing me of not giving it to you?"

"Don't play innocent with me, Beverly. I want the truth! Georgina didn't call only once. She called three different times, and I didn't get one message. Not one!"

There was no need to panic. She would acknowledge her mistakes and shoulder whatever blame Scott felt should be pointed at her. "You know how melodramatic Georgina can get in a crisis. I really didn't think there was a need for you to return to New York. We had just arrived in St. Thomas and you needed some time to relax. I was only doing what I thought best."

"You were only doing what you thought was best for yourself! You should have left that decision to me. It was mine to make, not yours." Scott shook his head. "You always resented my father. Why?"

"It wasn't intentional! In the beginning I tried to understand. But then he began taking away more and more of your time. You were always at the hospital. Our relationship has been in limbo. Was I supposed to not let that bother me? Was I supposed to hide my feelings?"

"You should have been more aware of *my* feelings," Scott angrily accused. "My God, Beverly, what if he had died while we were in St. Thomas?"

Beverly lowered her eyes, tracing the rim of her glass with a finger as she projected an image of contriteness. "I'm sorry. Why don't we put this behind us and start over?" She retrieved Scott's tie from the floor, intending to place it in the front pocket of his blazer. As she leaned over, Scott grabbed her by the arm, drawing her close to him.

"I don't believe you! Do you honestly think we can put this behind us because my father is dead? Maybe you can, but I can't! You knew my time with my father was limited, but you wouldn't accept that. You wanted me all to yourself."

Scott meshed his lips with Beverly's. The glass of Perrier splashed onto the green settee as she struggled against his embrace. "Well, congratulations," he snarled, attempting to unbutton her dress. "You've won. It's time to collect your winnings."

"Stop it," she protested. "Scott, this isn't right."

"You've never refused before."

"No! Not like this! Not when it isn't going to mean anything!" She pulled away from him with a strong tug, agonizing to hear the dove-gray silk tear. Rearranging her torn dress, she exploded at him. "What just happened was totally uncalled for! I think you'd better leave. Go back to your apartment, shower, change, and have some coffee. When you're civilized again, give me a call. We'll discuss whatever you want then." Her tone was firm and authoritative, leaving little room for argument. "Just leave! Now! I know you've suffered a loss, but that's no reason to take things out on me. I've admitted contributing somewhat to the situation and I've apologized. What more do you want?"

Beverly was confident that Scott would be at a loss for words. It was her turn to play injured party.

He stared hesitantly at her for a moment.

"Well?" she haughtily demanded, "haven't you anything to say?"

"I want an end to this relationship," he quietly stated.

For once Beverly did not know what to do or say. Throughout her entire relationship with Scott she had orchestrated their every move. She had made all the decisions, had pulled the strings. She had always intended to become Mrs. Scott Kendall. She wasn't about to lose that dream without a fight.

"It's over between us," he continued. "A relationship is supposed to consist of mutual love and trust. We never had that."

She began shaking her head wildly. "You're drunk. You don't know what you're saying."

"I've never been more sure of anything. What I've said is true. You know it is."

"You're drunk," Beverly reiterated, clinging to the one reason which made sense. "I love you. How can you say such things to me?"

"The only person you've ever thought about in this relationship is yourself." Scott gestured at the elegant surroundings. "You saw us as the perfect couple fitting into your perfect world. All you care about is appearances. You don't love me, Beverly; you never did. You only see me as one of your possessions. That's the only reason why you don't want to lose me."

"You can't leave me. Scott, I need you! I'll do anything to keep you! Anything! I'll change! I swear I will!" From Scott's stance she could see he remained determined to leave. Desperate not to lose him, she tore at the double strand of black pearls at her neck and wrists, scattering them to the floor. Pulling the pins from her hair, she shook her French twist free. "Tell me what you want and I'll do it, only don't leave me! I love you, Scott."

He shielded his eyes with the palm of his hand. "Don't do this to yourself. I'm not worth it," he pleaded. "You weren't the only one at fault. With my father ill, I wasn't ready to handle a relationship. You wanted one thing and I wanted another. Our expectations were too high. Somewhere along the way we lost each other. We were never there when we needed each other."

"Whenever you showed up I never turned you away."

"There's more to a relationship than just sex. We never found that. In all the times we spent together, we never opened ourselves up. I feel as though I hardly know you."

Beverly's rage was past the boiling point. Yet she was still able to assess the situation at hand. Clearly she had underestimated Scott Kendall and what he wanted. This round went to him. Tantrums and screams would be useless. He had made up his mind and nothing was going to change his decision. She would bow out a graceful loser for the moment, quickly going to work on her strategy for getting him back.

She managed to maintain her poise. "Contrary to what you felt about me, I'll always treasure the time we spent together."

"I know you must be hurting, but in time you'll see I'm right. We weren't meant for each other. You'll find someone else. Just like I will."

Beverly refused to look at him. She had to convince him she had accepted their breakup. "Perhaps," she said with anguish. "I think it would be better if you left. I need to be alone."

"I'm sorry for my behavior."

"Just go," she pleaded, deliberately allowing her voice to quiver. "You've made your feelings clear."

Not knowing what else to say, Scott left the duplex. After he had gone, Beverly headed for the bedroom, retrieving a framed photograph of Scott from her bedside. Clutching the brass frame to her chest, she sank upon her bed, oblivious to wrinkling the satin bedspread or the many ruffled pillows.

"I'll never find anyone else," she whispered with determination into the twilight-darkening room, "and neither will you."

That following week, Beverly had left New York for an excursion to Europe, and last month, upon her return, she slipped back into a pattern of social functions. However, she was still determined to win Scott back.

Since they traveled in the same social circles, she was certain they would bump into each other. First, she would make Scott believe she had gotten over him, letting him mistakenly think she only wanted to be friends. From there it would be much easier to trap him.

Whenever she ran into Scott, it would be as though nothing had happened between them. A pleasant greeting, a few minutes of conversation and then a return to the event at hand. She was going to give a wonderful performance.

Beverly knew he wasn't seeing anyone seriously. Apparently Wellington Cosmetics was consuming all of his time. In addition, so-called friends were always willing to keep her up-to-date on Scott's extracurricular activities, should she ever desire the information.

Still, Beverly never liked taking chances, which was why her top priority since returning to New York was reestablishing her friendship with Georgina Kendall Richards. With Scott's sister as her best friend, she would be sure to know his every move.

5

The sound of the alarm clock jarred the early morning stillness. Georgina Kendall Richards groaned loudly, reaching out with a grasping hand to discontinue the harsh jangling. Chasing away the last vestiges of sleep, Georgina stretched languidly against the satin sheets of her bed, contemplating the last few weeks. She couldn't believe it! For the first time in ages she actually felt good about herself. When was the last time that had happened? Things were looking up. She wasn't drinking as heavily as she normally did, and she found herself armed with a new sense of confidence and vitality. She couldn't wait to start modeling again. How she felt would surely show in her work before the camera.

The clinic in Denver had done wonders. Although she had been reluctant to enter, she would be the first to admit it had helped.

There had been a messy incident in the Hamptons involving her Corvette; luckily no one had been injured. Thankfully, the accident she had caused had been kept out of the papers; the parties in the other car had been using cocaine, and the judge at her hearing had been lenient, suspending her license for only a month. He had further instructed both parties to seek professional help for their addictions.

Georgina had fumed upon hearing those words. She had only had a few drinks at a garden luncheon. It wasn't as though she were an alcoholic. She could stop drinking anytime she wanted—she had proved that up in Denver. She only drank socially or when she needed to deal with a situation. She didn't drink from dawn till dusk. Alcoholics did that, and she certainly wasn't an alcoholic. She was a top fashion model in the same ranks as Christie Brinkley and Kim Alexis.

It was true that her career had slowed down a bit in the last year, but that didn't mean anything. Reduced drinking, exercise, and a strict diet had all worked wonders. She was ready for whatever came her way.

She sprang from her bed with a bounce. There was to be a meeting this morning at Wellington Cosmetics. Although she wasn't sure what Scott's plans were now that he had taken over, she was nonetheless confident she was going to be playing a key role in Wellington's future growth and success. After all, hadn't she successfully represented Wellington for the last five years?

As she slipped into a royal-blue fitted Perry Ellis suit, her eyes came to rest upon her wedding picture. She grimaced, removing the framed photograph and placing it facedown in a drawer.

Putting on her earrings, she wondered where Lance was. He rarely came home to their town house on West Seventieth, preferring to remain in his Greenwich Village loft where he did most of his work . . . and his play. Staying down in the Village was so much more of a convenience, Lance had told her on more than one occasion. Yet when

Georgina would tell him in advance of her plans for using the loft, she would still find herself alone at nights, yearning for some warmth and affection, questioning Lance's absence. In the past she had shrugged off Lance's indiscretions with an air of indifference and the sip of a drink. Without her liquor, Lance's indiscretions stood out jarringly.

In Denver she had made a decision. If Lance wanted to continue slumming with one of his many girlfriends, he was more than welcome to do it. But not while she was paying the bills. Lance was only a modest success with his photography, and he had expensive tastes. She was the one who brought home most of the dollars, although Lance was the one who spent them. Not anymore.

Where had their marriage gone wrong? Had there ever been any love? She honestly couldn't remember. As the money from her career had started pouring in, each had become absorbed only in themselves, exploring new avenues of life without the other. Who was to blame for their drifting apart? Georgina knew they had both contributed equally, yet she had never been unfaithful to Lance. Why take a lover when she could always take a drink?

The weeks in Denver had allowed her to do some serious thinking. She was creating a new image for herself, and Lance was the only black spot on it. She didn't intend to allow that black spot to remain. For once in her life she felt as though she were in control and the only person she had to please was herself. She knew what she wanted—the satisfaction of her modeling career. She had allowed herself to coast for far too long, instead of enjoying the benefits of her hard work. It was time to change all that.

Glancing at the time, Georgina gave her silky blond hair a quick brush. Gathering up her handbag and black leather gloves, she took a final look at the closed drawer with her wedding portrait. Out of sight, out of mind. Changes were definitely in the making.

Lance Richards pointed his camera at the naked young girl as she pranced before him, gathering her scattered articles of clothing from the floor.

"Stop that!" she teased, tossing a pillow at him as she struggled into her bra. "Can't you see I'm late for work?"

Lance paused. "I'm a photographer. When an artistic mood hits me, I can't control myself." He continued snapping away.

She zipped her skirt. "Did you mean what you said about helping me get into modeling, or was that just a line to get me into bed?"

Lance pretended to look crushed. "Sherry, what kind of a guy do you think I am?"

She crawled into bed next to Lance, kissing his naked chest and reaching beneath the sheet. "A horny one," she replied, ducking her head between his legs.

Lance pressed her face forward as she went to work with her lips. He could never get enough. When her head popped back up, she gave him a naughty grin. "I think I would have brought you home last night even if you hadn't made all those promises."

Lance tapped his camera. "We shot plenty last night. Once I develop these, all your dreams are going to come true."

"You're really an angel. Lock up when you leave, okay?" She kissed him one last time before jumping out of bed. "I'm running late and my boss is going to throw a fit. Call me tonight." She rushed from the bedroom, still talking over her shoulder before slamming out of the apartment.

The moment she was gone, Lance went into the bathroom, flushing his roll of film down the toilet. Watching the water drain, he thought of Sherry and the many other women he had had because of the unkept promises he had made with his camera.

Using his camera to satisfy his sexual appetite was a device he had been employing for many years, much to his advantage. Flashing his camera while traveling with an entourage of models only made things easier for him. Of course, there were his looks as well. His eyes were the color of cold pewter; his hair dirty straw; his features rough and impassive; his stance belligerent. Tight faded jeans, unbuttoned white shirts, and black cowboy boots were the staples of his wardrobe. Women flocked to him in droves. There was something cold and calculating about Lance Richards that made women want to reform him. None had ever succeeded. Lance only thought of himself, taking what he wanted when he wanted, and not giving a damn about anyone else.

He preferred one-night stands, always following the same pattern. He never brought anyone back to his loft, and he never gave out his real phone number. If someone was truly worth seeing again, then he would compromise, but very rarely. Georgina was enough of a headache to deal with.

As he wandered around Sherry's apartment, he reflected on the changes he had recently noticed in Georgina. She had cut down on her drinking considerably, and the insecurity which had always been her trademark was gradually being replaced by a new air of self-confidence. Lance didn't like it. The only time he could be sure of anything was when Georgina was drunk. Now he didn't know what her next move would be or how he should counter it.

Returning to the bedroom, he started to dress, deciding it was time he took another look at his marriage. After all, there was a five-million-dollar trust fund to consider, as well as all the other fringe benefits that came from being married to Georgina. He needed to do some serious thinking. There had to be some way for him to have it all. But without Georgina.

At ten o'clock precisely, Georgina sauntered into the executive offices of Wellington Cosmetics, waltzing past the receptionist without even a second glance.

"Excuse me," the woman called after her, springing from behind her desk. "Where do you think you're going?"

"I have a ten o'clock appointment with Scott Kendall," Georgina sniffed, affronted by the woman's accusatory tone.

"Your name?"

"What?"

The woman returned to her desk, keeping a wary eye on Georgina. She retrieved her appointment book. "Are you Georgina Richards?"

At the point of exasperation, Georgina decided to clear a few things up. "My name is Georgina *Kendall* Richards," she corrected. "Does the name sound familiar? Your boss is my brother. Secondly, take a look at these walls. Whose face is adorning them? Mine. I've helped sell Wellington for years, and I'll continue to do so. Therefore, I do not expect to be treated in this manner."

The woman flushed. "Do forgive me, Ms. Richards. I had no idea. This is my first week." She turned to her telephone console. "Let me check if Mr. Kendall is free."

"Dear woman, you should try to be more aware of the world around you." Georgina made herself comfortable in the reception area, pleased with the groveling tone she heard in the woman's voice. "In any event, of the more important individuals. Like me." She looked at the selection of magazines available. When was the last time she had appeared on a magazine cover? Too long.

Pulling out her compact, Georgina gave herself a quick inspection. Flawless complexion. Startlingly clear blue eyes. Striking features. She still had what it took to be the best, even though she would be the first to admit she had been neglecting things.

"Georgina?"

She looked up. Standing before her was a stunning redhead with emerald-green eyes and the creamiest skin. Erica Shelton. Georgina had worked with her on many Wellington shoots. Although the young model had only just started in the business, Georgina thought she had a promising career ahead of her.

"Erica, it's good to see you."

"Same here. You're looking marvelous."

Georgina accepted the compliment modestly. "What brings you up this way? Wellington thinking of using you?"

"Hardly. They've just released me from my contract. My agent and their lawyers are going over the paperwork."

"I'm sorry," Georgina sympathized.

"Don't be. I'm being well compensated. The grapevine says Scott is preparing to launch a new face. Is it true?"

Georgina's insides grew cold. "Really? It's news to me." She decided to shift the conversation. She couldn't deal with the thoughts suddenly racing through her mind. "Tell me, are you still seeing Jeff Porter?"

"We've moved in together. We may even tie the knot at the end of the year."

"Congratulations."

"Did you want a business card? Anyone you know thinking of a divorce?" Erica reached into her handbag. "Jeff insists I keep a supply."

Georgina accepted the card, slipping it into her purse. Erica was looking at her expectantly. Was she waiting for some morsel of gossip about her marriage to Lance? Georgina studied her coolly. Was Erica really as innocent as she came across? Certain sources linked Erica and Lance together. Was Erica another one of Lance's playmates? The odds were slim. She really couldn't see Erica sleeping with Lance—she had too much brains for that.

"Thanks. Never know when I might need it."

The receptionist came forward. "Your brother will see you, Ms. Richards."

"I've got to run," Erica said. "Give me a call. We'll do lunch."

Georgina managed a response before heading in the direction of Scott's office. No matter how hard she tried, she couldn't prevent the one thought that kept repeating itself over and over in her mind: God, do I need a drink!

6

Erica was waiting for the elevator when a pair of male hands covered her eyes.

"Guess who?"

Erica whirled around in annoyance. Standing before her was Lance Richards. "What do you want?" she asked in a surly tone.

Lance gave her a grin. "What I've been after all along." He snatched at her waist while leaning to give her a kiss. His lips missed their target as she shoved him away.

"What do you think you're doing? The receptionist will see."

"So?"

"Don't you know that's how rumors get started?"

"Having everyone think I'm sleeping with you is better than nothing at all."

Erica gave an exasperated sigh. She really couldn't tolerate any more of this, and was almost thankful her days at Wellington were over. At least she wouldn't have to deal with Lance Richards anymore. Since their first meeting over a year ago, he had made it obvious that he wanted to sleep with her. She had repeatedly let him know she wasn't interested. Having him as the photographer on most of her Wellington shoots hadn't made things easy.

As was the case at this moment, Lance Richards was a man who didn't like being refused. His interest only increased. Whenever their paths crossed, he let her know he was still willing to sleep with her. Despite the fact that Lance was attractive, she wasn't going to feed his inflated ego. He had no qualms about casting his lovers aside after growing tired of them. She had no plans to add her name to his list of conquests.

The elevator arrived and Erica jumped in, trying to close the doors on Lance. He managed to squeeze in.

"Ever make love in an elevator?" he asked, pushing the stop button.

Erica seriously considered kneeing him in the groin. He was worse than a horny teenager! She pushed Lance to one side, releasing the stop button and allowing the elevator to continue its descent.

"Leave me alone. You're married and I'm involved with someone."

He grinned. "So?"

"Doesn't commitment mean anything to you?"

"I'd rather have a good time." He tried to wrap an arm around her, but she wormed her way free. They were rapidly nearing the lobby.

"What about Georgina?" she asked.

"What about her?"

"Ever stop to think she might deserve a little respect?"

Lance looked bored. "I never think about Georgina. All she cares about is her booze."

The elevator doors opened and Lance sauntered out. "Besides, respect don't keep the sheets warm." He sent her a lewd wink before heading for the street. "And I hate for my sheets to be cold."

Scott was not looking forward to his meeting with Georgina. As much as he loved his sister, he couldn't shield her from the problems she had caused for herself. And he could no longer allow Wellington Cosmetics to be susceptible to them.

Where had his sister gone wrong? She had started her career at eighteen and it had skyrocketed. Constant exposure in all the right magazines. Television commercials and talk shows. An occasional movie appearance. Six-figure deals. Always in demand for New York and Paris fashion shows.

It had all been too much too soon. Georgina had amassed so much that she had been unable to handle it. Though she wouldn't admit it, she had constantly lived with the fear of one day losing it all. She started drinking to forget the pressures, and somewhere along the way she had lost control. After ten years in the business, her career was about to come crashing down.

Scott had to help her before it was too late. He only hoped she understood.

He turned from the window as Georgina entered. Giving her an affectionate kiss on the cheek, he led her to the chair in front of his desk. "I'm glad you could make it. Would you like some coffee?" Scott stepped behind his desk, preparing to ring his secretary.

Georgina waved away his offer. "Wherever did you find the pit bull? She's positively beastly."

"Ms. Davis? Her bark is worse than her bite."

Georgina gazed at Scott behind his black granite desk. "Impressive! Incidentally, I love what you've done with the outer office. All that glass and chrome is so modern. You're really upgrading Wellington's image."

"Image sells."

"Is my image tarnished, Scott?"

The remark caught him off guard. He gave his sister an

uncomfortable look, wondering what she knew. He hadn't wanted anyone else to break the news.

"I ran into Erica Shelton out in reception. We chatted. She dropped a few clues, but I'm still in the dark. Care to enlighten me?"

Scott suddenly felt like a little boy again, remembering the times when Georgina had been displeased over something he shouldn't have done. Her voice held the same tone. "Georgina, this isn't easy."

"Get to the bottom line. Is Wellington dropping me?"

"I hope you'll let me explain."

"Yes or no?" she harshly asked.

"Yes."

"You can't," she adamantly ordered. "My modeling is all I have."

"Wellington is only one of your many assignments. It's hardly a loss to lament."

"I'm Wellington's top model, and right now Wellington is the hot word in the industry."

"You used to be Wellington's top model," Scott interrupted. "You have no one but yourself to blame for this."

"Can't you see what this will do to me professionally?" she implored. "When word of this gets out, I'll be ruined."

"You're exaggerating."

"I'm not," she shrieked.

"We can tell the press whatever you like. I'll make sure you come out of this untarnished."

"How? Everyone is watching Wellington; everyone says you're going to be able to turn the company around. Scott, I want to be a part of Wellington's success, not a remnant of its failure. Can't you give me one more chance?"

"You've been given one chance too many." Scott reached for a report, leafing through it. "Arriving late, reshoots, showing up drunk, having outbursts." He spread a mass of photographs on his desk, shuffling through them. "Take a look at these. Do you really think these pictures sell beauty and glamour?"

Panic bubbled through Georgina as she flipped through the photographs. She couldn't even remember when the shoot had taken place. She certainly didn't look her best. It had to have been before she had checked into the Denver clinic. "It was a bad day," she explained weakly. "I had a terrible cold and overslept. The makeup girl was horrid and the photographer wasn't very good. His impatience made me very nervous. You can see how it all shows."

"The only thing I see," Scott reluctantly stated, "is a hangover."

"It won't happen again. I promise."

"You've made promises before and broken them."

"Scott, you have to give me another chance. I'm your sister."

"Don't try to make me feel guilty for your mistakes," Scott flared angrily. "I can't afford to keep doing things over, nor can I make exceptions. How will the board take me seriously? You're my sister and I love you. You know I would never do anything to intentionally hurt you." He came around the desk. "You've been pushing yourself for far too long. Don't you think it's time you took a break?"

Georgina rose defiantly. "I've already returned from a vacation. It's time I resumed my career."

"Not at Wellington," Scott firmly stated. "The board has already approved my plan to find a new model for the Fresh and Lovely line." He placed a hand gently on her shoulder, trying to soothe her fears. "Try to understand. All I'm doing is taking away some of your responsibilities. I'm not shutting the door in your face. Maybe Wellington will be able to use you down the road, but for the moment I need a new face. Can't you see what I'm doing is for the good of the company? Don't you want me to succeed?"

Georgina angrily shook off her brother's hand. "At what cost? Congratulations, Scott. I see you've learned the first rule of business. Be absolutely ruthless. Allow nothing to stand in the way of your ambitions. Not even family."

The impact of his sister's words crushed him. "You know that isn't true."

Georgina locked eyes with Scott, trying to intimidate him as she had when they were children. "Prove it," she challenged. "Let me remain the Fresh and Lovely Girl."

"I can't."

"Is that your final word?"

"Georgina, why won't you try to give some thought to what I've just said?"

She gave him a condescending look. "If that's your final word, then give some thought to this." She pointed an angry finger at him. "Unless I get to come back as the Fresh and Lovely Girl, I have nothing further to say to you. Ever."

She slammed her way out of Scott's office.

7

Lance pulled his black Maserati into the parking space behind Georgina's red Corvette. From the haphazard way the Corvette was parked, it didn't take him long to surmise how his wife had spent her afternoon. Lance wasn't displeased. Quite the contrary. It was always much easier to have one's way with Georgina when she was drunk.

There were a great many things Lance expected to get today.

Slamming into the entrance hall, he glanced into the library and living room. Logical places to look, considering both had well-stocked bars. No Georgina. He headed into the kitchen. "Bettina," he bellowed to their housekeeper, "where's Mrs. Richards?"

Bettina came running to Lance's side, wiping her hands on a dish towel. "Mrs. Richards is resting. She isn't feeling well."

Lance peeked into the bowl Bettina had abandoned, scraping a fingerful of frosting. "I can't seem to find her."

Bettina removed her bowl from his reach. "Have you checked the bedroom?" she asked, returning to her cakes.

He started climbing the back staircase. "I saw Mrs. Richards's car outside. Did she happen to have a liquid lunch?" he innocently asked.

Bettina sent him a dark look. "I wouldn't know, sir."

Lance shook his head woefully. "I certainly hope not. We wouldn't want to lose all that hard work in Denver."

"Certainly not," Bettina sniffed, affronted.

Lance came back down the staircase, reaching into one of the cupboards and removing an unopened bottle of scotch. "I think I'll give Georgina a little test. See how strong her resistance is." He started back up the staircase. "I'll be sure to let you know how things turn out."

Lance knocked twice on the bedroom door. Receiving no answer, he entered slowly, walking into darkness. The drapes were closed and all the lights were off except for a small lamp by Georgina's bedside. She was on the bed, tossing fitfully. Lance stood at the foot of the bed, staring down at his wife as she fought the demons of her sleep.

He moved closer and was about to shake her from her nightmare when he stopped, noticing her open purse. Most of the contents had fallen to the floor while the open purse teetered on the edge of the nightstand. Jeff Porter's business card was in plain sight. Lance picked up the card, staring at it uncomprehendingly. Divorce? How long had Georgina been contemplating divorce?

He brought his face down to hers. From her breath it was obvious she had been drinking. But from her tearstained cheeks, she had also been crying. Why?

Lance stared at the dresser directly across from the bed. For some reason Georgina had neatly aligned her best photographs in a row.

He went over to the photos, studying them. This had been Georgina's best work, when it had been almost too easy for the camera to capture her beauty and vitality. She had possessed a special magic back in those days, but now it was gone.

What was it about these photos that kept jogging his memory? Of course! All were from ads Georgina had done for Wellington. Lance replaced a framed photo. It didn't take long to put it all together.

Today had been Georgina's meeting with Scott. Something had to have gone wrong, otherwise why would she have removed these photos from various rooms in the town house? And why would she have started drinking again?

He went to a wall switch, flooding the bedroom with light. "Wake up!" he screamed, roughly pulling Georgina by the arm as he started shaking her. "You lost it all, didn't you?"

Georgina mumbled incoherently, trying to push him away. "Leave me alone," she muttered.

"So you're no longer the Fresh and Lovely Girl," he grandly announced. "Doesn't surprise me . . . doesn't surprise me at all."

"What?" Instantly, Georgina was awake. "What did you say?"

His guess had been right on the money! He couldn't wait to start stringing her along. "Didn't you hear me the first time?"

"How did you find out?"

"Does it matter? My dear, you're going to be *the* hot topic of conversation for weeks. The columns are going to eat it up."

Georgina trembled. Gone was the image of sophistication she had created that morning. Her eyes were swollen from crying and her hair was messily tousled. Her Perry Ellis suit was wrinkled and her silk stockings torn. She was no longer on top of the world.

"Scott," she mumbled, trying to recall the conversation they had had. "Scott said he would take care of everything. He said I would come out of this untarnished."

"And you believed him? How long have you lived in this town, sweetie? The real story always comes out." He dragged her by the arm into the bathroom, forcing her face against the mirror of her vanity as he turned on the lights. "Take a good look, baby. See the tiny wrinkles? See the dark circles? They're not going to go away. Not at the rate you're drinking. They're here to stay because you've lost the tools of the trade. It doesn't matter what Scott says. All it takes is one look at you and the entire story is there."

Georgina turned away from the mirror. "I'm still the best," she stated. "Still the best."

"Who are you trying to convince? Me or you? Where's the poise? The vitality? The glamour and sensuousness? Where's the most important thing of all? Where's the beauty?" He pressed his lips to her ear, whispering fiercely. "It's gone."

He held up the bottle of scotch he had brought from the kitchen. Georgina eyed it hungrily. "This is all that matters to you, isn't it? You live for your liquor." He twisted open the sealed top, waving the open bottle beneath her nose. "Smells heavenly, doesn't it? Bet you can't wait to taste it sliding down your throat." Lance pressed the bottle to her lips. "Go ahead. Take a chug. I'm sure that's how you drink it when you're alone. Why bother with glasses?"

A taste of scotch touched Georgina's lips. Her tongue darted out of her mouth, trying to catch the falling drops dribbling down her chin.

"Why so reluctant?" Lance placed the bottle in her hands. "It's all yours."

Georgina started to accept the bottle with trembling hands, then shoved it back to Lance. "Stop it," she screamed, tearing herself free and running back into the bedroom.

Lance left the bottle of scotch in the bathroom. "Where are you running to?" he taunted, following her. "There's no place to hide."

"Don't look at me that way," she pleaded.

"I've got news for you. I don't ever want to look at you again." He headed for the closet, removing his suitcases. Georgina stared at them in disbelief.

"What are you doing?"

Lance tossed the suitcases on the bed, starting to empty drawers. "This marriage is over. You're a loser. I don't associate with losers."

"Don't call me a loser," she screamed in agony, covering her ears.

"Why not?" Lance smiled maliciously. "You *are* a loser. Everyone knows it. Why do you think your father let you stick around at Wellington for so long? He knew no one else would ever hire you." Georgina stared at him wild-eyed, stock-still, hands still over her ears. "Scott had the guts to do what he couldn't," he whispered with deadly softness. "He got rid of Georgina the loser."

She dropped her hands from her ears. "Don't leave me. I need you."

Lance ignored her, continuing to pack. Georgina spoke to him again. When he wouldn't answer, she started unpacking his things.

"What do you think you're doing?" he asked.

"You can't leave me. I won't let you."

Lance tore his shirts viciously from Georgina. "The hell you won't." He placed his shirts back in his suitcases, zipping them shut. Then he took one last look around the bedroom. "If I forgot anything, just send it down to the loft."

Georgina grabbed at him. "You can't go. Lance, I need you!"

He laughed harshly, shoving her to the floor. "You need me? What a farce!" He waved the business card he had retrieved from her purse. "Looks like you were intending to divorce me." He flung the card at her with scorn.

Georgina caught the card in her hands, proceeding to rip it to shreds. "I wasn't planning on getting a divorce. Erica Shelton gave me the card this morning. I was going to throw it out. I need you Lance. I'm begging you to stay."

"If I stick around, things are going to have to change," he ordered.

"Anything," she agreed.

"No more questioning my comings and goings," he instructed.

"Yes." She nodded her head vigorously.

"I'd also like to be able to draw larger amounts from our joint accounts. Arrange with the bank to get rid of my limit."

Georgina checked the time. "I'll arrange it with the bank first thing in the morning."

"All bills sent to you are to be paid without question." Lance softly caressed Georgina's cheek, ready to make the promise that would keep her in his control. "I was wrong before. You still have a few good years left. All you need is the right photographer . . . someone who knows the way you photograph."

"Like you, Lance?"

"Who else? I think I can find some time for you in the next few weeks. We'll see how things work out. In the meantime, I've got to get down to the loft. See that my suitcases are unpacked." He headed for the bedroom door.

"When will you be back?"

Lance froze and a note of displeasure crept into his voice. "What did you say?"

Georgina stared forlornly at the bedroom floor, then retrieved the bottle of scotch from the bathroom, taking it with her as she crawled back into her bed. Clutching her pillow with one hand and the bottle of scotch with the other, she crunched herself into a tight ball, slipping under the sheets.

"Well?" Lance coldly asked.

Georgina brought the bottle of scotch to her lips. "Nothing," she whispered meekly. "Nothing important."

Beverly looked totally hot. She was wearing a burnt-orange, body-molded leather slip dress. Her hair, instead of being worn in its usual French twist, had been moussed and blow-dried into a wild, sexy mane. Makeup was liberally applied, and her favorite fragrance, Christian Dior's Poison, scented her body.

From the hungry stares and open invitations sent her way, Beverly knew she was producing results. And was pleased. She was on the prowl, ready to play her favorite game.

Beverly liked to play a game called "tease." The purpose was to dress provocatively, find a man, sexually arouse him, and then leave him unsatisfied. Each time Beverly played the game, she reveled in the power it offered. Men were so easy to manipulate. A slight brushing of the lips. A hand placed lightly on a groin. The glimpse of a shapely leg encased in silk. The gentle licking of an earlobe as false promises were whispered. Beverly relished the skills she had mastered to turn a man on.

Tonight there was going to be a new twist to the game. If she found someone appealing enough, she might sleep with the man she chose to toy with. She just might.

She was at the Palladium, immersed in a throng of hot, pulsating bodies. The smell of sweat from the hot summer night and frenzied dancers was thick in the air. Beverly inhaled deeply as she moved to the center of the dance floor.

Robert Palmer's "Simply Irresistible" was blaring from the speakers. The song fit her perfectly as she gyrated her body. All male eyes were glued to her. No man could ignore the brazen signals she was sending out. Now came time to decide. Who would it be? As long as he was good-looking, she was satisfied.

Her eyes darted around the dance club. Who should she settle for? Decisions, decisions.

Then she saw him. How could he possibly be missed? Straight black hair, piercing dark eyes, and a body demanding release from the clothes covering it. He was a live one. Definitely looking for some action. Beverly slid off the dance floor, positioning herself at the bar.

"Can I buy you a drink?"

Beverly turned her head with practiced disinterest. He certainly hadn't wasted any time! "Why not?"

"Any preference?"

"You order. I like the unexpected."

The drink Beverly sipped at was a strong concoction of rum and several other liquors. "Come here often?"

"Often enough. You?"

"Occasionally. I keep hoping I'll meet someone, but I don't know why I bother. This place is such a meat market."

"Lonely?"

She moved closer to him, placing a hand on his chest. "Very."

He closed the space between them, nestling her in the crook of his arm. His fingers feathered across the smoothness of her shoulders and down to the top of her breasts. "I could help you."

Beverly moved her hand from his chest, a coy smile on her lips. She wedged her leg between his, pressing against his straining erection. "Could you? I'd hate to go home alone to an empty apartment."

She meshed her lips against his, tasting rum as she pushed her tongue into his mouth for a deep and prolonged kiss. Her hands went around his waist, caressing his buttocks.

He broke the kiss. "What are we waiting for?" he rasped. "My name's Ken. Let's go."

"Ooh, aren't you an anxious little boy," Beverly cooed. She started unzipping his pants.

"Hey! What are you doing?" Ken panicked. He looked around to see if anyone was watching, but the other patrons and dancers were too involved with their own rituals.

"Relax, sugar. This is what you want, isn't it?" Beverly rubbed her fingers against his hot, pulsing flesh. If there was one touch she'd always loved, it was the feel of a man's throbbing erection. "Feel good?" she purred.

"The best," he moaned. "I don't think I'm going to be able to control myself."

Beverly whipped out her hand, playfully swatting his chest. "You try to hold on. When we get to your place, I promise you a hot time. Go get your car and meet me outside. I came with a girlfriend and I want her to know I scored extremely well."

Ken puffed up at the compliment. Beverly scornfully watched him leave before heading for another exit. She wished she could see the look on his face when he discovered she was gone. He'd be furious. Too bad she hadn't wanted to try him out. She was positive Ken would have been excellent in bed. But if she had decided to sleep with Ken, she wouldn't be having as much fun as she was having right now. The night was still young, and she was eager to play the game again.

8

"May I take your order?" Robyn asked perkily, flashing a smile.

She had been at the diner for a month with no complaints. The people she worked with were friendly; her salary more than adequate and the tips quite generous; Earl was a lovable grump, and Ruby was turning out to be a good friend.

She learned to balance trays and pick up her orders with

speed. She cleared away unsightly dishes and kept coffee cups filled. She moved from one table to the next with a smile glued on her face, even if she was exhausted from being on her feet.

Robyn had a lot to thank Ruby for. Not only for her job, but a whole lot more. Her sister Lydia's boardinghouse was a dream come true, and Robyn instantly fell in love with the room offered to her. Fresh sheets, crisp curtains, and bright bursts of sunshine were a much appreciated contrast from the hotel on Twenty-third Street.

Robyn thrived on all the new changes. She was surviving —making a living like everyone else. She was building a new life for herself.

After settling in at the boardinghouse, she had written an extensive letter to Quinn, updating him on the changes in her life. She didn't mention her first rough months, only telling him that she had been so caught up with job hunting and life in New York that she hadn't the time to write, hoping he understood.

She tried to write to Quinn at least once every two weeks. She wouldn't call him. In the four months she'd been in New York, she'd only called him once, and that had been to tell him about his stolen check. Although their conversation had been warm and friendly, she had kept it brief. She had to put some distance between herself and Quinn. Calling him with updates on her life would be too personal. Letters were much more suitable for the relationship she wanted to establish.

Quinn never failed to answer her letters, and he always sent back replies filled with support and encouragement. One day at the restaurant Ruby found her reading a new letter from him.

"Is this Quinn someone special in your life?" she asked.

"He's only a friend. He helped me through a rough time."

"Is there a future with the guy? Any possibility of wedding bells?"

"Of course not!"

"You could have fooled me, the way the two of you write back and forth. You hardly give the ink a chance to dry."

Robyn returned Quinn's letter to its envelope. "We're just friends."

Ruby shrugged. "We'll see. Call me a romantic. Listen, some of us are going dancing Friday night. Want to come?"

Robyn remembered her last night out at a dance club. She and some of the other waitresses had gone to the Limelight. Although they arrived in a group, everyone left as a pair. Except her. It wasn't that she hadn't had the opportunity. A number of men had offered to dance with her, talk with her, buy her drinks. She hadn't felt comfortable with any of them. What they wanted to do when the evening was over was made perfectly clear, and she didn't want to lead anyone on.

"Thanks, but I think I'll pass this week." She closed her locker and tied an apron around her waist, checking for her order pad and pen. "Do you think Earl would mind if I asked for some extra hours? I really don't have anything to do with my time off."

"Sure, but why ask for extra hours? Why work yourself to death? Why don't you do something else with the time? Something constructive."

"Like?"

"Take a few secretarial courses at one of the colleges. Weren't you originally looking for an office job?"

"Yes, but I don't want to leave here."

"No one is telling you to leave, but what could it hurt to have a few hidden skills to fall back on? Take a word-processing class and a shorthand class. Maybe in a few months you'll decide you want a change of pace. There's nothing wrong with working here, but Robyn, you were meant for bigger and better things," Ruby urged.

"You really think I could do it?"

Ruby nodded enthusiastically. "I do. Why don't we go over to NYU early on Saturday?"

"Won't you be getting in late Friday night?"

Ruby waved a hand at her. "The hell with dancing, boozing, and picking up men. I'll spend the night at Lydia's. We'll pop some popcorn, rent some videotapes, and plan our strategy."

"Strategy?"

Ruby draped a reassuring arm around Robyn. "Honey, you've got to shake off your modesty. You're going places."

"How can you be sure?"

Ruby gave a confident smile. "Easy. You've got the look of a winner. One day you're going to have it all. Mark my words."

Scott tried to sleep but found he was unable to. A haunted image kept appearing in his mind, never giving him a moment's rest. No matter how hard he tried, he couldn't escape the look of defeat and resignation in Georgina's eyes when he had told her she was no longer the Fresh and Lovely Girl.

He told himself he had been totally justified in doing what he had done. Wellington Cosmetics came first. He wasn't doing Georgina any favors by disguising the truth. If anything, he was helping her face some harsh realities. Maybe now she would start to straighten out the mistakes in her life.

If anyone else had been head of Wellington, Georgina would have been out ages ago. Nor would the situation been handled as delicately. He had tried to break the news to her in the most gentle way. He wasn't the one at fault, but Georgina didn't feel that way. She still refused to speak with him and still refused all his calls.

But Georgina was only part of the problem. The pressures were building at Wellington. Scott found himself putting in twelve-hour days as they prepared for the Fresh and Lovely campaign. Meetings were nonstop, and so many decisions had to be made. New packaging, new colors, and a new logo had to be chosen, and the most important choice of all had to be made: Who would be the new Fresh and Lovely Girl? Thousands of photographs were being sent in daily. Only one girl would be the winner. Which one?

Scott couldn't explain his feelings, but he was forming a composite of the woman they were searching for. Naturally she was beautiful, but there was more to her beauty than physical appearance. Her beauty radiated from within. All that was needed was a smile or a sparkle in her eye, and she would capture anyone's attention.

So far they hadn't found her. With each passing day the search became more intense. Time was running out. A decision would have to be made soon. Scott knew his Fresh and Lovely Girl was out there. Somewhere.

Georgina buried herself deeper into her mattress, pulling her pillow and comforter over her head. The phone beside her bed continued to ring incessantly. Finally unable to ignore it, she answered.

"Who is it?" she screeched into the receiver.

Beverly Maxwell's voice came over smoothly and gently, impervious to Georgina's crass tone. "Georgina, darling, it's been ages."

Georgina moaned softly, struggling into a sitting position. When was the last time she had spoken to Beverly? Theirs had been nothing more than a casual acquaintance, even when Beverly had been seeing Scott. She wondered what she wanted.

"Georgina, are you there?" Beverly asked into the silence.

Georgina contemplated if she should be rude or nasty. At eight in the morning she was in no mood for talking, especially to Manhattan's leading ice princess. She decided to see how the conversation progressed. "Beverly, what a surprise to hear from you."

Beverly's voice turned low and confidential. "Darling, I've been catching up on all the news. You simply must tell me everything about your demotion."

Georgina settled on nasty. "Give me the inside dirt on why Scott dumped you and I'll be more than happy to share my tale."

Beverly let the remark slide. "I didn't mean to sound negative," she soothed. "What Wellington did to you was deplorable. Couldn't Scott have prevented it?"

"Whose idea do you think it was?"

"Really? I noticed an article on Wellington's search for a new Fresh and Lovely Girl in the morning paper. Scott's idea as well?"

"Another one of his brainstorms. Does he honestly believe this search is going to benefit the company?"

"Of course not!" Beverly emphatically answered. "Georgina, you represented Wellington for five years. The public identifies with you. Scott made a grave mistake in letting you go."

Georgina softened at the compliment. "It's too complicated to get into over the phone. Why don't we meet for lunch?"

"Le Cirque? Around one?"

"See you then."

"Let's take a five-minute break. Erica, you're looking good."

"Thanks, Ray."

Erica was filming a series of commercials for Midnight perfume. The commercial she had just finished was set to air in three months. As she was walking off the set, she heard her name called.

"Ms. Shelton?"

Erica turned to the voice, smiling at the young girl before her. "Yes?"

"Jeff Porter called. He'd like to meet you for lunch at Le Cirque at one." The girl blushed. "He asked if you would wear something sexy."

"Did he?" Lunch with Jeff, possibly followed by dessert. Erica arched an eyebrow as she started contemplating her wardrobe. "Thanks for the message."

9

Beverly sipped Perrier from a wineglass while waiting for Georgina. Since she was always on time for her appointments, it infuriated her that Georgina was late.

Her eyes wandered to the entrance, widening slightly. Lance Richards. What was he doing here? She watched as the maitre d' led him to a secluded booth. Interesting. Perhaps he was meeting with a mistress. She wondered how Georgina would react if she knew Lance was here.

"Sorry I'm late but traffic was horrendous."

Beverly looked up, startled from her thoughts. In watch-qing Lance she had failed to notice Georgina's entrance. If anything, Georgina's outfit was less than conventional. She was wearing jeans so faded, the color was white rather than blue; a tight-fitting T-shirt; thigh-high black boots; huge silver bangle earrings and, of course, Georgina's trademark once the fall season in New York began, her oversized silver fox fur.

Beverly couldn't understand how Georgina wore the bulky thing. She preferred sable or mink. Both were tasteful statements of wealth and elegance, unlike Georgina's creation. You'd think the woman would have the decency to present herself in a way suitable to her station in life rather than looking like a refugee from SoHo. Beverly always made sure she looked her best. It was expected. Today she had outfitted and accessorized herself with some of her favorite designers. She had on a red wool crepe suit by Valentino. On her feet she wore Chanel slippers. Her gold charm bracelet was designed by Edouard Rambaud, and her bag by Hermés. As always, her scent was Poison.

She leaned across the table, brushing cheeks with Georgina. At first she didn't know what to say. "Georgina, you look heavenly," she finally managed. What a lie! The woman looked positively bedraggled, and what had she done to her hair? If there was one thing Beverly had admired about Georgina, it was her hair. It had always been a long mass of golden silkiness. Now it was cut in a shag style and layered with dark streaks. The entire mess was tied up in a red bandana, the bangs coming loose and feathering Georgina's forehead. The entire look reminded Beverly of a sheep dog.

"You're an angel for lying." Georgina removed her sunglasses. "There's so much to discuss. I don't know where to begin. For weeks I've been holed up in my town house feeling sorry for myself."

Beverly signaled for a waiter. "Make yourself comfortable," she coaxed, pouring Georgina a glass of Chablis from the chilling bottle on their table.

Georgina shrugged out of her fur, bringing the wineglass to her lips. "I really shouldn't be doing this," she explained after taking a sip. "I'm trying to cut down on my drinking."

"Nonsense. What's one glass of wine? We're about to have a lovely lunch with some wonderful conversation. Pamper yourself, Georgina. You're worth it."

Georgina took a longer sip from her wineglass. "You're right," she instantly agreed.

"I'm meeting Jeff Porter. I believe he has a one o'clock reservation."

"Mr. Porter has already arrived. If you would come this way."

As Erica weaved through the tables, she could sense all male eyes in the restaurant following after her. Well, Jeff had said to dress sexy. She had selected a tight black leather miniskirt with a mint-green silk blouse provocatively unbuttoned. Black silk stockings and high heels made her legs look delectably long and smooth. Her flaming red hair was flowing, tossed over one shoulder.

"Here we are." The maître d' handed her a menu. "Mr. Porter stepped away for a few minutes. When he returns I'll send a waiter to take your orders. Would you care for anything from the bar?"

Erica slid into the secluded booth. A gift-wrapped box along with a bouquet of red roses was on her plate. A bottle of champagne was chilling. How romantic! Could this be the day Jeff proposed?

"Everything's fine," she told the maître d', picking up the small box. "I'll just wait for Mr. Porter."

Erica shook the box against her ear, tempted to open it. She really should wait for Jeff, but she had never been good when it came to presents. She ripped away the wrapping in seconds, unveiling a box from Cartier. Opening it, she gasped. Nestled against the black velvet interior were two intertwined hearts on a thin gold chain.

She slipped the necklace on, gently patting the two hearts as they fell in the folds of her blouse. She loved it! She couldn't wait to tell Jeff how much.

"Do you like it?"

Erica looked up, a flash of annoyance on her face as Lance slid next to her.

"That's none of your business. Anyway, I'm meeting someone for lunch."

"Are you?" He seemed amused.

"Yes, I am. You'd better leave. Jeff can get very jealous."

Lance cupped a hand under his chin. "Really? Mind if I stick around till he gets here? I'd love to meet your infamous white knight."

"Mr. Porter, I see you've returned," the waiter said, standing next to the table. "Are you ready to order?"

Erica stopped fingering the hearts. She wasn't sure if she'd heard correctly.

"We'll be a while longer, but do you think you could uncork the champagne?" Lance asked.

"Certainly, Mr. Porter."

The cork was popped and the champagne flowed. Lance lifted his glass in a toast. "To us."

"You set this whole thing up!" Erica exploded. "How dare you trick me!" she ranted.

"Calm down," Lance soothed, sipping his champagne. He held out his glass. "Would you like a taste? It's delicious."

Erica shoved away the glass, tempted to toss the champagne in Lance's smug face. "You've got nerve."

Lance pondered the statement. "I'll agree. But if I had called and invited you to lunch, you never would have come."

"You've got that right." Erica looked at the chilling champagne, the roses, and the seclusion of the booth. All were part of a stage set for seduction. "I'm leaving."

Lance took another sip of his champagne. "I only wanted to make things up to you. My behavior in the past has been atrocious." He pressed a menu on her. "Please stay. Order whatever you like. Can't you see I'm trying to apologize?"

To avoid making a scene, Erica accepted the menu in a huff, sitting back down. It was time to teach Lance a lesson. Maybe in the future he wouldn't be so quick to toy with her. "Fine," she snapped.

The waiter returned. "Are you ready to order?"

"Erica?"

She smiled sweetly at Lance, then turned to the waiter, proceeding to order the most expensive items on the menu.

"Anything else?" the waiter asked.

Erica sipped at her champagne with distaste. "Yes. Get

rid of this stuff and bring us your most expensive bottle of Moët."

"And you, sir?"

"The same," Lance responded without hesitation. "When it comes to the lady, money is no object."

Beverly picked at her salad with disinterest, staring at the rich pasta Georgina had ordered.

"Aren't those calories murder to your figure?" she asked as Georgina sprinkled a liberal dose of Parmesan cheese.

Georgina reached for a roll, not forgetting to butter it before taking a bite. "Of course, but I'm out of work. I might as well indulge while I can."

"I know you've suffered a setback, but that's no reason to throw in the towel. You'll work again."

"I spoke to my agent last week. The few offers I've gotten aren't worth my time. The advertisers, at least the ones who count, have forgotten me."

"Why not look into the offers you've gotten? At least you'd be working until something better comes along."

"I'm not taking anything less than what I'm accustomed to."

Beverly bit her tongue. In the last half hour all she had heard from Georgina were complaints. Didn't she realize the downfall of her career had started snowballing long before Scott had taken over Wellington?

"Besides," Georgina continued, "the new Fresh and Lovely campaign is bound to turn into a fiasco. Scott will have to take me back."

"How can you be so sure? You can't pick up a newspaper or magazine without being bombarded by his ads. Same thing with TV and radio. He's generating a lot of interest."

"How successful do you think Scott is going to be with an amateur in front of the camera?"

"How is the search coming along? Have they found someone?"

Georgina shook her head. "I'm as much in the dark as anyone else."

Beverly delicately fingered her wineglass. "How's Scott?" she casually asked. "Do give him my best regards. Are you two talking?"

"Let's forget Scott. Tell me about Europe. Do much shopping?"

Beverly hid her annoyance as she tried to think of another way to route the conversation back to Scott. She wasn't going to suffer through Georgina's self-centeredness without coming away with some morsel of information. "Most of my time was spent on indoor activities, if you know what I mean." She took a long sip from her glass.

Georgina gave Beverly a skeptical look. Beverly Maxwell sleeping around? It was too much. But she wanted to find out more. "Anyone in particular you'd like to mention?"

Beverly paused for a moment. "There were so many. It's hard to keep track of the names. There weren't any emotional attachments. You must understand. Scott and I had such a passionate relationship. I had to forget him, and I did so in the only way I knew how."

Georgina nearly choked on the breadstick she had been lazily chewing, quickly reaching for her water glass. Scott and Beverly in a passionate affair? Was she kidding? The woman was *the* ice princess of the old-money generation in Manhattan. Georgina wouldn't be surprised if you slit Beverly's wrists and found ice water in her veins. The woman was always cool and reserved, constantly keeping her emotions in check, living her life as an example meant to be followed. Georgina studied Beverly, trying to visualize her in bed, not only with Scott, but with any man. Useless. She kept drawing a blank.

"It's best to try and move on to other relationships," Georgina commented, for lack of anything better to say.

"I agree totally, but there wasn't any chemistry between myself and any of the men I met in Europe. But I'm still searching."

Despite the instances when she indulged in playing "tease," Beverly loved having a man pumping within her as she locked her legs around his waist. She hadn't been lying when she'd told Georgina about her men in Europe. They'd been handsome, magnificent lovers, willing to sexually satisfy her. For a price. Why bother with the hassle of a relationship or the bother of playing "tease" when all you wanted was a good fuck? After all, there was nothing money couldn't buy.

There had been Niles in London. He'd been such a wicked delight with his bondage tricks, manipulating her with his tongue as she twisted against her bonds and screamed for him to enter her. In Germany a friend recommended she sample Damian if she wanted to be daring. Never one to turn down a challenge, Beverly gave Damian a call. During her entire time in Germany she became a willing participant in Damian's leather games, looking forward to the sensuousness of his leather sheets, the sinisterness of his leather mask and the sting of his leather whip. Once settling down in Italy, she craved a gentler touch. Giorgio, with his skillful hands, sensuous lips, and bottles of warm oils, allowed her to indulge in multiple orgasms as he sexually catered to her.

Yet none of her hired lovers compared to Scott. When it came to lovers, he was in a class by himself. Scott knew how to please a woman without being told. All he had to do was take you in his arms, and he instinctively knew what to do. Whether it was a caress or a kiss or a gentle touch that grew into more, Scott always managed to cast a spell.

He made love with abandon, and Beverly grew breathless as she recalled their lovemaking. He *would* be hers again, she vowed. It was only a matter of time before Scott realized his mistake and came back to her. For the moment all he wanted was his freedom and Wellington Cosmetics. Eventually he would tire of both. Then he would come to realize his life was empty and meaningless, unless he shared it with someone. *She* would be that someone. No one else.

"Shall we order something rich and sinful for dessert?" she asked Georgina. "I'm feeling positively wicked."

"You hardly touched a thing."

From the Newfoundland lobster to the Russian caviar, Erica had purposely picked at the delicacies on her plate. "I wasn't as hungry as I thought."

"Try one of these." Lance picked up a fresh strawberry, dunking it in a pot of chocolate sauce.

"I really don't want one," Erica refused.

"Come on. Open wide." Lance brought the strawberry to her mouth, forcing her to accept it.

An older couple passed the table as Erica bit into the

strawberry. The woman smiled at them, whispering to her husband, "Doesn't that remind you of the days when we were first in love?"

Lance slipped the rest of the strawberry into Erica's mouth, fingers tracing her lower lip before moving away. "Good?"

She swallowed the strawberry. "Delicious," she reluctantly agreed. "Will you excuse me?" She rose from the table. "I need to use the ladies' room."

Lance popped a strawberry into his mouth. "I'll be waiting."

"Is that Lance over in the corner?"

Georgina looked up from her chocolate cheesecake. "Lance?"

"Over there," Beverly pointed out.

Georgina followed Beverly's finger, expecting to find her husband with his arm draped around another woman. She gave an inward sigh of relief. He was alone.

Beverly sipped at her cappuccino. "Are you going to go over?"

"Of course not," Georgina indignantly retorted. "I wouldn't want to disturb him. He could be in the middle of business."

Or an affair, Beverly thought. She was tempted to tell Georgina of the striking redhead who had momentarily disappeared, but decided to wait a bit longer. "Does he meet with models?"

"Naturally. He's a photographer." Georgina put down her fork. "Will you excuse me?"

She headed for the ladies' room. It looked like Lance was getting ready to pay his bill. If he was with another woman, she didn't want to see her. She would stay hidden until she felt sure Lance had departed.

Pushing open the door of the ladies' room, Georgina came face to face with an exiting Erica.

Erica choked on her words, not knowing what to say, until she found her voice. "Georgina, what a surprise."

"Same here."

"Are you alone?"

"I'm lunching with a friend. You?"

"Jeff and I just finished," she lied.

"Could I meet him? You're always raving about him."

Erica laughed nervously. "I know. Am I the only woman who constantly talks about her boyfriend? I would have loved for you to meet Jeff, but he had to run back to the office." Erica knew she was babbling, but she couldn't stop. "Our schedules have been so hectic lately. I'm lucky I got him to spare me an hour. I'm sorry you missed him."

Georgina's eyes came to rest on the intertwined hearts around Erica's neck. "Obviously he found time to buy you that." She moved closer to examine the necklace. "It's gorgeous."

Erica looked down at the hearts in shock. In her anger with Lance, she had forgotten to take off the necklace. How could she have been so stupid? "It's nothing, really."

"Are you kidding? I wish someone would buy me a bauble like that. You must be really special to Jeff."

Erica's heart went out to Georgina and the pain Lance constantly caused her. Suddenly she felt uncomfortable with her lies. "I have to run. I'll talk to you soon."

Outside the ladies' room Erica yanked the necklace from around her neck, cupping it in her palm as she headed for the entrance. She couldn't risk returning to Lance's table. The lies that had passed her lips had been to spare Georgina's feelings. She couldn't have told her she was having lunch with Lance. Georgina would have invariably jumped to the wrong conclusion. She knew how she would feel if she came across Jeff lunching alone with an attractive woman. Sparks of jealousy, no matter how small, were sure to arise.

Alone in the ladies' room, Georgina wondered about Erica. Why had she seemed so nervous? Could she have been having lunch with Lance? If so, why not admit it? Unless it had been more than lunch. She couldn't help but notice the way Erica had been dressed.

She didn't want to believe it, and tried to banish the thought from her mind. Yet it kept returning. Could Erica and Lance be having an affair? But why?

Speculation wasn't going to get her answers. If she really wanted, there *was* a way she could find part of the answers. All it would take was a phone call. Perhaps she'd make that phone call later in the afternoon.

Lance flagged down the passing maître d'.

"Excuse me, but my lunch companion has been gone for some time. She stepped into the ladies' room. Could someone check on her?"

The maître d' disappeared as Lance settled with a glass of remaining champagne, contemplating the afternoon ahead. Perhaps he could convince Erica to come back to his loft. Alone, she might be more receptive to his advances. He couldn't remember the last time he had wanted a woman as badly as he wanted her. She was more than beautiful. She was breathtaking. All he wanted was to smother himself in her flesh, tasting her sweetness as he pushed himself deeper and deeper into her, feeling her body writhe beneath his.

The maître d' returned. "Sir, I'm sorry, but the young woman you were lunching with left a few minutes earlier. She sends her apologies for departing without notice and thanks you for the lunch." The maître d' reached into his jacket, removing a sealed envelope. "She also asked that this be returned to you."

"Thank you." Lance opened the envelope, revealing the intertwined hearts.

"Will there be anything else, sir?"

"Just the check."

Lance took one final look at the hearts before returning them to the envelope. Then he picked up the roses he had left on Erica's seat when she had gone to the ladies' room. He sniffed the petals gently before crushing them in his fist and letting them flutter to the floor.

His frustration, as well as his desire, was doubling. So far he'd been playing by Erica's rules. He'd give her some more time.

And then he'd play by his rules.

"Are you sure you don't want to share a taxi?"

"It's the perfect day for window shopping," Georgina stated.

"Only the impoverished window shop," Beverly remarked drolly. "It's because they can't afford to buy everything they see and need to shop wisely. Unlike me." She signed the check, watching as Georgina deliberately kept her back to Lance's table. "Too bad Lance has already left. You could have asked him to join you."

"Has Lance gone?" Georgina turned slowly toward his table, as though not trusting Beverly's words.

"He left alone," Beverly stated.

"Really? How surprising." Georgina's face was impassive, devoid of any emotion. "Lance never fails to have a beautiful woman on his arm."

"She *was* beautiful," Beverly conceded, preparing to divulge the information she had withheld earlier.

Georgina was puzzled. "Who?"

Beverly's words were delivered with a touch of innocence and an air of distractedness. But she knew they would cause Georgina alarm, and she savored it. "The striking redhead who was lunching with Lance."

After departing from Beverly with the promise that they would meet again soon, Georgina headed for the nearest pay phone, dialing information. After getting the number she needed, she deposited her coins with shaking fingers. The line rang and rang before a harried voice answered.

"Holt, Winfield, Daniels, and Rogers."

"Jeff Porter."

"One moment."

The line was transferred, ringing once before being picked up. "Jeff Porter's office."

Georgina tried to muster a tone of confidence in her voice. "Yes, may I please speak to Jeff Porter."

"May I ask what this is in reference to?"

"Are you his secretary? Perhaps you can help me. Mr. Porter had lunch this afternoon at Le Cirque. He accidentally left his credit card behind. Would it be possible to have someone pick it up?"

"There must be some mistake. Mr. Porter didn't go out for lunch today. Every Thursday the lawyers have a luncheon meeting. The meeting is still going on. Are you sure you have the right number?"

Georgina continued playing along. "Does Mr. Porter have a girlfriend? A redhead?"

"Yes, he does. Erica Shelton."

Georgina pretended realization. "That must explain it. She was the one who had given me the credit card. I assumed her companion was Mr. Porter."

"Would you like to have someone pick it up? I can send a messenger."

"Highly unnecessary," Georgina rushed. "I see Ms. Shelton headed my way. She must have remembered leaving the card behind. She's so attractive. I'm sure Mr. Porter wishes he had been lunching with her."

"I'm sure he does. He's been stuck in his meeting for close to three hours."

"Thank you for your help."

The phone was replaced numbly. In a daze, Georgina started walking back to her town house, fighting against the tears threatening to escape from the corners of her eyes. "It doesn't matter," she whispered. "It doesn't matter."

10

Ruby pressed a newspaper clipping into Robyn's hand. "Read this," she urged.

Robyn scanned the piece of paper. "It's an ad for a secretarial position."

Ruby gave a huff. "Would you mind telling me why you've been taking those classes?" She didn't wait for an answer. "So you can move on to bigger and better things! Robyn, you're too good for this place. You've got to go somewhere else, where you'll be able to build a future for yourself. If you stay here, you're headed for nowhere."

"That's not true!"

Ruby ignored Robyn's protest. "I have taken the liberty of

making you an appointment for ten o'clock tomorrow morning at Wellington Cosmetics."

"Oh, Ruby, you didn't! Do you really think I could handle it?" Robyn hesitantly asked. She didn't know why, but she was starting to get excited. Maybe she was ready for a new challenge.

"Honey, I've already got the Help Wanted sign ready," Ruby boasted.

"Ruby!" Robyn mocked sternly. "Trying to get rid of me already?"

"Of course not. I'm only looking out for your best interests," Ruby stated plainly. "You belong out in the world, Robyn, not hiding in some diner."

Robyn knew Ruby was right. She *was* hiding from the world. Although the pieces of her life had fallen into place, there was still one elusive piece missing. Her past. Although she spent as much time as she could trying to remember, she came up with nothing. How long *was* she going to hide?

Robyn made a decision. Her past was a mystery and would remain that way, but her future was a fresh, clean canvas she could create upon in whatever way she liked.

No more looking back.

"Ruby, you love playing mother hen. Don't deny it and don't ever change." Robyn fingered the clipping. "I'll go!"

The woman waltzed into the reception area with an officious air, giving a quick glimpse to the clipboard in her hands. "Robyn Prescott."

Abandoning the magazine she had been trying to read in her nervousness, Robyn gathered up her coat and hurried after the woman. "I'm sorry, but I didn't catch your name," she called.

The woman, having assumed Robyn was right behind her, had started speaking. She stopped her speech, turning around in annoyance. "I'm Angela Kraft," she replied before continuing down the corridor. "My office is right this way."

Once in her office, Angela Kraft settled herself behind her desk before offering Robyn a seat. "Tell me, Ms. Prescott, what office experience do you have?"

"To be quite honest, none."

A pointed stare was directed at Robyn. "Really? What makes you think you're qualified to work for a company as prestigious as ours? Why should we hire you?"

The questions were rapid-fire, and Robyn hurried to find answers, wanting to make a good impression. Before she could open her mouth, Angela Kraft asked to see her résumé.

"Résumé?" Robyn's cheeks turned red. "I'm afraid I don't have one."

Angela Kraft's voice was incredulous. "You don't have one? Ms. Prescott, that's not at all professional."

"I know," Robyn hurriedly apologized, "but there really wasn't much for me to put down on paper. You can call my boss, though. He'll give you a reference and tell you what a hard worker I am."

"Who's your current boss?"

After Robyn's answer, there was a disdainful sniff. "I would hardly put much stock in the word of a short-order cook. Waitresses are hardly the type we're looking for."

Robyn silently burned. If Ruby had heard those words, she'd have gone through the roof. Nonetheless, she continued smoothly. "My office skills are flawless. All you have to do is give me a chance."

Angela Kraft sighed. "I'm sorry, Ms. Prescott, but this interview is over." She handed Robyn back the application she had filled out. "You've wasted more than enough of my time, and I have other more qualified applicants to see."

"But you haven't even tested me or let me interview with the person looking for the secretary. Shouldn't the decision be theirs?"

"Ms. Prescott, you're trying my patience. My job is to screen applicants for Wellington. In order to get anywhere in this company, you've got to get past me first. You've failed to make an impression on me. Come back in six months with a little more experience and maybe we'll try again." She returned her attention to the papers on her desk. "Until then this interview is over. Good day."

Robyn was halfway out of the Wellington Building before deciding on a course of action. Turning around, she headed back to the waiting elevators.

Although she understood Angela Kraft's point, that still didn't mean there couldn't be exceptions. She had come to interview as a secretary, and that was what she was going to do.

There had been other forms on Angela Kraft's desk. Robyn couldn't help but notice them. The secretarial job was for an executive named Scott Kendall. His office was on the thirty-sixth floor.

Robyn stepped into a waiting elevator, pressing the button for the thirty-sixth floor.

"Scott, we're up against a wall. Everything's set to go into motion but we're still looking for a Fresh and Lovely Girl. Why do you insist on being so stubborn? Make a selection!"

"It's not as easy as that."

Kyle Masters threw up his hands in exasperation, shaking his sandy haired head ruefully. "Some answer! Why am I putting up with this?"

"Because you're my best friend, and they were wasting your talents at Grey Advertising. Wellington will never let that happen."

"We'll never know unless we find a girl to use in our campaign." Kyle held a photograph before Scott. "What's wrong with her? She's certainly more than attractive."

Scott stared disinterestedly at an amber-eyed brunette. "I've said it before and I'll say it again: None of these girls have what I'm looking for."

"Scott, I don't think you even know what you're looking for. My staff and I have been sifting through hundreds of photographs for weeks, narrowing down the entries. Nothing seems to please you."

Scott ran his fingers over the pile of photographs on his desk. "Keep looking."

"What are you looking for?" Kyle asked, his blue eyes puzzled. "Do you even know?"

"We need a special girl to represent Wellington. I'll know her when I see her." Scott grabbed a handful of photos. "You can get rid of these."

"Scott, time is running out," Kyle reminded him. "The board isn't going to be patient much longer. They want to see results. That was the whole reason why you were given a chance to try and save the company."

"They'll get their results and a whole lot more. Soon," Scott vowed. "In the meantime, keep searching. I know the Fresh and Lovely Girl exists. I'll know her when I see her."

Robyn took a deep breath before barging into Scott's office. "Mr. Kendall?"

A look of exasperation and surprise crossed over Scott's face at the unexpected interruption. He was seated behind his black granite desk, sleeves rolled up as he pondered the mound of photographs before him.

"Yes?" The woman in the doorway was a complete stranger. He'd never seen her before. And yet he couldn't take his eyes from her.

Robyn didn't dare take a step farther into the office suite. She was starting to regret her impulsive decision. It was obvious that Scott Kendall was an important man. The sheer impressiveness of his expansive corner office astounded her. Plus there was the fact that he didn't look too pleased at being disturbed.

But she had come with a purpose, and she wasn't going to leave until she carried it out. Robyn began her speech without hesitation. "You don't know me," she began, "but I've just come from Personnel. Angela Kraft didn't seem to think I was qualified for the position I came to interview for, but I think she's wrong. She hardly gave me a chance to prove myself, and I wouldn't be standing here if I didn't think I could do the job."

"Why did you come to me?"

"The position was to be your secretary." Suddenly Robyn felt self-conscious, as Scott Kendall continued to study her intently. A silence filled the space between them, as there wasn't anything left to say. She felt like a fool. Why had she bothered Scott Kendall? He probably didn't even care what had happened down in Personnel. "I'm sorry for inconveniencing you," she apologized, backing out of the office. "I'll let you get back to your work."

Scott rose from behind his desk. "Don't leave. Maybe we can work something out."

Robyn didn't know why, but she wanted to stay and listen to his words. He was such a handsome man. She took a step forward, but then stepped back, running for the elevator.

"Wait!" Scott cried, following after her. "I don't even know your name."

The elevator doors closed behind Robyn, making it impossible for Scott to follow. "Damn!" He kicked a potted palm while pounding his fist on the closed elevator doors. He had to call Kyle. He had found their new Fresh and Lovely Girl. She had been bold and determined. Daring. But most of all, she had been beautiful, unlike any woman Scott had ever seen.

Yet he didn't know who she was or how he would be able to reach her. Then it dawned on him. A phone call to Personnel would give him the answers he needed.

Outside on Fifth Avenue, Robyn wistfully stared up at the Wellington Building. The image of Scott Kendall kept returning to her mind. There had been such a look of longing on his face when she had entered his office, like a child unable to solve a complex problem. But then his eyes had lit up as they focused on her. It was as though she had been the answer to his problem. She was positive she hadn't imagined it. At the same time, feelings she'd had with Quinn and no one else had begun to surface and stir within her again. And she had been frightened. So, despite her promise of the previous day, she had chosen to run.

When would she stop running?

Robyn lost herself in the shoppers and tourists cruising down Fifth Avenue, the world's most expensive street. She passed by Sak's, Cartier, Trump Plaza, and Tiffany's.

Would Scott Kendall have helped her stop running? Being his secretary certainly would have been an exciting experience. Would their professional and private lives have intertwined?

Robyn sighed, hailing a taxi. She was tired of asking herself questions.

After his late-afternoon conversation with Personnel, Scott slammed down his phone in frustration. "I can't believe it!" he raged to Kyle. "Our mystery lady took her application with her when she left. And Angela Kraft left early—for a two-week vacation. No one knows where she's gone or how to reach her." Scott pounded the top of his desk in frustration. "How are we supposed to find the woman I saw today?"

"Calm down," Kyle advised. "What I have to tell you may be good news. I spoke to the man who runs the corner newsstand. He remembers seeing the woman you described walk down Fifth and then grab a taxi. All we have to do is go down to the taxi company and talk to their drivers. If she's as beautiful as you say she is, I'm sure she won't be too hard to forget."

"Get to it, man," Scott encouraged, rising from behind his desk. "Call them and tell them we're on our way."

Robyn wiped the table clean, carefully arranging a place setting.

The diner was empty. As she gazed from booth to booth she wandered to the plate-glass window, staring out at the busy street. She folded her arms across her chest, burrowing deeper into her sweater.

Leaning against the glass, her thoughts kept returning to Scott Kendall and Wellington. Angela Kraft had probably already found someone to fill the secretarial position.

Deciding it would be better to keep busy rather than lose herself in her thoughts, Robyn left the window and began gathering salt and pepper shakers. A waitress named Cheryl looked up from her newspaper when Robyn approached the counter and clattered the shakers as she put them down.

"Do you always have to keep busy?" Cheryl complained. "It's so slow tonight. How can you stand it?"

"Slow is just the way I like it."

Robyn started unscrewing the shakers. "Anything interesting in the paper?"

Cheryl cracked her gum. "Not much, except that contest is still going on."

"Contest?" Robyn didn't know what Cheryl was talking about.

"For the new Fresh and Lovely Girl. Where've you been? It's been all over the papers, television, and radio."

"I must have missed it."

"How could you?" Cheryl shook her head wistfully. "What I wouldn't give to lead that kind of life. Whoever they choose is going to have it all. Can you imagine yourself in that position?"

"I don't know," Robyn honestly admitted. "There are some things money can't buy."

"Name one," Cheryl replied.

This time it was Robyn's turn to sound wistful. "Love," she replied.

11

Scott ignored the menu handed to him. He didn't know why he had agreed to dinner with Kyle, since he had no appetite. All he could think about was the beautiful young woman he couldn't find.

The taxi company wouldn't be able to help them until next week, when the driver Scott was looking for returned. The driver was moving furniture cross-country to his brother's new home in California. Like Angela Kraft, there was no way to reach him. Kyle kept telling him to be patient. Once the driver returned, Wellington would have its Fresh and Lovely Girl.

But Scott found it hard to be patient. He hadn't felt this excited in months, and it had more to do with than just the Fresh and Lovely contest. He had felt *something* deep within himself stirring when he had stared at his mystery lady. He hadn't felt this way in such a long time. There was definitely something special about her, and he wanted the chance to find out exactly what it was.

He wanted to get to know her. He felt like he wanted her to become a personal part of his life. After Beverly, there had been a few evenings with other women, but nothing more complex than dinner and a Broadway show. Friends were always trying to set him up on dates. He usually gave in to such prearranged evenings. Why not? He knew his life wasn't complete. It would be nice to wake up in the morning with his arms wrapped around someone special after a night of passion. He was tired of being alone and rattling around his Central Park apartment without anyone.

Yet there was never any chemistry between himself and the women he agreed to meet on blind dates. The same was true for women he met on his own. Did romance still exist? He was tired of being appraised by the quality of the suits he wore and the size of his checkbook. Scott knew he was considered one of New York's most eligible bachelors, and he hated it. His name appeared regularly in all the social columns and he was on everyone's party list. He was only judged by what appeared in print, never given a chance to reveal the real Scott Kendall. He was considered an attractive package of looks, wealth, and breeding. Yet all he wanted was to fall in love. Was that too much to ask for? he wondered. To find a woman he could love and cherish? For that, he'd gladly trade in everything he had.

Would he ever find such a woman? Or had he found her today and then lost her?

"Scott?" Kyle snapped his fingers. "You still here?"

Scott blinked. "Sorry. I got lost in my thoughts."

"I'll say. Our waiter will be back soon. Have you decided what you're going to order?"

Scott and Kyle were dining at La Caravelle, one of Manhattan's leading French restaurants. It was noted for its whole roasted ducks and chickens, as well as its elegant walls, decorated with murals by Jean Pages, and a highly rated wine cellar.

Scott skimmed the menu. "What are you having?"

"The roast rack of lamb stuffed with spinach and pine nuts."

"Sounds good."

"Darling, I hear it's *fantastic,* but take my advice and order the salmon fillet with three caviars in lemon sauce," a female voice declared. "It was exquisite."

Both Scott and Kyle looked up at the same time. Standing before them was Beverly Maxwell.

Scott didn't know what to say. It was the first time he had

come face to face with her since their breakup. He started to rise from his seat, but she waved him down, giving him a dazzling smile.

"Sit. Don't let us disturb you. We were on our way out." She indicated her male escort. "Where are my manners? Let me introduce Derek Nadler. Derek's a lawyer who worked on the Leona Helmsley case. Wasn't it horrible the way they attacked poor Leona? It's unbelievable the way the press always tries to crucify the rich."

"Isn't it," Kyle murmured, trying to suppress a grin as Scott kicked him under the table.

"I've heard all the latest about Wellington. Best of luck. If anyone will be able to turn around the company, it's you."

"Thanks for the vote of confidence."

"How's the search going?"

"We may be close to reaching a decision, although nothing has been decided. How was Europe?"

"Fabulous, except I overindulged and spent too much money. Like this dress." She was wearing a dove-gray dress that wrapped her body like a second skin. "I paid fifteen hundred dollars at Chanel in Paris for it."

"You look great in it," Scott complimented.

"Thank you. Doing anything special for Thanksgiving?"

"Is Thanksgiving here already?"

Beverly laughed. "You have been busy! It's next week."

"No plans yet." Scott regretted the words the minute they were out of his mouth.

"Really?" Beverly pounced. "I'm having a few people over. You're more than welcome to join us."

"Thanks for the invitation, but I don't think I should," Scott said, declining.

"Why? Because we were once lovers?" Beverly gave a mirthful laugh. "Darling, I'm quite over you. Isn't that right, Derek?"

Derek came from behind her, placing an arm around her. "That's right," he affirmed.

"If it makes you feel any better, I'll rescind the invitation. I just didn't think you'd want to spend Thanksgiving alone." Derek held out her mink, and she slipped into it. "We're running late so we'd better go. Enjoy your dinner, and for dessert order the raspberry mousse cake." Taking Derek's arm, Beverly departed with a wave of her fingers.

"Whew! I can't believe you were once involved with her!" Kyle exclaimed. "Consider yourself lucky to have gotten away."

Scott grinned. "Am I ever!"

Once outside La Caravelle, Beverly brushed off Derek's affections. "Must you glue yourself to me? I can hardly breathe."

Derek stepped back a pace. "Sorry."

"Darling, forgive me for being so beastly," she purred, "but I've suddenly developed the most excrutiating headache. I'm going to have to pass on the ballet."

"If you're not going, then neither am I," Derek firmly stated.

"You're an angel, but I won't allow you to make the sacrifice. You can't miss *Swan Lake.* I've heard that Baryshnikov has decided to break tradition and dress Odile, the wicked black swan, in white. You can't miss it!" She gave Derek a kiss on the cheek. "Run along to Lincoln Center. I'll be fine."

Derek knew there was no arguing with Beverly. "If you insist. I'll call in the morning to see how you're feeling."

Don't bother, she thought as she headed down West Fifty-fifth Street to hail a taxi on Fifth. Despite his wealth, Derek was a loser. He was nothing short of boring, and when it came to making love, on those few occasions when she had allowed him the privilege, he had been unable to satisfy her. Why had she gotten involved with him in the first place? He could never compare to Scott.

Scott. He had looked so wonderful. She'd hardly been able to contain her excitement after spotting him. But she had controlled herself, playing the role of self-absorbed socialite when all she had wanted was to sit at his table and stare at him for hours. How had she forgotten how deep his green eyes were? And she had wanted to run her fingers through his tawny hair, flicking back that persistent forelock that insisted on falling over his forehead. She had given a spectacular performance of controlled disinterest, although she'd slipped by inviting him over for Thanksgiving. Well, she'd withdrawn the invitation, and he thought she and Derek were an item.

Yet her insides were on fire and her senses stretched to the limit. She craved sexual satisfaction. Scott had ignited her sexual hunger, and it was raging. She had to have a man, any man, to satisfy her burning ache. Derek would never do, otherwise she would have brought him back to her duplex.

She needed a real man. Rough. Savage. Greedy. She wanted a man who would take her and pierce her with his shaft with only thoughts of his own satisfaction. Unknown to him, he'd be giving her the kind of lovemaking she wanted.

A taxi pulled to the curb and Beverly jumped in, away from the chilled November night. She gave directions to her duplex and then started planning the outfit she would wear when she came back outside.

Her "headache" was gone.

Inside her duplex Beverly tossed her mink and discarded her Chanel dress to the floor as she made a beeline for her bedroom. With mounting excitement in anticipation of what was to come, she pushed aside a panel of mirror, revealing her secret wardrobe.

Miniskirts and tight dresses and bustiers made of leather. Satin and lace merry widows and G-strings. Body stockings with low backs and scooped fronts. Leopard, zebra, and tiger print fabrics awaited her selection.

She slipped into a black lace body stocking. Then she chose a tight, faded denim miniskirt. She pulled on short white boots with spiked heels and left her pink silk blouse mostly unbuttoned.

Beverly twirled before her full-length mirror as she shook her French twist free. She looked so brazen! Her uptown crowd would have a coronary if they could see her now. She giggled, thinking of Scott. What would his reaction be?

Grabbing a silver-backed hairbrush, she brushed her chestnut hair into a wild, flowing mane. Sitting before her vanity, she applied liberal coatings of black mascara, ruby-red lipstick, green eye shadow, and thick slashes of rouge to her cheeks.

When she finished, she surveyed her completed image. How marvelously trashy! She was sure to attract a low-bred couth, not some white-bread loser like Derek. Not wanting to spend another second alone, she hurried from her duplex to find some action.

She took the subway down to the Village. Standing defiantly in the center of her subway car, she stretched and posed, basking in the catcalls sent her way. This was only a taste of things to come.

She went to Peggy Sue's on University Place near Thirteenth Street. It was located on the second floor above a pizza parlor and a Chinese restaurant. Black and white sketches, as well as magazine covers, sprinkled the walls. There was a bar, and Beverly headed for it, perching herself on a red plastic stool. After ordering a gin and tonic, she watched the dancers. There was a nice assortment of flesh on display, but nothing spectacular.

The sound of clicking billiard balls could be heard faintly through the pulsating music. With drink in hand, she headed in the direction of the corner billiard table.

Five men were playing, and one turned at her approach. He was shirtless, a black leather vest stretched tight over his well-sculpted chest. Tight black jeans were tucked into lizard-skin boots with silver tips. His left arm was tattooed with a coiled serpent ready to strike and his hands were rough and callused, the nails jagged and torn. His long, dark hair was tied back with a red bandana. Dark eyes appraised her as he removed the cigarette dangling from the corner of his mouth.

Beverly stopped in her tracks. She had hit the jackpot! She remained where she was, watching the game in progress and ignoring him until he inclined his head.

"Why are you standing so far away?" he asked.

"I don't want to break your concentration."

"What's your name?"

"Barbara. Yours?"

"Todd."

Beverly's eyes kept returning to Todd's tattoo.

"Want to touch it?" he asked.

"I want to taste it," she confessed.

"Go ahead."

Beverly moistened her lips and placed them over Todd's serpent tattoo. With her tongue she darted over the coiled design.

"Want a taste of something better?" Todd challenged.

Beverly looked at him beneath her lashes, moving her hands to his groin. "When?"

"Whenever you want."

She ruffled her fingers through Todd's hair as he clinched her around the waist. She rubbed her hands on his chest, thrilling at the touch of such sculpted perfection. "Do you lift weights?"

"Every day," he proudly revealed.

"Let's go to your gym," she urged, sticking her hands down the back of his pants and gripping his buttocks. She thrust her body against his as she gave him a long kiss. "We'll do it there."

Their sex was hot, wild, and savage. Beverly was a burning, wet center needing Todd's throbbing heat. He wasted no time with foreplay. Throwing her down on a sweat-stained mat in the deserted gym, he ripped away her denim miniskirt and plunged his erection through the paper-thin silk of her body stocking. He bit at her nipples and chewed at her neck as she repeatedly thrust her body at his. With guttural moans and rasping breaths, the two attacked each other with ferocity until their passions were drained. Then they started again.

"I'll bet a cunt like you never had it so good," Todd bragged. "You've probably spread your legs for plenty of guys, but none as good as me."

There was a tone of ugliness in his words. Beverly allowed herself not to panic. "How true." She gave him a kiss. "You're the best lover I ever had."

He caressed her throat. "How many guys have you had tonight?"

Beverly didn't like the hold he had on her throat, but she refused to flinch. "You're the only one."

He tightened his hold. "You better not be lying."

"Why would I lie?"

"All it takes is one squeeze," he informed her. "With one hard squeeze I could end your life."

"But you wouldn't, would you, Todd?" Beverly gave him a wicked smile. "You wouldn't want to risk prison. You wouldn't want to be pressed against a wall, especially at shower time."

He squeezed a little harder. "I could take a chance."

Beverly forced herself to remain calm. She swallowed twice before finding her voice. "But you'd lose. You don't have power and privilege," she sneered. "All you've got is a magnificent cock. I don't think it will get you many brownie points with a jury, but the boys behind bars will love it as much as I do."

His hand came away from her neck. "You're not worth the risk."

Beverly exhaled with relief.

12

Robyn's first Thanksgiving in New York, spent with Lydia, Ruby, Earl, and others from the boardinghouse, was wonderful. Lydia outdid herself in the kitchen, preparing a thirty-pound turkey with mashed potatoes, candied yams, stuffed mushrooms, string beans, and hot biscuits. There was homemade apple cider, and for dessert, a choice of either apple, cherry, or pumpkin pie with whipped cream or vanilla ice cream.

Quinn had invited her to come out to Chicago for the holiday, but she had turned him down. As much as she would have liked to see Quinn again, Robyn found herself constantly thinking of Scott Kendall. And she didn't know why. They had met for less than five minutes! True, he was strikingly handsome and she'd had to fight the urge to walk right up to him and brush back the forelock falling over his forehead. But it was more than just his looks. Scott Kendall had seemed real. There hadn't been any pretense or aura of importance in his words and gestures.

Part of her had hoped he would call her back for an interview. Yet so far she'd heard nothing.

"I'm stuffed!" Ruby exclaimed, tossing down her napkin. "Looks like I'll have to wash some dishes if I want to burn off a few calories." She started clearing away dishes. "You men settle yourselves in front of the TV. I know there's a football game you can't miss."

Robyn had to get her mind off Scott. She started piling dishes, and followed Ruby into the kitchen. "Want to wash and I'll dry?"

Ruby shooed her away. "Go relax. You work hard enough at the diner."

Robyn started wrapping leftovers. "I don't mind helping. It'll stop me from thinking how much I really wanted that job." She started filling the refrigerator. "I guess I might as well forget about Wellington Cosmetics."

Scott poked morosely at his frozen turkey dinner. Dressed in jeans and a Harvard sweatshirt, he was settled on his couch with the remote control.

Why had he been so stubborn? He had been given an invitation to a Thanksgiving dinner, and knowing he would be alone, had still turned it down. Georgina, who still wasn't talking to him, had flown to Los Angeles for a shot at a possible commercial. And Kyle was with his family in Boston. So what if the dinner was with Beverly and her uptown crowd? He'd survived plenty of her dinners before. He could do it again.

He checked the time. Three o'clock. Was there still time to call? Why not swallow his pride? It was better than being alone. There was nothing wrong with accepting Beverly's invitation, he told himself. It wasn't like they were going to be all alone.

He reached for the phone and dialed her number.

She'd done it again! Beverly proudly admired her Thanksgiving menu. First there would be beluga caviar on rye toast triangles. Then came a hearty oyster bisque. Turkey wouldn't be appearing on her menu today. It was such common fare, and so tasteless! Instead she had decided on roast goose with chestnut stuffing and creamed onions. Her one concession to holiday tradition was cranberry sauce. Waldorf salad with Roquefort dressing would be served as a side dish. And a dessert of mincemeat pie with whipped cream would complete the feast. The champagne she had chosen was a Veuve Clicquot 1982. After dessert there would be Rhum St. James in snifters as the women nibbled on Godiva chocolates and the men smoked Partagas cigars.

"Ms. Maxwell?"

Beverly looked up from her menu at her young maid. "Yes, Dagmar?"

"Mr. Kendall is on the line."

Scott? Calling today? Beverly's lips twitched into a satisfied smirk as she picked up her phone. "Scott, Happy Thanksgiving."

"Happy Thanksgiving. I hope I haven't caught you at a bad time."

She decided to dangle a carrot. "I was checking a few last-minute details. My guests won't be arriving for another hour. What can I do for you?"

Scott cleared his throat uncomfortably. "I know I turned down your invitation and this is very last-minute, but is your offer still open?"

She'd let him squirm. "What happened to your other plans?"

"My hosts had a family emergency."

Beverly clucked sympathetically. "Too bad for both of you. Darling, you know I'd love to have you over, but I've had the dinner catered. Individual meals have already been prepared."

"No big deal. I've got other people to call. I just thought I'd call you since you'd been the first to invite me."

"Are you sure? We could probably fiddle with the dinners. Although there's still the seating to deal with, I wouldn't want you to be alone on Thanksgiving. We can squeeze you in."

"Thanks, Beverly, but it sounds like too much trouble. Let me accept one of my other invitations. Have a great day."

"You too." She hung up her phone with glee. Let Scott wallow in his loneliness. Let him see how it felt to be alone. Did he really expect her to believe he had other dinner invitations? If he had, she'd have been the last person he called. She could have easily invited him to come over, but why make things easy for him? He still had a way to go before she accepted him back into her life. On her terms. She was more than willing to be patient. When the time came for Scott to grovel for her forgiveness, she intended on enjoying every minute of it.

Had he been crazy or just plain desperate? Scott stared at his phone incredulously. Had he been nuts?

Scott clicked on the football game, digging into his turkey dinner. The first forkful tasted like dried cardboard, but he chewed it. Anything would be better than a seat at Beverly's table. He started watching the football game. He couldn't wait till Monday. Hopefully by then he'd have found his mystery lady, and maybe, just maybe, he wouldn't be alone next Thanksgiving.

"Are you sure you don't mind locking up?"

Robyn pushed Earl forward with a gentle shove. "Will you get going? By the time you get to the hospital your new niece or nephew will have already arrived."

"You're a lifesaver. Don't worry about tomorrow morning. Ruby has her own set of keys. She'll open up."

"Go," she commanded, holding the door open.

"Want any help cleaning up?" Cheryl asked after Earl had gone.

"Don't you have a date?" Robyn asked.

Cheryl stifled a yawn. "It's only Bobby. We're just going to be watching 'Monday Night Football.' "

"But he'll be expecting you. Would you rather spend the rest of the night with Bobby or a sinkful of dirty dishes?"

Cheryl acted as though she was afraid that Robyn would change her mind. She quickly bundled herself up and hurried outside. "See you tomorrow."

Robyn locked the door after Cheryl, wistfully watching after her. It must be wonderful knowing you mattered in someone else's life, she thought. She began turning off the lights, heading toward the kitchen. She had reached the swinging doors when someone began tapping on the front-door glass. She squinted into the interior gloom of the diner, trying to catch a glimpse of the figure standing out in the shadows. It was hard to do. He was wearing a trench coat with the collar drawn up and a hat rakishly tilted to one side of his bent head.

"We're closed," she called out.

The figure shouted back an answer, but Robyn was unable to hear the words. Edging forward a few steps, she repeated her earlier statement.

This time she was able to hear the words. This time she was able to identify both the figure and the voice. It was Scott Kendall. She ran to the door, fumbling with the keys as she unlocked it. "I'm sorry I left you out there for so long," she apologized, holding the door open.

Scott entered the diner, his green eyes glistening mischievously. Suddenly Robyn became aware of her appearance. She looked like a harried waitress, not a well-groomed secretary. She nervously tugged at the ribbon that held her hair back in a ponytail. "I must look a sight."

"Nonsense. You're a beautiful woman," Scott complimented.

At a loss for words, Robyn seated Scott at a table, her waitressing skills springing into action. "Can I get you anything? Coffee?"

Scott laughed, clearly amused. He extended his arm to the seat across from him. "I think it's better that you be sitting when I tell you what I want. First of all, what's your name?"

"Don't you know it?"

"No. Don't ask why. It's a long story."

"My name is Robyn . . . Robyn Prescott."

Scott smiled. "Well, Robyn, shall we get down to business?"

Robyn tried to control her excitement. "Does this mean I've got a shot at the job?"

Scott unfolded the newspaper he had been carrying under his arm, spreading it open on the table as he began flipping through the pages. "No," he answered, "you haven't gotten the secretarial job."

The hopes that had started rising fell. Robyn fought back

pangs of disappointment. If she hadn't gotten the job, then why was Scott Kendall here? Why had he gone to the trouble of tracking her down?

Scott finally found what he'd been searching for. He twisted the paper around to Robyn, pushing it toward her. "Wipe away that look and read this."

It was a full-page ad in *The New York Times* for the new Fresh and Lovely Girl. There was a model, but her face was blank, replaced by a question mark. Below was the logo for Wellington Cosmetics, asking "Who will be the new Fresh and Lovely Girl?"

Robyn looked from the ad to Scott. "Am I missing something?"

"I've been searching for the new Fresh and Lovely Girl, and now I've finally found her."

"Me?" she asked incredulously, the realization of Scott's words dawning on her. She pointed to the ad. "You want my face to go there?"

"Not just there, but everywhere!" Scott enthused. "Billboards, magazine covers, television commercials."

"But why me?" Robyn persisted.

"Why not?" His palm traveled slowly along her cheek before he bent his lips to hers. "I know I've already said it, but you're an exceedingly beautiful woman," he whispered.

She received the kiss before abruptly pulling away. Although she wanted to let her lips linger against his, she refrained from doing so. Suddenly she was uncertain. Control of her emotions was slipping away. Feelings and sensations were running rampant throughout her body, and all she wanted to do was prolong the pleasure. But she stopped herself, not knowing how she should react. This was happening so fast!

"I'm sorry," Scott apologized. "I shouldn't have done that."

"No harm done." She gave an embarrassed smile and rose from the table. "You've certainly given me a lot to think about, Mr. Kendall."

"Call me Scott and tell me what there is to think about. Wellington Cosmetics is presenting you with the opportunity of a lifetime. Any woman in America would be willing to trade places with you. Don't you understand? The search is over. Wellington has found its Fresh and Lovely Girl."

"But why me?" she asked again. "I don't know the first thing about being a model."

Scott spoke to her in a reassuring tone. "I'll be there to help you."

"Will we be working closely together?"

"Would that make a difference in your decision?"

"It might," she revealed.

"For a while, yes. Robyn, there are no strings attached to this offer. Forget about what happened a few seconds ago. If all you want is to be the Fresh and Lovely Girl, fine. If anything else is meant to happen, it will. Otherwise, it was never meant to be. Okay?"

Those were exactly the words she had been waiting to hear. Learning to trust again wouldn't be easy, but she had to take a chance. She would take a chance with Scott Kendall. Her instincts told her he wouldn't hurt her. She looked into his eyes. "Are you sure you know what you're getting into? This will all be new to me."

"I'll always be there if you need someone," Scott promised. "Will you take the job?"

Robyn considered her options. Being the Fresh and Lovely Girl would be a dream come true. She knew it wouldn't always be easy, but it would be fun and exciting. The money was a temptation, and there would be other opportunities should she ever decide to explore them. Based on those factors alone, she would be foolish not to accept. But there was one overriding factor that made up her mind: Scott Kendall. When he had reassured her earlier, Robyn had seen the sincerity of his words in his eyes.

"My answer is yes," she told him.

Scott released a hearty yowl of satisfaction, drawing her into his arms for a hug. "Fantastic! I knew you wouldn't let me down." He released her and then started leading her to the front door. "Come on, we've got to celebrate."

Robyn released her hand from his. "Sorry, but I can't. Until I become the Fresh and Lovely Girl, I'm still a waitress. I've still got responsibilities, including a sinkful of dirty dishes."

Scott started unbuttoning the cuffs of his shirt, rolling up the sleeves. "Lead the way."

Robyn was aghast. "I can't make you do dishes," she protested.

"I'll wash and you dry. If I leave you here alone, you'll probably end up daydreaming till dawn." He cocked his head in the direction of the kitchen. "Coming?"

Robyn followed him, not wanting to let him out of her sight. "You bet I am."

13

The morning after accepting Scott's offer to become the Fresh and Lovely Girl, Robyn met with him at the Wellington offices.

"Before we start going into details, there's someone I'd like you to meet," he said.

"Who?"

"Your agent, Samantha D'Urban."

The back of Scott's swivel chair turned, revealing Samantha D'Urban. She was a ravishing woman in her early forties with jet-black hair worn in a blunt cut and piercing gray eyes. She had a preference for wearing only white silk blouses, black leather skirts, and gold jewelry; she always looked stunning in the outfit. A former model herself, she had decided to open her own agency, Ravish, once her career had begun to slow down. Though her agency was small, consisting of thirty models, they were the most sought after and highest paid in the industry.

Samantha's voice was low and husky. "Scott had me on the phone all of yesterday afternoon, raving about you. I can see why."

Though the conversation began hesitantly, with Samantha doing most of the talking, the pace soon picked up. At first Robyn was tongue-tied being in the presence of a woman as beautiful and successful as Samantha. But Samantha was so warm and engaging that Robyn began to open up. Samantha entertained her with stories of her modeling days, along with vivid descriptions of the locations she had been to: Paris, Athens, London, Milan. Robyn was mesmerized by her storytelling, and astonished when Samantha told her the same experiences were awaiting her.

Scott was nothing less than impressed with Robyn. She possessed both a self-reserve and modesty that was a startling contrast to her exceptional beauty. It was a hard combination to find. It looked as though he had a winner.

After a while Scott decided to break into the conversation. "Robyn, you've gotten to talk with Samantha. Is she the type of person you'd like representing you? The decision is yours. But I want you to know she's one of the best."

"The best, darling," Samantha corrected.

"I like Samantha very much," Robyn said. "I think we'd get along well. But I only have one question. I hope you don't think it's a foolish one." She looked first to Scott, then to Samantha and back. "Will I really be needing an agent? Is being the Fresh and Lovely Girl going to keep me *that* busy?"

Samantha lit a cigarette. "Hardly. Wellington will take up a small but substantial portion of your time. Once your face hits the public, you're going to be in demand."

"She's right," Scott concurred. "Wellington is going to be your main priority, but offers will be pouring in. You'd be foolish not to capitalize on them."

"Do you really think so?"

"Don't take this as an insult," Samantha stated, "but your lack of confidence is refreshing. Most girls in this business think they're going to conquer the world with their face."

Robyn turned to Scott. "If you think I need an agent, then I'd like Samantha to represent me."

"Wonderful. I knew you were Ravish material," Samantha drawled while exhaling a puff of smoke. "Let me start spreading the word. I've a few jobs in mind that I think you'd be perfect for." Samantha got to her feet. "I've got another appointment to run to. Scott's going to tell you all about the Wellington contract. I couldn't make any changes since this was a contest, but the terms are very good." She brushed cheeks with Robyn before leaving. "I'll call you later in the week."

The rest of the morning was spent in going through the Wellington contract point by point, with Scott explaining each clause as simply as possible.

"Any questions?" Scott asked after they finished discussing the contract.

"None. Let me sign before you change your mind."

"That would never happen, but are you sure you want to sign?"

Robyn began signing while Scott was still advising. "What more could I possibly want? Wellington's given me practically everything on a silver platter." She signed each page with flourish, handing the gold pen back to Scott with three signed copies of the contract. "Including a handsome boss."

"The months ahead are going to be wonderful," Scott said.

"Promise?"

He gave her a wink. "Promise."

Erica Shelton sat in her agent's office while her portfolio was being inspected. She was sure Constance would have no complaints. She had managed to compile a montage of her best and most recent work.

Compliments were rare and few from Constance Carter. At sixty-five the silver-haired woman was still grande dame of the modeling world, dividing her time before and behind the camera. Models who worked for her made it to the top because Constance pushed them there. She wouldn't accept anything less.

"Wonderful book," Constance enthused. "I'm so glad you're keeping it up to date."

Erica beamed with pride. Constance was usually so hard to please.

"Where are the Wellington photos?"

Erica's feeling of elation passed. She didn't like the phrasing of the question. It had been a demand. When Constance demanded, she expected.

"I got rid of them."

"Are you insane? Those photos were phenomenal."

Erica had wanted no reminders of her days at Wellington. That's why she had disposed of the photos. Anyway, her portfolio was strong enough without them. "They weren't so great."

"I disagree. Get them back," Constance decreed. "Without them this portfolio doesn't merit my attention."

"But why?"

"I'm in this business to make money for both you and me. All I have to do is flash those Wellington photos and I'll double your fee." She dismissed Erica with a wave of her hand. "Contact the photographer. Wasn't it Lance Richards? I'm sure he has duplicates."

Erica sighed, closing her portfolio. Just when she thought she had finished with Lance, another round of sexual tag was about to begin.

14

Robyn's life began to change drastically. Caught up in a whirlwind of glamour and excitement, she found herself the center of attention, loving every minute of it.

Her days were jam-packed during the month of December, and most of her time was spent with Samantha, rather than Scott. Although Wellington had sent out press releases with a few preliminary photos of her to all the major newspapers, magazines, television and radio stations, the first press conference intended to introduce her wasn't scheduled until March.

"We want to build anticipation," Scott explained. "Right now everyone is caught up in the holiday spirit. We want full attention, and March is the perfect month to grab it. All of our work will be taking place in January and February. After you meet with the press, Wellington intends on flooding the market with the new Fresh and Lovely campaign. In the meantime, you're going to be seen around New York at some of the poshest places with some of the biggest names from other industries. Your name is going to be dropped in columns and excitement is going to build. Everyone is going to wonder where you've come from, and the answer will be found in only one place: Wellington."

Robyn was taken on an elaborate shopping spree with Samantha for creating her new image. As they were being driven in Samantha's chauffeured limousine, Robyn asked how much they would be spending.

"Forget the prices." Samantha fanned an array of credit cards. "We'll be using plastic. If something catches your eye, let me know and we'll buy it. Let me know your preference in color and style so I can keep my eyes open. Don't worry about paying me back. I'll recoup the costs from my commission. Our goal is to make you look stunning."

They started with the European designers. At Laura Ashley Samantha loaded Robyn with off-the-shoulder sweaters with pearlized snaps in black, white, yellow, and red, as well as a strapless dinner dress in a rich burgundy and a deep emerald shirt dress with pleated yoke shoulders.

At Yves St. Laurent Robyn fell in love with a beaded silk tulle top and matching silk pants, as well as a hot pink linen dress with a bare crisscross back. The Chanel Boutique, famous for its cream-and-black lacquered walls and mirrored staircase with wrought-iron handrail, left Robyn breathless. Samantha insisted on purchasing her a blue silk crepe evening gown decorated with a mother-of-pearl necklace. They also picked up a two-piece charcoal-gray Chanel wool suit.

At twelve-thirty Robyn and Samantha walked down to West Fifty-seventh and had lunch at the Russian Tea Room.

"You must have the blinis," Samantha recommended after she ordered herself a vodka.

While they were having lunch, a number of people came up to their booth. Samantha took great pride in introducing Robyn as her newest Ravish model, promising great things were on the horizon.

After lunch they tackled the American designers at a number of department stores. At Sak's they purchased a violet Perry Ellis dress with a stand-away collar; at Bonwit Teller's they found a red leather cropped jacket and slim skirt by Carolina Herrera; Bergdorf Goodman's offered a white cotton suit with brass buttons by Anne Klein and a red crepe evening gown by Valentino; at Bloomingdale's they jumped on a pale peach double-breasted blouse with shawl collar and long fluted skirt by Liz Claiborne.

La Bagagerie was a pit stop for clutch bags, shoulder bags, large totes, luggage, and vanity cases by Chanel, Gucci, Vuitton, and Fendi. Shoes made of ostrich, crocodile, alligator, lizard, and leather, in a rainbow of colors, came from Maud Frizon and Charles Jourdan. Lace camisoles, slips, bras, and string bikinis in the softest materials were purchased at Victoria's Secret. Swiss-made stockings were picked up at Fogal on Madison Avenue.

At Goldin-Feldman on Seventh Avenue, Samantha had three furs custom made for Robyn. One was a black mink, the second a gray raccoon, and the third a red shearling. Robyn was shocked by the extravagant fur prices and told Samantha how she felt.

"Darling," Samantha drawled in her smoker's rasp, "you have an image to build."

"But I'm really uncomfortable with spending all this money." Robyn had been keeping a running tab the entire day. If her calculations were correct, they had spent close to fifty thousand dollars.

"Robyn, you're going to be the modeling world's newest star," Samantha patiently explained. "We can't have you seen in a cloth coat!"

At the end of the day Robyn was smothered with packages. "I don't know where I'm going to put all this!"

"Why not get an apartment of your own?"

Robyn was hesitant. "I like living where I am. I don't think I'd want to live alone."

Samantha, being Samantha, was blunt and to the point. "Then consider a roommate. You're going to be traveling in a different world from the people you live with. Sooner or later you'll have to make the break."

"Then I'll settle for later." Robyn struggled to gather the rest of her packages. Kevin, Samantha's chauffeur, raced to assist her.

Samantha gestured wildly with her cigarette lighter. "Whatever." She lit her cigarette. "Get a good night's sleep. Tomorrow we start working on your portfolio."

"Okay. Thanks for today. It was great."

Samantha released a puff of smoke. "Robyn, you ain't seen nothing yet!"

The following morning Samantha arrived at ten.

"We want your photos to look as good as you do in person," Samantha explained. "It's not going to be an easy feat, but when you have some of the best people in the business working for you, it becomes possible."

Robyn was intrigued. "How possible?"

"I've called in a few favors. José Eber has flown in from Beverly Hills. He's going to work magic with your hair. Adrien Arpel herself will work on your face. Once they're finished, you'll be clad only in Bob Mackie and Nolan Miller creations. Then you'll be immortalized on film by Francesco Scavullo."

Robyn gave Samantha an incredulous look. The names, such famous names, were stellar. "Are you serious?"

Samantha patted Robyn's knee. "Never more."

The creative geniuses Samantha had gathered together all worked their special brand of magic, and Robyn enjoyed every minute of attention lavished on her. Samantha was ferocious with all of them, including Robyn, demanding their best because she knew they had it in them and nothing else would do.

After twelve hours Samantha called the day to an end. Robyn, clad in a jade silk crepe gown, her hair in a thick, long braid, smiled gratefully at the departing talents as they left the studio Samantha had rented for the day. When they were gone, she kicked off her heels. "I'm exhausted."

"Sorry if I cracked the whip too hard, but wait till you see the results. I guarantee brilliance," Samantha promised.

Robyn turned the last page of her portfolio. She still couldn't believe the face she was seeing was *hers*. She looked so sophisticated, worldly, glamorous, wealthy . . . beautiful.

She turned back the pages. Was this *really* her? She had never seen this image in her mirror before. Never.

"Am I as good as my word or what?" Samantha boasted.

"Is this what people see when they look at me?" Robyn asked.

"More or less. Your image is extremely polished in those photos, but it's you."

Robyn was at Samantha's West Fifty-seventh Street office. From her window there was a glorious view of Central Park. The furniture was all modern, consisting of glistening metal and glass, sprinkled with abstract sculptures and paintings. The floors were shiny hardwood, and the walls a cool white decorated with photos of Samantha's other Ravish models. Robyn knew her photo would soon join the others.

"What's next?"

"Time for me to earn my commission. I'll start sending out your portfolio and look through the assignments that have come in. Word will spread like wildfire once they hear there's a hot new face on the block. Trust me. They'll be lining up outside the door."

"Is there anything you want me to do?"

"Concentrate on looking your best. We're going to be hitting the party circuit. I'll let you know when and where you have to be to knock New York's socks off!"

Within a week Robyn's name and face started appearing in New York gossip columns. Suzy described Robyn's new wardrobe in lavish detail. Liz Smith got catty about the rivalry between Eileen Ford and Samantha, asking how Eileen had let Robyn slip through her fingers.

Robyn attended a number of Christmas parties with Samantha and was constantly being introduced. At a party given by Lancôme at Tavern on the Green, Robyn met Isabella Rossellini and found her to be lovely and gracious. At the Rainbow Room she met the legendary silver-haired Carmen, and marveled at the older model's flawless beauty.

Although the parties were fun, Robyn found them exhausting. She had attended so many that she hadn't even gone Christmas shopping yet, and Christmas Eve was only six days away! Feeling guilty about all the money she had spent on herself, she decided that those on her Christmas list would receive only the best. With her first check from Wellington, she knew she could afford to splurge.

Not wanting to be the least bit glamorous, Robyn slipped into a pair of jeans, an oversized sweater, and sneakers, pulled her hair into a ponytail and grabbed her ski jacket, ready to hit the stores.

Surrounded by piles of her finest winter clothing, Georgina carefully eyed her three empty Vuitton suitcases. Was she taking too much? Nonsense! She had to look her best at all times. Better to pack more than less, although it looked like she was pinched for space.

"Bettina," she called, "have Henry bring my Vuitton trunk."

Georgina was spending Christmas and New Year's in Aspen. She had to get out of New York. She was sick of being bombarded by Robyn Prescott's name and face. The worse was still to come once Wellington revved up its new Fresh and Lovely campaign.

Georgina knew her career was in serious trouble. Although she had gotten the commercial she had auditioned for in L.A., the product was hardly glamorous. Who wanted to be associated with a dandruff shampoo? The only other offers her agent had recently gotten were for tampon and deodorant ads. Georgina refused them. She had her pride, and her heart was set on becoming the next L'Xuriance blonde.

L'Xuriance Hair Color was getting ready to launch a new campaign featuring a blonde, redhead, and brunette. Georgina was pushing her agent to do all she could to get her the job. Who was blonder than she? Women would kill for her hair color. Look at how L'Oréal had boosted the careers of Meredith Baxter Birney and Cybil Shephard. The people at L'Xuriance would have to be nuts not to choose her.

Henry came in with the Vuitton trunk. After putting it down, he asked, "Shall I retrieve Mr. Richards's luggage?"

"Lance will be spending the holidays alone. I'll be leaving on the twentieth and returning on the fifth. You and Bettina are to take that time off. Lance will take care of himself."

"Very good." Henry withdrew from the bedroom.

Georgina started wrapping her clothes in tissue paper. She couldn't wait to tell Lance he'd be spending Christmas alone. It served him right for all the nights he'd left her alone. Last year had been the ultimate humiliation. She had planned a Christmas Eve dinner for the two of them, and he never bothered showing up. She had also spent hours shopping for his gifts, and he had given her nothing. This year she was returning both gestures.

There was a discreet knock on the bedroom door. "Come in."

"Mrs. Richards, your brother is on the phone," Bettina said as she entered.

"Is it business?"

Bettina shook her head. "He'd like to know your holiday plans."

Georgina gave Bettina a stern look. "I left specific instructions if Scott was to call." She continued wrapping her clothes with tissue paper. "Tell him I'm unavailable."

Bettina left the bedroom without argument, and Georgina refused to dwell on thoughts of her brother. She wouldn't wonder if Scott was going to be alone. He probably had plans for the holiday. If not, he could consider working on a reconciliation. He knew what would patch up their differences: her return to Wellington.

The phone rang again, and she snatched it up. "Yes? Scott?"

"It's Lance."

"What can I do for you?" she coolly asked. She hadn't seen or heard from him in a week. She couldn't wait to drop her little bombshell. "When will you be dropping by?" This *had* to be done in person.

"I won't."

"Why not?" she demanded, losing her cool. "It's Christmas. I'm your wife."

"I've got to fly off to Switzerland on assignment. I tried to get out of it, but these things can't be helped."

Georgina heard several high giggles in the background. "I'll bet," she spat out. "Hopping away with some snow bunnies?"

"Have a happy holiday, love. Don't drink too much eggnog, and watch those rum balls!"

He'd beaten her to the punch. He'd screwed her again! "Fuck you, hubby dearest," she snarled. "I hope your dick freezes off on the slopes!"

It was the day before Christmas Eve, and Robyn was immersed in rolls of wrapping paper, bows, and ribbon. She knew she had gone overboard with her shopping, but had been unable to resist. As she was placing her last package under the tree, she heard the door bell. Seconds later Lydia announced she had a visitor.

"Who is it?"

"He wouldn't give his name, but he's gorgeous!" Lydia raved. "Shall I show him in?"

It had to be Scott. Robyn's heart raced as she checked her image in a mirror. Why did she always *not* look her best when she was least prepared to see him? She played with her bangs before racing back to the tree and retrieving his present. Nothing extravagant. Only a Swiss-made watch with a sunburst dial. Kind of a thank-you for the opportunity he had given her. She scooted Lydia out of the living room, holding the present behind her back. "Show him in."

At the sound of approaching footsteps, Robyn's face broke into a smile. She was looking forward to seeing Scott alone. Their paths had hardly crossed since he'd offered her the job.

When Quinn entered the living room, his arms full of beautifully wrapped gifts, Robyn's smile faltered. Quinn was the last person she had expected to see. What was he doing here?

"Is that any way to greet an old friend?" he asked while setting down his pile of packages.

What was wrong with her? She was thrilled to see him. His unexpected visit had only taken her by surprise. She was just disappointed that Scott wasn't the one standing before her. She put down the gift she had been hiding behind her back and warmly embraced Quinn.

He held her tightly . . . too tightly for her liking. There was something intimate in his embrace. Months ago she would have thrilled to have his arms around her like this. But not today. Her feelings for Quinn were merely of friendship. After a quick kiss on his cheek, she broke the embrace. "Quinn, it's good to see you. Why didn't you let me know you were coming? I would have made special plans."

"I wanted to surprise you." He gave her a wide smile. "Robyn, you're still as beautiful as ever. No wonder they chose you to be the Fresh and Lovely Girl."

"You sound like you haven't seen me in ages. It's only been six months."

"Six months too long. It seems like forever. I've missed you."

"And I've missed you," she honestly admitted. "You're one of my closest friends."

"Is that all?"

Robyn sighed. "Quinn—"

He held his hands up in surrender. "Sorry. It's Christmas. Let's not spoil the season. Okay?"

"Okay," Robyn agreed in relief. Sooner or later she was going to have to have another talk with Quinn, but now wasn't the time. As he'd said, it was Christmas. "Why don't we go out for dinner tonight? My treat. We can do some catching up."

"That's an offer I can't refuse."

"How long will you be in New York?"

"Two weeks."

"Great. I can play tour guide. I don't start work till after New Year's."

Quinn indicated his pile of gifts. "Want to open a few?"

"We have to wait till Christmas," she scolded, eyeing the large pile. "You shouldn't have spent so much. Don't you know good things come in small packages?"

"Is that a hint?"

She looked at him in confusion.

"I saw the gift you were hiding behind your back when I came in. It's for me, right?" He made a beeline for it. "Can I shake it?"

Robyn raced ahead of Quinn in panic, managing to grab the package before he did, thrusting it behind her back. "You have to let me give it to you." She tore away the tag with Scott's name, crumpling it in her fist. She couldn't give Quinn the sweater and cologne she had originally purchased for him. He deserved a special gift. He'd done so much for her. Yet why did she feel like she was betraying Scott by giving away his gift?

She made sure there was a smile on her face as she handed Quinn the gift. "Merry Christmas."

Should he or shouldn't he? She probably had plans for Christmas. Maybe. Maybe not. He wasn't going to find out unless he called.

Scott, as nervous as a teenager, was at his desk at Wellington Cosmetics, contemplating a call to Robyn. What was the big deal? He had made dates before with other women. But they hadn't made him feel the way Robyn did, and if she was unable to spend Christmas with him, he was going to be immensely disappointed. He knew he might be moving too fast—after all, they had agreed to take things slowly—but there was a chemistry between them. Scott couldn't explain it, but whenever he was around Robyn, he felt different. Special. He picked up the phone and dialed. Before he knew it, Robyn was on the line.

"It's nice to hear from you," she said. "I was beginning to forget the sound of your voice."

He plunged right in. "Why don't we fix that? Do you have any plans for Christmas?"

"I'm sorry, but an old friend dropped in."

She sounded as disappointed as he felt. Or was he hearing what he wanted? He decided he would make a sacrifice. "Why don't you bring her along? Maybe I can get Kyle to join us." Seeing her with others was better than not seeing her at all.

"I don't think Quinn is Kyle's type."

Her friend was a man! Was he her boyfriend? She had never mentioned having a boyfriend, but then again, he'd never asked, and her private life was her own business. What if she was serious about this guy? No, she couldn't be. She'd been in New York for six months. Any man who'd let her get away would have to be a fool. And she had indicated interest in him. He hustled for an excuse, since he didn't know what direction the conversation should take. Damn, but he was feeling jealous! "I'd better go. I'm running late for a meeting. Have a wonderful Christmas."

"You too."

After he hung up, Kyle stuck his head in. "Why so glum, chum? Beverly extend a Christmas invitation?"

Scott shook his head. "She's in Paris for the holidays. I ran into her at Bloomingdale's last week and got her full itinerary."

"What are your plans?"

"At the moment? None."

"How about coming out to Boston? My family would love to see you."

Scott snatched the invitation. He wasn't about to replay his Thanksgiving. "Sounds terrific."

"Care to explain the frown you had on your face?"

"I want you to be a witness," Scott stated.

"To what?"

"My New Year's resolution."

"Namely . . ."

Scott looked at Kyle with determination. "In 1989 I'm going to win Robyn Prescott's heart."

15

Life as the Fresh and Lovely Girl started in January with Robyn's first day before the camera. Shooting was for a series of print ads that would appear in a majority of women's magazine's; *Cosmopolitan, Elle, Vogue, Mademoiselle.* The photographer was Lance Richards. Along with the usual entourage of assistants, hair dressers, and makeup people, Scott, Kyle, and Samantha were also present at the shoot.

Robyn had no problems with posing before the camera. The shoot she had done for her portfolio had gone smoothly, and she was looking forward to getting to work. Yet once Lance started shooting, giving her directions and instructions, fear suddenly enveloped her. She froze. An image flashed through her mind. She was no longer in New York, but Chicago. She was on a set, surrounded by other people. She didn't want to be in front of them, but knew she had to do what they wanted. If she didn't, they would get angry and hurt her. She felt vulnerable . . . exposed. A man's face emerged from the hazy memory . . . his face was the one she had visualized at Quinn's apartment. Who was he? Why did he scare her so? The memory started to fade and Robyn fought to retain it. Yet it kept slipping away, leaving behind a frustrating void.

Lance, notorious for his short temper, exploded. "What the hell is going on?" He handed his camera to an assistant, heading over to Robyn. "Loosen up, you're as stiff as a board." He tried to tilt her head at an angle, but Robyn violently pulled away, mistaking him for the unidentified man.

"Don't touch me!"

Lance threw up his hands in exasperation. "Jesus Christ, I'm only trying to do my job." He turned to Scott. "Would you explain things to her? I haven't got all day."

A voice boomed from the darkness surrounding the set. "Don't even bother asking, Lance. What can they do with an amateur?"

All eyes turned as Georgina strolled onto the set. "You promised to take some photographs, darling. Let's show her how a professional gets things done." Georgina gave Robyn a gentle shove, pushing her to one side as she took center stage beneath the lights and backdrop. She tossed her fur to an assistant, running her fingers through her hair as she started posing. Lance retrieved his camera and started shuttering away.

Robyn watched from the shadows as Georgina's professionalism came into action. She was a natural before the camera and knew all the right moves.

The angry whispers floated over, and Robyn couldn't help but overhear them.

"What's she doing here?" Samantha furiously demanded. The agent in her had risen, ready to do battle for her client. "How did she find out about the shoot?"

"Lance must have mentioned it," Kyle stated.

"I want her off the set." Samantha stubbed out her cigarette. "This minute."

"Let Georgina stay. I think Robyn should watch. Can't you see this might do us some good?" Kyle reasoned. "Maybe it will help Robyn know what to do before the camera. You have to admit she does need some polishing."

"I agree," Scott stated, "although it's probably only stage fright. Having Georgina around might raise her competitiveness."

"Let's hope so, otherwise we're in trouble," Kyle said.

"The shoot isn't a total waste," Scott pointed out. "We're getting some spectacular shots of Georgina."

Samantha refused to be ignored, wanting action for her client. "Scott, what are you going to do about this? I want Georgina removed. This isn't helping Robyn at all."

"True, but my sister can be good when she wants to," Scott admitted. "Don't worry, Samantha. Robyn is still our number-one girl. I'll go have a talk with her. We're losing money just standing around."

Robyn didn't want to hear false words of sympathy. Before Scott could reach her, she ran to her dressing room, locking the door behind her as the tears began to fall.

The makeup that had been so delicately applied was ruined, and Robyn felt like a little girl playing dress-up. She wasn't a model. What was she doing here? Why had she deluded herself into believing she could do it? Reaching for a clump of tissues, she wiped away both her tears and smudged makeup.

A tentative knock came from the door, but Robyn ignored it. She couldn't face Scott. A more forceful knock followed. "Go away," she said.

"Somebody's in there! Thank God! Listen, I'm desperate to use the loo."

The voice wasn't Scott's. Curiosity aroused, Robyn unlocked the door. A dark-haired model who had also been on the set dashed into the dressing room and headed for the bathroom.

"You really saved the day," she called out. "Another second longer and I would have burst." The toilet was flushed and the model reappeared, turning her back to

Robyn. "Mind zipping me up? Thanks." She turned to face Robyn once the task was completed. "Allow me to introduce myself. I'm Kristen Adams."

"Robyn Prescott."

Kristen walked over to a small refrigerator, removing a container of plain yogurt and a jar of wheat germ. "Would you care to join me?" she asked while mixing the two. She saw Robyn's hesitation and brushed it aside. "Don't feel obligated. I'm on a diet, so I'll probably feel the same way you do in a month." She stirred the yogurt ruefully. "I've got to lose five pounds. Once I've shed them I'll be okay." Kristen swallowed a spoonful of yogurt and wheat germ as she wandered over to the couch, kicking off her high heels and gratefully wiggling her toes. "So tell me, is the shoot still on?"

Robyn found herself immensely liking this bubbly, talkative model, and decided to open up. "I'm scared. I didn't know that until I was in front of the camera. I don't think I can go back out there."

"Let me give you some advice. I've been modeling for five years, and the first time is always the hardest. But it's probably twice as hard for you. Not only are you modeling for the first time, but everyone's watching. Wellington has got a lot at stake. Everyone's asking if you can help save the company. If you don't believe me, just go out there and listen. You're the hot topic of conversation. I can understand the pressure."

"What if I freeze up again?" What if the memories returned? Robyn fearfully wondered. She didn't like the bits and pieces she was recalling. What was she going to learn about her past?

"Some more free advice," Kristen continued. "Take a lesson from me. When you're out there, let your mind go blank. Ignore everyone else. Concentrate on the camera, the photographer, and on having a good time. After all, that's what you're getting paid for. It always works for me."

"What if I'm not good enough? What if they compare me to her?"

"Who?"

"The model Lance is photographing."

"Georgina?" Kristen hooted with laughter. "Are you ready for a news flash? You're the one who replaced her!"

"What?" Robyn couldn't believe it. What possible reason could there be? Georgina was so beautiful. It was obvious she had spent years before the camera. How could she be replaced?

Kristen was able to read the thoughts flashing through her mind. "I've worked with Georgina before. We've shared dressing rooms. She drinks. Her drinking got out of control and she let it come before her modeling. Don't feel sorry for her. She purposely showed up today to unnerve you."

"It worked," Robyn confessed.

"Temporarily," Kristen confirmed. "I just set you straight. Look, Robyn, no two models are exactly alike. Each one has a special quality that the camera is able to capture. For me, it's my brashness. For Georgina, it's her cool elegance. But who knows what the camera will capture in you? There's only one way to find out, and you can't do it hiding in here. You've got to get back out there."

"Will you come with me?"

"Would you like me to?"

Robyn gave Kristen an encouraging smile. "I think it would be easier if I had a friend watching."

Robyn's second attempt before the camera was a success. After having her hair and makeup repaired, she strolled back onto the set with an air of renewed confidence.

Lance was skeptical at first but willing to try again. Georgina sulked in the shadows while Scott, Kyle, and Samantha watched hopefully.

At first Robyn was tense. It didn't help when Lance started cursing. But then, from the corner of her eye, she caught sight of Kristen and remembered their pep talk. Kristen's words worked, and by the end of the afternoon Robyn felt as though she had always been intended to be in front of the camera. She was disappointed when the day's shoot came to an end. It seemed like she had only started.

"You were wonderful," Scott congratulated. "I can't wait to see the photographs. Why don't we go somewhere and celebrate your first day?"

"Sounds inviting," Samantha interjected, "but I've still got a busy schedule." She touched arms with Robyn. "I'll call you tomorrow about some possible job offers." She gave an encouraging wink on her way out. "The shoot was spectacular. Looks like you're on your way."

Robyn was flattered by the remark. Samantha's confidence in her had been unwavering, but Scott had been another case. She had heard the faint traces of uncertainty in his voice, and she couldn't forget his remark that she was wasting the company's money.

"Guess it's only you and me," he secretly whispered.

She gave Scott a chilly smile. "I've already made other plans."

"With who?" Could she have plans with Quinn?

Robyn couldn't think of a name to give. Then, seeing Kristen pass, she grabbed her arm. "Kristen and I are going to Chinatown."

"We are?" Robyn discreetly gave Kristen a poke in the ribs. "Yeah! Right! Chinatown." Kristen gave Scott a full smile. "Love to chat, Scott, but we've got to change."

"We'll have to celebrate another time," Scott said, trying not to look too disappointed. At least Robyn was going out with Kristen and not Quinn. When she had said she had other plans, he had again felt an unfamiliar pang of jealousy.

"Maybe lunch," Robyn proposed vaguely, purposely trying to dispel any of Scott's romantic intentions. It would be some time before she was willing to forgive Scott for his remark. Perhaps as long as a week. After all, how could any woman hold a grudge against him?

Scott closed the door to his office. "Just what kind of a stunt were you trying to pull?" he demanded.

Once Robyn had regained her composure and the shoot had continued as scheduled, he had pulled Georgina to one side, requesting a meeting for later in the afternoon.

"What are you getting so upset about?" she huffed. "I showed the girl how things are supposed to be done. The shoot was a success."

"It could have backfired."

Georgina dismissed Scott's reasons. "But it didn't. You

got some adequate shots of her and some spectacular shots of me. Scott, I want to come back to Wellington. I need to come back," she implored. "Working here is where I had the most confidence in my work. You saw the shoot this morning. You saw how together I am. My drinking is under control. Please, Scott, I'm begging you. I need to spend some time with Lance. Our marriage is in trouble. This is all we have left to share. With some luck, we could salvage what we once had. You saw how well we work together. Not only would I be able to resurrect my career, but also my marriage. What do you say?"

Scott wanted nothing more than to make amends with his sister. Yet before he made any reconciliatory offers, he wanted her to be aware of the situation. "You realize that you wouldn't be returning as Wellington's top model."

"I understand."

"That spot belongs to Robyn," he pointed out.

"Of course."

"Make sure you *do* understand," he firmly reminded her. "I don't want to deal with tantrums later on."

"I give you my word."

"Your work load will be much lighter. For the next few months the focus will be solely on Robyn. Even after all the excitement dies down, she's still going to be the face that Wellington pushes. Can you handle that?"

"With less time in front of the camera and more time to myself, I'll be able to give you my best."

"That's all that Wellington ever wanted," Scott grudgingly stated. "You're my sister and I love you. I only want you to be happy."

"Does this mean I'm back?"

"Looks that way."

"My ego's been drastically reduced," Georgina remarked, "so you needn't worry. I'm sure Robyn and I will get along splendidly."

Scott held out his open arms. "How about a hug for your brother? I've missed you."

Georgina threw her arms around Scott. "I've missed you too. I'm sorry for being such a bitch. I love you, Scott. Thank you for giving me another chance."

16

Beverly set down a pitcher of martinis on a glass-topped table. "Olive?" she asked, pouring Georgina a drink.

"Why not? We're celebrating, aren't we?" Georgina eagerly accepted the glass, taking a delicate sip. "Beverly, you make the absolute driest martinis in Manhattan. Fabulous. Aren't you going to have one?"

Beverly settled across from Georgina with her usual Perrier with a twist. "Once I've acquired a taste for something, I often find it hard to give up. Anyway, I thought you told Scott you weren't drinking anymore."

"No. I merely told him my drinking was under control, which it is," Georgina quickly added while pouring herself a second martini.

"Tell me what went on in his office."

"It went exactly as we planned."

"You'll have to be on your best behavior. You have to make Scott believe you're satisfied with no longer being in the spotlight."

"But I'm not," Georgina complained. "I gave five years to Wellington and now I've been discarded to the side."

"Only temporarily," Beverly soothed. "You have to have patience. We can't change things overnight. Let's be satisfied that we've gotten you back in the company."

"I don't know how long I'll be able to stand it."

"You'll tolerate things for as long as necessary," Beverly intoned forcefully. "You aren't going to jeopardize my plans once we get started. Make up your mind, Georgina. I can't stand indecisiveness. Do you want to be Wellington's Fresh and Lovely Girl again?"

"More than anything else in the world. You know that."

"Do you believe I want to help you?"

"Why wouldn't I?"

"Because you aren't trusting my judgment," Beverly snapped, slamming her glass down. "You'd still be spending your afternoons in bars if I hadn't decided to help. I'm willing to put a lot of time and planning into this, but I can't do it alone. You have to help me, Georgina."

"But I will! I'll do anything." Georgina rose clumsily to her feet, spilling her third martini onto the carpet. "Oh, I'm sorry."

Beverly grasped Georgina by the arm, leading her to the door of the duplex. "It's been an exhausting day, Georgina. You'd better head home."

"The spill. Let me clean it up."

"Don't worry. The maid will get it."

"It'll stain." Georgina tried to wiggle free from the iron grip Beverly had on her arm. "You're hurting me," she whimpered.

Beverly squeezed tighter. "Pay attention, Georgina. The next few weeks are crucial. Scott is going to be watching you like a hawk. If he even suspects anything amiss, your pretty little ass is going to be out on the street faster than you can say cheese." She released Georgina's arm. "All you need to do right now is smile and pretend everything is wonderful. Leave the rest to me. Understand?"

Georgina gave Beverly an indignant look while rubbing her arm. "Of course."

Beverly put a reassuring arm around Georgina as they walked out to the elevators. "We can't afford to make mistakes."

The elevator doors opened and Georgina stepped into the waiting car.

"Why are you helping me?" she suddenly asked. "There's nothing in this for you."

Beverly gave Georgina a wounded look, holding open the doors. "How can you ask such a question? I thought we were friends." She released the doors, imparting one last bit of advice with a false smile. "Aren't friends supposed to help each other?"

When Beverly returned to her duplex she found Dagmar attempting to remove the stain.

"What do you think you're doing?" she demanded in her iciest tone.

The young maid, clearly intimidated, as always, kept her eyes downward. "Cleaning the carpet."

"Don't be ridiculous!" Beverly snapped. "Tomorrow I want the entire living room stripped. Carpets, drapes, wallpaper, furniture. I want everything gone. I'll be out most of the day so I expect this room to be bare by the time I return."

"Everything?" Dagmar echoed, staring in wonder at her plush surroundings.

"Everything," Beverly confirmed. "It's time I redecorated. Georgina's carelessness speeded my decision." She waved a dismissive hand. "That's all, Dagmar. I'll see you in the morning."

When the young maid reached the front door of the duplex, Beverly called to her. Dagmar hesitantly turned.

"Yes, Miss Maxwell?"

Beverly gave her a sly look. "I want everything trashed. Don't try to scavenge anything."

Dagmar's cheeks reddened as she hurried out.

Beverly let out a laugh, relishing the discomfort she had caused her maid. She'd needed to sharpen her claws. Dealing with Georgina always left her so tense! She didn't know how much more she could handle. Yet it was her manipulation of Georgina that was going to get her closer to Scott.

All it had taken were a series of carefully placed suggestions in which she had pretended to sympathize with Georgina. At first Georgina had been hesitant about returning to work as a model, but she'd been no match for Beverly's determination and persistence.

There had been a number of teasers in the reigning New York columns: Where was Georgina Richards? When would she return to the modeling scene? Would her return mark a comeback?

Then there had been the parties, where Beverly always had someone latch onto Georgina and bombard her with questions, asking why her career was in neutral and when would she be getting things off the ground. And then there was Beverly herself: "Georgina, you can't give up, not at this point in your career. You're only twenty-eight! You've got plenty of years left. Don't you realize that you're at an advantage? All you need to do is capitalize on it. Go back to Wellington and stay in the shadows for the next six months. By that time the new Fresh and Lovely Girl will be history. Scott's taking a gamble with an unknown, and he's going to lose."

"But he could win," Georgina worried. "She's got Samantha D'Urban as an agent and she's already getting tons of exposure. After going back to Scott and eating humble pie, I could still be a loser."

"You can still come out on top. I'd see to that." She gave Georgina a fixed stare. In her eyes was a reflection of the power she held; a privilege of being part of the monied set. It was there for Georgina to see—to entice her. "I could do it if you wanted it badly enough."

Beverly didn't need to say anymore. She could see Georgina had succumbed. Though Georgina was too proud to admit it, she wanted her help—she needed it. Beverly was her last chance to get back on top, where she desperately wanted to be again.

"Your return to the top will be *the* topic of conversation, eclipsing anything done by Scott. The public loves scandal—they love family feuds, especially among the rich. Scott's ousted you, but you're going to go back to Wellington and this time you're going to win."

"How am I going to do that?"

"Open your eyes! You've got the key back to Wellington right under your nose."

"I do?"

"Yes! Lance!" She could see the confusion and complexity on Georgina's face. "It goes without saying," Beverly patiently explained, "that Lance is an excellent photographer. Scott is going to use him whenever he can. He's going to want his first shoot with his new model to be as successful as possible. Obviously, he's going to use Lance. All you need to do is find out from Lance when and where the shoot is going to take place."

"And then?"

Beverly bit her tongue, something she did a lot when she was around Georgina. Was this bitch dense? "Haven't you made the connection yet? You made the observation weeks ago. Whoever this new girl is, she probably isn't going to have much experience in front of the camera. It'll take some time to smooth away the rough edges. Time is money, and at this point Scott can't spare much of either. When you show up on the scene, Scott is going to be made even more aware of that fact. Once you get in front of the camera and show what you can still do, he's not going to want to lose you again. You're an asset Wellington needs."

So far the pieces were falling into place. Beverly was slowly inching her way back into Scott's life, although her work would be cut out for her. She had to make sure Georgina remained at Wellington. One slip and Scott would throw his sister right out the door. Having Georgina in the Wellington Building would be nice. She could drop by for lunch and "accidentally" bump into Scott. The possibilities were endless.

Georgina was a fool for believing she truly wanted to help her, Beverly thought. Even more so for believing her a friend. The only interests concerning Beverly were her own. Anything she did for Georgina would be done to serve herself. She intended to keep using Georgina, making false promises and telling lies until she had what she wanted. However, once she had Scott, Georgina would no longer be of use. Until that day arrived, she had to keep herself under control. She couldn't let Georgina irritate her. She needed to relax and relieve her tensions. She knew just the thing.

Beverly headed for her bedroom and her secret wardrobe with mounting excitement.

"How could you pass up an evening with Scott Kendall?" Kristen reached for a container of chicken chow mein. "What gives? I'm flattered you chose to spend the evening with *moi,* but wouldn't Scott have been better company?"

Robyn stared at her chopsticks with dismay while Kristen deftly maneuvered her own. After three attempts she still hadn't gotten the hang of it, succeeding only in scattering her food around her plate.

"Let me get you a fork," Kristen volunteered, heading into the kitchen.

After Robyn had cleared Kristen's confusion about the dinner date they had never made, Kristen had suggested they get Chinese takeout and bring it back to her Greenwich Village apartment.

"Scott Kendall isn't the man I thought he was," Robyn said.

"What do you mean?" The clatter of drawers opening and closing filtered into the living room.

Robyn nibbled on a few grains of rice. "He's a hypocrite."

"Sorry to be taking so long, but I know I've got silverware somewhere." Kristen could be heard shifting through a sinkful of dishes. "Will a spoon do?"

"Fine. Anyway, Scott said certain things to me and he clearly didn't mean them." She could still vividly recall his remarks to Kyle at the photo session.

Kristen returned to the living room, drying Robyn's spoon with a dish towel. "Don't let this afternoon throw you off." She handed the spoon to Robyn, resuming a cross-legged position on the floor. "Who do you think sent you that pep talk?"

Robyn looked at Kristen with wide eyes. "Scott?"

"Who else? I was glad to do it. I would have done it even if he hadn't asked me." Kristen bit into her egg roll. "But he did ask," she stressed.

Robyn shrugged her shoulders indifferently. "What does that prove?"

"In my book it proves he had faith in you. Don't try to pretend you don't care. You may shrug your shoulders, but your eyes say something else."

"We're just friends," Robyn stated noncommittally.

"Hoping to be more?"

"Maybe I'll give Scott another chance," Robyn alluded.

"You'd be a fool not to," Kristen advised.

"Is there anyone special in your life?"

Kristen took a sip of white wine. "I wish there were."

"Lance Richards was showing an interest in you today."

"Lance Richards *is* attractive," Kristen conceded, "but he's also egotistical and married. I really don't want to be another notch on his bed post."

Robyn was surprised. "I would have hardly thought he was married, from the looks he was sending your way. Who's his wife?"

"The prima donna who tried to upstage you."

"Georgina? Why would Lance cheat on someone as beautiful as her?"

"One of life's little lessons is that everything is not always what it seems. Lance and Georgina are married, but Georgina loves only two things: her face and her liquor. Lance only loves sex with other women."

"Has she lost Lance?"

"Why do we keep returning to Lance?"

"Answer the question," Robyn persisted.

Kristen sighed. "Yes, she's lost Lance, although I can't believe she ever loved him. Georgina only loves herself."

"That's pretty harsh. Why do you keep blaming her? Maybe Lance is equally at fault. After all, he's the one cheating on her. Maybe that's why she drinks so much."

"Or maybe her drinking drives him to other women," Kristen countered.

"Ah! A touch of sympathy. Tell me, if their marriage is in such a shambles, why have they stayed together?"

"Do I look like a marriage counselor?"

"Would you be interested in Lance if he weren't married?"

"If I answer this question, can we change the subject?"

"Whatever you like," Robyn promised.

"Maybe."

"That's not an answer!" Robyn protested.

Kristen smiled sweetly, gathering the empty containers. "Yes it is. Well, maybe it's not, but it's the only one I have right now."

Robyn followed Kristen into the kitchen. "You win for the moment. The subject is dropped. Anything you want me to do to help?"

"You can toss those dishes in the sink."

Robyn approached the filled sink with caution, wondering if the teetering combination of dishes, glasses, and silverware would collapse if she deposited the dishes they had just finished using.

"Neatness is not one of my virtues," Kristen apologized. She shifted a few piles before finding room, then took the dishes from Robyn and put them in the space she had provided. Then she squirted the whole mess with dishwashing liquid before turning on the hot water. "These can soak overnight."

"How much stuff do you have in there?"

"Three weeks' worth, I'm embarassed to say." When the dishes were smothered in suds, Kristen turned off the water. "Doesn't that look much better?" She wiped her hands with a paper towel. "Would you like a grand tour?"

Robyn followed Kristen out of the kitchen, shutting off the light behind them. "That mess isn't going to go away."

"It's not so bad. You should have seen this place before Sandy left. What a disaster area!"

"Sandy?"

"My old roommate. She was worse than me. She went off to Europe with a musician. I think his name was Julian. She's his problem now." Kristen started taking Robyn from room to room. "At first I enjoyed the idea of having the place to myself. But I'm tired of being alone. As you can see, there's plenty of space and privacy."

"Are you hinting at something?" Robyn asked.

"Look, I can easily afford this place myself, but I don't want to. How would you like to be roommates?"

"Are you serious?"

"Would I be asking if I weren't? I've been rattling around this place for three months. I'd love to have someone around who I could talk to." Kristen's smile brightened. "Think of all the fun we'll have," she urged. "It's a golden opportunity made even more golden with me thrown in. How can you pass it up?"

"Golden opportunities seem to be crossing my path a lot these days," Robyn remarked.

"So you're moving in! Yes?" Kristen excitedly asked.

"Yes!" Robyn exclaimed.

17

"These are phenomenal. If this doesn't sell Wellington, nothing will!"

Scott and Lance were scrutinizing a series of print ads. All were of Robyn. The first set presented her as the all-American girl. Dressed in active wear and ready for a day of fun, she conveyed a pure and simple beauty. This set of ads was intended to be aimed at the thirteen-to-eighteen age group, appearing in all the leading teen magazines.

In those magazines aimed at the twenty-one-and-over group, Robyn was presented as the all-American girl grown up in a sleeker, more sophisticated manner.

Lastly there were the most stunning ads of all. Sensual. Sexy. Dazzling. Depicted as the epitome of glamour, Robyn was every woman's fantasy come to life. No expense had been spared in creating a look of grandeur. These ads would appear in the most elite women's magazines.

Robyn's beauty shined through in each set of ads. She had the look that women of all ages strived for.

The new packaging and design for the Fresh and Lovely line had already been designed and manufactured. The pale beige background that had carried the Fresh and Lovely name in gold script was gone. The new design was definitely eye catching, and would cause female consumers to stop and examine what was on display. Now there was a bright, solid white background with *Fresh and Lovely* scrawled in brilliant bloodred foil type.

Wellington had never used television to promote its cosmetics. Soon there would be an all-out blitz. A series of commercials had been shot around Manhattan. In all of them, the camera followed Robyn until focusing on the Fresh and Lovely product she carried. Background consisted of parties and beautiful people. The message—wear Wellington cosmetics and live in a world of glamour and excitement.

Lance nodded in agreement. "I have to admit she's got a lot more than I first gave her credit for." He chose a photograph that was his favorite, handing it to Scott. "This one is a definite winner."

It was a full facial shot from the shoulders. The look was wild and sexy yet subtly elegant. Robyn's makeup had been lightly applied to highlight her features. The silk bodice of the evening gown she wore was barely visible, while her shoulders were smooth and bare. She wore shiny black gems around her neck, and her ash-blond hair was teased and sprayed in a wild, windblown style.

"Totally hot," Lance stressed.

Scott nodded absently as his thoughts turned to Robyn. He couldn't explain why, but whenever he was around her, he felt special. Maybe it was because she wasn't after anything from him. His wealth didn't impress her. She saw him for himself. Quite a contrast from Beverly. As much as he hated to admit it, becoming involved with Beverly had been a mistake. Everything in her life, including himself, had been an object of status. He didn't ever want to feel that way again.

Scott had the impression that Robyn was always genuinely pleased to see him. Whenever she was working on anything for Wellington, he always paid her a visit, just to make sure things were running smoothly. Upon seeing him, her eyes would light up and she would smile more brilliantly. He was sure he wasn't imagining it, and sensed that similar feelings were stirring within her. The attraction had been evident since their first meeting. But something was holding her back. He didn't know what it was, and he didn't intend to push things. He was willing to wait until Robyn was ready.

Kristen entered the dressing room, pulling off the outfit she wore. Dropping items as she went along, she ducked behind a dressing screen and slipped into a kimono. She took a seat next to Robyn at the vanity table, dipping her fingers into a bottle of cold cream. She smeared the cream over her face, wiping away the makeup she had worn for her just-completed shoot.

"Why are you staring?" Kristen asked. "Do I look that bad without makeup?"

"Have I told you you're a great friend?"

Kristen grinned. "Only about a hundred times, but keep telling me. My ego loves it."

The apartment-sharing between Kristen and Robyn was working out perfectly. Kristen was warm, open, and funny. She was constantly talking, and Robyn already knew her life history. She was the oldest of three daughters raised in Texas. Her father was a pharmacist and her mother a teacher. She had come to New York after being first runner-up in the Miss Texas pageant. When she first arrived in New York the work had been scarce. All she had done for six months was print ads for department stores. Then she got lucky. She was asked to substitute for a model at an exclusive Calvin Klein showing. After Calvin got a look at her, he chose her to be his model for a new line of jeans he was launching. From there her career skyrocketed.

There were commercials. She was still the Lustre shampoo girl. She did commercials for American Express, Honda, and Ivory soap. Her face appeared on a number of Harold Robbins novels. Just recently she had been considered for a bit part in an upcoming James Bond film.

Kristen stared straight into the mirror at Robyn. "Doing anything special this evening?"

"No. How about you?"

"My slate's clean." Kristen discarded her kimono, changing into street clothes. "Yours shouldn't be. We'll have to change that." She took Robyn by the hand, leading her to the elevators.

"Kristen, what are you doing?"

She pressed a button. "Trust me."

"These elevators go to the executive offices. That's where Scott is."

"Your powers of perception are extraordinary."

"I'm not going up there." Robyn tried to pull away, but the elevator doors opened. Kristen pushed her forward, causing her to collide with the person already in the elevator.

"I'm terribly sorry," Robyn began apologizing, looking up at the gentleman she'd barged into. It was Scott.

"Isn't this a lovely surprise," Kristen exclaimed as the doors started closing. "Robyn was just on her way up to invite you to dinner."

The elevator doors closed, leaving Robyn and Scott alone in their ascent.

"Were you on your way up to invite me to dinner?" Scott asked. "Kristen's words seem to have caught you off guard."

"Kristen is hardly subtle, but asking you to dinner had crossed my mind."

"Well?"

"Well what?"

"Aren't you going to ask me?"

"I just did."

"No," Scott mused, "Kristen said you invited me to dinner, and you said you were considering it, but you never really asked me."

"So you want the personal touch, do you?"

"It would be nice."

"Scott, would you like to have dinner with me this evening?"

"Why?"

"Excuse me?" she asked in disbelief.

"Why do you want to have dinner with me?"

"I don't believe this," she sputtered.

"It's a simple question. There must be a reason why you'd like to see me."

"You're asking for it, buster," Robyn playfully warned.

"Come, come, Ms. Prescott." Scott feigned impatience. "Time is money."

"Scott, would you like to have dinner with me this evening so we can get to know each other better? You're a perfect gentleman, handsome, very intriguing, and you make me laugh despite your sometimes pompous air." She ran out of breath. "Good enough?"

The elevator doors opened and Scott stepped out. "Good enough. I'll make the reservations and pick you up at seven."

* * *

"I could kill you for that stunt in the elevator," Robyn screamed at Kristen on her return to the dressing room.

"What did he say?" Kristen gushed.

"Wouldn't you like to know," Robyn teased.

"Robyn!" Kristen wailed.

"He said yes," Robyn shrieked.

Kristen started jumping up and down hysterically. "I knew it! I just knew it! The two of you are perfect for each other." She ran to Robyn, giving her a hug. "I'm so happy for you. Scott is such a great guy."

"Did I hear mention of my brother's name?"

Both Kristen and Robyn turned at Georgina's imperial entrance.

"Sorry to interrupt, but this is my dressing room as well." She sat at the vanity, removing the pins from the elaborate hairstyle she had worn for her just completed shoot, shaking her hair free. "Do continue," she commented, brushing her hair. "Your cackling could be heard all the way down the hallway."

Kristen looped her arm through Robyn's, preparing to leave. "We thought we were having a private conversation," she sniffed frostily.

"I must say you're different from some of the other women my brother has dated."

Robyn faced Georgina. "Different? How?"

Georgina started pacing around Robyn, glancing at her from side to side. "You're quite attractive, but with Scott that's always a prerequisite." Georgina laughed. "What am I saying? You're beautiful. You replaced me as the Fresh and Lovely Girl." She reached for a pack of cigarettes, lighting one and taking a deep puff. Ever since she had cut back on her drinking, she found herself smoking more and more. At least it kept her sober and in front of the camera, but what she wouldn't give for a cold vodka gimlet!

She waved the cigarette back and forth, dispersing smoke as she paced around Robyn. "Scott's dated a variety of women. As I've said, they've all been beautiful, but they've also been rich and powerful. 'Independent' is really the word I mean." Georgina tapped a manicured nail against her lips, studying Robyn intently. "Being the Fresh and Lovely Girl is certainly going to give you that same independence, but do you want to know something? You're not going to let fame and fortune go to your head. Wise decision." She tapped at her cigarette, scattering ashes. "I should have made that same decision years ago," she bitterly remarked.

"Your advice overwhelms us," Kristen said sarcastically before Robyn could respond. "Too bad we can't stay and listen to any more of it."

Kristen and Robyn hurried to the arriving elevator, rushing by an exiting Beverly Maxwell.

"They were certainly in a hurry," Beverly commented.

Georgina flopped on a dressing room couch, stubbing out her cigarette and lighting a fresh one. She started blowing smoke rings at the ceiling. "Tell me what you thought of the blonde and I'll let you in on a little secret."

"She was lovely." Beverly decided to slip in a small dig. "Beautiful. She reminded me of you in your early days."

"She's the new Fresh and Lovely Girl."

"Your replacement?" Beverly tried not to smirk. She was *supposed* to be on Georgina's side. "How could I not have recognized her? Her face is everywhere. What's her name again?" She examined herself in a mirror, deciding her makeup needed a light touch-up.

"Robyn Prescott." Georgina paused for dramatic effect. She really wanted this to sink into Beverly's aristocratic skull. "She's also Scott's latest plaything."

Beverly cracked her eyebrow pencil in two. "How clumsy of me."

"Surely you're not jealous of that bit of fluff?" Georgina innocently asked.

"Why would I be jealous? It's over between Scott and me." Beads of perspiration started to break out on Beverly's forehead. She dabbed them away with a tissue. "Is it hot in here?"

Georgina languidly raised a stockinged leg, smoothing away the wrinkles. "I'm perfectly comfortable. Tell me, Beverly, why did you and my brother break up? We've never really discussed it."

"Scott and I were hurting each other and decided to put an end to our relationship. We weren't meant to be together."

"But you wanted to marry him. Do you think you pushed him away by being too possessive?" Georgina went behind the silk screen. "I don't think Robyn is like that. I think she's exactly what Scott's been looking for."

Beverly swallowed over the lump in her throat. "Really? How wonderful. I certainly hope she can give Scott what I wasn't able to. He deserves to be happy. How long have they been seeing each other?"

Georgina emerged from behind the silk screen, wearing her oversized silver fox fur. "Tonight is their first date. I have no idea what Scott sees in her. If you want my opinion, Robyn Prescott is just a temporary amusement. She's only a new piece in the game he's playing." She squeezed Beverly's arm. "I was only teasing before. I know you're still getting over Scott. Why don't you come over for dinner?"

Beverly gave Georgina her most dazzling smile. "Thanks for the invite, but I've already made plans. Why don't I give you a call later in the week? I need to freshen up. Run along without me."

The moment Georgina disappeared from sight, Beverly began searching the dressing room, creating a state of disarray. She was looking for anything of Robyn's that would give her a clue as to how she had managed to captivate Scott. She found nothing, and began pulling at her hair in outrage. It was only when she caught sight of herself in a mirror that she stopped.

Beverly stared at her bedraggled reflection with horror. She had been losing control. She took a deep breath, counting to five. Taking deep breaths, she started repairing the damage she had inflicted on herself. She had to remain in control! Only then would she find the answers she was looking for. She smoothed her French twist back into place, straightening the collar of her silk blouse. She needed to be patient. Why did she always forget that? Given enough time, she would find out all she needed to know about Robyn Prescott.

There were two things she was absolutely sure of. One was that Georgina was going to pay for the hell she was putting her through. And the other was that she would always hate Robyn Prescott.

* * *

Georgina stared at her image in the mirrored elevator walls. Something was wrong. Something was missing. Frowning while trying to remember what it was, she tilted her head back, running a brush through her hair. When the back of her hand flicked by her earlobe, she knew what it was. She had forgotten her earrings.

At first she was going to take the elevator down to the lobby and back up to the dressing rooms. But then she remembered. She had taken the earrings off during her afternoon shoot. They hadn't gone well with the evening gown she'd had to wear. She'd been chilled by the air-conditioning and had worn a smock when she wasn't before the camera. The earrings had been placed in one of the pockets. When the shoot had ended, she had discarded the smock and forgotten all about them.

She pressed for the eighteenth floor. When the doors opened she hurried into the darkened studio.

There were a series of pegs on the far wall. Hanging on them were a variety of smocks. Rummaging through the pockets, Georgina found her earrings. Thankful they hadn't been stolen, she kissed them before fastening them on her ears. As she was about to leave she heard voices at the far end of the studio.

Curiosity got the better of her as she silently approached the voices, hoping to overhear some juicy gossip.

"Is Jeff a better lover than me?"

A coy female voice answered. "How can I answer that question?"

"With practice."

"How?"

He picked up her hand, placing it on the front of his denim jeans. "I think you've got plenty to work with."

Georgina froze in her footsteps. There was no mistaking the male voice: Lance. Sounded like he wanted a performance rating from one of his sluts. Which one was it? She inched closer. The voice sounded so familiar.

"I can't wait to make love with you," Lance said.

"Neither can I."

He took the woman in his arms, burying his face between her breasts. His lips moved up her neck before meshing with her lips. He twisted her body sideways, bringing her into the light. Georgina gasped. It was Erica Shelton. Georgina dropped her purse to the floor. The sound startled her, but Lance and Erica were oblivious. They only had eyes for each other.

Choking back a sob, Georgina fled from the studio. There was no longer any denying it. Lance was having another affair.

Erica pulled herself from Lance's embrace. "I can't go through with this."

"Take it easy," he soothed. "We're just getting started. I'm not going to disappoint you."

"I've changed my mind. Lance, let me go."

He planted another kiss on Erica's lips, ignoring her pleas for release. "Why don't we go back to my loft?" His eyes traveled around the deserted studio. "Or would you prefer here? The idea of getting caught turns me on."

Erica shook herself free. "Didn't you hear me? I said I've changed my mind."

"What gives?" Lance's eyes narrowed. "You're the one who called me, remember?"

Erica suddenly felt afraid. Lance didn't seem too pleased by her change of plans. She couldn't believe she had seriously considered sleeping with him just to get the pictures she wanted. She would never sleep with Lance. Never. Simply asking him for the photos would have gotten her nowhere, and after the stunt she had just pulled, asking for them now would be useless. He had her in a corner even though he didn't know it. She had to figure out a way to outfox him, but that task would have to wait for another day. Right now she had to appease him.

"Don't take it personally. When I called, I did want to make love. You were all I was thinking about. But now I'm starting to feel guilty. I can't betray Jeff."

"Why not?"

The question caught her by surprise. "I-I-I love him," she stammered.

"So why did you call me in the first place?"

Erica's mind raced for an answer. "We had a fight. I wanted to get even—hurt him and make him jealous. I knew making love with you would do that." She glanced at her watch. "I've got to go. I'm running late." She tried to wedge around Lance, but he blocked her way with his arm.

"Slow down. You drag me all the way down here and now you're running off? I don't like being used and I don't like having my time taken up," he whispered, his fingers caressing her face, "especially when it doesn't bring any results."

Erica smiled nervously, reaching into her handbag for her checkbook. "Would you like me to pay you for your time?"

Lance ignored the checkbook. "Know what else I don't like?"

"What?"

"Teases."

Erica's pen, poised over her checkbook, trembled. Lance removed his arm. "Forget the check. Run along."

Erica wasted no time heading for the elevators. "I really am sorry."

Lance studied her with hooded eyes. "Sure."

She pressed for the elevator, keeping her back to him. When she got in, Lance called to her. She held the doors open with one hand, reluctantly bringing her eyes to his.

"We still have a debt to settle," he promised. "I won't forget."

Suddenly frightened, Erica's hand slipped away from the open doors, which closed on Lance's grinning face.

Robyn stared in her closet with dismay. Scott was taking her out to dinner and she didn't have a thing to wear!

"Why didn't I buy a new outfit this afternoon?" she wailed to Kristen. Scattered on the floor and bed of Robyn's bedroom were discarded blouses, skirts, and dresses. "What am I going to do?"

Kristen held up a lavender blouse and black silk skirt. "What about this?"

"Too informal."

"How about this blue strapless?"

"Too formal," she protested. "We're just going to dinner, but I want to look special."

"Because Scott is a special guy?" Kristen hinted.

"Does it show?"

"You beam at the mention of his name."

"I never thought I'd feel this way about anyone."

"Not even Quinn?"

Robyn had told Kristen about her friendship with Quinn, but hadn't revealed the circumstances under which they'd met. "Quinn's just a friend. He's very special to me and will always have a place in my heart. But we'll never be lovers."

"How come? I've seen his photo. He's a handsome guy. Rich too."

"Don't forget to mention that he's warm and caring," Robyn chided. "Circumstances weren't right for Quinn and I to become lovers, and now we've traveled in different directions. I'm not the same person I was when we first met." She continued searching her closet. "I can't go into it tonight. Tonight belongs to Scott."

"Hey, you've got a right to privacy. Whenever you're ready to talk, I'm here for you."

Robyn smiled her thanks. "I know. Soon—not tonight. I don't want anything to spoil this evening, even though it looks like I'm off to a pretty good start." She slammed her closet door in frustration. "Damn! Not a thing to wear."

"I'll be right back," Kristen said mysteriously.

Robyn plopped down on her bed, wondering about the evening ahead. Although she was a bit nervous, she was looking forward to spending the entire evening in Scott's company . . . being near him . . . wanting to touch him . . . having him touch her.

"Would I stand in the way of true love?" Kristen held up a hanger. "Behold one never-before-worn Halston. Live it up, kid."

Robyn's spirits instantly revived at the sight of the simple sheath of midnight green. "It's perfect." She started accessorizing. Which shoes? What jewelry? How should she wear her hair?

"Enough!" Kristen ordered, as though reading Robyn's mind. "Just put on the dress and wait for Scott. No matter what you wear, he's still going to be crazy about you."

Scott arrived promptly at seven in a chauffeur-driven black stretch limousine. Stepping into the rear interior, Robyn was amazed by what she saw. Not only was there a chilling bottle of champagne, but a miniature wet bar, television, and telephone.

"First dates always force me to make an impression," Scott revealed.

"How come?"

"So you'll say yes the next time I ask you out."

"But *I* was the one who asked you out," Robyn reminded. "Doesn't that count for something?"

"It shows you have excellent taste," Scott said.

"Is your ego always this inflated?" Robyn teased.

"When a woman as beautiful as you asks me out, a guy starts feeling kind of tall."

Robyn blushed at the compliment as she gestured at the items around them. "None of this really matters. Scott Kendall is who impresses me."

"Really?"

"Really," she honestly answered.

Scott reached for a bouquet of roses: red, yellow, white, and pink. "I didn't know which color was your favorite, so I got them all."

Robyn sniffed at the delicate petals. "They're lovely. How thoughtful. Thank you." She put them down. "Where are you whisking me off to?"

"I thought we'd try something different tonight. Since this is our first date, I figured privacy would be the most important thing."

Robyn nodded. "I'll agree."

"I knew you would."

"Where is this intimate little Casbah?"

"Right here." Scott flicked a switch and a smoke-colored partition divided them from the driver. "Complete privacy. No interruptions. Thomas will drive us around Manhattan."

Robyn was thrilled with Scott's originality. A date in a limousine! "What will we eat, or do you have a chef hidden in the trunk?"

Scott revealed two picnic baskets. "We have cheeses, crackers, oysters, cold chicken, and fruit."

"Sounds great."

Scott put the baskets to one side. "Before picking you up I was famished. Now my appetite seems to have mysteriously disappeared. Can you explain why?"

"I haven't the foggiest."

"Any idea how I could get it back?"

"Maybe you need a taste of something sweet," Robyn suggested.

"Like?"

She pressed her lips against his, not believing what she was doing. Once, she had thought she would never be able to feel this way again. But Scott disproved that. He was igniting desires and emotions she'd long believed forgotten and dormant.

Yet because her feelings were so new and she needed to get readjusted to them, she didn't want things to go any further. In her heart she knew Scott would never hurt her, but she was still hesitant. She wasn't sure if she wanted to take the risk of an emotional betrayal. She continued kissing Scott. Look at the man she stood to gain!

"I don't know about you," she stated, removing her lips from Scott's, "but I'd like to start on those picnic baskets."

Scott returned her kiss, planting it on her cheek. "Whatever you want is fine."

For the next four hours they existed in their own world, talking about everything. When it seemed they had exhausted all possibilities of conversation, they found new topics to explore.

Scott deliberately avoided mentioning Quinn. Tonight belonged to him and Robyn and he didn't want the magic of their evening spoiled. He didn't want to consider the possibility that a relationship with Robyn wouldn't be possible. He'd have to find out, but until he found his answers, he was going to enjoy every minute he had with Robyn and make every effort to sweep her off her feet.

They arrived back at Robyn's apartment at midnight.

"I feel like Cinderella," she confessed. "Tonight was fabulous."

"Poor Cinderella lost everything at the final stroke of midnight."

"Will that happen to me?" she asked.

"No," Scott vowed, embracing her passionately, wanting to show her the effect she was having on him. He didn't want the evening to end this way. He wanted to spend the night with her, making love . . . holding her in his arms and never letting go. He watched as she headed up the front steps, and wanted to hurry after her . . . to ask if he could go in with her.

Robyn turned when she reached the front door. Her eyes had a dreamy look. "Thank you for a wonderful night." Forbidden thoughts of Scott started creeping into her mind, but she banished them. It would be so easy to invite Scott upstairs, but she couldn't. She wasn't ready. Not yet.

Scott returned to his limousine. When he reached the car he turned back. "Your Prince Charming is here to stay," he promised.

18

The press conference was a success. Photographers' cameras clicked incessantly and the reporters were charmed by Robyn. Both groups felt that Robyn's face was guaranteed to sell. Dressed in a black gabardine Chanel coat dress with notch collar and gold-tone buttons, she was an image of elegant simplicity. After being introduced by Scott, she wasted no time in establishing an immediate rapport. The first few questions were standard:

"How does it feel to be the Fresh and Lovely Girl?"

"Wonderful, frantic, thrilling, nerve wracking. My answer changes almost every hour."

"What was your reaction upon hearing you'd been chosen?"

"I couldn't believe it—some days I still can't."

A curve ball: "Do you think there's anything special about you that separates you from other women?"

"Absolutely not. I may be attractive, but there are plenty of other attractive women in the world. Anyone else could easily be standing in my place. The people at Wellington saw something they liked in me. If I hadn't come along, they certainly would have found someone else. It was a matter of luck and timing."

Personal: "What are your plans for the future?"

"Right now I'm having a lot of fun and taking one day at a time. Who knows what the future will bring? Being the Fresh and Lovely Girl means responsibility and dedication. It's an important part of my life. But there are other important things in my life as well."

"Sounds like you're committed to someone. Care to mention his name?"

"At this moment I'd like to keep him to myself."

The questioning and photographing continued until Scott finally managed to get himself before the microphone. "Ladies and gentlemen, our time is up. A buffet has been set up in the next room." He offered Robyn his arm. "Let's make a run for it. Mention free food and people turn into vultures."

Robyn laughed, happily hooking her arm through Scott's.

"She's right, you know."

"About what?" Kristen turned. Standing beside her was Lance Richards.

"Anyone else could have been chosen to be the Fresh and Lovely Girl."

"Like me?"

"Why not?"

"They were looking for a new face."

"You could be just as big as Robyn Prescott."

"I don't have any complaints with my career."

"You should. Kristen, you're just as beautiful as Robyn. All you need is the right exposure."

Kristen scrutinized Lance. "Meaning?"

"I can give you that exposure."

"How?"

"By becoming your agent."

Kristen laughed. "Are you serious? Constance Carter is my agent, and she's the best in the business. I'd have to be insane to drop her."

"You're insane to keep her," Lance stressed. "How often have you worked in the last six months? Not enough. Constance no longer wields any power in this town. She doesn't have the connections anymore. You need some new blood. I can take you just as far as Samantha D'Urban will take Robyn."

"You sound confident of results."

"And you sound hesitant of my ability. Why are you holding back? Is it because of Robyn? Constance? You don't owe either one a thing. The only person you owe is yourself."

"Why are you so willing to help me? Why not Georgina? If anyone's career needs salvaging, it's hers."

"Georgina lost her career years ago. There's no hope of salvaging it. I'd only be wasting my time."

"Does that way of thinking also apply to your marriage?"

"Why does my marriage interest you?"

Kristen flushed. "It doesn't. But how can I be confident of your success if your marriage is such a failure?"

Lance advanced on Kristen, placing a hand beneath her breast. He gently squeezed through the silk material of her blouse. Despite herself, Kristen placed a hand on the front of Lance's jeans. The hardness against the palm of her hand caused her to flush again. She took away her hand, reaching for a glass of champagne from a passing tray. She deliberately avoided Lance's eyes.

Lance moved behind her, rubbing the back of her leg with his knee. "You'll have to take your chances. Consider the options. Business. Pleasure. Or both. The choice is yours. Let me know what you decide."

Robyn sipped at a glass of orange juice, her throat parched from all the talking she had done. She turned to Ruby and gave her an affectionate hug. "Thanks for being here. I needed the moral support."

"Nonsense, you were wonderful. You handled them like a pro. Those reporters were eating out of your hand."

Scott joined Robyn and Ruby. "Wasn't she wonderful? By this evening every woman in America will be green with envy and every man fraught with desire."

"Including you?" Robyn teased.

"I've been fraught since the moment I first laid eyes on you."

Robyn moved closer to Scott, kissing him. "Me too."

Scott returned the kiss. "We better be careful." He kissed her again. "The eyes of the press are watching."

"I don't care."

Scott's next kiss lasted longer as he allowed his lips to linger on hers. "Neither do I."

"No one has ever made me feel the way you do," Robyn confessed.

Scott gave Robyn a mischievious smile. "How do I make you feel?"

"Wonderful."

"You make me feel the same way."

"Do I?"

"Why do you sound so astonished?"

Before Robyn could respond, Kyle hurried over to Scott, telling him the reporters had some additional questions.

"We'll continue this later," Scott promised.

Robyn kept her eyes on Scott as he walked away. Ruby leaned her head toward Robyn's. "I'll bet any woman would love to get her hands on him."

"You know, Ruby," Robyn thoughtfully replied, "I think you're right."

There were some days when Beverly just didn't feel like playing "tease," but wanted the pleasures of a man. When those days rolled around, she called Male Express. All she had to do was give her desired preference, name the time and place, and then show up. The five-hundred-dollar fee was money well spent, and payment was done over the phone by credit card.

Lounging against her satin lilac sheets and lace-frilled pillows as thoughts of Scott ran rampant through her mind, Beverly decided today was one of those days. Last night she'd had the most wonderful dream. Scott had been making love to her over and over, declaring his love. When she had awoken, she'd been immensely disappointed to find herself alone in bed. Her dream had ignited a yearning that *had* to be satisfied.

She picked up the phone and dialed Male Express, specifically requesting a green-eyed, tawny-haired blond.

Lance was leaving the Wellington Building when he collided into Erica. "Isn't this a surprise," he exclaimed. "Just the person I was looking for."

"Were you?" Erica brushed herself off. "Why?" she suspiciously asked.

"I have a business proposition."

After having been unable to reach Lance by phone, Erica had decided to seek him out. Constance kept harping to her about the missing Wellington photos almost every day. "What kind of business proposition?"

"Let's not discuss it here." Lance hailed a taxi. "Why don't we go back to my loft?"

Lance seemed to be in a good mood, and Erica didn't want to ruin it. If she feigned interest in his proposition, it might make getting the duplicates of the photographs much easier.

"Where to?" the driver asked.

"Eighth and Broadway."

"What's your proposition?" Erica asked. Maybe they could cover everything, including the photographs, during the drive. She wasn't too keen on the idea of being alone with Lance again.

"Patience," he said, placing a hand on her knee. "We'll discuss all in the privacy of my loft."

Cartier. The perfect place to spoil oneself.

Georgina studied the dazzling displays of diamonds, rubies, and emeralds. Exquisite antique brooches and bracelets of perfect workmanship. Chic earrings, rings, and necklaces made of gold. All were nestled against crisp folds of black velvet and secured behind shimmering glass. The richness of colors was luminous, catching one's eye at every turn.

Georgina's eyes skimmed from right to left as she walked down the aisles, taking her time as she savored the sights before her. Next to buying furs, she adored purchasing jewelry. The cool glitter of gems was an allure she could never resist.

Setting her eyes on a diamond bracelet with emerald chips, she closed the distance between herself and the display case. Her fingers brushed against the glass as though hoping they could pass through. Lifting her eyes, she saw her favorite clerk heading her way.

"Mrs. Richards, always a pleasure," he enthused in his high voice.

"Cary, you're looking marvelous. I love the suit."

He preened at the compliment. "It's an Armani."

"I could tell," she confirmed.

He puffed up even more. "What may I help you with?"

Georgina pointed to the bracelet. "That."

"Exquisite," he raved, opening the case and removing the bracelet. He draped it lovingly upon Georgina's offered wrist. "It'll go so well with your diamond hearts."

Georgina stopped admiring the bracelet, puzzled by the statement. "Diamond hearts?"

"The two diamond hearts on the gold chain. The necklace Mr. Richards purchased." Cary slapped a hand to his shocked mouth. "I hope I haven't spoiled the surprise."

Cary's words suddenly clicked. Georgina knew of only one necklace with two diamond hearts. The one she saw Erica Shelton wearing.

Georgina returned the bracelet to Cary. "Of course not. Lance gave me the necklace weeks ago."

"At Le Cirque?" Cary eagerly asked.

Georgina choked out the words. "How did you know?"

Cary revealed his knowledge proudly. "Mr. Richards told me that he planned on having a romantic setting when he gave you the gift. Champagne, roses, the works!" He nestled closer to Georgina. "You must give me the details. Didn't you almost die when you opened the box and saw the necklace? Lance is such a love. He insisted on seeing only our most expensive pieces." Cary playfully tapped Georgina's arm. "Don't let that man go."

Georgina pulled away her arm, halting Cary's gushing discourse. "I'll pass on the bracelet," she tersely snapped.

Cary watched as Georgina stormed out of Cartier. What had gotten into her? All of a sudden she had turned moody. He returned the bracelet to the display case, plastering a smile on his face as he moved on to his next customer, once again thankful for preferring his own sex.

Erica tensed once Lance closed the door behind him. Her reaction wasn't lost on him.

"Calm down. I'm not going to bite." He seemed amused, which put her a bit at ease. "Why not make yourself comfortable?" He indicated an arrangement of leather pillows in the middle of the loft. "Would you care for a drink?"

Perhaps a drink would calm her nerves. "Rum and coke," she answered.

While Lance prepared the drinks, Erica surveyed the loft. Every inch of wall space was covered by photographs. Her eyes stopped. Among the many photographs were her Wellington photos enlarged and framed.

"Admiring yourself?" Lance handed her her drink, steering her back to the black leather pillows. He flopped down on them, encouraging Erica to join him. She took a sip of her drink before hesitantly sitting next to him.

"Isn't this nice?" he commented.

Erica felt uncomfortable with Lance so near. She sipped at her drink again. "What did you want to discuss?"

Lance threw his leg over Erica's, moving closer. "It can wait."

Erica drained her glass, pushing it at Lance. "Could you fix me another?"

Lance obliged, speaking from the kitchen. "Have you ever thought of switching agents?"

"Why?"

"It's time you did. Constance Carter is old news."

"I've always been satisfied with her." A lie. The woman was driving her crazy with her demands for the missing Wellington photographs. Since her meeting in Constance's office, she hadn't worked as often as she usually did. Constance claimed the offers weren't pouring in as quickly as they had, but Erica knew that was a lie. Constance was holding back. She wanted her to know who held the power in their business relationship.

The thought of switching agents had been crossing Erica's

mind a lot lately. Other models did it, but she was afraid it wouldn't reflect well on her professionally if she switched agents so soon. After all, she had only been modeling for a year.

Lance returned with a fresh drink. "You need someone capable of representing you."

Erica accepted her drink. "Like?"

"Me."

Erica almost choked on the liquor sliding down her throat. "Get serious," she sputtered between gasps for air. "How can you expect me to get along with you professionally when we don't get along personally?"

"Then why did you come back with me?" Lance narrowed the space between them, pushing Erica back among the pillows. He placed a hand on her shoulder, moving toward her breasts. Erica pushed away his hand, struggling into a sitting position.

"Stop it! I thought I could trust you. This is just what I was afraid of happening."

"You're lying." Lance noticed Erica's eyes kept returning to the photographs on the wall. "You came for something."

Erica tried to rise to her feet, but suddenly felt dizzy. She shouldn't have had two drinks on an empty stomach. The last time she had eaten was the previous evening. "I did not," she hotly denied. The loft was starting to spin. She fell back among the pillows as Lance drew closer.

"Close your eyes," he whispered. "You need to rest."

"Don't feel good," she mumbled.

"Just sleep. Sleep is all you need."

Lance left Erica on the leather pillows, retrieving his camera and then undressing her. When he had positioned her among the pillows in the most explicit of poses, he started shooting.

The sedative he had given her would keep her out for a few hours. During that time he would be taking lots of pictures in a variety of poses. In some he'd include himself posing with her. Admiring Erica's body, Lance found himself becoming aroused. He forced away the thought. There was no way he could have sex with her. Not yet. When she awoke she had to believe that she had passed out from the drinks she'd had.

But soon they would make love, and it would be on his terms. The pictures guaranteed it. He knew Erica would do anything to stop them from being published. The ultimate piece of evidence would be the model's release she signed. With that piece of paper she'd be unable to stop him and she'd be under his control.

Pretending he was interested in starting his own agency had been a stroke of genius. Talking with Kristen Adams had only been a smokescreen, but she was a sexy piece of ass. Maybe he'd while away his time with her before putting the squeeze on Erica.

He finished one roll of film and began another.

The tawny-haired man stared at the woman. What was her problem? She looked all together, but obviously had a few screws loose. As a gigolo he had spent some strange afternoons with women, but nothing like this.

Upon arriving she had insisted he shower. When he emerged from the shower he noticed she had changed the sheets on the hotel bed. Weird, considering they were at the Helmsley Palace.

Only after inspecting his body, the wet towels, and used shower stall, would she allow him to touch her body. He told her his name, but she insisted on calling him "Scott," and when they were making love, instructed him to tell her he loved her.

"I love you, Beverly."

"I love you, Scott," she whispered passionately, savagely raking her nails against his back.

He jerked back in pain, but she pulled him deeper into her, grinding her hips against him while locking her legs around his waist.

Once he had climaxed, she went to take a shower. She spent a half hour beneath the water. When she returned a cloud of steam followed, angering him. Didn't she think he was clean? He was one of the highest paid gigolos in Manhattan. His body was his business, and he took care of it. But the worst had been a few minutes ago. After turning on the TV, she had freaked. She had picked up a lamp, throwing it across the room, where it crashed to the floor in pieces.

"How could you do this to me?" she shrieked.

He pulled on his pants and shirt, not caring about the blood on his back. He slipped into his shoes and grabbed his sport jacket while hurrying to the door.

"Why are you doing this to me? Why are you betraying me? I love you, Scott. I love you. How could you make that whore the Fresh and Lovely Girl? How could you take her into your life?"

He looked to the TV. Some sort of press conference. A good-looking guy had his arm around a strikingly beautiful woman. They made the perfect couple. No big deal. What the hell was going on in this chick's mind? Was this some sort of fantasy? Was he supposed to be participating?

She began frantically changing the channels with the remote control, becoming more and more enraged. Another lamp flew across the room. He hurried out of the hotel suite. This wasn't his scene. This chick's anger was too real. Crazy. He didn't want to be at the end of it.

Beverly hardly noticed the door slam shut. She kept changing the channels. On every station all she saw was footage of Scott and Robyn from the Wellington press conference held early that morning.

She was still no closer to reclaiming Scott. Although she had been satisfied with the casual friendship she and Scott had established, Beverly knew she now had to consider Robyn Prescott a threat—a threat that had to be eliminated. Her eyes locked back onto the TV screen. Scott and Robyn were smiling at each other. She hated the sight of them together! You had to be blind not to see that a romance was budding. This had to stop, before things progressed any further.

Sweeping through the debris cluttering the carpet, she went to the phone, dialing a number. "Calder Investigations? This is Beverly Maxwell. I need to employ your services. I'd like your agency to locate some information on someone. I want results, so I'll double your regular fee. I can't give you much except a name: Robyn Prescott. Remember it. I want every skeleton from her past uncovered and delivered to me."

* * *

Erica opened her eyes groggily. "What happened?"

"Why didn't you tell me you couldn't handle your liquor?" Lance kidded.

Erica struggled into a sitting position, trying to clear her head. "What time is it?"

"Almost five."

She jumped to her feet. "I'm supposed to meet Jeff."

"Let me call you a taxi," Lance insisted. "You shouldn't be wandering the streets in your condition." He pressed a steaming cup of coffee on her. "Take a sip of this."

She accepted the coffee, sipping slowly while she tried to reconstruct what had happened. Clearly she was at fault. She had been so nervous about being alone with Lance that she hadn't monitored her reaction to the liquor.

"The taxi should be here in ten minutes." He pointed to her rumpled clothing. "Did you know you constantly twist and turn?"

Looking down at herself, Erica suddenly felt self conscious. Why did she feel uncomfortable in her own clothing? "How long was I out?"

"The entire afternoon. At one point I had to leave you alone. I had an appointment I couldn't cancel."

"Another woman?"

"Am I that predictable?"

Erica grinned in spite of herself. "Yes."

Lance sighed. "I might as well confess. The lady in question is Kristen Adams. I made her the same offer I made you."

"Did she accept?"

"She's seriously considering a move."

"She hasn't done that badly with Constance."

"Neither have you, but the two of you can do much better. What do you say to my offer, Erica?"

The taxi honked from the street. Although Erica had been more at ease with Lance than earlier in the day, she was still relieved at the taxi's arrival. "We'll see," she stated noncommittally, heading for the door.

Lance's answer was unexpected. "Take your time. Don't rush. Whatever you decide will be fine by me. You're the one who's going to have to be ultimately satisfied." He took her arm. "Let me walk you out. By the way," he announced, handing her a manila envelope, "I thought you'd like copies of these."

"What are they?"

"Open it and see."

Erica opened the manila envelope, gasping with surprise. "My Wellington photos."

"I thought you might like a few extra copies. I couldn't help but notice the way you were admiring them on the wall."

Erica was thrilled. "Thank you, Lance. You don't know how much this means to me."

"Think nothing of it." He held out a piece of paper and pen. "Do you mind signing for them? It's only a receipt. It'll help me at tax time."

Erica didn't even look at the paper, signing away while smiling at Lance. "Could I be mistaken or are you becoming a nice guy?"

"Nah," Lance replied, folding the signed sheet of paper in half and tucking it in his jacket pocket. "I'm still the same scoundrel."

Georgina watched in the shadows, checking the time as Lance walked Erica to a waiting taxi. Five o'clock. They had been alone for nearly five hours. She had no difficulty imagining what they had been doing.

After Cary's revelation, she had returned to the town house, rummaging through her monthly bills until she had found the receipt she was looking for—the receipt from Cartier signed by Lance—the receipt for the diamond necklace given to Erica.

Rage had coursed through her as she studied the receipt. Lance was spending *her* money on his mistress. Every month they had their accountant handle the bills. If it hadn't been for Cary, she never would have known of Lance's spending.

With the receipt in hand she had stormed to the loft, stopping in her tracks when she saw Lance and Erica approaching from the opposite side of the street. She had ducked into a coffee shop, taking a seat by the window as Lance led Erica up the steps.

Situated where she could see all, Georgina patiently waited for Erica's exit. She consumed cup after cup of coffee as images of Lance and Erica skittered through her mind. At one point she was tempted to barge in on them, then realized she would be at a disadvantage. Knowing Lance, he wouldn't be ashamed of being caught. He would probably laugh in her face, relishing her humiliation at seeing him in bed with another woman.

Looking up, she caught sight of them departing the loft. Lance had his arm around Erica in a comfortable, reassuring way and she was smiling amiably at his words.

Leaving a few scrunched dollars on the table, Georgina hurried outside, stepping into the alley while her eyes remained glued across the street. Lance opened the taxi door for Erica, then kissed her on the lips. The kiss was more than friendly, then Erica slammed the car door, giving instructions to the driver as they merged into traffic. So much for Erica's words of love for Jeff.

Lance stood watching with a satisfied grin on his face. Only after the taxi disappeared from sight did he head back into the loft.

Georgina stared at the receipt clutched in her hand. When had Lance ever spent this much on her? Never! She began furiously tearing the receipt to shreds.

"Bastard," she cried out under her breath as the torn pieces fluttered to the sidewalk. "You're going to pay for this. Both you and Erica are going to pay."

19

Beverly angrily tore the report in two. Anthony Calder, an expression of wary disbelief etched on his face, remained behind his desk.

"Exactly what am I paying you for?" she demanded,

tossing the shredded pieces of paper in the air. They scattered to the floor, where Beverly trampled on them, furiously pacing before him. "It's been a month since I've employed your services, and you've come up with nothing."

"That's not true," Calder countered, eyes resting on the pieces of his report.

Beverly stopped pacing, fixing a penetrating stare on him. She still couldn't believe Anthony Calder was a private investigator. With his silver hair, continental tan, and three-piece suits, he looked more like George Hamilton. Yet his icy blue eyes were cunning. There was power in them—raw power able to expose and unearth secrets, given only the smallest of clues. The fact that he was going to help her destroy Robyn thrilled Beverly, but she wasn't satisfied with the results he had provided so far. "Really? Do explain."

Calder cleared his throat. Having overstepped his bounds to express an opinion in his favor, he knew it would be in his best interests to placate Beverly. "Given only a month, my agency has been able to sketch in a few basics. Robyn Prescott came to New York from Chicago. Before coming to New York she was a patient at Chicago General Hospital. She was in a coma for six months after being hit by a car. She has no memory of her life before the accident."

"Is that good or bad?"

"What do you think?"

"I think there might be a reason why Robyn Prescott doesn't want to remember her past." She gave Calder a pointed look. "You're going to find that *dirty* reason, aren't you?"

He raised an eyebrow. "Dirty? Hmm. Yes, you could be right. Ms. Prescott probably isn't as lily white as she'd like us to believe."

"How right you are," Beverly purred.

"Let's individually examine each piece of information that we have." He passed a pile of photographs to Beverly. "These are the items she was found wearing. Quite a provocative outfit. I'm sure many heads turned."

"Looks like Robyn was a naughty girl. Her wares were definitely on display." Beverly discarded the photos. "Next?"

"Next we have the area where the accident took place. She

was found between Halsted and Ashland. That's a punk and gay quarter where anything goes."

"Meaning?"

"Drugs, prostitution, etcetera. Why would someone of Ms. Prescott's . . . caliber be in such an area?"

"You tell me. I'm the one signing the checks."

"She had to have some sort of business there that night."

Beverly gave Calder a coy smile. "How intriguing. I like the direction you're headed in. Continue."

"Robyn Prescott had to have been involved in *something.* Right now we're still in the dark, but my men are presently combing the area she was found in, flashing her picture and asking questions. Sooner or later we're bound to find someone who remembers her." Finished with his presentation, Calder gave Beverly a satisfied look.

"Wipe that smarmy grin off your face," she coldly demanded. "Is that all you have for me?"

"There is one other bit of information," he remembered.

Beverly was irritated that her bitchiness hadn't bothered him. "Yes?"

"There's a man in her life."

"No? Really?" Beverly sarcastically questioned. "Who the hell doesn't know that? Everyone in New York knows Robyn Prescott and Scott Kendall are an item. I'm not paying you for information that's in every gossip column in every major newspaper."

"There's a man in Chicago," Calder quietly stated.

"Who?" she pounced.

"Dr. Quinn Marler."

"What's their relationship?"

"At the moment, strictly platonic. But Dr. Marler would like something more from Robyn."

"What's his background?"

"Rich, influential, and connected."

"Quite a catch," she mused.

"I would tend to agree."

"How did they meet?"

"He was her psychiatrist. He tried to help her remember her past. Despite being one of the best psychiatrists in Illinois, he was unable to help her."

"Do they still keep in touch?"

"Considerably. Letters. Phone calls. He spent two weeks with her at Christmas."

Beverly pondered over Calder's latest bit of information. There was another man in Robyn's life. This was good. She could breathe a bit easier. Robyn couldn't be too serious about Scott if Quinn Marler was still in the picture. But how to use this to her advantage? If only Dr. Marler were in New York . . .

Beverly whipped her checkbook out of her Fendi bag. "Pursue whatever leads you can find," she instructed. "If your men think they've found something, let me know at once. Day or night."

Calder fingered the check handed to him, eyeing Beverly shrewdly. "Mind if I ask why you have such an interest in Robyn Prescott?"

Beverly's lip curled in disdain. "Frankly, yes. But since you're so curious, I'll tell you. Leverage."

"Don't you mean blackmail?"

"The two *are* synonymous," she agreed. "Just do your job and I'll keep writing you checks. Understood?"

"Of course. I hope you were pleased with this week's report."

"It was adequate," she admitted nonchalantly, not wanting Calder to see how excited she was. Quinn Marler had become the light at the end of her tunnel.

The table was set with candlelight. Silverware sparkled and dishes and glasses gleamed. The tablecloth was fine lace upon which there were an assortment of multicolored roses in a crystal cut vase.

Robyn thought she looked very elegant and sophisticated with her hair swept up, and attired in silk lounging pajamas. Yet for the third time she checked her image in a mirror.

"Looking pretty snazzy tonight," Kristen remarked.

"You're not going to believe this, but I feel like I'm playing dress-up."

"How come?"

"I want to make a good impression on Scott, but I feel like a vamp!" She twirled before Kristen. "I specifically bought this outfit at Victoria's Secret this afternoon. There's only *one* reason to buy *anything* at Victoria's Secret. I feel like I'm getting ready to pounce on Scott!"

"What woman wouldn't like to pounce on him?" Kristen grinned. "Look, you told me you invited Scott over for a casual evening, right?"

"Yes."

"Then let's give him that!" Kristen headed for her closet, rummaging through the mess at the bottom. "My magic closet was able to help you once before." She pulled out an oversized football jersey as well as a pair of faded jeans ripped at the knees. "Let's leave a little to his imagination. Think this will throw him a curve?"

Robyn was already slipping out of the silk pajamas, removing the pins from her hair and shaking the ash-blond strands free. "I love it!" she exclaimed.

The phone rang, and Kristen tossed the clothes to Robyn before answering. "Hello."

"Kristen, I'm glad I caught you."

It was Lance Richards. Although she didn't know why, Kristen was thrilled by the sound of his voice. Aside from his offer of representation, he had been on her mind lately. "What can I do for you?"

"I was wondering if you'd like to meet this evening. Since we're in the same neighborhood, how about the Lone Star Café?"

She didn't bother to ask for a reason. "I'm on my way."

"Who was that?" Robyn asked after Kristen hung up.

"An interesting prospect." Kristen shed her jeans and sweater, going through her hangers. "Looks like I'm the one who's going to be needing a sexy outfit. Let's see if my magic closet works for me."

Robyn had decided to follow Kristen's advice. A casual evening was what she had promised Scott, and that was what he was getting. Gone was the elaborately set table, replaced by paper plates, napkins, and plastic utensils. In the kitchen the gourmet meal she had prepared was wrapped and hidden in the freezer, replaced by a substitute.

The door bell rang. She hurried to answer it, then waited for it to ring again before opening the door.

"Don't you spend enough time primping in front of a mirror during the day . . ." Scott's words trailed off at the sight of Robyn's appearance.

She managed to keep a straight face. "Right on time." She took his attaché case while leading him in. "Like a drink?"

"Actually, I'm starving." Scott sniffed in the direction of the kitchen. "What have you whipped up?"

"Franks and beans."

Scott blinked, looking at Robyn skeptically. "You're kidding, right? I haven't had franks and beans since I was a kid."

She took him by the hand, taking him into the kitchen and uncovering the simmering pots.

"Franks and beans," he stated incredulously.

"You told me not to go to any special trouble," she stressed.

"I had expected maybe a little pampering," he confessed, pinching his fingers together.

"Poor baby," Robyn consoled, kissing him. "Make yourself comfortable and I'll bring everything in."

Scott headed for the living room but kept looking back at her, shaking his head in bewilderment. Robyn managed to keep a straight face until she was alone in the kitchen. She couldn't believe the shock on Scott's face. For once she had gotten the better of him.

She prepared a tray for both of them and proceeded into the living room. When she got there the tray almost toppled from her hands to the floor.

"Like the duds?" Scott asked.

Gone was his perfectly cut charcoal-gray Armani suit, Gucci loafers, Oxford shirt, and silk tie. Instead he was wearing cutoff jeans, deck shoes, and a Mets sweatshirt and baseball cap.

"What happened to your clothes?" She steadied her grasp on the tray before setting it down.

"I was entirely overdressed. You said the evening was going to be casual. I should have listened."

"But how did you change so fast?" she sputtered. Now she was the one thrown for a loop. She could tell Scott was loving every minute of her confusion. There was no mistaking the look of amusement on his face. His lips wouldn't stop twitching into a smile. "Where did you get the clothes?"

He patted his attaché case. "I always keep a change of clothes with me. Pays to be prepared." He reached for a hot dog, but Robyn snatched it away.

"Hey, I'm starving!"

Robyn waved the hot dog in Scott's face before biting into it. "Unlike this hot dog, your story isn't kosher." She took another bite. "Try again."

"Will you give me all the hot dogs I want?" he bartered.

"All you want," she agreed.

"And dessert?"

"I didn't make dessert."

"Can't you whip something up?"

"Like?"

"A taste of the forbidden?" he suggested.

Robyn nodded. "Okay, but only a taste."

"Deal!" Scott reached for a hot dog. "I met a neighbor of yours in the hallway. He was willing to swap." He bit into his hot dog before noticing it was plain. "Got any sauerkraut?"

Robyn shook her head.

"Mustard?"

"All out."

"Some date," Scott grumbled, returning his attention to his half-bitten hot dog.

"What about dessert, wise guy? Forget all about that?"

Scott perked up. "Dessert. Will it make up for the missing sauerkraut and mustard?"

Robyn removed the hot dog from Scott's grasp. "Definitely."

"I like the way you plan a meal."

Scott wrapped his arms around Robyn, fully embracing her as he drew her into his lap. As their lips met, both felt a renewed passion surge through them.

Scott's lips were gentle and firm against Robyn's yielding sweetness. He couldn't remember the last time he had experienced such a full range of emotions. Simmering love. Burning desire. Tender caring. Making love with Robyn would unite the three and show her how deeply he felt about her.

With closed eyes Robyn allowed her fingers to caress Scott's face, billowing through the softness of his tawny hair. Immediately his image was formed, burning her soul with desire. She wanted to make love with him. Tonight. Desperately.

Robyn only allowed herself to think of Scott and how he made her feel. When Scott was around she was never happier. His brilliant green eyes always glowed with love and passion. Scott made her feel beautiful and desirable in a way no other man ever had. All it took was a look or a word or a smile. Scott always saw her as a matched equal, not as someone who needed to be taken care of. He loved her for who she was.

Undecipherable flashes from her past started creeping in, but Robyn pushed them away, locking them behind a steel door. If she had her way, they would remain there forever. Tonight belonged to Scott. Nothing else mattered except being in his arms and having him make love to her.

Their lips separated but Scott pressed his against Robyn's again, his tongue skillfully exploring and entwining with hers. Robyn kept her lips locked in place, responding to Scott's urgency.

"Scott, I love you," she whispered fervently.

"I love you, Robyn, more than I've ever loved any other woman."

They were the words she had so wanted to hear. Scott loved her! "Make love to me."

"Are you sure?"

Robyn placed her hand in Scott's, leading him in the direction of her bedroom. Once inside, Robyn turned to him, stripping away her football jersey and jeans. "We've waited long enough."

Scott was mesmerized by her beauty. With the softest of touches his fingers moved from her cheeks to her lips, delicately tracing their contours. He lavished the proud arch of her neck with a trail of passionate kisses before moving around, above and below her nipples. Cupping her breasts in his hands, he brought them to his lips for a devouring taste.

His touch left Robyn breathless. She quivered with desire and anticipation as Scott's tongue darted from nipple to nipple, manipulating the soft bits of skin into hardened points. His lips returned to her neck, and when they reached her lips again, she met them with an all-consuming hunger. Never before had she felt this way! All she wanted was for Scott to satisfy her.

She slipped her hands around his waist, pulling at his cutoff jeans. Scott shed them, along with the sweatshirt, freeing the surging power of his erection. Robyn brushed her fingers along the sculpted ridges of his exposed chest, thrilling at his hard, smooth bronzeness. Her heart raced as Scott captured her in his embrace, pulling her close in his arms. The joining of his bare flesh with hers was like a drop of water on a hot skillet. Sizzling. Passion and desire bubbled through Robyn's veins, aching for release.

Her fingers found his erection, caressing the velvety heat of his shaft as they walked backward to her bed. They fell upon the mattress together, Robyn's legs widening as Scott easily slid into her awaiting wetness. His rhythm was slow and unhurried as he rocked deeper and deeper.

Robyn gasped with delight at each movement, experiencing a swirl of exquisite sensations. Scott's every touch only intensified her pleasure, and at the approach of his frenzied climax, Robyn surrendered to the ecstasy building within her.

Scott's climax was the trigger that set her free. Crying aloud, she buried her fingers in Scott's hair, tightening her grip. Twisting Scott's head back, her lips found his, instantly locking before pushing open his mouth, savagely probing with her tongue.

He responded with equal fervor. The sight and smell of Robyn sent his senses reeling. He buried his face between her breasts as his fingers probed her glistening wetness. No matter how much time he was given, he'd never get enough of her. She was his dream lover finally brought to life.

They explored each other's bodies with the passion and awareness of new lovers, never tiring, reveling in their union.

When they were drained of all passion and initiative, they collapsed in each other's arms, content to spend the rest of the evening with the intimacy of soft words and declarations of love.

20

Kristen was glad Lance had chosen the Lone Star Café. With its sawdust-covered floors, checkered tablecloths, and country and western atmosphere, she always felt at ease.

She was sipping a beer, listening to the live band, when Lance arrived, taking a chair beside her.

"Hi," he greeted, kissing her without hesitation. "What are you having?"

"Rolling Rock."

"I'll have the same," he told the approaching waiter. After the waiter left, he returned his attention to her. "I'm glad you came."

"Who said you could kiss me?"

Lance laughed. "Come on Kristen, let's get serious."

"About what?"

"Us. There's no denying there's an attraction. Why fight it?"

"Because you're married," she pointed out. To Kristen's ears the words sounded lame and dated. Why was she making excuses? What Lance said about their attraction to each other was true. But she had been unable to admit that to herself. She had been using his offer of representation as a way of keeping in touch with him, hoping for more. Now they were together with unspoken words hanging between them, leading to more if they wanted it.

Why did she feel so guilty of her attraction to him? His marriage had been in a shambles long before her arrival. True, her becoming involved with Lance wouldn't help his marriage, but the damage had already been done.

"Reason enough for you, but not for me," Lance said. The waiter arrived with his beer. Lance didn't bother with a glass, drinking straight from the bottle. "What are you doing here if you feel that way?"

"You invited me."

"You accepted without question," he retorted.

Kristen stuck out her tongue. "Smartass."

"What would you say if I told you I had planned a seduction?"

Kristen took a sip of her beer, twisting her head around the crowded bar. "In front of all these people? Intriguing."

A savage rock and roll beat had been started by the band. Lance took her by the hand, leading her out onto the dance floor. He placed his hands on the back of Kristen's jeans, lifting her up and pressing himself forcefully against her. Kristen's arms flew around Lance's neck and his arms locked tightly around hers.

"How long can you hold out?" he asked, looking directly into her eyes.

She was hypnotized by his gaze. Undisguised passion stared at her. Mesmerized by what she saw in his eyes, she could only imagine the results. "Long enough," she whispered dryly, struggling against the responses her body was experiencing by having him so close.

"Let's change that." He moved his hand to the back of Kristen's head, gripping her short hair tightly before pulling down sharply. Upon placing his lips to her exposed neck, currents of pain became ones of searing pleasure. "Still want to hold out?"

Kristen felt her resolve slipping away and didn't care. "Let's go to your loft," she said breathlessly.

Enveloped in darkness, Lance and Kristen moved together as one, instinctively knowing where to place their hands, lips, and tongues to illicit the most pleasure.

Lance buried his face between Kristen's breasts, moving his tongue from one nipple to the other. As his taste for her grew, his licks turned into bites and she screamed in ecstasy. Arching her back, Kristen wrapped her legs around Lance's waist as he prepared to enter her, immediately pulling him deep into her pulsing depths.

Her lips licked the droplets of sweat beading his chest

while he sucked at her erect nipples. Their lips then joined together, tasting of themselves and each other.

Wrapping their arms around each other's shoulders, they braced themselves against the approaching climax. Kristen's arms clutched at Lance as he pressed her farther into the mattress. When the moment of release arrived, they shuddered with excrutiating pleasure, collapsing among the pillows and remaining entwined. Breathing was heavy. They separated, settling into more comfortable positions, studying the other's silhouette.

"Hungry?" Lance asked.

Kristen shifted in the darkness. "Kind of."

"Want to get something to eat?"

"Sure." She got up from the bed, standing naked before the window in the incoming moonlight. "Will we do this again?"

"Why do you ask?"

Kristen gathered her clothes off the floor, heading for the bathroom. "You have a reputation."

"Fuck 'em and leave 'em?" Lance propped himself on an elbow, studying Kristen intently. "Do you want to do this again?"

Making love with Lance had been sheer bliss. Kristen absolutely couldn't wait until the next time. She nodded her head. "I do."

Lance relaxed among the twisted sheets of their spent passion. "Then we will." He held out open arms. "Want to build up an appetite?"

Kristen dropped her clothes, wasting no time in rejoining him.

•

Robyn was the first to awake the following morning. The first sight she saw was Scott. Kissing him on the cheek as she remembered the evening before, she bounded into the shower and dressed quickly, deciding bagels and lox would be a nice way to start the morning. She left Scott a note and then left the apartment.

She basked in the morning sunlight as she walked, smiling at whoever she saw.

Deciding she wanted only the best, Robyn went to

Balducci's. There she bought a dozen bagels, fresh lox, cream cheese, and strawberries. On the way back to the apartment she also bought a bunch of wildflowers from a corner vendor, adding them to her purchases. Oblivious to everything except her newfound happiness, Robyn began humming a tune.

She failed to notice the car with darkened windows that had followed her every move.

Bettina knocked tentatively on the bedroom door before entering. Georgina was in bed, an ice-filled compress held to her forehead. "Yes?" she asked wearily.

"You have a phone call, Mrs. Richards."

"Ask them to call back."

"It's the police."

The compress slid to the side of her head as she sat up. "The police? What do they want?"

"I have no idea."

Georgina's mind started racing. Could something have happened to Lance? Had he finally been caught by a jealous husband or lover and met his end? She began envisioning herself at his funeral, dressed smartly in black, preparing to begin a new life. Perhaps she'd even wear a trace of red. The idea of it all was almost too tantalizing. She jumped for the phone, jarring the remnants of the previous evening's hangover.

"Damn," she muttered, waving away a concerned Bettina.

Her agent had called yesterday afternoon to tell her that the L'Xuriance hair-color people hadn't given her the job. They'd wanted to go with a "fresher" face.

Georgina had taken the news calmly, but after hanging up with her agent, had needed to talk to someone. She'd wanted to confess her fears. She was afraid she'd never model again. She felt so *useless*. What did she have beyond her modeling? Nothing.

There had been no one for her to talk to. So she'd taken a drink . . . only to calm her nerves. One drink soon led to another and another and another. She didn't remember when she'd passed out or how she'd gotten to her bedroom.

Needing to dull the edge of the throbbing in her head, she

reached for a glass with a fingerful of scotch, swallowing it as she pressed the phone to her ear. "This is Georgina Richards." She coughed as the scotch burned down her throat.

"Mrs. Richards, this is Officer Mitchell. We need you to come down to your husband's loft."

"What's happened? Has something happened to Lance?" She wondered if she sounded a bit too eager.

"Your husband's loft was broken into early this morning. As far as we can tell, he wasn't here at the time. Sorry if I alarmed you."

Georgina slumped dejectedly among her pillows. "What does any of this have to do with me?"

"We need you to come down and take a look around. See if anything is missing."

"Can't Lance do it?" she snapped irritably. "After all, it is his loft. I hardly ever go down there."

"We've tried locating your husband, and can't afford to spend any more time. We've questioned the neighbors, and no one saw or heard anything after your husband left this morning. We can't keep our eyes open for anything stolen if we don't know what we're looking for. You must have some idea of what your husband kept here."

"Hardly."

"If you're not going to come down, Mrs. Richards," the voice complained as it turned impatient, "we're going to have to mark this case closed."

Wouldn't Lance love that! She could just hear him bellowing at her once he learned of the break-in. He'd say she'd been too drunk to go down to the loft. Even if nothing was missing, Lance would still go on and on. He never passed an opportunity to criticize her.

"All right," she sighed, banishing thoughts of Lance from her mind as she reached for a discarded skirt and blouse. "I'm on my way."

"Once again, thank you for your help, Mrs. Richards."

Georgina gave a weary smile before closing the door on the departing officers. They seemed satisfied now that they had a list of items to hopelessly attempt to recover. Once she called a cab and had a quick drink, she would be the next to leave.

The idea of remaining alone in the loft was insane. Not because of the thieves who had left the place ransacked. No sense of security had been violated here. This place wasn't a home. A stereo system, color TV, and a few cameras had merely been taken. Easily replaceable. It was the women brought here that made Georgina's blood boil—women like Erica, who didn't give a damn about anyone but themselves.

She still hadn't found a way to get even with Erica, but she would. When she did, it would be a staggering blow to the picture-perfect world Erica believed she lived in. After all the years of passively watching Lance have affairs, she was finally going to take some action.

When the officers had been there, Georgina had avoided going into Lance's bedroom, telling them there was nothing of value in the room. Now, drawn by a morbid sense of curiosity, she found herself entering the bedroom.

Surprisingly, the room was untouched. She remained rooted in the doorway, staring at the bed. Before she knew what she was doing, she moved to the drawers, opening one after the other, rummaging through Lance's clothes. Then she found the lingerie.

Georgina stared, sickened, at the rainbow colors of silk and lace before becoming consumed by rage. Within seconds the lingerie was tossed helter skelter around the bedroom.

When the phone rang, she stopped, listening as the answering machine clicked on. It was a female voice: "Guess you're not in. Give me a call when you get a chance. I'm hungry for some love, and you're on the menu. Bye."

Suddenly the walls of the bedroom felt like they were closing in on Georgina, getting ready to crush her with its secrets. She had to get away from the evidence of her failed marriage.

Rushing through the cluttered mess of papers thrown around by the thieves, her foot slipped and she skidded to the floor. As she fell, the contents of a manila folder fanned out.

Georgina landed with a thud, her eyes falling to the photographs spread out before her.

They were nude photographs . . . nude photographs of Erica Shelton.

With a mixture of repulsion and thrilled fascination, she examined photo after photo before dropping each back to the floor. In most of the photos Erica posed alone. But in a select few she posed with a nude Lance in the most intimate of embraces. With her closed eyes and lips pouted in a sensuous bow, she had a look of dreamy satisfaction etched on her face.

At first Georgina didn't know what to do. Then she began gathering up the photographs, sticking them neatly back into their manila folder. When she had collected them all, she got back to her feet. She left the loft with the folder under her arm.

Georgina was no longer angry or upset. Why should she be? She finally had what she needed to destroy Erica.

21

As predicted by Scott and Samantha, Robyn's career skyrocketed. After the Fresh and Lovely campaign was launched, the offers poured in.

Samantha carefully sifted through all of Robyn's offers, recommending only those that were the most lucrative and promised the highest visibility.

First Robyn did a series of commercials for Smooth, Silky, Sexy Panty Hose. In the commercial Robyn was seen racing from one activity to another as the camera zoomed in on her legs and the panty hose's three intertwined S's. Cuts were interspersed with three different men admiring Robyn's legs. One called her legs smooth, another called them silky, and the third called them sexy. At the end of the commercial Robyn held up a fan of Smooth, Silky, Sexy Panty Hose in a number of colors.

For a European designer, Robyn slipped into a pair of Sensation! jeans and was soon appearing on billboards from coast to coast. The print ads and commercials on TV showed a bare-backed Robyn drenched in sweat, wearing a pair of Sensation! jeans. A male hand caressed one of her denim clad legs as the logo declared: "Feel the Sensation!" The ads were considered the hottest thing since Brooke Shields and her Calvin Klein days.

Bloomingdale's wasted no time hiring Robyn as their spokeswoman, replacing Erin Gray, and used her exclusively for all their advertising. The same was true for Farthington Furs and Lamour Leathers.

Robyn soon lost count of the number of magazines she posed for: *Vogue, Elle, Mademoiselle* and *Cosmopolitan. International Sport* flew her to Barbados and put her on the cover of their June swimsuit issue, easily beating the sales figures of *Sport's Illustrated*'s swimsuit issue from February.

L'Xuriance Hair Color fell in love with Robyn and had to have her as their blonde for their commercials. The company eagerly met Robyn's fee.

Although Robyn was kept busy throughout the summer, darting from one assignment to the next, she always found time for Scott. Once they had become lovers, the two never seemed to get enough of each other. Whenever possible they spent evenings together. Some evenings they went out. Other times they settled in front of the TV with a stack of videotapes and a pizza. On weekends they were inseparable, going to art galleries, museums, and other interesting places as they learned more and more about each other.

When work called one away and the other was able to rearrange their schedule, there were fun-filled days and passionate nights in Paris, London, Beverly Hills, and the Bahamas.

Scott and Robyn never tired of being in each other's arms, exploring the other's body with as much passion and abandon as if it were the first time their bodies were joining together.

For the first time in a long time, both Robyn and Scott felt their lives were complete.

In early September Robyn came home from a shoot and found every room of her apartment filled with orchids. She could only stare at the exotic purple and white flowers in amazement. They were gorgeous! Only one man would go to such extravagant lengths. She dialed Scott's private line at Wellington with a smile.

"Scott, the flowers you sent are gorgeous, but you shouldn't have gone so overboard. There isn't an inch of space available. Kristen is going to go wild."

"What flowers?"

"The orchids," she answered.

"What orchids?"

"Stop teasing. I know you sent them."

"Robyn, I have no idea what you're talking about."

The confusion in his voice was unmistakable. "You mean you *didn't* send the orchids?"

"I wish I had," he ruefully admitted. "Sounds like you've got an admirer. Is there a card?"

"I didn't think to look for one." Suddenly Robyn realized who the orchids were from, but she didn't want Scott to know. Not yet. "They're probably from a satisfied advertiser. I'll take a look for a card and give you a call later. Love you, sweetie."

"I love you, Robyn."

When Robyn found the card, she wasn't surprised to find Quinn's name. The card fell from her fingers to the floor. There was no longer putting off what had to be done. Quinn had to get on with his life. He had to stop believing they had a chance. She had to tell him the truth about her feelings, something she should have done months ago. She'd never love Quinn the way she loved Scott. Quinn had to understand that he didn't have a future with her. Scott Kendall was her future.

There wasn't a doubt in Scott's mind as to who had sent the orchids: Quinn Marler. Who else would it be?

Scott fought against his feelings of jealousy—and insecurity. Robyn loved *him*. He needed no proof of her feelings.

The times he had asked about Quinn, Robyn had told him that Quinn was only a friend. He had believed her and not asked any other questions. Her relationship with Quinn was really none of his business.

Then why did he feel threatened? Why did he suddenly

feel like he was on the outside looking in? Robyn was the love of *his* life. Quinn Marler had no claim to her heart. *But,* if for some reason Quinn decided to go after Robyn, then the man had better get ready for battle. Scott was ready to fight. Quinn Marler would never have Robyn. *Never.* Scott was determined he wouldn't lose her.

Quinn was staying at the Plaza. Robyn gave him a call and asked if they could meet in the Oak Room bar.

"I'll be there," he promised. "Were you surprised by the orchids?"

His orchids had forced her to face a situation she had wanted to avoid. But she couldn't tell him that over the phone. "They're lovely. I'll see you in an hour."

When she arrived at the Oak Room bar, Quinn was already waiting in a booth, sipping a scotch. He held out his arms and Robyn gave him a warm hug.

"You're as beautiful as ever," he raved. "More so than the last time I saw you. I can't believe over a year has passed since you left."

Robyn slid into the booth. "Enough with the compliments. I look the same."

"You don't," Quinn insisted. "You've changed, Robyn." He studied her intently. "You've become elegant and sophisticated, but it's more than that. You glow. You seem happy . . . very happy. It looks like moving to New York was a step in the right direction."

How could she tell him her happiness was due to Scott and not New York? This was so hard. She didn't know where to begin.

"Think moving to New York would work for me?" he asked.

Robyn gave Quinn a puzzled look. "What are you talking about?"

"Bellevue Hospital called me last month. I've been flying back and forth on interviews." Quinn's eyes gleamed with excitement. "Today they gave me the news. They want me to head their psychiatric program."

Even though Robyn knew Quinn's answer, she asked her question. "Are you going to accept?"

"Of course," he exclaimed. "Why wouldn't I?"

Robyn tried to keep smiling as she felt her stomach tighten. She knew she was grasping at straws, but she'd do whatever she had to in order to spare Quinn whatever pain she could. "I know accepting the position will be a big leap for your career, but it means relocating to New York. It means starting over. Are you sure you want to do that?"

"Sounds like you're trying to discourage me." Quinn laughed. "Robyn, I want to move to New York. I want to be closer to you. Don't you see? This is our chance for a relationship." He took Robyn's hand in his. "I know I messed things when we were in Chicago, but this time there won't be any mistakes. Everything will be perfect. I promise." Quinn noticed the look of distress on Robyn's face. "What's wrong?"

"Quinn, there can never be anything between us." She looked into his eyes. "We can only be friends. Never lovers."

"Aren't you being a bit rash? How can you make a decision like that without giving us a chance?"

Robyn revealed her news as gently as she could. "I'm involved with someone."

Quinn released her hand. "Is it serious?"

"Yes," she quietly admitted. "I love him very much. Scott is the man I want to spend the rest of my life with. I don't know what I'd do without him. Scott brings out a part of myself I never knew I had. When I'm with him I feel like an entirely different person."

"And with me?"

Robyn gave Quinn a warm smile. "When I'm with you I feel safe . . . protected."

"Is that so bad?"

"Don't you see? You deserve someone who will love you with all her heart."

"Couldn't you try loving me?"

"I love Scott."

Quinn gave Robyn a rueful smile. "Sounds like your mind is made up."

Robyn nodded sadly. "It is. I never wanted to hurt you, Quinn. I was hoping we would never have this talk. I thought you would find someone else. You have to let me go. We both deserve our own happiness."

Quinn finished his scotch. "Looks like I won't be moving to New York."

"Are you sure you want to turn down this opportunity?" Robyn truthfully asked.

"I have to. Don't worry, there'll be other opportunities. Getting over you in New York would be too hard. Our paths would be bound to cross. Anyway, you were the real reason I would have relocated. I wonder what the board would think of my professionalism if they knew that." Quinn rose from the booth. "I'll only be a few minutes. I have a phone call to make. There's a job I have to turn down."

Beverly was speaking with the director of Bellevue's psychiatric program over the phone.

"Dr. Marler turned down the position? I see. Yes, I agree. He must be crazy to turn down our offer. What more could he want? We were giving him a six-figure salary, an all-expense-paid apartment and the freedom to head up whatever programs he liked. Yes, it is regretful. Well, thank you for calling."

Beverly slammed down the phone. She whirled around in her black silk dressing gown and stared out at the starry night.

Quinn Marler had ruined her plans. She had hoped to divert Robyn's attentions away from Scott by bringing Quinn to New York. This wasn't good. Quinn must have met with Robyn and she must have set him straight. She must have told him that he didn't stand a chance and that Scott was the only man she'd ever love.

All Beverly could see was red. She'd wasted so much time calling in favors and pulling strings in trying to get Quinn to New York. Her efforts had been useless. Quinn was gone and Robyn was still around.

Beverly didn't like the look of things. She didn't like the look of things at all. She'd better give Anthony Calder a call. He'd better have found something from Robyn's past . . . something scandalous. Beverly no longer wanted Robyn out of Scott's life. She wanted her out of New York.

She intended on destroying Robyn and having her lose it all. She wouldn't settle for anything less.

* * *

"Scott?"

"In the bedroom."

Robyn followed a trail of orchid petals to her bedroom and found Scott in her bed covered only by a blanket of orchid petals.

"What are you doing?" she exclaimed.

"Waiting for you."

Robyn raised an eyebrow. "For what possible reason?"

Scott grinned, holding out a hand. "Come find out."

Robyn entered his arms and allowed herself to be nestled against the velvety smoothness of the petals. "This feels nice," she said. She brushed away a few petals, uncovering Scott's chest. "But I like what's hidden." She started kissing his chest.

"Robyn, I love you," he declared.

Robyn rubbed against him. "I can tell," she teased.

"I'm serious."

The intensity of his words cut through her humor. "I know. I love you too."

"I don't know what I'd do if I lost you," he confessed, cradling her head against his chest.

Robyn looked up at him. "You're not going to lose me," she promised. "I love you more than any other man."

Scott had to put his fears to rest once and for all. "Including Quinn Marler?"

"Including Quinn Marler," she confirmed. "Tonight I met with Quinn and we settled everything once and for all. He's only a friend, Scott." She clicked off the bedside lamp. "Quinn and I never shared anything like this." She gave him a passionate kiss. "I told him there was only one man in my life—only one man I would ever truly love. You're that man."

"I believe you."

Robyn slipped off her dress and brushed away the rest of the petals. "Then make love to me like you never have before, and when it's over, start again."

Scott was only too willing to comply.

22

"Look at all those people," Robyn whispered, peeking out at the audience.

Kristen pulled Robyn's arm, allowing the heavy curtain to fall back into place. "Come on, we've got to get ready," she urged, leading Robyn to the racks where a multitude of gowns hung in clear plastic wrappings.

The scene was backstage at the Waldorf Astoria. In a few minutes a charity fashion show was about to begin. The biggest names in fashion, modeling, and design had joined forces for a thousand-dollar-a-plate luncheon to benefit the homeless. In addition, each outfit worn would be auctioned off, with the proceeds contributed to the funds.

For weeks the columns had devoted themselves to the sold-out event. Manhattan's elite had been unable to refuse the call. Now all were in attendance, waiting for the curtain to rise. Among the models giving freely of their time were Kelly Emberg, Paulina, Patti Hansen, and Iman. The designers included Calvin Klein, Ralph Lauren, Bill Blass, and a score of others.

"Honey, I've got to take those curlers out of your hair," a hairdresser called to Robyn.

"See you in a few minutes," Kristen said, heading off to have her face made up.

Robyn took a seat before the woman, staring at the bevy of activity around her. Dressers, assistants, and an assortment of others scurried back and forth, shouting orders.

"Where are those pumps?"

"I need accessories! Where are those bracelets? Jesus Christ, can't you see the tags don't match? I need the bracelets for the Nolan Miller, not the Givenchy."

"How much longer till we begin?"

"More blush! She'll look like a ghost under those lights."

"My God, how much weight did you put on since that last fitting? We can hardly squeeze you into your gown."

The rollers were removed one by one and the hairdresser's brush moved swiftly and smoothly over Robyn's head, resulting in a sleek bob of shimmering ash.

Next Robyn headed for the Givenchy gown waiting for her. It was a tube of glittering silver overlaid with emerald drops and bared only on one shoulder. Cut high in the thigh, it showed off her black-stockinged legs and black lizard pumps. Emeralds and diamonds dripped from her neck, ears, and wrists, while a white mink stole was draped around her shoulders.

Kristen was zipping herself into a ruby-red Oscar de la Renta with spaghetti straps and a plunging neckline. Her short hair had been moussed and spiked.

"Looking good," Robyn complimented.

Kristen shimmied before Robyn while fiddling with the straps of her gown. "When you've got it, flaunt it." She studied her face in a compact. "Feeling nervous?"

"Kind of. All those eyes are going to be watching us."

Kristen grinned, putting away the compact. "Don't you mean the clothes on our backs?"

"How could I have forgotten?" Robyn gushed with relief before becoming panicked. "But what if no one bids on what I'm wearing?"

"It'll never happen."

"Why not?"

"Scott's in the audience. At least one sale is guaranteed."

"Have I missed anything?" Scott took the seat next to Kyle Masters at the damask-covered table.

"It's about time you showed up," Kyle commented.

Scott smiled confidently while exchanging greetings with the others around the table. "My meeting took longer than expected."

"Good news?"

"Phenomenal. The Fresh and Lovely line is moving off the shelves. Orders are pouring in."

"Congratulations."

"Don't give me all the credit. This was a team effort." He glanced at his watch. "Any idea when the auction starts?"

"Any minute. You got here just in time."

"Seen any signs of Robyn?"

"She was hovering around the curtain last time I saw." Kyle spread some caviar on a sliver of toast. "She was probably looking for you."

"Well, I'm here. Let the show begin."

"I was asked to participate but refused," Georgina commented at another table. "Once everyone starts jumping on the bandwagon, exclusivity is gone, don't you agree?"

Beverly lifted a finger and instantly a fluted glass of champagne appeared before her. When out at social gatherings, she drank whatever everyone else was drinking. Today champagne was the order of the day.

There were a number of reasons why Beverly had decided to attend the fashion show. The first was simply because everyone who mattered in Manhattan was attending. Secondly, she wanted a closer look at Robyn Prescott in action. Anthony Calder had still found nothing she could use. Hardly surprising. Her patience with him was wearing thin. Each passing day meant Robyn still remained a part of Scott's life, and that infuriated her.

Beverly picked at the offerings on her plate. Scotch-smoked salmon. Lobster patties. Oysters on the half shell. Grapes wrapped in salmon. She sipped at her champagne while Georgina continued babbling. How had they managed to be seated at the same table? Actually, she knew she had no one to blame but herself. Everyone assumed she and Georgina were the best of friends. Why not? Beverly had done everything in her power to promote that illusion.

She planned luncheons and dinner parties around Georgina. They went shopping together at Tiffany's, Sak's, and Bonwit Teller's. Had facials and their hair done at Liz Arden's. So far Georgina had been good for nothing but aggravation. Things had to change soon.

"Do you intend on bidding on anything?" Georgina asked. "Bid high enough and your name is sure to make one of the columns."

"My name always makes the columns," Beverly sniffed frostily. "I doubt I'll buy anything. Buying at an established price is much more dignified than haggling over a few thousand dollars. That's what distinguishes the rich from the nouveau rich."

Beverly's eyes started to wander as Georgina responded. Her heart froze. Scott was sitting across the room. He didn't see her. What should she do? She instantly decided. There was nothing wrong with going over to him and exchanging a few pleasantries. All perfectly innocent. As she started rising, the lights dimmed and a rock and roll beat began.

"Where are you going?" Georgina asked, holding Beverly down in her seat. "The show is about to begin."

Resisting the urge to shake off Georgina, Beverly sat back, biting back the ugly stream of words she was ready to spew forth. The lights dimmed further and the music grew louder. Keeping her eyes glued on the runway, Beverly settled back in her seat. Her mind wasn't focused on the fashion show. Instead she was biding her time until the lights came back up and she could meet with Scott.

"I can see Scott." Robyn exhaled with relief as the lights started to dim. "I'm so glad he's here."

"He wouldn't have missed this for the world." Kristen took her place in line behind Robyn as they prepared to make their way down the runway. "Relax," she coaxed, gently squeezing Robyn's shoulders. "You're so tense. They're going to love you. After all, you're the new darling of the press."

It was true. Robyn's name had become a fixation in all of the columns. Whether at work or at play, her name was mentioned, her photograph sought. Invitations to dinners, parties, clubs, and opening nights flooded her daily. There were so many to choose from that she hardly had any free time. New York had become mesmerized by her looks, her rise to fame, and most of all, by her romance with Scott.

If there was anything she treasured above all she had achieved in such a short time, it was her love for Scott. She was happiest when they were together. No matter where they went or what they did, the rest of the world ceased to exist. Just a look or a touch conveyed more than spoken words. Their desire and passion for each other kept growing with each passing day.

"You're so calm," she remarked to Kristen. "Don't you ever get nervous before a show?"

"Nah, I love it." The drapes on the stage were parting as the music increased. Spotlights began dancing on the stage and runway. "All the attention gives me a rush. I'm a natural showoff. All those eyes are my mirrors." The models before Robyn started moving forward. "We're on," Kristen gleefully cried, twisting Robyn face forward and following after her into the lights.

Backstage was a frenzy of activity as models appearing in more than one gown or outfit made quick changes. Among them was Erica Shelton, who was slipping into a black velvet Donna Karan. She stopped dressing as bits of conversation floated over. What she was hearing sounded familiar.

"So she went back with him to his place," an auburn-haired model explained. "And then accepted a drink."

A second auburn-haired model turned to the other listeners, nodding sagely. "Spiked."

"She passes out and he whips out his camera. When she wakes up, he takes the legitimate photos and gets her to sign a release. Next thing you know, she's spread all over the pages of a porn magazine."

"Is she still trying to make it in the business?" a hairdresser asked.

The first model sprayed herself with Giorgio. "Hopped on the next plane back to Kentucky."

"Did she have a chance to make it?" another hairdresser asked.

"Yes, she was very beautiful."

The second model tossed her auburn head, sniffing disdainfully. "Just as well she's gone. We don't need the extra competition." She held up a swimsuit to the others. "Can you believe I'm only getting to model this? I turned down a more expensive shoot to be here today. My agent thought it would be good exposure."

Erica stopped listening to the conversation. What had

happened to the model from Kentucky sounded too much like her afternoon at Lance's. He had given her a drink and then she had passed out. But she hadn't gone there to take pictures, and he couldn't have taken any. He had told her he'd left her alone and spent the afternoon with Kristen Adams.

But she only had his word that he hadn't taken advantage of her, Erica thought. She tried to calm down. She was jumping to conclusions. Why would Lance have done such a thing? What could he possibly have to gain from nude photographs of her? He couldn't use the photos if he had taken any because she hadn't signed a release. Or had she? She remembered signing for duplicate photographs, but she hadn't read the paper Lance had shoved at her. Erica suddenly felt ill. What was Lance up to?

She was due to follow in the second group of models, and Kristen was still out on the runway. She would have to talk to her after the show.

Erica pressed her palms into the folds of her skirt, praying Kristen would give her the answer she hoped for.

Robyn carefully slid from her Givenchy gown into a terry-cloth robe. Relieved to be out of the expensive gown, which had gone for ten thousand dollars, she waited for Kristen to scurry offstage.

"They're certainly in a spending mood," Kristen commented. Her gown had gone for seven thousand. "You've gotten the highest price so far."

"Think they'll go any higher?"

"Not unless the bidder is male and we come along with the rest of the package." Kristen slipped into her robe. "What are you wearing next?"

"Lingerie."

"Lucky girl. You don't have to go back out till the end of the show."

"What else are you in?"

"Swimwear."

"Doing anything special after the show?"

"Hopefully. How about you?"

"Nothing's definite, but I do have something in mind."

"Care to divulge?" Kristen prodded. "You've got the

naughtiest grin on your face. Keep it on. It'll enhance the lingerie."

The bidding began.

"Do I hear three thousand? Three thousand dollars. Do I hear three thousand five? Three thousand five. Four?" The rapid voice of the auctioneer, which actually belonged to one of the leading auctioneer's from Sotheby's, increased along with the price. "Five. Do I hear six? Surely we can do better than five thousand dollars for this lovely Nolan Miller creation. Let's dig into our wallets. Remember, this auction is for the homeless."

Robyn wore a negligee of pale blue silk which complimented her coloring. The bodice was low and trimmed with lace that matched the trim on the Edwardian sleeves of the matching dressing gown.

"Seven thousand dollars. Do I hear eight? Eight thousand dollars? No? How about seven thousand five? Seven thousand five? No? Okay! Seven thousand dollars. Going once . . . going twice . . ."

Before he could conclude, a male voice boomed, "Twenty-five thousand dollars."

A collective gasp traveled through the audience as all heads, including Robyn's, turned to the man who had made the highest bid of the day.

It was Scott Kendall.

Beverly crumpled her program into a ball. It was obvious why Scott was bidding on the negligee. She didn't have to stretch the limits of her imagination. She knew exactly when and where it would be worn. She knew whose body it would be worn upon before being peeled away by Scott's hands.

It would be Robyn's.

As much as Beverly wanted to outbid Scott, she knew she couldn't. Tongues would start wagging and rumors would surely fly. But this *was* a golden opportunity. She couldn't let it slip by. She knew what she had to do.

Beverly slowly raised her hand.

Scott stared across the crowded auction at Beverly. Rushing in as late as he had, he hadn't noticed anyone except those in the vicinity of his table. She gave him a friendly smile before rising to her feet. He returned the smile, all along wondering what she had up her sleeve.

Was she going to bid on the negligee out of spite, so he couldn't have it? If so, she'd better be prepared to spend. He intended on doubling any offer she made.

The eyes at the auction shifted between Beverly and Scott. Most knew the history between the two and breathlessly waited for Beverly to speak.

"Ladies and gentlemen," Beverly confidently began, "we have gathered today for a special cause, to help the homeless. We've all given generously of our time and money, but special recognition must be given to Scott Kendall. His bid of twenty-five thousand dollars is one that comes from the heart. I don't know about the rest of you, but suddenly I'm suffering from pangs of guilt. There's only one solution." She reached for her checkbook. "I'm matching Scott's bid and donating twenty-five thousand dollars to today's fund for the homeless."

There was a round of applause as champagne glasses were toasted to both Beverly and Scott. At the same time, others began reaching for their checkbooks.

Beverly lifted her own champagne glass, winking at Scott. Around her congratulations were being offered. Smiling at all, she sipped contentedly at her champagne. Score one for her.

"Bet you never thought you'd own such an expensive negligee."

"Can't say that I have." Robyn twirled before Scott. "Can't you see me wearing this while I'm making coffee and frying eggs with my hair in rollers and my face without makeup?"

"Never," Scott vowed. "You'll always have breakfast in bed and you'll always look as ravishing as you do right now." He held up a hand. "Scout's honor. Do you like it?"

Robyn grinned. "For twenty-five thousand dollars, I'd better."

Scott's fingers traced the blue silk. "You'll have to wear it at least once."

Robyn sighed reluctantly. "I suppose you're right."

His fingers moved down to the lace embroidered sheath. "Such enthusiasm," he mocked. "Any ideas?"

"One did cross my mind."

"Care to share it?"

"It will be a very special showing. Only two people will be there."

"Which two?"

Robyn looked deeply into Scott's eyes before bringing her lips to his. "Us."

"The two of you make such a wonderful couple," a female voice announced.

Startled, Robyn and Scott broke their kiss. Beverly was standing before them.

"I didn't mean to interrupt," she apologized. "One of the designers invited me to the backstage party." Beverly noticed Robyn was still wearing the negligee. "Can't take it off, can you? Actually," she confided, fingering the lace on the sleeves, "I was tempted to outbid Scott for it until I realized why he was bidding on it. I'm hardly one to stand in the way of romance. Wear it well, Robyn. You look lovely in it."

Robyn smiled her thanks before flashing Scott a questioning look. She didn't want to appear rude, but who was this woman? Her face was familiar, but she had no idea who she was.

Scott caught Robyn's look and wasted no time in making introductions. "Robyn, this is Beverly Maxwell." He paused for a moment, debating his next words. "Beverly and I were once involved."

Robyn hoped she didn't look surprised. Naturally there had been other women before her. Scott was an attractive man. Keeping a smile on her face, she took a closer look at Beverly, comparing and contrasting herself. The woman was stunning. How could Scott have let her go?

"Ages ago," Beverly glibly explained. "Scott was the one who realized we weren't suited to each other. He saved us years of heartache by breaking things off, but at the time I was the stubborn one. Yet after examining our relationship and the mistakes I made, I can admit Scott was right."

Scott was amazed by the change in Beverly's attitude. This was the first time they had actually discussed their breakup, and he'd expected her to be nothing less than bitter. Instead, she was bubbling with friendliness. "You're looking wonderful," he stated sincerely.

"I can't compare with Robyn." Beverly turned to Robyn. "You really are beautiful. I've been following your ads and they don't do you justice."

"Thank you."

"I must say Scott, it was a stroke of genius choosing Robyn to be the new Fresh and Lovely Girl. Don't let her get away."

Scott gave Robyn a loving look. "I don't intend to."

"I'd better change." Robyn disengaged herself from Scott, extending a hand to Beverly. "It was nice meeting you."

Beverly gripped Robyn's fingers as she continued to ooze with warmth. "The pleasure was all mine. I hope we meet again. Perhaps we could have lunch."

Robyn let her hand drop. She didn't know why, but she felt wary of Beverly. Maybe it was because she had once been involved with Scott. "Be right back," she told Scott, giving him a kiss.

Beverly's eyes followed after Robyn before returning to Scott. "I really do like her. I'm glad you've found somebody."

"I don't know what I'd do without Robyn. She means everything to me."

"Will we be hearing wedding bells soon?"

Scott didn't think it wise to be talking of marriage to another woman with his ex-lover. "We're taking things slowly."

"I'm sorry. I didn't mean to make you uncomfortable. Let's change the subject. Congratulations on the success of Wellington. No one deserves it more than you."

"Thanks. It's been an uphill battle and we've still got a way to go, but I think we're going to make it."

"I'm sure you'll succeed. You've never been a quitter."

"How are things with you?"

"Much better. It took me a while to get over you."

"I never meant to hurt you."

"I know. I never meant to hurt you either. But that's what we both managed to do. I'm just glad that we're able to put it all behind us and become friends."

There had once been a time in Scott's life when he never would have entertained such a notion. But speaking to Beverly and seeing how she had changed caused him to reconsider. She was obviously trying, and he wasn't going to deny her efforts. "I'm glad too."

"Wonderful," Beverly gushed. "I see Robyn is returning, so I'll run along. It was good talking with you. Maybe we'll run into each other again soon."

"That would be nice."

"Take care, Scott."

"You too."

Beverly left as Robyn came up at Scott's side. "Still talking with her?"

"Is that a twinge of jealousy I'm hearing?" Scott teased.

"A tiny twinge," Robyn admitted.

"I know the feeling. I'm sorry I didn't tell you about Beverly sooner, considering that we're bound to run into her occasionally."

"You had your reasons."

"Our relationship started off okay but then turned ugly. Our memories together are painful ones."

"You both seem to have overcome those memories."

"We have, haven't we? Actually, I was surprised by Beverly."

"How come?"

"I never thought of her as the 'forgive and forget' type. I always envisioned her as being vindictive."

"My perception exactly," Robyn teasingly agreed.

"But she wasn't," Scott corrected. "She was very pleasant to both of us. Anyway, what happened in the past is over and done with." He wrapped his arms around Robyn, hugging her closely. "The future is all that matters . . . our future."

"Come on," Robyn said, "let's get to your apartment. I promised you a private fashion show."

Scott offered Robyn his arm. "Let's not waste any more time."

23

The backstage party was in full swing. Everyone was in a celebratory mood, ready to cap off an extraordinarily successful day in the most sinful way possible. Yet Erica was oblivious to it all. As she wove her way through the throng of bodies, her eyes kept searching for Kristen.

Where was she? Erica wondered. She had canvassed the backstage area twice and there was still no sign of Kristen. Could she have already left? If she had, where could she find her? She had to speak with Kristen today.

Erica closed her eyes wearily. Ever since overhearing that conversation, she felt as though she had been sucked into a nightmare. The pieces fell together so easily. Speaking with Kristen would either cause the pieces to scatter or lock into place. Her eyes started searching again, moving from face to face. Then they stopped. Kristen was across the room, heading for an exit.

Erica pushed through the crowd, not bothering with apologies. "Kristen!"

Kristen didn't hear her, and Erica called louder. But still Kristen didn't respond, slipping outside as Erica broke free of the crowd. Erica caught up with her as Kristen entered a cab.

"Kristen, I need to speak with you. Please wait."

Kristen was seated in the cab, reaching to close the door. "Can this wait? I'm running late."

"This won't take long," Erica implored, getting in next to her. "I promise. I need to ask you a few questions."

"Hold on a minute," Kristen said to the driver, then turned back to Erica. "Questions about what?"

"Lance Richards."

"What kind of questions?"

"Were you with Lance on a Wednesday afternoon in March?"

"Erica, I can't remember what I had for lunch yesterday let alone who I met with eight months ago."

"Does the date help? It was the fifth."

Kristen shook her head. "Sorry, I'm drawing a blank. I'll think about it. If I remember anything, I'll give you a call."

Erica's voice was tense. "I called Constance this afternoon and checked on your scheduling. She said you were doing a commercial for Lustre shampoo. Does that help your memory?"

There was no way Kristen could have forgotten that afternoon. It had been one of the worst. They had washed and blow-dried her hair eight times. The studio where they had shot the commercial had been freezing, and as a result of the multiple shampoos she had left with the beginnings of a head cold. Back at the apartment she'd taken a hot bath and gone straight to bed. She hadn't seen Lance at all that afternoon. In fact, their affair hadn't even started yet.

"I didn't see Lance that afternoon," Kristen answered.

"Are you sure?"

"Positive." Kristen's curiosity was aroused. "What's this about?"

Erica ignored the question. She got out of the cab. "Thanks for your help."

"Are you okay?" Erica had paled considerably, and Kristen thought she might faint. "We can share my cab if you like. I can drop you off wherever you want to go."

Erica shook her head. "I've kept you long enough. Honestly, I'm fine."

Kristen didn't believe Erica, but there was nothing more she could do. Lance was coming over to the apartment, and she had a very special surprise in store for him. Of course, there would be no surprise unless she got the items she needed.

"You look like you could use a drink."

Erica smiled feebly. "I need more than a drink to solve my problem."

Kristen gave Erica a curious look before giving her

instructions to the driver. Then she settled in the back seat, grinning in anticipation of the evening she had planned.

Erica watched as Kristen's cab disappeared from sight. Suddenly she felt a chill, and realized she had chased after Kristen wearing only the black velvet gown she'd modeled. She'd better get back inside.

Erica didn't know what she was going to do. Kristen's answer only proved that Lance had lied to her. But why did he lie? What could have happened that afternoon?

Rejoining the party still in full swing, Erica headed for the dressing rooms. The commotion around her was nerve wracking. She needed some peace and quiet in order to think. She also needed a drink. A strong one. After changing, she decided she would head for the bar on the corner.

Contrary to what she had told Beverly, Georgina hadn't been asked to participate in the fashion auction. She had actually volunteered her services, but they had been politely refused.

Georgina brought her glass to her lips. This afternoon would have been the perfect opportunity to revive her career. She could have shown them all that she still had it—that she was still a winner. Columns would have been devoted to her comeback, and fashion spreads within her reach. Within no time she would have been back on top where she belonged. Yet now all she could do was bide her time with one drink after another.

Her loss of the L'Xuriance account was still a blow. The world of advertising and fashion revolved solely around Robyn Prescott. She was sick of it. She wished Robyn Prescott were dead! Maybe then some work would come her way.

"Bartender," she called, holding up her empty glass. "Another."

A fresh gin and tonic was placed before her. As she was reaching for it, a hand clamped around her wrist. "You don't really want that drink."

"Don't I?" Georgina snatched her wrist out of Kyle Masters's grasp. "What are you doing here? Why aren't you celebrating with the others?"

"I could ask you the same question."

Georgina deliberately held her gin and tonic before Kyle's eyes before drinking. "I'm drowning my sorrows."

"Over what?"

Georgina stared at Kyle's handsome face incredulously. "Don't you keep up with the gossip mill? I'm always a hot topic of conversation."

Kyle signaled the bartender, ordering a seltzer. "You're a beautiful woman. What do you care what they say?"

Georgina was speechless at Kyle's words, looking at him in amazement. Not knowing what to say, she pointed to his arriving seltzer. "How come you're drinking that?"

"I don't drink. I'm an alcoholic."

Georgina looked Kyle dead in the eye. "Is that supposed to get a reaction out of me?" She saw his eyes travel to her glass and immediately bristled. "Are you serious? Are you trying to say I'm an alcoholic?"

"I didn't say that."

"I'm not," she screeched.

"Then prove it. Ask the bartender to remove your drink."

"I will not," Georgina refused. "I've already paid for it, and I'm not going to waste my money."

Kyle took Georgina's drink, leaned across the bar and poured it down the sink. Then he reached into his wallet and removed a ten-dollar bill, placing it before her. "This should cover the cost."

Georgina gave Kyle a chilling smile. "I'm capable of making my own decisions. I can stop drinking any time I want. Right now I don't want to stop." She called to the bartender. "Give me a refill."

"Funny, I used to say the same thing," Kyle mused. "I'd tell myself I needed only one more drink and then I'd stop. I'd make excuses and keep turning away the help offered to me, stubbornly refusing to accept the truth until finally I hit rock bottom. Georgina, I can see the signs. Let me help you . . . before it's too late."

Georgina stared into her untouched drink. "What if I don't want your help?" She looked at Kyle brazenly. "I'm not admitting I'm an alcoholic. I just like to drink. It helps me relax and forget my problems until I feel strong enough to face them."

"Then I wish you all the luck in the world," Kyle replied. "All you're doing is hiding, and until you decide to stop hiding, you're going to have a hard lesson to learn."

"Meaning?"

"It's time to get on with your life. Forget your modeling. It's over."

Georgina slammed her glass down on the bar. "My modeling career is not over! It'll never be over!"

"Why not?" Kyle asked.

"Because it's all I have left," she brokenly sobbed.

Kyle gently placed a hand on Georgina's heaving shoulders. "Maybe it's time you started over and did something new."

"Like what?" she angrily demanded.

"Weren't you once interested in acting? Didn't you do some off-Broadway at one time? Why not pursue that?"

"No," she flatly refused, reaching for her glass.

"Why not?" he asked in angry exasperation.

Georgina wiped away her tears. "I can't take the risk. Don't you understand? I might fail."

Kyle could no longer stand to be in Georgina's presence. He put some bills on the bar and left his stool. "I *don't* understand. Only you can make your dreams happen. They can't be found at the bottom of an empty glass."

"You're right," Georgina responded, her words beginning to slur as she drained her gin and tonic, "but they sure as hell can be kept alive."

Kyle didn't notice Erica as he left the bar, and she didn't notice him. Taking a stool, she called for the bartender, ordering a bourbon.

Taking a deep sip, Erica made a face as the burning liquid went down her throat. Coughing, she nursed the rest of her drink as she tried to contemplate her next step.

She would have to face Lance. There was no way around it. She would confront his lie about having spent the afternoon with Kristen. If the answer he gave wasn't a plausible one, she would then ask him about nude photographs. She didn't know what she would do if he confirmed her suspicions.

Erica wanted to handle the entire matter on her own,

without bringing Jeff into it. She didn't want him knowing about the nude photographs, if there were any. What would he think of her? Would he take the time to listen to her side of things? Damn Lance Richards! How could she have been stupid enough to trust him?

"Well, look who's here! What's the matter, Erica? Lance getting it somewhere else? Can't satisfy your man?"

Erica looked up in surprise. A very drunk Georgina stood before her.

"Why would you say such a thing?" Erica asked.

"You are fucking my husband, aren't you?"

Erica's cheeks turned crimson. "I'm not having an affair with Lance," she flared. Why was Georgina acting so hostile? Weren't they friends?

"So you say," Georgina muttered, sipping from the glass in her hand. "Tell me, does Lance bring you to multiple orgasm?"

"I've had enough of this!" Erica shouted. She paid for her bourbon and prepared to leave, aware of the eyes in the bar watching the exchange between herself and Georgina. "You've had too much to drink and don't know what you're saying. I'm not going to stand here and be insulted."

"Can't face the truth?" Georgina sneered.

"What truth? What are you talking about? I'm your friend, Georgina."

"Some friend you are," Georgina snorted, "screwing Lance behind my back."

Erica's anger exploded. "Your husband is scum. I wouldn't let him touch me, let alone make love to me. You've let him walk all over you for years. Don't take your anger out on me. Find the guts to take it out on him."

"I still can't believe you're denying it."

"If you're so sure I'm having an affair with Lance, prove it," Erica challenged.

"Fine, I will." Georgina went back to her bar stool, retrieving her shoulder bag. She dug into it, finding a manila envelope and opening it before Erica, allowing the contents to spill onto the top of the bar.

"Still going to deny your affair?" Georgina crowed triumphantly.

Erica couldn't believe what she was seeing. These were

nude photographs . . . of her. Lance *had* done it! With trembling hands she examined the photos. The sight of them sickened her. The photos slid from her fingers and back onto the bar, where Georgina quickly scooped them up.

"W-w-where did you get those?" Erica stammered.

"Lance's loft—or should I call it your love nest?" Georgina answered. "I saw both of you enter the loft one day and not leave for hours. I found the bill for the necklace that Jeff supposedly bought for you when it was really Lance. Did the two of you think I was so stupid that you could flaunt your affair in front of me?"

"You're making a mistake. Let me explain," Erica whispered.

"A mistake?" Georgina raged. "Do you take me for an idiot? I saw the two of you in the studio at Wellington talking about making love. What more do I need? You're going to pay for this Erica! I swear to God you're going to pay!"

Georgina stormed into the night, clutching the photographs to her chest. Erica remained standing at the bar, staring after her. Reaching for the remainder of her bourbon, she emptied the glass in one gulp.

Despite the shock of the photographs, Erica's mind was clear. There was only one thing on her mind.

Revenge.

If anyone was going to pay for this, it was Lance Richards.

"Kristen, why didn't you answer the door?"

Lance had been given his own key to Kristen and Robyn's apartment. Letting himself in after repeated ringings of the door bell had gone unanswered, he found signs that Kristen was home.

"I'm in the tub," she called.

Lance glanced at his watch, grumbling. "You aren't ready? Forget it. We've lost our reservation. We'll never make it on time."

"I wasn't really hungry."

"I was," Lance sulked, plopping himself down on the sofa. "The food at this place is fabulous, and the desserts are stupendous."

"Poor baby. I forgot you have a sweet tooth. Would you like a banana split?"

Lance perked up at the idea. "Sounds good."

"Come into the bathroom."

"Huh?"

"Just come in here. Trust me."

Lance headed into the bathroom, wondering what Kristen wanted. At first he thought she was taking a bubble bath. As he moved closer, he realized his mistake. She was smothered up to her neck in whipped cream.

Kristen lifted an arm dripping with whipped cream and chocolate sauce out to him. "Like a taste?"

"Yes."

"Then don't be bashful. Come on in."

"Where are the bananas?"

Kristen looked pointedly at Lance. "Where do you think?"

The image of Kristen's satiny smooth skin covered with whipped cream and chocolate sauce instantly aroused him. Shedding his clothes, he prepared to jump into the tub.

"Hold on." Kristen reached for a can of whipped cream, spraying a spiral around Lance's erection. "I'd like a taste too," she said.

The coldness of the whipped cream and the heat of Lance's throbbing erection blended deliciously in Kristen's mouth. As her tongue licked away at the spiral, Lance held back his ejaculation. When the last bit of whipped cream was gone, Kristen sighed contentedly. "You can come in now."

Joining Kristen in the tub, Lance buried his face between her legs, finding the banana she had promised. Kristen moaned in ecstasy as his tongue and fingers probed deeper and deeper into her vagina as he ate away at the banana. When it was all gone, Lance plunged his penis in.

"Which is better?" he gasped, pumping away.

Kristen dipped her fingers in the chocolate sauce, covering his nipples. She sucked greedily at both. "You are." She massaged his shoulders and chest with whipped cream, wasting no time in sampling the taste.

They kept at each other for an hour, using the spare cans of whipped cream. The sweetness of sugar combined with the acidic bite of sweat from their sex was like a nectar neither had ever before tasted.

"Is your sweet tooth satisfied?" she asked.

"Quite satisfied."

"Why don't we take a shower?"

They moved to the glass-encased stall, soaping each other down under the steaming jets.

"We really should do this again," Lance commented.

"Are you serious?" Kristen shampooed at her hair vigorously. "Do you know how many cans of whipped cream and chocolate sauce I had to buy to fill up that tub? It's going to be murder to clean."

Lance moved behind Kristen, pressing his soapy hands between her legs. "I'll be happy with just a banana," he whispered into her ear.

"We really should clean ourselves up," she murmured weakly as Lance's new erection pressed against the back of her thighs.

"Wouldn't you like another taste?" Lance asked, pressing harder.

"Yes." Kristen whirled around, spreading her legs and slipping Lance into her. Never before had she felt this way with a man. Vital. Daring. Alive. Lance had charisma and raw sexuality. She couldn't help responding to it.

They made love in the shower, then returned to the bedroom where Kristen slipped into a red teddy while Lance lounged on the bed.

"Would you like to stay tonight?" It was the first time Kristen had asked the question. Usually Lance left an hour or two after they made love. Tonight she wanted him to stay. She didn't want to be alone. Thoughts of Robyn and Scott kept returning. How she wished she and Lance could have the same type of relationship. But they couldn't. He was married, and she had her pride. She wasn't going to force him to choose. Eventually he would have to make a decision himself.

Lance stretched lazily across the sheets, patting the spot next to him. "Sure, why not?"

* * *

Robyn slipped into Scott's bedroom the moment she arrived and changed into her negligee. She couldn't wait for the expensive silk to be pulled from her body and pooled on the floor in a twenty-five-thousand-dollar pile.

Scott knocked on the locked bedroom door. "Aren't you going to let me in?"

Robyn gave her hair a quick brush and sprayed herself with Giorgio. She unlocked the door, and when Scott walked in, wrapped her arms around him.

His shirt was unbuttoned and she could feel the strength of his chest. Surging desire raced through her. She wanted his body pressed upon hers with nothing between them.

"At last!" Scott nuzzled her neck. "I was giving up hope. I can't wait to make love to you," he declared.

"Was I worth the wait?"

Scott pressed an open mouth to Robyn's, kissing her with a devouring passion. "Definitely."

They approached the bed together, gently settling down on it. Scott removed his shirt. Robyn couldn't help but put a hand upon the smooth, bronzed hardness of his chest. The feel of his flesh was like a jolt of electricity, and she thrilled at the excitement coursing through her.

Fingering the negligee, Scott slowly slipped it away from Robyn's shoulders, spreading his fingers through her fan of golden hair. "You're so beautiful," he whispered in awe, kissing her.

Their lovemaking was slow and extended. Scott explored every part of Robyn's body, beginning with her face. Every detail of her exquisite beauty was memorized by his lips. Eyes, nose, lips, and cheeks were all lavishly kissed and adored. Moving to her breasts, Scott luxuriously teased them with his tongue, taking her hardened nipples into his mouth as gently as a newborn infant. Then he progressed to her tawny, glistening patch with the hunger of an adolescent, probing with fingers and tongue as her juices flowed.

His hands traveled down her shapely legs with the appreciation of an artist. The smoothness of her legs as they moved over his felt like satin, and he wanted nothing more than for them to lock around his waist. The instant Scott entered Robyn, their bodies welded together, rocking in a fever pitch.

"I love you," Robyn said as her breathing accelerated, looking into his green eyes as he moved deeper within her, feathering her fingers through his tawny hair. "I love you so much."

When they climaxed, it was as one. Arching his back, Scott pressed deeper into Robyn while she lifted herself up to him. Mouths opened, tongues explored and lips meshed. When they were drained of all passion, they collapsed back among the pillows, talking softly and giggling, playfully continuing to kiss and caress until they fell asleep in each other's arms.

Kristen paraded naked with a hairbrush before Lance in the morning sunshine. "Did I tell you I ran into Erica Shelton yesterday?"

Lance sat up in bed, keeping his tone casual. "What did she want?"

"She was acting really strange. She had all these questions about you. She wanted to know if we had been together on a certain afternoon." Kristen put down the hairbrush, reaching for a can of mousse.

Lance's voice was tight. "What did you tell her?"

Kristen squirted a ball of mousse into her palm. "The truth. We weren't together that day."

"Damn you! Why didn't you tell her we were?"

The can of mousse clattered to the floor. Kristen looked at Lance in shock. "What's the big deal? We *weren't* together."

"Erica Shelton is a thorn in my side. I don't want any involvement with her."

"Am I supposed to be a mind reader?" Kristen raked her fingers through her hair, satisfied with her spikes. Giving herself a spray of Obsession, she headed for the bathroom with her makeup bag. "Let me know when you're in a better mood."

Lance wondered about the purpose of Erica's questioning. Could she suspect something? He punched the pillow balled under his arm. Shit! He swore under his breath. He was going to have to handle Erica soon.

* * *

Beverly woke up in a sleazy hotel off Fourteenth Street. At first she didn't know where she was or how she had gotten there. But then she remembered.

Following in Scott and Robyn's footsteps after the fashion show the previous evening, she had witnessed every laugh, smile, and kiss exchanged. She'd been furious at the sight of them together, and it had taken all her restraint not to tear them apart. How she had wanted to pull Robyn from Scott's side . . . sinking her nails deeply into Robyn's arm. How she had wanted to slap Robyn's face and yank out her hair. By all rights she should be the one at Scott's side. If Robyn hadn't come to New York, none of this would be happening. Scott would have already been hers again.

She had watched as the lights in Scott's apartment went off within seconds of being turned on. They were making love. *Her* Scott was making love to Robyn. It wasn't the first time, but it still hurt.

Unable to spend the rest of the night watching in the shadows because it was too painful, Beverly had returned to her duplex. There she put together her trashiest outfit: tight red leather miniskirt, leopard-print bra with beads and fringe, black seamed stockings and stiletto heels.

It was the exact same outfit Robyn had been found in.

Beverly wasted no time. She knew exactly what she wanted and where she could get it: Peggy Sue's.

When she got to the bar she made a beeline for Todd. He was playing pool, standing in a cloud of gray smoke, a cigarette hanging belligerently from his mouth.

"Remember me?" she asked.

A flash of recognition appeared, but was quickly masked. She could see his lips curl into a smirk of satisfaction . . . and anticipation. He took a drag from his cigarette, crushed it beneath his boot heel and followed with a swig of beer. "Refresh my memory."

Beverly arched her back, brazenly shaking the fringes of her bra. She turned on her heels, strutting before the other men to howls of appreciation. She cocked an eyebrow at Todd. "Refreshed?"

He aimed a ball for a corner pocket, missed and cursed. He finished his bottle of beer, paid off his bet and then grabbed Beverly by the arm.

"Let's get reacquainted," he growled. He gave her a closer look. "What's your name again?"

"Robyn," Beverly promptly cooed, running her fingers down his arm as she molded herself against him. "My name is Robyn. I'm a cheap slut and I want you to degrade me."

His arm tightened around her waist as he bent his head to her neck, sinking in his teeth. "I haven't got a problem with that."

Beverly let him do what he wanted, and did as he demanded. All she wanted was to feel pain. As Todd rammed himself into her again and again, she kept visualizing Robyn . . . feeding her fury. Robyn was going to pay for this.

"Don't just lie there, bitch!" Todd's ringed hand slapped her across the face. "Let's see some action." He seized her head. "Get down on me."

Beverly's mouth was forced open. Todd didn't even give her a chance to do it on her own. He wound his fingers through her hair and pulled with sadistic glee as he forced her to swallow him.

How Robyn was going to pay!

When Todd had finished with her, he left, and Beverly's battered body had fallen into an exhausted sleep. Opening her eyes, she had remembered it all. And her determination to destroy Robyn was refueled with an even greater intensity.

She covered herself with the trench coat she had carried, gently easing her stiffened limbs. The first thing she was going to do when she got back to her duplex was have a nice, long bath.

The second was to call Anthony Calder.

24

The headaches started in October. At first Robyn thought nothing of them. They were simply a dull throbbing at the base of her skull, easy enough to ignore with aspirins. But then the aspirins stopped working and with each passing day the headaches returned with greater ferocity. Soon the dull throbs turned into piercing jabs, splintering throughout Robyn's skull.

Her first thought was migraines. She went to a doctor and he gave her a prescription. The pills prescribed didn't help. Robyn's next thought was overwork. She was doing too much. She asked Samantha for fewer assignments and tried to slow down her pace. All she needed was some relaxation. For a while it worked. Then the headaches worsened and the nightmares began.

She was alone in a dark tunnel until a man and a woman appeared before her. Robyn's heart quickened with fear at the dangerous looks on their faces. They wanted to hurt her. Robyn tried to run, but couldn't move. She remained frozen in place. Then a mirror appeared before her, her image in it. Robyn cringed with horror. She was wearing the outfit she had been found in after the car accident. Globs of excess makeup were painted on her face, and her hair was teased to an extreme. She'd never looked so cheap and horrible. She pounded her fists into the mirror and it broke into a thousand shards.

The mysterious woman was suddenly in front of her. In her raised hand she gripped a sharp shard as blood oozed down her hand. She aimed the shard for Robyn's heart with a malicious grin.

"I'm going to kill you," the woman shrieked.

The nightmare always ended there, as Robyn awoke with

a scream before the shard ripped into her heart. Whether Kristen or Scott raced to her side, Robyn always had the same answer, "It was only a nightmare," she assured. "Only a nightmare."

But it wasn't. Although the nightmare was unexplainable, it held grains of truth. The figures in the nightmare weren't phantoms—they were real.

At the end of October she called Quinn, not knowing what else to do. The headaches and nightmares were taking turns in making her life miserable.

Quinn listened in silence, speaking only after she had finished. "I don't want to raise your hopes," he said, "but it looks like your memory is getting ready to return."

"Why? Why after all this time?"

"I don't know," Quinn honestly admitted. "Your life is in order. Perhaps your subconscious feels it's time you remembered."

"I don't want to remember," Robyn stated fiercely. "I don't need to know about my past."

"I'm afraid you have no choice. When your memory returns, you're going to have to deal with what you learn."

"When will that be?"

"From what you've told me about the headaches and nightmares, soon. Very soon."

"I think you'll be pleased with this week's report."

Beverly gave Anthony Calder a dubious look. "I doubt it."

"I've been able to find out some more on Robyn's past."

"How much more? Anything I can use?"

"Not yet."

Beverly's eyes narrowed dangerously. *"Not yet?"* she shrieked in outrage. *"When?"*

Calder held up a halting hand. "We're on the right track. Listen to what I have to say."

"I'm listening," Beverly hissed.

"Robyn Prescott was born in Springfield, Illinois, and moved to Chicago after her parents died in a car crash. She moved in with her grandmother, Miriam Reilly, but left home when she was sixteen."

"Where did she go?"

"That's where we run into a brick wall. According to the

neighbors, Miriam Reilly told them she had been unable to control Robyn and sent her to stay with other relatives."

"Why do you sound so skeptical?"

"Robyn's only living relative was Miriam Reilly. Both her parents had no siblings, and her paternal grandparents were deceased before she was born. So far we haven't been able to uncover anyone else, and the neighbors all recall Robyn as being a good kid. She hardly ever caused trouble, but life with her grandmother wasn't so hot. Miriam was a religious fanatic. We're assuming Robyn became a runaway."

"Assumptions are meaningless. If Robyn was a runaway from the time she was sixteen until she arrived in New York, then how did she survive? That leaves five years of her life unaccounted for."

Calder sat back smugly in his chair, folding his hands together. "You tell me. You're a smart woman, Ms. Maxwell."

Beverly closed the distance between them. Her eyes glistened with fury and impatience. "No," she refused, a tinge of iciness coating her words. *"You* tell *me."*

Calder found himself becoming aroused by Beverly's forcefulness. He stood up, placing an arm around her shoulders. She was dressed totally in black leather, with her hair artfully styled in a wild disarray. Chunks of gold jewelry adorned her neck and wrists. Usually he tried not to become involved with his clients, no matter how attractive they were. Yet there was always the exception. Beverly Maxwell was the exception. He couldn't seem to resist the physical pull she was ensnaring him in. But it was more than her looks. There was something savagely ruthless about her, and it excited him.

"Investigations require patience," he soothed, allowing his hands to nonchalantly travel down her shoulders to her leather-encased breasts.

"So does dealing with you." She placed a hand on his groin, squeezing his erection tightly. "My patience is wearing thin."

Calder's hand dropped from Beverly's shoulders. "There's only one way for runaways to survive on the streets."

"How?"

"Prostitution."

Beverly released some pressure but softly massaged Calder's fabric-encased erection. "Continue," she purred.

"My people are searching the underbelly of Chicago, asking questions and flashing Robyn's picture. It's only a matter of time."

Beverly released her hand, allowing Calder to straighten his appearance. "You'd better be right. I want some ammunition, and I want it soon."

Calder, red-faced from excitement, was taking deep breaths. "Don't worry. Someone out there has all the answers you're looking for."

"Reassure me when we meet again next week." Beverly's voice turned low and seductive as she appraised Calder from head to toe. "A bonus might be negotiable."

"Doll, you were the greatest lay I've had in ages." The man left a tumble of bills on the dresser. He turned to the woman smoking a cigarette in bed. "If I want to see you again, can I find you at the same place?"

Her voice was bored, devoid of emotion. "Sure."

When he was gone, she remained in bed. Except for the glowing tip of her cigarette and the bright lights of Las Vegas outside, the hotel room was in darkness.

Tiffany Hunt remained in bed for a long time. Then she took a shower and dressed, preparing to sell her body once again.

Tiffany's life had hardly changed for the better after leaving Chicago, and Vaughn Chandler was still a threat she feared.

Arriving in Las Vegas, she had tried to make it as a showgirl. Lacking talent, the only parts offered were in the bedroom. She refused. Finding straight work as a cocktail waitress was a thrill at first, but soon turned to boredom. She hated the long hours and constantly being on her feet. Although the money she made was good, she wasn't satisfied. She had to have more, and soon found herself addicted to the casinos, losing paychecks and tips in record time.

As she got deeper into debt she started supplementing her income by returning to her former profession. It still wasn't enough. Desperate for cash, she started stealing from the register at work. She got away with it twice before being caught and promptly fired.

She lost her apartment and was forced to move in with another girl, also a prostitute. Gambling soon became a forbidden fruit. She knew she was never going to pull herself out of the hole she was in unless she stopped going to the casinos. But she kept believing that one win was all it would take to wipe the slate clean. Unable to pay her debts, she was harshly beaten by a loan shark for a debt she owed. The money was forgotten, but Tiffany was unable to look at herself in a mirror for a month. Some of the scars still remained, and Tiffany stuck to the streets.

During all this time her hatred for Robyn grew. She read of the Fresh and Lovely contest and raged after learning Robyn had been chosen. Robyn was the one who had it all: a new life, money, fame, beauty. What did she have? Nothing.

Tiffany emptied the envelope she carried with her at all times. When she had been a little girl she'd loved playing with paper dolls, poring over fashion magazines and cutting out pictures of models for hours.

She still liked playing with paper dolls, only this time her collection consisted only of cutouts of Robyn. She fingered the slips of paper. Here was Robyn in a mink. Here was Robyn in a Bob Mackie gown. Here was Robyn in a pair of Sensation! jeans.

Tiffany crumpled the paper dolls in her fist and threw them in an ashtray. Then she lit a match and watched the images of Robyn burn. The pieces of paper crinkled and curled, and Tiffany imagined hearing Robyn's agonized screams.

She watched until the flames died and only a heap of ashes were left. How easy she wished it could be!

It was then that she made her decision.

It was time for Robyn's nightmare to begin.

Kristen stuck her head in Robyn's bedroom. "Phone call."

"Who is it?"

"She wouldn't say. Only said she was an old friend."

"Really?" Robyn headed for the living room phone, trying to figure out who could be calling. "Hello, this is Robyn Prescott."

There was only silence at the other end.

"Hello," Robyn repeated. "Is anyone there?"

The voice that answered was one of controlled fury. "Hello, Robyn. Remember me?"

At the sound of Tiffany's voice, Robyn dropped the phone to the floor, stepping away from it in horror. A flood of images, no longer undecipherable fragments, assaulted her. The images erupted with uncontrolled speed and everything fell into place with horrid clarity. The degradation, horror, and hopelessness of her past life returned in vivid color.

"I remember," Robyn gasped. "I remember."

— BOOK THREE —

Chicago
1979–87

25

"Keep your elbows off the table! Sit with your back straight! How many times have I told you not to dawdle at the table? Finish your supper and then return to your bedroom."

Twelve-year-old Robyn Prescott barely heard one command before another was given. That was the way it had always been since she had come to live with her grandmother. For as long as she could remember, she had never had a place in her grandmother's heart. Orphaned after the death of her parents the previous year, Robyn had been forced to live with a cold and bitter woman who hardly made an effort to accept her into her life.

Robyn stared down at her plate with disgust. The steak placed before her was barely cooked. She cut a small piece from the oozing red mass, aware of her grandmother's eyes studying her.

Miriam Reilly, a thin, pinched-looking woman with steel-gray hair worn in a tight bun, sipped at her tea, staring at Robyn with disinterest. "Is there a problem?"

Robyn swallowed over the lump in her throat. Why did she always feel placed on the defensive when speaking to her grandmother? "I can't eat this."

"Why not?"

"It's raw."

"Rare."

"Raw," Robyn insisted, determined not to back down.

Miriam's cold gray eyes remained hard and unflinching. "If you look in the kitchen you'll see I slaved over a hot stove."

"You didn't cook it enough."

Miriam poured herself a second cup of tea. "I haven't the time for arguments. Finish eating."

The commanding tone of Miriam's voice ignited Robyn's stubbornness. She was tired of being told what to do. "I won't eat it. I'll get sick." Robyn rose from the table, pushing her chair forward. As she did, the teapot fell over, splashing the white lace tablecloth.

"Grandmother, I'm sorry," Robyn apologized, all previous traces of bravura gone. She rushed to blot up the mess with trembling hands. "I didn't mean to push my chair so hard."

"Idiot! You never think!" Miriam ranted. "You're exactly like your mother. You never think of anyone but yourself. Look at what you've done." She pushed Robyn away, dabbing at the stain herself.

"Will it come out?"

"Do you care if it does?"

"I offered to change tablecloths before setting the table. You told me not to."

"Don't blame me for this," Miriam flared. "Your mother used to do the exact same thing. You're following in her footsteps, and I will not tolerate it! I will not have another sinner in my home!"

Robyn stared down at the floor, edging away from her grandmother. She knew what was going to come next. Why had she made such a fuss?

"Where do you think you're going?" Miriam demanded in a steely whisper.

"Nowhere," Robyn stammered, keeping her eyes locked on the floor.

Miriam advanced on her granddaughter, gripping her firmly by the shoulders, forcing her down on her knees. "Pray to the Lord for mercy! It's not too late to salvage your soul! Your mother was a sinner! A taste for male flesh consumed her soul, and she thought nothing of seduction to satisfy her hungers. By the time I learned of her actions, it was too late. She was already soiled . . . impregnated with you."

Robyn shook her head, tearing herself free. She covered her ears, refusing to listen to another word. She had gone up to the attic one day and gone through her mother's scrapbooks and diaries. None had lent support to Miriam's accusations. If anything, they had painted a picture of loneliness, similar to the life Robyn was leading. Yet all that had changed for her mother when Andrew Prescott entered Nicole Reilly's life. Andrew and Nicole fell instantly in love, deciding to elope, and leaving Miriam and her religious fanaticism behind.

"You're lying," Robyn stated. "My parents were married for two years before I was born. You always lie when it comes to my mother."

Miriam's face contorted with rage. "How dare you talk back to me!" She ripped the lace tablecloth from the table, sending china and silverware crashing to the floor. "This is all your fault, child! Your greed and covetous thoughts led your parents down death's path. How symbolic that the fruit of their sins caused their destruction. You weren't satisfied with what you had! You had to have more! Their love wasn't enough, and so the Lord took it away! Your selfishness resulted in their deaths! Repent, child! *Repent!*"

In her early days of grief, Robyn had believed Miriam's words, but then had realized she wasn't to blame. It had been an accident. Her parents' car had stalled on a railroad track. Neither the engineer of the train nor her parents had been able to prevent the tragedy. Andrew and Nicole Prescott had been crushed to death, along with the ten-speed bike hidden in their trunk. It had been the present Robyn had so wanted for her twelfth birthday.

Ever since the death of her parents, Robyn's days had been a nonstop stretch of loneliness. Uprooted from the neighborhood she had grown up in, she'd been moved to Chicago. Her old friends had been left behind and new friends had been hard to find. Some days Robyn wondered if her grandmother was purposely trying to make her life miserable.

The death of Robyn's parents had left her with nothing. All she had left were her memories . . . memories of being loved. More than anything else in the world, Robyn wanted to be loved again. She wanted to feel the warmth of a hug and the gentle softness of a kiss. She could still remember the way her parents had lavished her with affection. She refused to forget, and she ignored the fear growing daily within her.

Robyn was afraid no one would ever love her again.

"Grandmother, why won't you love me?" Robyn asked in a small voice. Despite her resolve, tears were falling down her cheeks. In the past year she had been exposed to the ugliest of emotions, and hated it.

"Love must be earned rather than given," Miriam imperiously proclaimed.

"Tell me what to do," Robyn begged, "and I'll do it."

Miriam regarded Robyn with a long, thin sneer. "It'll be quite some time before the evil of your soul is expunged. You have a long road to travel before you'll be worthy of my love. Be warned! I'll be keeping my eye on you at all times. You won't deceive me as Nicole did. I won't make the same mistakes twice." Her eyes settled on the mess she had created. "Clean this place up," she ordered.

Miriam left the dining room, still ranting under her breath. With churning emotions, Robyn watched her go. Once again she had opened her heart and had it stomped on. This was the last time.

One day she was going to find a special person to love.

26

Despite Miriam's attempts to smother Robyn's beauty as she grew older, the miracle of adolescence still took place. Suddenly Robyn's legs became long and lean. Curves appeared in the usual places, resulting in a small waist and slender hips. Her breasts became full and firm, and Robyn's ash-blond hair became a richer, more luxuriant color.

Every morning Robyn left for high school at seven-thirty, dressed in the clothes her grandmother insisted she wear. Once around the corner and out of Miriam's sight, an amazing transformation took place.

First, Robyn would remove the thick rubber band holding her hair back, allowing it to flow loosely down her back the way she loved best. Next, the top three buttons of her blouse were undone, showing a peek of round softness. Standing before the still closed grocery store, Robyn would use its plate-glass window as a mirror, deftly applying mascara, eye shadow, blush, and lipstick. When finished, the transformation was amazing. Lips that had been soft and sweet became sensual and seductive. Her hair became a mane meant to be tossed proudly, while the mascara intensified her liquid green eyes. In minutes she went from shy schoolgirl to an alluring young woman.

More than anything else, Robyn wanted to go on dates and attend dances, but Miriam had forbidden it. Thus, Robyn didn't allow herself to be friends with the other girls, because they would talk about their boyfriends and the parties they had gone to. Listening to the gossip about what she also wanted to participate in would be too much to handle. The safest thing, she decided, was to distance herself.

Every Monday and Friday Robyn left school an hour

earlier, her classes finished for the day. She didn't tell Miriam about her early dismissals, knowing her grandmother would insist she immediately return home. That was the last thing Robyn wanted. She was tired of being treated like a prisoner. Usually she went to the local ice cream parlor for a taste of freedom.

Today she was sitting on her usual stool beside the jukebox. "Strawberry sundae," she told the counterman, reaching into her shoulder bag for her favorite magazine. She whipped out the latest issue of *Vogue,* eagerly flipping through it. Both the sundae and magazines she purchased came from not spending the lunch money her grandmother gave her daily. Better to starve a little for a few small luxuries. Robyn became so engrossed in the pages of designs and models that she didn't notice the stranger who sat down next to her.

She sighed, wishing she could become famous and successful. Then she could leave Chicago and its painful memories. Her mind began to wander. Did she really want fame, or was there something else? Did she want love? She wondered what it would be like to just have love.

The clatter of the spoon on her dish caused her to look up from the magazine. She smiled her thanks, reaching for the spoon. Robyn slowly scooped vanilla ice cream and strawberry sauce together. The mixture slid deliciously down her throat, filling her stomach with an intense chill. She shivered.

"May I offer you my jacket?"

Having been unaware of the stranger beside her, Robyn looked into his smiling face for the first time.

"Allow me to introduce myself," he said, extending a hand. "My name is Vaughn Chandler."

Always eager to meet a friendly face, Robyn opened up to his warmness. "I'm Robyn Prescott."

Vaughn took his bearded chin in his hand, stroking it gently as he studied Robyn intensely. "You're quite lovely."

Robyn blushed, taken aback by the compliment. "Do you come here often?" she asked offhandedly. "I've never seen you before." If he said yes, Robyn intended on making more frequent visits.

"No, this is my first time. I think I may be returning,

though, considering how pleasant the atmosphere is." Vaughn smiled, spooning some of Robyn's melting sundae into his mouth.

"Hey, you didn't ask," Robyn scolded teasingly.

"You sounded like a little girl just then. Tell me, how old are you?"

"Sixteen," Robyn sadly admitted, knowing someone as handsome and charming as Vaughn would never be interested in her. She didn't know what it was, but there was a magnetism to him. Every time she looked at him she felt a strange stirring inside.

"Why so down? Sixteen is a wonderful age." Vaughn whistled softly. "If this is what you look like at sixteen, I can imagine what you'll look like in five years."

"You're sweet. Thank you for saying such nice things."

"You're not used to compliments. I can tell; you keep blushing. We'll have to change that. Why don't you give me your number and I'll give you a call? Maybe we can get together later in the week."

Was she hearing things? Vaughn wanted to call her! He was at least twenty-five and he was interested in her! He wanted to take her on a date! But her elation soon disappeared. There was no way Miriam would allow her to go on a date, let alone with an older man.

"I can't," Robyn whispered wistfully, staring longingly into Vaughn's dark brown eyes. They were two glistening drops shining beneath tapered brows. His matching beard and mustache were as rich and thick as the hair on his chest. He was wearing khaki-colored slacks and a red knit shirt. The neck of the shirt was open, revealing a thin gold chain, and his arms were well-proportioned and tanned. Finding herself thinking the most unusual thoughts as she studied Vaughn's body, Robyn quickly turned away. "It isn't because I don't want to," she hastily interjected. "I'd love to see you again. It's just that my grandmother won't let me date."

"You live with your grandmother?" Vaughn asked.

"My parents died when I was younger."

"Tough break. It's hard to lose someone you love," Vaughn sympathized.

Robyn was amazed at the understanding she could hear in

Vaughn's voice. He was almost identifying with her loneliness.

"Let me pay for this," he announced, digging into his pocket. "It isn't very often that I get to chat with someone so nice. Why don't we meet here again, since I can't take you out?"

"I'd like that." Robyn tried not to stare at the roll of bills Vaughn had removed from his pocket. She'd never seen so much money before.

Vaughn waved the bills before Robyn. "From my business. I've got a few connections on the West Coast. Maybe one day I'll fill you in."

Robyn only nodded her agreement. Although she would have liked to hear more, simply to listen to Vaughn talk, she didn't want to appear too nosy. "I'd like that."

"Great." He gave her a devilish grin. "I promise not to disappoint you."

For the next month Robyn eagerly went to the ice cream parlor, hoping to meet Vaughn again. She took extra care with her appearance, wanting to look her very best. She wanted to impress Vaughn because it was the first time that someone had taken an interest in her.

And if she saw Vaughn again, Robyn knew she wanted to go out with him. Her grandmother had forbidden dates, but she would figure out a way to get around that. She'd been denied so much for so long. She was tired of being unwanted and unloved. She wasn't going to allow the opportunity to slip by.

After a month of sundaes and no sign of Vaughn, Robyn came to the conclusion that he wasn't going to reappear. One afternoon, sighing, she signaled for her check, rummaging through the clutter of her shoulder bag.

"Leaving already? Just when I've arrived?"

Robyn spun around on her stool, coming face to face with Vaughn. He was standing before her with a smile on his face. Impulsively, she drew a hand to his cheek, stroking his beard.

"I'm sorry," she said, drawing away her hand. She looked into his eyes, unable to suppress the grin spreading across her face. "It's really you."

"Didn't you think I was coming back?"

Robyn looked down at her lap. "I was hoping you'd come back."

Vaughn reached into his leather jacket, pulling out a small pink package. With a grand gesture he placed it before her, twisting the curled ribbon around his finger.

"For me?" an amazed Robyn asked. She toyed with the box, shaking it gently against her ear. "Thank you."

"Don't thank me just yet. You might not like it."

"How could I not like it?" she exclaimed, ripping away the pink paper and bow. She couldn't remember the last time she had received a present.

Lifting the top of the box, Robyn's eyes fell on one of the most exquisite rings she had ever seen. She held the ring of tiny diamond hearts up to the light, marveling at the way it sparkled and glittered. Slipping it on her finger, she held her hand out to Vaughn to admire.

"Do you like it?" he asked. "As soon as I saw it I knew it was for you."

The smile on her face said it all. Robyn admired the ring one last time before replacing it in its box and reluctantly returning it. "I can't accept your gift."

"Why not? Would you like me to exchange it for something else?"

"Vaughn, please don't get upset. I love your gift. The fact that you even thought to buy me a present is enough. I'd like to keep it, but I can't. My grandmother would never let me keep such an expensive gift from a man." Robyn rose from her stool, gathering her books.

Vaughn placed a restraining hand on her arm. "You're not going anywhere," he stressed. "The ring is yours to keep. It was a gift. Do whatever you want with it. You're a lovely young lady who I'd like to consider a special friend." Vaughn placed the ring back on her finger, giving her his devilish grin. Chills of excitement traveled down her spine. Vaughn was so gorgeous! She couldn't stop the images racing through her mind. "What your grandmother doesn't know won't hurt her, and my sources tell me you've eaten quite a few sundaes."

Robyn blushed, hiding her face. Vaughn went behind her, placing his arms around her shoulders. They were strong arms, and Robyn liked how they felt around her, hugging her tightly to his chest. His embrace gave her a feeling of comfort and protection. As she ran her fingers lightly over his muscular arms, she decided it was a feeling she would like to experience again.

"I want to get to know you better," he whispered into her ear.

Robyn's heart pounded. "I want to get to know you better. I'll keep the ring," she promised, "and wear it only when I'm with you." She turned around, smiling into Vaughn's eyes. "You've made me happier than I've ever been in such a long time."

Vaughn placed a chaste kiss on the top of her head, bringing her silky tresses to his lips as he hugged her tighter. "I'm never going to let you go, Robyn. I have a feeling that we're both going to make each other very happy."

Vaughn continued to give her gifts: charm bracelets, earrings, perfumes, even a selection of expensive silk and lace lingerie. She tried to refuse each gift given to her, but each time it became harder to turn Vaughn down. She told him that being in his company was enough to keep her happy.

Each succeeding gift was even more lavish than the last. Robyn kept them hidden in the top drawer of her dresser. Whenever possible she would gently finger the gifts, remembering the occasion in which Vaughn had presented them to her. If she heard Miriam approaching, she would cover the items quickly, rushing to her bed and pretending to read until she heard Miriam's receding footsteps, waiting until she was sure it was safe to uncover them again.

At first she and Vaughn met in the day, so as not to arouse Miriam's suspicions. On weekends they went to outdoor concerts staged at the Petrillo Music Shell and cheered the Cubs at Wrigley Field.

But soon this wasn't enough for Robyn. With each departure her longing for Vaughn grew. She needed to see him more and more. He was the only one who cared, the only one who showed an interest in her life. He was the reason she faced each new day. She began meeting him at night. The meetings were never long, an hour or two at the most, but they were enough to satisfy the stirrings growing within her with each passing day, causing her to fall deeper and deeper in love.

Her relationship with Vaughn was progressing at a steady pace. It was almost as though he was afraid of pushing her too fast. He was the only man she had ever been involved with, and she was falling in love with him. When she was in Vaughn's arms, she experienced the warmth and comfort she had been denied. His kisses started out light and feathery, but could quickly turn passionate and demanding. Vaughn awakened a side of her that she hadn't known existed. There was a new awareness to her senses as Vaughn's hands traveled over her breasts and his lips meshed hungrily over her own. She wanted him to make love to her. But Vaughn never did. He always restrained himself from going one step too far.

"It's so easy to become caught up in the moment," he had whispered one evening. "I want your first time to be special."

"It will be," she murmured. "It will be with you."

"We have to wait," he stated, disengaging himself from her embrace. "You have to trust me. I only want what's best for you."

Naturally Robyn did as Vaughn wanted. She *did* trust him—implicitly.

One afternoon in July, Robyn and Vaughn had a picnic at Fullerton beach. Robyn used the excuse of hospital volunteer work to slip away from Miriam's ever watchful eye. It was a Saturday, and she met Vaughn in front of her high school, sliding across the leather seats of his red Mustang.

When they arrived at the beach, Robyn spread out the blanket, kicking off the shorts and T-shirt she had worn over her white bikini. Turning to Vaughn, she stood absolutely still for his inspection.

Robyn knew she looked irresistible. For hours she had stood before her full-length bedroom mirror, unable to believe that the image she was seeing was really her own. She had never owned a bikini before. Sneaking it into the house, she'd been petrified of getting caught. The thin wisps of material kept her modestly attired while at the same time displaying the beauty of her body. Her grandmother would go wild if she could see her now!

Vaughn patted the spot next to him on the blanket. "Why don't you take a seat next to me?" He gave her his devilish grin. "I promise not to bite," he teased.

Robyn caught sight of Vaughn's erection straining against the front of his shorts. The mystery of what was hidden behind his tattered shorts drew her like a magnet. She knelt next to him, and he took her hand in his, pressing her fingertips against the cloaked throbbing. "How does this feel?"

Robyn swallowed hard. She knew she should take away her hand. She began hearing Miriam's voice: "Nice girls don't go all the way! Only wicked girls with evil souls sacrifice their virginity!"

Robyn shut out the voices. She didn't want to take away her hand. She liked the way Vaughn felt. There was nothing evil or wrong about making love, especially if you loved the person you were with. Robyn knew she loved Vaughn.

"You're doing this to me," he whispered. "Being so close is sending my blood racing." He released her hand, but Robyn left it in place, softly rubbing through the denim.

Vaughn undid the string of her bikini. The skin exposed was a creamy white, contrasting with the rich darkness of her tan.

Vaughn's lips meshed to her nipples. Robyn's skin rippled with pleasure as his mouth closed. She fell back onto the blanket, and Vaughn covered her with his body. He reached for her bikini bottom and slipped it away, exposing the dark triangle. There were glistening drops of wetness, and Vaughn brushed his fingers over them, causing Robyn to twist from left to right as the sensations escalated.

"Make love to me," she urged.

"Are you sure?"

She kissed Vaughn long and hungrily. The feelings she had kept locked away for so long were finally free. She wasn't going to deny them any longer. "Yes."

Vaughn tried to be gentle. At first, as Vaughn plunged inside her, Robyn felt pain. Then she met his thrusts, arching her body upward. Soon Robyn was gasping with delight, her initial hesitation replaced by exhilaration as Vaughn probed deeper, harder and faster. Her hands traveled over Vaughn's body. She touched his chest, caressed his face with long strokes.

Making love with Vaughn was one of the most sensuous experiences imaginable, and Robyn couldn't wait until the next time. There *would* be a next time, if only to hear Vaughn whisper the words he had whispered before climaxing.

"Robyn, I love you. It's never been like this with anyone else."

With tears in her eyes, Robyn nodded back. After so many years, the love she had been denied was back in her possession. "I love you too, Vaughn. I'll never be able to tell you how much you mean to me."

Robyn continued her secret meetings with Vaughn throughout the summer. Each time they made love, Robyn's body responded in ways she had never before imagined. But the best part was always when Vaughn told her he loved her.

There were times when Vaughn would disappear for days at a time. When he reappeared it would always be with a smile, an apology, and a gift.

"It's business," he would explain.

Robyn knew Vaughn was involved with films, but other than that, she was completely in the dark. The few times she had questioned him, he had merely avoided answering.

"It's nothing to concern yourself with. Someday I'll tell you all about it. Right now we're having too much fun. Who knows? Maybe one day you'll help make me rich."

Robyn had let it drop at that. The important thing was Vaughn. Did she care enough about his business to make it an issue in their relationship? Not really.

One evening in late August, Robyn arrived home after having spent the afternoon at the Museum of Contemporary Art. It had been a peaceful, relaxing day, as she and Vaughn had admired paintings and sculptures. Later that night they would be going to a movie, and for the first time Robyn contemplated staying out all night. It would be wonderful if she could spend the night in Vaughn's arms, waking up with him in the morning. What did it matter what Miriam had to say? She had Vaughn to protect her.

Bouncing into her bedroom, she decided to take a shower before dinner. She went to her dresser, slipping her hand into the top drawer for the familiar lace garments that always met her touch.

Robyn felt her insides grow cold at the realization that they weren't there. As quickly as the thought entered her mind, she pushed it away. Miriam never went into her bedroom. Robyn pressed her hand farther into the drawer. It didn't jangle the way it usually did when opened.

Robyn pulled the wooden drawer out, dumping the contents out on her bed. At first she searched nervously, then frantically, as her suspicions were confirmed. The jewelry wasn't there. Neither was the perfume nor the undergarments. They were all gone.

Robyn closed her eyes in resignation, sinking onto her bed as all the good feelings from that afternoon slipped away. What was she going to do? Miriam had found out she was seeing someone. Was she going to lose Vaughn?

Determination gradually replaced Robyn's initial fear. It was her life and she could do anything she pleased with it. Where did Miriam come off dictating how she should lead her life? Robyn remembered the way she used to view each new day with a feeling of despair. There had been nothing to look forward to. Until Vaughn. She wasn't going back to the way life used to be.

Robyn threw her things back into the drawer before heading down into the kitchen. With her mind flooded with images of Miriam throughout the years, contrasting with the most recent images of Vaughn's love and affection, she grew more and more enraged. Thinking about her missing things made Robyn feel violated. What right did Miriam have to invade her privacy?

She stood in the kitchen doorway. "Were you in my bedroom today?" Miriam was at the stove, standing before a simmering pot. She didn't answer. "Did you go through my things? What you've done is no less than stealing. I want my things back."

Miriam put down the wooden spoon she was using. She turned to stare at Robyn, her eyes narrowing to two tiny slits. Her words were uttered with hissing softness, then she turned back to the stove. "Watch your tongue, girl. This is my house, and as long as you're under my roof, you'll abide by my rules. Did you think I was a fool? Did you think I wouldn't notice the signs?"

The tone of her grandmother's voice chilled Robyn. Her only defense was to retaliate with anger. She went over to the stove, pulling Miriam by the shoulders to face her. "You didn't answer me," Robyn demanded. "What did you do with my things?"

"Jewelry? Perfume? Garments that only a whore would wear?" Miriam recanted the list in a singsong tone of voice. "They're all gone."

"You had no right to take those things," Robyn cried, shaking her grandmother furiously. "Those were gifts given to me."

"Don't you mean purchased with your flesh, girl?"

"My name is Robyn! Why won't you say it? In all the years I've lived with you, you've never called me by my name."

"The mere sound of your name disgusts me. It's synonymous with whore." She pushed Robyn away. "Get your hands off me. Your touch sickens me." Miriam's eyes glinted with a touch of danger. "Whore!" she spat out furiously, spraying Robyn's face with a fine mist of spittle. "You're exactly like your mother. You both wanted pretty things, and you both did the same things to get them." Miriam gave Robyn a sneer. "There's no mistaking the smell of a bitch in heat."

Robyn slapped Miriam across the face. Once. Then twice. "For years I've listened to you tear away at the memory of my mother! I won't stand for it any longer. All we wanted was for you to love us! That's all! We didn't ask for anything else. Wasn't that enough? What more do you want?"

"Your words of evil fall on deaf ears," Miriam roared, "because that's all you are. *Evil!* I knew it from the first time I laid eyes on you, but I ignored it. Why is the Lord testing me this way? Why have I been betrayed twice?" Miriam gazed at Robyn with blank eyes, staring off into the distance. So fixated was her stare that Robyn turned around to see if there was anyone behind her.

While Robyn's back was turned, Miriam reached for the boiling pot on the stove, pulling on a pair of oven mitts. "I must cleanse your soul of all evil. Only then will you be saved."

Robyn turned back and, realizing her grandmother's intent, jumped out of the way as Miriam splashed the pot of scalding water where she had stood only seconds before. Robyn watched as steam came off the water-spattered wall nearby, and she shuddered, imagining what would have happened if the water had hit her skin.

"You're crazy! I'm not staying in this house another minute," Robyn screamed, backing out of the kitchen.

She raced to her bedroom, taking the stairs two at a time. Pulling her suitcase from her closet, she began throwing in everything that would fit. Rushing to Miriam's bedroom, she searched for the old woman's jewelry box. It was on the dresser. Though locked, Robyn opened it easily with a hairpin. Her hunch proved correct after the locked top popped open, spilling out the items given to her by Vaughn. Taking only what belonged to her, Robyn added the jewelry to the rest of what she had already packed.

In the living room she found Miriam praying on her knees. Robyn banged her suitcase on the floor when she reached the bottom of the staircase.

"I'm leaving. I can't stay in this house another minute!"

Miriam got off her knees, going to the bookcase where she kept her religious statues, removing one Robyn had bought as a Christmas present years before. "Don't forget this one, harlot. I'm sure you fucked real hard to earn it. Even as a child you knew which tricks to use on a man."

The statue came flying hard across the room, smashing at Robyn's feet. She stared down at the broken pieces, remembering how hard she had saved to buy the statue in the hopes of winning the heart of a woman who did not have one; a woman incapable of loving or of being loved.

"I hate you, old woman," Robyn raged. "Live with your loneliness. I don't need you."

With those final words, Robyn picked up her suitcase and walked out into the night, never once looking back.

"What's with the suitcase?" Vaughn asked when he picked her up.

Robyn hurriedly got into his car, tossing the suitcase in the backseat. "I've left home," she stated flatly.

"Just like that? What are your plans now?"

"I don't know," Robyn cried, her shoulders starting to shake. The aftermath of her confrontation with Miriam was starting to take its toll. In a matter of minutes she was in tears, huddling against Vaughn as she retold her story between sobs and gasps. "Please hold me. I don't know what to do. I can't go back there. I'm afraid to. She might try to kill me."

"You don't have to convince me of anything," Vaughn soothed. "I'll take care of you."

Robyn sniffed, brushing at her tearstained cheeks. "Will you?" It was almost too much to hope for. Someone to take care of her. Someone to love her forever. "I have no money. What's going to happen when classes start in the fall?" Suddenly it didn't seem that the pieces were going to fit together as easily as she hoped. She burst into a new wave of tears. "I'll have to go back," she wailed.

Vaughn had pulled his car to the curb while Robyn had told him her story. Now he pulled the car back into traffic.

"Where are we going?" she sniffed.

"Dry those tears. You're coming home with me. You can stay as long as you like. I've got plenty of room. You're sixteen years old and free to do as you please. You don't have to go back to high school in the fall. I'm sure we can find some kind of work for you to do."

Robyn looked at Vaughn with eyes filled with trust and admiration. "You're wonderful," she shouted, throwing her arms around him. "A few hours ago I thought my world had come to an end. Now you've opened a whole new one. You've saved my life, and I promise to pay you back. Maybe you could find me a position in your company? I've taken a few secretarial courses."

Vaughn pulled to the side again, taking Robyn in his arms

while he slowly caressed her. "I'm sure I could find something for you. Everyone loves a pretty girl, and I'm no exception. I'm always looking for new talent."

"I'll do anything you want me to," Robyn promised.

Vaughn stroked Robyn's cheek, staring into her eyes. "That's all I needed to hear."

27

During the drive to his apartment, furtive glances were sent back and forth between Vaughn and Robyn. Suddenly Robyn felt shy with him. They were entering a new stage in their relationship, a stage dedicated to commitment. Would the relationship remain the same? They had already given so much to each other, but the hardest part was still to come. They needed to adjust to one another and would have to reveal parts of themselves that they had kept hidden. After all, they would be spending much more time together. There was still so much to be learned about Vaughn, she thought.

Once they closed the door to Vaughn's apartment, they were upon each other. Kisses were hot and passionate, tongues insistent and probing. Vaughn's hands glided along the summer skirt she wore, lifting the material up her legs. Her hands first explored along the muscular hardness of his chest before resting upon the hardness beneath the zipper of his faded jeans. They made love on the foyer floor. Only wanting what the other had to offer, they were too impatient to go into the bedroom.

Vaughn later carried Robyn to his bed, laying her gently on the blue satin comforter. Nestling against the pillows, she pulled Vaughn next to her, wrapping a possessive arm around him.

"Just hold me," she whispered into the darkness.

Vaughn obliged her, and Robyn pressed her nose to his

skin, inhaling the lingering scent of his cologne and sweat. There hadn't been any such smells while living with Miriam. Her grandmother had existed in a cold and sterile environment. Robyn had despised every aspect of it, and inhaled deeply again, thankful that she would never have to return.

"Were you sincere about my staying?" Thoughts of Miriam had caused her doubts to resurface and she needed to be reassured.

"Would I have asked if I hadn't meant it? There'll be some inconveniences, but we can handle them."

Robyn bolted up. Taking a deep breath, she tried to keep her voice steady. She didn't want her words to tremble nor for Vaughn to see how he had unnerved her. "What kind of inconveniences? I'm not an imposition, am I?"

Vaughn laughed at Robyn's worried frown. "I can put up with sharing my closet space, but no panty hose in the bathroom!"

"You're terrible!" She flung a pillow at him. Relief flooded her body. He had only been kidding. He wanted her here.

Robyn threw her arms around his neck. "I love you so much. It seems I can never tell you enough. You've given me something I thought I would never have—a chance to love."

Robyn's happiness with Vaughn grew with each passing day. They went on shopping sprees and spent evenings at restaurants and night clubs. Within months Robyn was transformed from a high-school girl to a sophisticated young woman. Gone were her days of chocolate malts and sneakers. Now she indulged in dry martinis and the finest silk stockings. Robyn was a student eager to learn the lessons that would make her fit in with others. Wherever she went she watched and listened and learned.

The only mystery that existed between Robyn and Vaughn was his business. The hours he kept were sporadic, and often he would disappear for hours, not telling her where he was going, only mentioning that it had something to do with films. Afternoons were spent locked behind his study doors where he had his own private phone line. Whenever she ventured to ask a question, he immediately brushed it aside or refused to answer at all. She and Vaughn couldn't share every aspect of their lives, she reasoned, squelching her curiosity. Certain parts had to be kept separate and distinct. Besides, his business life was separate and she really knew everything she needed to know. She didn't push Vaughn for answers, and he didn't provide any.

Robyn knew she was lucky. There wasn't a day when she didn't realize just how much Vaughn had changed her life for the better. There seemed to be no end to the surprises he had in store for her . . . until the fateful night in January when all the cards were laid on the table and her newly constructed world came tumbling down.

Robyn awoke on January 21 to an empty bed, missing Vaughn's reassuring warmth next to her. She peered at the alarm clock with eyes still squinty with sleep. It was eleven.

"Morning, sleepy head." Vaughn sauntered into the bedroom. He was already dressed, knotting his tie and slipping into a sport jacket.

"Why did you let me sleep so late?"

"You looked like Sleeping Beauty, and I didn't want to wake you."

"You're supposed to kiss Sleeping Beauty."

"I did, but she's a sound sleeper. My kisses were powerless."

"How did you kiss her?"

"Like this," Vaughn demonstrated, leaning over to kiss her. Robyn wrapped her arms around him, not wanting to let go. Suddenly she was afraid and didn't know why.

"Hey," Vaughn laughed, "you're squeezing pretty hard."

"I'm sorry. I needed a hug."

"Any time, with pleasure. You know that. Just have to ask."

Robyn slipped into a lavender robe edged in lace, relishing the cool silkiness against her skin. "Where are you off to?"

"Few business-related errands, but here's something to put a smile on your face. Tonight I'm taking you out to dinner with a client, so I want you to look your very best."

"I always try to look my best when I'm with you, Vaughn."

"Wear that clingy black number that I bought you last

week. I don't think you've worn it yet. You know, the one with the turtleneck and no sleeves. And try to do something with your hair. Use your hot curlers. I love it when your hair is long and wild."

"Anything else?" Robyn edged her voice with a tinge of sarcasm. It sounded as though Vaughn wanted a ready-made date.

"For accessories wear those large silver hoop earrings along with those silver bangle bracelets. See if you can dig up a wide belt. Don't worry much about your makeup. Your face is perfect just the way it is."

"Vaughn! Are you for real?"

Vaughn looked at Robyn with deadly seriousness, and a chill traveled down her spine. "I don't ask for much, Robyn. The least you could do is try to look your best for me. Tonight is a very important meeting. You're an important part of it."

Robyn instantly felt contrite. "I'm sorry. Of course I'll wear whatever you want."

Vaughn lifted her chin, gazing into her eyes. Though there was a smile on his face, his eyes were still cold and distant. Once again Robyn felt a chill travel down her spine. Stop it, she scolded herself. You have nothing to be afraid of. This is Vaughn. He loves you.

"I knew you wouldn't disappoint me, Robyn."

Robyn gazed into the mirror, wondering again if what she was wearing was appropriate for a business dinner. The tube of black silk she was wearing clung to her body like a second skin. She felt uncomfortable staring at her reflection. Little was left to the imagination, as her breasts strained against the thin material and her legs rustled seductively with her every step. Her normally straight hair was a jumbled mass of wildness.

Again she wondered if she should change what she was wearing and dress in what made her most comfortable. Then she remembered Vaughn's phone call earlier that afternoon. He had apologized for his behavior but hoped she could understand. He was proud of her and wanted to show her off. Was there really anything wrong with that?

There wasn't, she had realized, immediately feeling guilty. Vaughn had given so much to her, and all she had been able to do was give him a hard time. She couldn't disappoint him.

The phone rang and Robyn turned from her reflection. From the corner of her eye she could see the silk material twisting with her every move. It was only for one evening, she told herself again. She would be able to get through it. The phone rang again, and Robyn ran toward it, hobbling on the spiked heels she wore. They were uncomfortable, but Vaughn had also wanted them to be included in the ensemble.

"Hello?" She concentrated on the phone, ignoring her reflection.

"Robyn?"

"Vaughn, where are you? It's getting late. We should be on our way to the restaurant."

"Problems, babe. I can't go into much detail, but I'm at the airport. A crisis came up with another client. You run along to the restaurant. I'm sure you'll be able to keep my client entertained until I get there."

"Didn't you tell the client you're with now that you had previous plans? Vaughn, I don't know what to do."

"He wouldn't let me get a word in edgewise. Don't worry, all you have to do is have dinner with Mr. O'Connor and explain why I couldn't make it. I'll try and get there as soon as possible, but it's absolutely vital that you go to the restaurant. I've made reservations at La Tour. This evening means a lot to me, Robyn. You'll be helping a great deal. If I had been able to cancel, I would have, but he's probably on his way to the restaurant."

"Why not call the restaurant and leave a message?"

"After all the trouble he's gone through to get there? Does that seem very professional?"

Robyn knew Vaughn had a point. "All right," she acquiesced. "Just let me change."

"No!" Vaughn shouted over the line. "Keep what you have on. You are wearing the clothes I asked for?"

"Yes, but—" Robyn bit down on her tongue. She wasn't going to protest. She was going to do this for Vaughn. He had already done so many wonderful things for her. It was her turn to reciprocate. "I hope I look the way you wanted me to. If we were going together, you could correct any mistakes. I don't want to disappoint you."

"You could never disappoint me, Robyn. I'm sure you'll come through this evening with flying colors. Have a wonderful time."

Vaughn had been wrong. She wasn't having a wonderful time. She was having a miserable time.

She had arrived at the restaurant before Mr. O'Connor. After being shown to her table, she ordered an extra dry martini. She was poking at her olive with a toothpick when Mr. O'Connor finally made his appearance.

Robyn nearly swallowed the toothpick she had brought to her lips as she stared at the man towering above her. He was huge, with large hands sprouting from the sleeves of a suit that seemed too small for his excess bulk. Pockmarked cheeks and a bulbous nose were situated above a leering smile.

Summoning up all her courage, she rose from the table, offering a smile and her hand in greeting. I'm doing this for Vaughn, she told herself. The waiter pulled out their table, and Mr. O'Connor slid next to her, deliberately pressing his body against hers. Robyn tried not to cringe, grasping for her martini and quickly draining the glass.

"I didn't catch your name," he said.

"I'm Robyn."

"I'm Louis, but most people call me Lou." Raising his eyebrows, he sent her a lewd wink. "Vaughn sure picked a winner this time. The guy always comes through."

The comment made no sense to Robyn, unless Lou was making references to one of Vaughn's previous girlfriends. "Shall we order?" she asked, shoving a menu at him.

Throughout the meal Robyn had the distinct impression that Lou was appraising her. She felt as though she were on display, and again wished she wasn't wearing what she had on. Perhaps if Vaughn had been there she wouldn't have felt so uncomfortable. And perhaps Lou would have been better behaved. He was touching her every chance he got.

"Your skin is so soft," he murmured at the conclusion of dinner, lifting his second brandy to his lips. "I've been wondering what it would feel like next to mine."

That was it. Lou had obviously had too much to drink, and she didn't want to stay for anything else. Vaughn was going to regret having made her suffer through this evening.

"I'm sorry, Lou, but as you can see, it's ten o'clock, and Vaughn said if he didn't show by nine, that we shouldn't wait any longer." Actually Vaughn had said no such thing, but she had to get away from this man. "I really must go." She rose from the table.

"Not so fast," Lou said, gulping down the rest of his brandy. "We still have a few things to settle at my apartment."

"Like?"

His answer was succinct and to the point. "Business."

Robyn was exasperated. She couldn't fathom the idea of being with this man in a restaurant filled with people, let alone the privacy of his apartment. "Can't it wait?"

He tossed a few bills on the table. "We've waited long enough."

Robyn reluctantly followed Lou out of La Tour and into a waiting taxi. She deliberately sat as far away as possible.

Inside his apartment Lou asked Robyn if she wanted a drink. She politely refused, wanting to put an end to the task as quickly as possible.

"Calm down," Lou stressed, putting the chain lock in place and staggering to the bar. "You'll have plenty of time to get home and warm Vaughn's bed"—he took a long sip of brandy—"after you've warmed mine."

Robyn passed off the remark as she had so many others during the course of the evening. Lou was drunk. Though she didn't want to admit it, seeing the chain lock in place made her nervous. It would be hard to get away in a hurry.

"Can we get down to business?" she asked. She didn't like being alone with him. She just wanted whatever it was he had to give her and then to leave.

"Of course, it's the reason you're here. Let me step into the bedroom." Lou pointed an unsteady finger at her. "Don't run off."

Robyn checked the time on her watch after ten minutes. Where was Lou? It was getting late, and she didn't like being out alone at this time of night. She hoped he hadn't passed out. It would mean having to go into his bedroom to find out.

"Lou," she called out into the hallway, "are you all right?" No response. Again she called, this time louder and more urgently. Still no reply. Suppose he had fallen and hit his head?

Robyn knew she would have to check on him. She couldn't leave him in the condition he was in. She hesitantly walked down the hallway as though she were entering forbidden territory. The only sound was the soft rustle of the silk she wore. A door was ajar, light spilling out into the darkened hall. Lou was slumped facedown on the bed, appearing either asleep or passed out. Robyn wanted to make sure he was asleep. She went over and nudged him in the ribs.

"Lou? It's Robyn. I'm leaving."

In an instant he sprang up from the bed, grabbing her hand and pulling her on top of him. The action took Robyn totally by surprise. She gasped as her beaded purse flew to the top of the bed and her fur stole was torn from her shoulders. His hands began pawing her body, attempting to pull away the black silk. His breath was thick and foul, causing her to choke for air. He began massaging her breasts, trying to squeeze his thick hand between her skin and the delicate material.

"Stop it," she cried, starting to fight back.

"Quiet, bitch, I know how your type likes it. Hot and rough, isn't that right? You want me to take it myself. I have to admit the idea turned me off earlier, but as you can see," he stated, unzipping his pants and removing his penis, "the idea of raiding your cookie jar has turned me on."

He was going to rape her! How had this happened? She continued to twist and struggle. There had to be a way for her to get away. She stretched her hands toward the purse she'd dropped.

"Decided to give up and enjoy it?" he cackled.

Robyn's beaded purse was a heavy bag, filled with makeup. Once her hands were around it, she began to pound it against the side of Lou's head. She brought the beaded bag down harder and harder, until Lou tried to seize it from her.

"What the fuck is going on?" he demanded, releasing his hold. Robyn took the opportunity to slide out from under him, falling to the floor. Holding her purse as a weapon, she got to her feet and slowly began backing out of the bedroom.

"Stay where you are, you bastard. If you think you're getting away with this, you're sadly mistaken. I'm going to have you up on charges so fast it'll make your head spin."

Lou sat on the bed, vigorously rubbing the side of his head with a puzzled look. "What gives? I paid your pimp two hundred dollars for tonight. I don't know what kind of stunt you're trying to pull, but if you're looking for more money, it's not going to work. Vaughn got paid, and you'll get your cut from him. I'm not shelling out anything else."

"Pimp? Vaughn? I-I don't understand."

"Aren't you one of Vaughn Chandler's girls?"

"No!" Robyn shrieked.

"He isn't getting away with this," Lou stated, picking up the phone and starting to dial. "I've done business with Vaughn before, and he's always been straight with me."

Robyn didn't hear the rest. As soon as she had made the connection between Vaughn and what Lou was saying, she had run from the bedroom. It couldn't be true! Vaughn loved her. He had told her so on countless occasions. He wouldn't lie to her. He wouldn't! He would never, could never, betray her trust in him. He was her whole world. He knew how much he meant to her. He had saved her from a life of loneliness and had taught her how to love again. Why would he have given her so much if only to take it all away again?

She pulled away the chain and lock with trembling fingers. There had to be a mistake. Yes, it was all a mistake. Lies. It was all lies. Lou was lying. He had made up a phony story about whores and pimps to cover his tracks. Vaughn would deny everything. She knew he would. He had to.

Vaughn was waiting for her when she returned to their apartment. She ran sobbing into his arms. As the tears fell forth, so did her story. Vaughn crooned to her gently, smoothing her hair. When she was finally finished, he stepped back and asked her if that was all there was.

"Yes," she sniffed, brushing away a tear from the corner of her eye.

"Good," Vaughn said. "I'm glad to see you're so calm." He then slapped her across the face. The blow was hard and stinging, sending her reeling against the wall.

"You stupid bitch!" he ranted. "Haven't you put two and two together yet? Didn't you realize something was wrong or were you so wrapped up in yourself that you didn't bother to notice?"

Robyn cowered against the wall, terrified by Vaughn's display of violence. Suddenly she was a child again, at the mercy of Miriam's wrath. She thought she would never have to experience such fear again. But this time it wasn't Miriam inflicting the fear. It was Vaughn, and he was screaming a whole slew of ugly remarks at her just as Miriam had always done. The only difference was that she loved Vaughn, and his display of anger doubled her fear. She looked at him in horror as fresh tears streamed down her cheeks.

"You almost lost me a valuable client this evening. Do you know how long it took me to smooth things over with O'Connor? Do you know how much money he brings me each month? Plenty! But you don't care. None of this matters to you. You only care about yourself. When did you become so modest, Robyn? When did you start guarding your chastity? Saving it all for me? I've got news. It's time to start sharing with others." He leaned over her, pressing his face closely against hers as she tried to pull away, averting her face. "Look at me!" he ordered. "Don't you know you've been my whore all along?"

Robyn shook her head at Vaughn, covering her ears and trying to block out the hateful things he was saying. This wasn't happening. It was all a nightmare, her worst dream come to life: Vaughn denying he loved her.

He pulled her to her feet, pushing her into the bedroom. There he opened the closets and drawers, pulling out items of clothing and scattering them to the floor.

"Do you see these?" he asked, holding a handful of dresses and negligees. "To you they're nothing more than pretty outfits designed to make you more appealing." He threw them in her face and went over to her vanity table, rummaging through the various bottles of cosmetics and perfumes. "Look at all this shit. Lipsticks, eyeliners, eye shadows, blushes." He emptied out the drawers, scattering the bottles to the floor. "Do you know what you look like when you wear this stuff?" he screamed. Robyn didn't answer. "Do you?" he screamed again. The tone of Vaughn's voice caused her to cringe, but she forced herself to answer.

"I don't know," she whispered.

His answer surprised her. "You look attractive."

"Everything I've ever done has been for you," she whimpered.

"I understand that, sweetie," Vaughn cooed, wrapping a comforting arm around her. "But now you must understand that the rules have changed." He gestured at the soiled clothing on the floor, the broken bottles of cosmetics and perfumes, the scattered jewels. "These items only serve one purpose: to sell you."

Robyn broke from Vaughn's embrace and ran out onto the balcony. Icy winds tore at her skin but she was oblivious to them. Nothing could compare to the pain she was feeling inside. She heard Vaughn's footsteps behind her and she turned to face him. She wasn't going to let him humiliate her in this way. She wasn't going to be afraid of him. She had options and choices. She wasn't going to do anything she didn't want to do.

"I was almost raped this evening. Doesn't that matter to you?"

Vaughn was brusque and to the point. "You're young and beautiful. Men *want* to have sex with you. They'll pay whatever it takes to get you into their beds. Hungers need to be satisfied, and I intend to make a profit from it. Lou O'Connor wanted you. He was willing to pay. It can hardly be called rape."

The wind was whipping at Robyn's hair, and she brushed it away from her face. "It's called rape when it's done without consent, and Lou O'Connor did *not* have my consent to sleep with me, let alone touch me." She hunched her shoulders at Vaughn. "I refuse to be a part of it."

Vaughn's fingers dug deeply into her shoulders, crushing the skin against her bones. Yet the pain was nothing compared to the emotional pain she was suffering. He wanted her to do this. He wanted her to be a prostitute. Robyn twisted away from him, running back into the bedroom. She felt as though she were in a dream and there was no means of escape. A feeling of helplessness choked her and she could barely get out her words.

"You used me! You tricked me! This was your intention all along, wasn't it? You never loved me. You lied to me. Everything you ever told me was a lie," she screamed.

Deep in her heart, Robyn didn't want to believe what she'd said. Maybe it was all a horrible joke. After seeing how much he could get away with, Vaughn's face would break out into a grin and he would take her in his arms, apologizing for the pain he had put her through.

"I've always believed in the truth," Vaughn exclaimed, sitting himself down, "and I see no reason why I should start lying now. You were nothing more than an investment. The first time I saw you, I saw your potential, and under my guidance it's blossomed. I've improved your looks, your tastes, and most importantly, your lovemaking. You were an adept student and learned your lessons well. All the time and money I've invested in you is about to pay off. You know what pleases a man, and those lessons will serve you well in your new area of employment: the bedroom."

"I won't do it," Robyn emphatically stated. "I'll go to the police. They'll believe me and they'll protect me."

Vaughn laughed. "Still deluding yourself, I see. After the way you've been living with me, who's going to believe you? The only thing that you'll convince them of is that you're a jilted lover out for revenge, and that's not going to do you any good.

"Consider the facts if you leave. You're a high-school dropout whose grandmother will gladly admit that her granddaughter has the morals of a whore. If you leave me, you'll have no place to go, except juvenile hall, and you don't want to go there. Those places aren't nice. They're cold, lonely places, and they aren't safe. A pretty little thing like you wouldn't last very long. The girls would get to you long before the boys did." Vaughn grinned wickedly. "You'd still have the pain and humiliation. The only difference is that you wouldn't be getting paid for it."

"Nothing you say will scare me or cause me to change my mind. I'm still leaving." Robyn started walking away. Vaughn watched her with an air of detachment, not saying anything. The silence was nerve wracking. It couldn't be this easy. He wasn't going to let her just go.

"I'd reconsider if I were you," he instructed with steely determination.

She stopped, turned. "Never."

Vaughn walked over to her, placing a hand against the side of her face, slowly rubbing his hand up and down her cheek. His touch repulsed her, as Lou O'Connor's had, and she jerked away. "I'm not sure of that," he said. "If you walk out that door, I can't guarantee you'll stay in perfect health. I don't like to make threats."

Robyn faced Vaughn with her head held high. "You couldn't be capable of such violence."

"You belong to me, Robyn. If you walk out that door, I promise that within the next twenty-four hours your grandmother will be dead." A length of silence ensued before his next sentence. "And twenty-four hours after that you'll be dead. But your death will be slower and more painful."

Robyn closed her eyes in resignation. He had her. She had lost. There was nothing she could do to guarantee that she would be able to safely get away from him. She would always be living in fear, and she didn't want to live that way. Nor did she want to die. She wanted to live. Then there was Miriam. No matter what the old woman had done to her, she couldn't take a chance with her life; she didn't want Miriam's death on her conscience. She had to take things one step at a time before making any drastic moves. For now, the only thing to do was to give in to him.

Vaughn's voice cut harshly into her thoughts. "Have you made a decision? You don't have to like what you're doing, but you *are* going to do it."

He sounded so sure of himself. Why wouldn't he? They had been living together for close to seven months. He knew everything about her, and she knew practically nothing about him. She had been such a fool, blinded by her love. She looked into eyes she had once adored. Instead of seeing love and passion, she saw violence and madness. She was dealing with an entirely different Vaughn. Saying no to him would be like trying to defuse a time bomb. Until she knew exactly what moves to make, she would do as he wanted.

"I won't leave," she promised in a barely audible whisper.

Vaughn smiled with content. "I knew you wouldn't disappoint me." He led her toward the bathroom. "Straighten yourself up and I'll get on the phone with Lou. He's going to be thrilled that you're coming back."

Robyn headed into the bathroom with her makeup bag under one arm. Spreading the cosmetics on the marble counter, she chose a ruby-red lipstick and began applying it to her lips. Over and over she kept applying the lipstick until the texture of her lips was thick and greasy. Next she applied the blush with long strokes, and heavily coated her eyes with mascara and eye shadow.

Usually when she wore makeup, the effect was one that enhanced her features rather than masking them. But tonight Robyn was building a mask to hide behind. She needed one to cower from her new life.

28

The first thing Vaughn did was take away whatever money Robyn had in her possession, along with the jewelry he had given her. "This is just a safety precaution in case you decide to run away."

"I wouldn't do that."

"It's better that you realize how vulnerable you are. Nothing belongs to you, Robyn, not even the clothes on your back. It's all mine."

"Won't I be making any money?" Robyn felt nauseated uttering the words, but she had to know. She wasn't going to be Vaughn's slave for the rest of her life.

"I'll arrange everything. Your johns, the locations, the exchange of money. Everything will be handled by me.

You'll get a small cut, but don't start getting any ideas." He sent her a chilling smile. "Whatever money you get from me is to be used on your appearance. I run a class operation, and it's up to you to look your best. All you have to do is obey my orders. Understood?"

Robyn tried to look defeated, mustering a tone of meekness. "Yes, Vaughn."

Next he moved her out of his apartment and into an apartment on the fringes of Wrigleville with two of his other girls. "This is where you'll be living from now on." He dumped her suitcases on the floor. "Make yourself at home. If you have any questions, the girls will be glad to answer them."

"Where are you off to?" she called sarcastically to his retreating figure, no longer able to keep her anger bottled up. "Out to replace me already while your girls show me the ropes? Going to prey on a lonely runaway? I'm sure you've gone that route before."

"I have," Vaughn boasted.

"You sicken me."

Vaughn brushed off her comments without even a look back, leaving Robyn alone with two strangers.

"Hey, my name is Cara."

Robyn accepted the proffered hand of a tall, lean black woman, approximating her to be in her late twenties. She had coffee-colored skin and a mane of luxurious black hair down to her shoulders. Sharply sculpted eyebrows over almond-shaped golden-brown eyes were the crowning glory on a face etched with the finest features. Robyn found herself admiring Cara's beauty and elegance. If she had ever passed her on the street, she would never have assumed her to be a prostitute.

Cara shook Robyn's hand vigorously, then pointed to a blue velvet sofa where a bob of curls alternated between a box of chocolates and a movie star magazine. "That's Tiffany. Girl, will you get your butt off that sofa and get over here?"

"Calm down, I was just on my way over," she screeched, rising from the sofa and straightening the hem of a miniskirt much too tight for her shapely form. The image of a porcelain doll came to mind as Robyn studied Tiffany's shiny red cheeks and pouty ruby lips.

"Let me take your other bag," Tiffany offered, squeezing around Cara. "Follow us and we'll show you to your room."

Cara put a reassuring arm around Robyn, leading her down the hall after Tiffany. "I don't know the whole story with Vaughn, but I know he twisted your arm to get you here. There's nothing I can do to change things, but I want you to know that it's okay to cry. If you ever need to talk, I'm here. I won't be able to change things, but I'll be able to listen."

"Finished with your little chat?" Tiffany asked in what Robyn took to be a too-cool tone of voice. "If you are, then take a look at this." She opened the bedroom door they had reached with flourish, standing to one side. "Cara and I decorated it ourselves."

"Do you like it?" Cara asked.

Robyn put down her suitcase, gazing at the gleaming furniture, the freshly ironed curtains and new bedspread. Whose room had this been before she arrived? Had it been used by Tiffany and Cara to entertain clients? Or had it belonged to another girl, a girl who had become lost in the life she had been forced to lead? She wouldn't ask. She didn't want to know.

The wallpaper was made up of tiny yellow roses. They looked so fresh and pure. They didn't belong in this room.

"Can I take the wallpaper down?"

Tiffany dropped the suitcase she was holding, her eyes enlarging with outrage. "Take it down? We spent two weeks—"

Cara cut Tiffany off. "Anything you want is fine. This is your room."

Robyn had to forget what she had lost. Gone were her days of innocence and trust. She had to adjust to the present situation. She had to get used to the idea that she was nothing more than a whore. She would accept money from men and then subject herself to their demands. When she looked at herself in a mirror, it would be with shame, wondering if she would ever regain the respect she had lost.

"Why don't we strip the entire room to the bare walls?

Would you like that?" Tiffany didn't bother masking her anger.

"I didn't mean to offend you," Robyn apologized.

"Whatever you want to do with the room is fine with us, so long as you're comfortable," Cara said.

"It's been a long day. Do you mind if I rested for a while?"

"We're out of here." Cara snapped her fingers. "Tiff, get your rollers. This morning you said you wanted me to do your hair."

Robyn watched them exit. As the door was closing she called out to Cara. "Did you really mean what you said before?"

Cara peered back into the room, her hand on the knob. "What in particular?"

"Vaughn. Surely you can't condone what he's done to me."

"I don't take sides," Cara stated flatly.

"What he's doing to me is wrong," Robyn persisted. "I don't want to be here."

"Honey, you've got a lot to learn. I can't help you get away. This world is different from the one you've come from, and you've got to learn the rules. Rule number one is survival. Think only of yourself and no one else."

"You're scared of him."

"Vaughn can be a real bastard when he wants to. He doesn't show that side often, but you want to keep clear of it."

"Meaning?"

"Rule number two. *Never* cross Vaughn, but if you do, I suggest you keep your tracks very, very well hidden."

Afterward Robyn threw herself on her bed, closing her eyes and hugging her pillow to her chest. She instantly opened them. Whenever she closed her eyes, one scene kept persistently replaying itself—the night she had spent with Lou O'Connor. His vile obscenities; the touch of his hands exploring her most intimate spots; his hot, foul breath; the scalding tears that had silently fallen down her cheeks; the shame and degradation she had experienced. All were recalled from the deepest, darkest shadows of her memory. No matter how hard she tried, she couldn't forget.

She allowed the tears to begin again. She had lost count of the number of times she had immersed herself in tears since Vaughn's betrayal. Each time she had cried she had sworn it would be the last time. Now here she was crying again. Did it mean something? Did it mean she was still willing to fight, or had she already lost? Should she start worrying about the day when there would be no more tears to shed?

After drying her eyes she fixed her rumpled bedspread and went into the kitchen. Tiffany's head was covered by pink rollers, hidden under a hair dryer. Cara was at her legs, administering a pedicure.

"Tiff, stop wiggling. You'll smear the polish."

Robyn sat next to Tiffany, thumbing through one of her movie magazines, not knowing how to start a conversation with the two.

"Vaughn called," Tiffany mentioned between snaps of her gum. "Your assignments are tacked on the fridge. You've got a busy night. Five in a row. Vaughn's really keeping you bed hopping." Tiffany giggled.

Robyn turned white as Tiffany's words sank in. Five men in one evening? Vaughn was doing this purposely, getting even with her remarks from earlier in the afternoon. She felt a stirring in her stomach and bolted from the kitchen, running to the bathroom.

"Can't you see she's upset?" Cara snapped.

"It's time she faced reality," Tiffany stated. "Pretending the situation doesn't exist isn't going to help matters."

"If I didn't know you so well, I'd think you'd done that on purpose." Cara hurried after Robyn.

Tiffany watched Cara leave with a shrewd look, snapping her gum loudly. "Maybe you don't know me as well as you think."

Cara found Robyn in the bathroom. Most of the color had returned to her face.

"I'm sorry for the way I'm behaving," Robyn said.

"Weren't you listening before? Everything is open here. It'll take time to adjust, but you will."

Robyn shook her head. "At first I thought I could do it, but I can't. Not again. I haven't been with anyone since Vaughn forced me that first time."

"You've got to! Remember what I told you about survival? Vaughn has a mean streak. Don't provoke him."

"What am I supposed to do? Lie there and allow myself to be violated?"

"No!" Cara commanded. "That's the one thing you don't do. When you're with a man, you're providing a service. At the price they're paying Vaughn, they expect the best. You've got to accommodate them. If the customers start complaining, you're in big trouble."

Robyn felt the tears building again as her body started to tremble. "What am I supposed to do? How can I pretend to enjoy it? I get sick thinking about it."

"Pretend you're with someone else. Detach yourself from the situation. Loosen yourself up with a drink or two. Do anything you can to get through the hour. The important thing is to create an illusion. If you can do that, you'll do fine."

Tiffany began pounding on the locked bathroom door. "Hey, let me in. I'm a working girl. I've got to get ready."

Cara unlocked the door. "You better start to get ready yourself."

Robyn smiled weakly. "I'll try to remember what you said."

Cara opened the door to a mud-packed Tiffany who was pulling rollers out of her hair. "You're going to make it, Robyn. You're a fighter. You've got determination. You're going to get out of this one day."

As the weeks turned into months, Robyn got to learn more about Tiffany and Cara and how they had gotten into prostitution.

Cara's story was a simple one. She had wanted a glamorous life and had done whatever was necessary to escape from the ghetto. She became part of a high-priced call girl operation when she was sixteen, and for the next ten years lived the life she had always wanted. But then her pimp had gotten too greedy with the Chicago mob and his body was found at the bottom of Lake Michigan.

Afterward Cara was stripped of everything she had accumulated over the years. All her money, furs, and jewelry were taken away. Left destitute and with no place to live, she had had no choice but to go out on the streets. It was there that she met Vaughn. Liking her looks and elegance, he offered to take her off the streets and set her up in her own place. At the time the offer had been too good to refuse. All Cara had wanted was to get off the streets. But then Vaughn had started to become domineering. Cara was no longer allowed to handle her own money, and Vaughn did everything. When she protested, he promptly beat her, telling her that her only worry was to lie on her back and spread her legs.

That had been a year ago. After the beating, Cara started saving whatever money she could get her hands on, planning, waiting for the day she would make her escape.

Tiffany's story wasn't as simple. Robyn learned the details one day when she and Tiffany were alone in the apartment.

They were in the kitchen making dinner, and Cara was out with a client. Feeling awkward because she and Tiffany barely talked, Robyn asked her how she had ended up working for Vaughn.

"Our stories really aren't that different," Tiffany began. "Same loneliness. Same emptiness." Her voice hardened. "Only you got the G-rated version and I got the X. My mother was a drunk who had nothing better to do than beat me. When I wasn't her punching bag, I was my stepfather's whore. From the time I was fourteen he raped me every night. I couldn't go to anyone. Burt said if I told anyone he would blame me . . . say I had seduced him." Tiffany's voice became a quiet whisper. "They would have believed him too."

"What about your mother?"

"She knew what was going on but chose to ignore it." Tiffany gave a harsh laugh. "Burt not bothering her for sex meant she had more time to swill gin. I stayed until I was eighteen, packing my bags the day I graduated. New York was my destination. I used to spend hours poring over fashion magazines. My dream was to one day work on Seventh Avenue, selling my designs to the world's most beautiful women."

Tiffany viciously stubbed out her cigarette. "Dreams die fast in New York. No one was interested in my designs. I couldn't even get my foot in the door. I would have taken any job involved with fashion. All I wanted was a chance to work my way up. When that was denied, I tried to sleep my way up. Promises were made in exchange for my body, but no one ever came through.

"One weekend I flew out to Chicago with one of my bosses. We went to a party, and it was there that I met Vaughn. The minute I laid eyes on him, I knew I wanted him. Vaughn's perceptive. He picked up my vibes and later dumped his date. We spent the entire weekend in bed. When Monday came I didn't want to go back to New York. Vaughn offered to let me stay with him for as long as I wanted." Tiffany started frantically chopping vegetables. "Settling in Chicago wasn't as easy as it had been in New York. Finding work was a nightmare, and in the back of my mind I knew relocating was a mistake. But I wanted to be near Vaughn. I could never get enough of him. Vaughn was the one who offered the solution." Tiffany viciously sliced at her vegetables. "Easy work with high pay and my own hours, leaving me with plenty of time to work on my designs. The offer sounded good enough. I decided I would do it until I had saved enough money and had restored my confidence. Only then would I return to New York."

Tiffany reached for her wineglass, rapidly draining it. "Bit by bit Vaughn managed to squeeze me out of his life, stealing my independence." Tiffany gestured expansively around the walls of the apartment. "And then I wound up here. I haven't picked up a sketch pad in two years and don't think I ever will again."

Tiffany swayed while reaching to refill her empty wineglass. Throughout her story she had kept filling and draining the glass. She grabbed for the bottle and it crashed to the floor.

"Let me help," Robyn offered, bending beside Tiffany. She placed her hand on Tiffany's. She felt as though a bond had formed between them, and wanted to strengthen it. Together they could help each other.

"I can do it myself," Tiffany shouted with venom, snatching her hand from beneath Robyn's. She waved the carving knife she had been using in Robyn's face and her eyes burned with fury. "You think you're such a martyr. I'm sick of it! Cara and I are no different than you. One of these days you'll learn your lesson. I can't wait till that day arrives."

True to Tiffany's word, Robyn did learn her lesson. It was an evening when she was alone in the apartment. She was before the fireplace, leaning against the mantel while gazing into the flames. Nine months had passed and she was still no further from square one. Vaughn still had her trapped in his web. Somehow she had to find a way to escape.

Hearing a key turn in the apartment door caused her to look up. Had Tiffany or Cara forgotten something? She was about to call out when she saw who was entering. Robyn's blood froze. Moving away from the fireplace, she clutched the flimsy negligee she was wearing closer to her body.

"What are you doing here?"

Vaughn closed the door behind him, securing the locks. "I thought we needed some time alone."

Robyn kept nervously pushing her hair away from her face. She had washed her hair earlier in the evening and it shone in the gleam of the flames. Approaching Robyn, Vaughn rubbed his fingers against its silky texture. He pulled her into his arms, breathing deeply of her perfumed scent. Robyn tensed, trying to remove herself from his grip. But Vaughn only tightened his arms around her before bringing his lips down to meet hers. They traveled from her lips down to her neck and between her breasts. Robyn moaned softly, struggling against the pleasure being rekindled.

"Stop it," she whispered, her resolve melting. Vaughn undid the string of her bodice, allowing the silky material to fall away. He slipped his hand between her breasts, cupping them gently.

"Robyn, I want you. Don't fight it. Don't you know how much I love you?"

The words were like a splash of water on a cold winter day. Robyn snatched the front of her negligee out of Vaughn's hands, covering her exposed breasts. She broke free of Vaughn's grip, pushing him away. "Keep your hands off me, you bastard! How dare you say those words to me?"

"Are old grievances coming back to haunt us? Look, I'm

not in the mood for games. Just get on the sofa and spread your legs."

"Don't tell me what to do!"

"You'll do anything I say." Vaughn advanced on her, grabbing her arm and pulling her to the sofa. She struggled against him, clawing and kicking. She wasn't going to allow this to happen. It would be the ultimate humiliation. She had sworn that she would never allow Vaughn to touch her again.

He threw her on the sofa, pinning her down with his knees. She attempted to scratch his face, but he undid his tie and used it to bind her hands above her head. She cringed upon hearing her negligee rip, trying to keep her legs tightly closed. The silk material was tossed to one side as Robyn continued to fight.

"Get off me!" she shrieked.

Managing to get a hand between her legs, Vaughn pried them apart. Robyn struggled even harder, but Vaughn was too strong. As he pressed himself against her, Robyn realized she wouldn't be able to stop him.

The weight of Vaughn's body suffocated her as he pumped furiously within her. She kept her eyes tightly closed. She didn't want to look at him. The sight of him would make her ill. Only when she felt him withdrawing did she open her eyes.

"You'll never do that again," she stated coldly, removing her loosened bonds. She covered herself with a quilt from the top of the sofa. "Unless you're willing to pay the next time, my body is off limits." With the quilt wrapped tightly around her, she moved past Vaughn in the direction of the bathroom. "Excuse me, but suddenly I've the urge to take a hot shower."

"I'll come around anytime I please, and you'll be waiting, no questions asked," Vaughn shouted. "As for a shower, don't you think that should be my option? After all, who the hell knows where you've been?"

Robyn stared at Vaughn with steely, hate-filled eyes.

"What's the matter?" he daunted. "Lose your tongue, cunt?"

She had only three words for him. "Go to hell."

Vaughn's fist plunged into Robyn's face with brutalizing

force. She staggered against the wall, ready to crumple to the floor. Vaughn reached out to grab her by the hair, then threw her across the glass-topped coffee table. Robyn slid across the table, feeling a sharp ache in her back as she pressed against sharp chrome edges. Vaughn dragged her off the table, smashing her onto the oakwood floor. The quilt was pulled away as she curled herself into a ball in a desperate attempt to protect herself. He began punching her body slowly and repeatedly, then rapidly and spontaneously. His sharp rings cut into her flesh, immediately causing bleeding. The pain throbbed intensely before transforming into a dull ache that soon spread throughout her body.

"From now on keep that tongue in place," he shouted, eyeballs bulging in a face gone wild. "You're lucky I didn't mess up your pretty face." He reached into his back pocket, pulling out a switchblade. "See how sharp and shiny it is?" He knelt beside Robyn, twirling it before her. "Can you imagine what it would look like dripping with blood?" Vaughn displayed the knife for a few more seconds before putting it away.

He went into the kitchen, returning with a bottle of scotch. Drinking from the bottle, he towered over Robyn. "You need to learn a few things. Especially when fucking. You were positively frigid. Do your johns put up with that? Don't worry, I'll be paying lots more visits, and we'll practice. Won't that be nice?"

Robyn squeezed her eyes tightly shut, not wanting to cry. How much longer was this going to go on? She had seen Vaughn angry at her once before, but this time it was different. This time there was a touch of madness infused with his fury.

"I've got big plans for you, Robyn. It's time we started putting things in motion. I'll let you in on the details the next time I visit." He slammed the door behind him.

Robyn remained curled in a tight ball, afraid Vaughn might return. Blood trickled from a cut on her neck. The pain was unbearable. What had she done to deserve this?

She slipped into unconsciousness, remaining on the floor until Tiffany and Cara returned home.

"How could he have done this?" Cara cried, rushing to Robyn.

"She got what was coming to her."

Cara gave Tiffany a strange look. "What the hell is that supposed to mean?"

"She pushed Vaughn too far. How many times did we warn her? We both had to learn the hard way. Now it's her turn."

"He didn't have to be so brutal."

"I feel sorry for her, but it was probably Vaughn's intention. She's learned a lesson she won't easily forget."

"We've got to get her off this floor and clean her up."

Tiffany went to get some warm water, antiseptic, and towels. Cara managed to get Robyn to her feet, bringing her to her bedroom.

"Come on, sweetie. Cara's going to make everything all right."

Robyn kept repeating Vaughn's name over and over. While Tiffany attended to Robyn's cuts, Cara went to the bathroom, returning with two Valium and a glass of water.

"Open up," she coaxed Robyn, placing the tablets on her tongue. "This will make the pain go away."

Robyn swallowed the pills willingly, hoping Cara would then leave. All she wanted was to be alone. Why wouldn't anyone leave her alone?

Tiffany and Cara took turns sitting with Robyn the rest of the night. At first she twisted and turned against the sheets, each move bringing additional pain. Cara wiped at Robyn's brow, debating on whether or not she should give her another Valium. But as dawn approached, Robyn settled down, much to Cara's relief.

The bruised and battered figure in bed tormented Cara's heart. There was not much she could do. The scars on the outside of Robyn's body would heal soon enough, but what would happen to the scars on the inside?

29

Vaughn's beating caused Robyn to remain in bed for several days. Most of the time she slept, with help from Cara's Valium. What had happened had been pushed to the back of her mind, though she distinctly remembered Vaughn's final words. He had said he had plans for the future; plans involving her. What was he up to? What new monstrosity would she have to endure?

She awoke to sounds of arguing. Cara was refusing to let Vaughn into the apartment.

"You're not coming through this door until you calm down," Cara said. "You've already done enough harm."

Vaughn's fists pounded the door. "Open up! Things have gotten too cozy around here for my liking."

"I'll let you in," Cara replied, removing the chain lock, "only if you'll stop ranting and raving."

"Where's Robyn?" he asked the minute he stepped through the door.

"Sleeping. There'll be time to talk another day. Sit down and I'll make you a drink."

"You can't protect her forever, Cara. I've got plans, and they're going to make me a lot of money."

"Not in the condition she's in. She's all battered and bruised. I hope you were drunk when you tossed Robyn around, because I don't want to believe you did that on purpose."

Vaughn accepted his drink. "Never mind what I did. You know what I'm capable of. It was time she learned my limits. Robyn had that beating coming. Next time she won't be so quick with her tongue." He drained half his glass. "How soon can she work?"

Cara shrugged. "I don't know. Three, four days. Vaughn, why don't you leave her alone? She isn't meant for this business. She doesn't belong here."

"Too bad. I say she stays." Vaughn handed Cara his glass, preparing to leave. "Don't get any crazy ideas about helping her get away."

"I may have a soft heart, but I wasn't born yesterday. Nobody crosses you, Vaughn."

"Keep that in mind. I'll be back in a few days. Have fun playing house."

"Don't you mean whorehouse?" Cara muttered, locking the door behind him.

When Robyn woke again, it was early evening. She found Tiffany sitting by the side of her bed.

"Hi, how you feeling? Cara's in the kitchen making like a chef. I get to play nurse. She'll be glad to see you're awake."

Robyn tried to pull herself into a sitting position, but collapsed back among the pillows.

"Let me help," Tiffany offered, putting down her magazine. She fluffed up Robyn's pillows and smoothed the sheets. "You must really be hurting." She brought forth a vial of pills, shaking out two. "These will help you feel much better."

"Are they addicting?"

"What do you care? You're only taking them because Vaughn beat you up. After next week, you won't need them again."

Robyn was uncomfortable with Tiffany's brazen answer. The pills were practically being forced on her. Still, she was hurting. She would only need the pills until the pain ebbed. She took them.

Robyn wasn't sure if it was her imagination, but after she swallowed the pills, Tiffany relaxed and began recapping the afternoon soaps she'd watched. At first Robyn listened intently, but soon Tiffany's voice faded. The pills were working, carrying her away. Robyn liked the way they made her feel. She could almost imagine she was somewhere else. And the pain was gone . . . not only the pain from her bruises, but the pain from the last few months. It was as though the pills were erasing the past, easing the ache in her heart and helping her to forget for a short time.

Five days later Robyn was out of bed and ready for whatever came her way. She didn't need to be afraid anymore. In the future, whenever she felt times were getting too rough, all she had to do was take one of her pills and all would be fine. She wasn't going to give up the pills, no matter what anyone said.

The morning Robyn got out of bed, Cara came to clear away a mass of accumulated dishes. Gathering them up, she casually asked if she could have her pills back.

"I'm sorry," Robyn lied, swallowing the pill hidden under her tongue, her back to Cara as she buttoned her blouse. "When I was returning them to the medicine cabinet they fell out of my hand. The top was loose and they spilled down the drain."

Cara gave her a look of skepticism. She wasn't too ready to believe Robyn, but Robyn had never lied to her before. If only she could get a look at her face, to search for signs of deception. Yet Robyn moved quickly around the bedroom, hardly remaining still. Cara decided to let the matter drop. She'd have to take Robyn's word. Even if Robyn still had the pills, once they were finished, she wouldn't be able to get a new supply.

Robyn discovered this one afternoon a week later. The vial of pills that had previously seemed numerous was now depleted and she desperately needed to obtain more. She couldn't get through a night of johns without them. She went to a drugstore, asking the pharmacist to refill the prescription. He refused, stating that he needed written permission from a physician to allow her more pills.

The scenario repeated itself in three other drugstores, and by the beginning of the evening Robyn was at her wit's end. Where was she going to get more pills? She desperately needed them—she couldn't imagine being with a john without them. Then she remembered. Why hadn't she thought of it sooner? Dr. Charles Haskell, her Friday-night john, would be able to help her get a refill.

* * *

Robyn knocked on the door of room 115, straightening a few loose bangs. She clutched her shoulder bag tightly, waiting for the door to open. When it did, she entered a dimly lit room. The drapes had been closed and the bed drawn. As the door closed, Robyn turned to look over her shoulder.

"On time as usual," Dr. Charles Haskell stated, checking the time. "Want a drink or should we get right down to things?"

Robyn let her cropped red leather jacket and bag fall to the carpet. "You make things sound so informal." She stripped down to her red teddy, studying the silver-haired doctor with soulful eyes. He was in good shape for his late forties, and of all her johns, he was the one she was most able to tolerate. "After all these weeks of meeting, you'd think we would have more to talk about than just business at hand." Robyn narrowed the space between them, placing a hand on his chest. "Of course, when I'm alone with you it's hard to keep my mind on other things."

He fingered the straps of her teddy. "Take it off," he urged.

She refused, preferring to toy with him, moving away as he kept closing the distance between them.

"Come take what you want, Charles. Show me what you want." She threw herself down on the mattress, lounging against the pillows. "I'm waiting," she seductively purred.

Dr. Haskell joined her in bed. Her teddy was shed and tossed to one side. Pressing himself against her, he allowed his tongue to travel along her neck and breasts. His touch was gentle, but it didn't matter. It was at this point that Robyn always closed her eyes, separating herself from the situation and what was going to happen next. She imagined herself elsewhere, while at the same time stroking Charles's back, whispering sweet words of encouragement and giving him what he was paying for. She wasn't consciously aware of what she was doing. It was all routine—the result of months of indifference.

When Charles finished and removed himself from on top of her, Robyn's attention returned.

"You were really charged up tonight," he stated admiringly.

Robyn jumped from the bed, stretching playfully while monitoring the gleam in his eye as he admired her naked body. Good. It would put ideas in his head—ideas only she could fulfill. When the gleam became hungry, she snatched her clothes off the floor, running into the bathroom.

"Charles," she called through the door, "lately I've had trouble sleeping at night. I'm so keyed up from my sessions that I usually don't get to sleep until four or five in the morning. I've been talking to some of the other girls and one of them told me Valium can help you relax. Is that true?"

"It can help somewhat," he agreed.

"I've been to three doctors and all have been reluctant to give me a prescription. They said I should get to bed earlier. Little do they know the line of work I'm in," she joked, coming out of the bathroom and baring her back. "Can you zip me? Anyway, I was wondering if you could write me a prescription."

Charles took Robyn in his arms, nuzzling her neck. "We don't want you overdoing things, and we certainly don't want you giving up your nighttime activities."

"I would hate to disappoint you, Charles," she said.

"My prescription pad is in my jacket."

Robyn raced to bring both pad and pen to Charles. After the prescription was written out, Robyn snatched the piece of paper from his hand, folding it in two and placing it down the front of her dress. "Many thanks."

Charles patted the spot next to him. Robyn sat beside him, but instead of falling into his arms, pushed him away. "Sorry, angel," she apologized, slipping into her high heels, "but I've got other customers." Gathering the remainder of her things, Robyn retrieved a white envelope containing her tip. After checking to make sure the hallway was clear, she exited.

Out in the hallway Robyn leaned against the closed door, pulling out the folded prescription. She stared at it lovingly before returning it safely away. She would definitely be returning next week and the week after.

The weeks progressed at an alarming rate and so did Robyn's dependency on Valium. At first Robyn would take a pill in the morning, and then again in the evening. However, one pill grew into two and then two into three as she kept popping pills whenever she felt the need. She kept returning to Charles with a variety of excuses, and each one was accepted without question. At the same time that her pill dependency grew, so did her increasing consumption of liquor. The only times she took care with her appearance was when she had to meet with her johns. The remainder of the time she was content to remain alone in her bedroom with only pills and liquor for solace.

"You're on something, aren't you?" Cara accused one day. "Is it the pills?" She took Robyn's hand in hers. "Honey, you don't need those pills. Remember how I told you about how I was saving my money? Well, Tiffany's been helping me. We're going to get out of here real soon. When that day comes, you can come with us. We won't leave you behind. We care about you. Try to be stronger a little while longer."

Robyn snatched her hand from Cara, pouring herself a hefty shot of gin. "What would you know about caring?" Her hands shook uncontrollably until she took a sip. "I know why you and Tiffany want me along," she screamed. "You want to get me in bed, isn't that right?"

Robyn knew there was more between Cara and Tiffany than just friendship, although what they shared behind their bedroom door was none of her business.

"You think just because you show me some compassion I'm going to be grateful," Robyn shrieked with rage. "Where was that compassion when I needed it months ago? When I still had a chance and was willing to fight? I heard you the day after Vaughn beat me, telling him you wouldn't be stupid enough to cross him. Why should I listen to anything you have to say? Why should I even trust you?"

"Because we're friends. I've never done anything to hurt you. I've tried to help you. I'm still willing."

Robyn lost interest in Cara, returning to the bar for a fresh drink. "Too late now. I don't want your help. I don't need it," she said resignedly.

"But you do," Cara began. "I'm going to forget all that's been said. I know that isn't the real Robyn Prescott talking. It's the pills and the liquor. The real Robyn Prescott is still here, deep inside you, waiting to come back."

Robyn slammed the bottle of gin onto the bar. She brought her hands to the sides of her head, tearing her fingers through her hair and clenching her teeth. "I'm going to scream if I hear another person say that to me. When Vaughn's pumping inside me he asks where's the hellcat from the night he raped me. You think the Robyn of yesterday is ready to reemerge, willing to spread sunshine to all. I've got news for all of you. There's nobody down there. Do you hear me? *Nobody!* I'm empty. I've been stripped of everything. There are no feelings; no thoughts; no emotions. *Nothing!* It's all gone."

"If that's true," Cara said quietly, "then you have no one to blame but yourself. You could have fought harder, held on longer, but you gave up. You took the easy way out, escaping with pills and liquor. What's it gotten you? Nothing. At least I still have my dreams, and I'll never give them up."

"Do you know how ridiculous your words sound?" Robyn spat out. "You've been in this business for over ten years and you're still in it. You're never going to get out of it." Robyn wanted her words to hurt and convey the pain she lived with daily. "Once a whore, always a whore."

"Maybe, but at least I've still got a chance. You don't."

Cara left the living room, and Robyn sank to the floor, burying her head on her knees. She was tired . . . so tired. Getting back to her feet, she staggered into the bathroom, staring at her reflection in the mirror.

"Mirror, mirror, on the wall, who's the fairest of them all?"

The bedraggled figure staring out at her didn't respond. Was that really her? She pushed a tangled mess of hair out of her eyes and the image did the same. Yes, it was really her. Bloodshot eyes, tangled hair, rumpled clothes. She reached for the bottle of gin she had brought, toasting herself.

"Obviously I'm no longer the fairest in the land, but that doesn't matter. Today is a special day. Do you know why, magic mirror? It's my birthday," she shouted with glee. "I'm nineteen years old, and because today is such a special day, magic mirror, I'm going to give myself a very special present. Would you like to know what it is?" She moved closer to her reflection, whispering confidentially. "Today is the day I kill myself."

That evening Robyn didn't go out with Tiffany and Cara, pleading a headache.

"This is the fourth time in the last two weeks," Tiffany whined. "When are you going to start pulling your weight around here?"

"Don't give me orders," Robyn snapped. "I work for Vaughn, not you."

"Let's go, Tiffany. You're wasting your time," Cara stated. "We'll be in by three, so don't put the chain on the door if you go to bed."

Ten minutes later they were gone and Robyn was racing to the medicine cabinet. A glint of light caught her eye on the top shelf. Reaching upward, she found a package of razor blades. She removed one, examining it carefully and turning it over in her hand. So small, yet so deadly. It was sheer brilliance. She would slit her wrists.

The only important thing left to consider was timing. She would wait until Tiffany and Cara returned. There was no telling who might show up or call before then. Once they were back in the apartment and settled for the night, then she would do it.

Robyn spent the evening on the sofa, sipping from a glass of scotch she never left empty. In a few hours it would all be over and then she would be reunited with her parents. Robyn's heart ached as she remembered the happy times they had spent together. Closing her eyes, she could see them as they once were.

"Why did you have to die?" she cried. "I needed you. I didn't want to be alone all these years. Why did you leave me?"

When she opened her eyes again, it was two-thirty. She heard a key turn in the door and froze as the night of the rape flashed through her mind. Then, seeing it was Tiffany and Cara, she relaxed. Both were laughing and talking, passing a bottle of wine. Robyn suddenly felt a pang of remorse over her imminent action. Despite the circumstances, they had tried to help her as best they could.

"Hi." Robyn tried to smile. "Looks like you had a good night."

"Are you still up? I thought you'd be asleep." Cara went around the living room, turning off the lights. "Feeling better?"

Tiffany looked at the clutter of glasses. "She's flying high. She's bombed out of her mind. Run out of liquor, Robyn? Is that why you're being so friendly after weeks of being a bitch? Want a sip of our booze?"

Cara stepped between the two, sensing a fight was about to start. "Tiff, Robyn doesn't need this. Everyone's had a long day."

Tiffany angrily pushed Cara to one side. "Why is it that you're always on her side? What's so special about her?"

Robyn found herself getting caught in a wave of anger. She pushed herself into Tiffany. "You've never liked me, and I don't really care. You're jealous . . . about me, about Vaughn, and about Cara. Don't worry, sweetheart. I'm not after your girlfriend."

Tiffany slapped Robyn across the face, and without hesitation Robyn returned the gesture. "Don't touch me," she lashed out, eyes glaring. "I may have to take that shit from Vaughn, but not you."

"Why don't you go out on the street where you belong? You've been nothing but trouble."

"Don't worry. I don't plan on staying around much longer."

Cara's ears immediately perked. "What did you say? What's this talk about leaving?"

Robyn nonchalantly shrugged her shoulders. "Who says I have to stay here forever? What can Vaughn do if I leave? Kill me?"

"Yes," Cara responded.

"Whatever happens, happens," Robyn answered succinctly. "I'm going to bed. See you in the morning."

Cara prepared to follow after Robyn, but Tiffany grabbed her by the arm, whirling her around.

"You've treated her like a queen ever since she's arrived. I'm sick of it."

"Robyn needs more attention than you, Tiffany. She doesn't want to be in this business."

"You think I do? Robyn is the lady and I'm the tramp?"

"You're blowing things out of proportion." Cara placed a reassuring arm around Tiffany. "I care for you, Tiff. You don't have to feel so insecure."

"Could have fooled me," she sniffed.

"Let me show you how much." Cara placed a hand on Tiffany's cheek, caressing it softly. "What do you say?"

Tiffany gave Cara an innocent smile. "Sounds like a good idea. You go ahead and warm the sheets. I'll be right in."

Tiffany watched Cara's retreating back with narrowed eyes. After she heard their bedroom door close, she picked up the phone, dialing a number. She cradled the receiver against her ear.

"Like Robyn said, whatever happens, happens."

After hearing Tiffany and Cara's bedroom door close a second time, Robyn jumped from her bed, creeping to her door and listening intently with one ear. They were making love. That meant they'd be busy for a while. When was she to slit her wrists? One of them might need to use the bathroom and find her in time. She decided to be patient, waiting behind her door until all was silent. On tiptoe she slipped down the corridor to the bathroom, checking over her shoulder to make sure she was unheard.

Inside the bathroom she began running hot water in the sink. Steam started to build, fogging the mirror. She rubbed away a circle, studying her reflection.

"Good-bye, Robyn," she whispered, taking a razor between her fingers and getting ready to slice through the tender skin of her left wrist. As the sharp blade was about to make contact, the bathroom door slammed inward. The banging of the door against the tiled wall startled Robyn, causing her to drop the razor to the floor.

"What the hell is going on?" Vaughn screamed, lunging for her. She pulled away from his outstretched arms, searching the floor for the razor. She tried to shove past Vaughn in order to run into the hallway, but he grabbed her arm, pinning her against the wall.

He took her face between his palms, squeezing her cheeks hard. "You just tried to kill yourself, didn't you? Thought you'd take the easy way out?" He grabbed her by the hair, pulling her head back sharply. Robyn winced at the suddenness of the motion. "Good thing I decided to come check things out. Surprise visits always pay off. Let's go see if we can find out what your roomies are up to."

Vaughn pushed Robyn ahead of him. She stumbled, putting her arms out against the walls for support. She had to warn them. But how? Should she scream? Would that give them enough time?

Vaughn opened the bedroom door, immediately switching on the overhead light. Robyn moaned, covering her eyes with her arms, afraid of not what she was seeing, but of what she would soon be witnessing.

Cara and Tiffany were naked.

In the same bed.

In each other's arms.

Vaughn exploded in a frenzy of violence. He slammed the door shut, throwing Robyn across the room. She landed with a thump, sliding to the floor. She cowered in fear of his next move. She looked to Tiffany and Cara. Both had been jolted from sleep. She could see the fear on Cara's face, but for some reason Tiffany did not seem upset. On her face was a look of sureness. Satisfaction. Robyn's stomach turned. Why wasn't Tiffany afraid?

"So this is what goes on when my back is turned," he ranted.

Cara edged off the bed, slipping on a robe. "Vaughn, calm down." She approached him slowly. "You're too excited. Tiffany and I aren't going to deny anything."

Consumed by his tirade, Vaughn did not hear her continuing words. He swept the dresser of perfume bottles, bringing them to the floor with a crash. Within seconds the cloying smells of different scents mingled in the air, making it difficult to breathe. Robyn watched as Vaughn pulled open drawer after drawer, tossing contents everywhere.

"Things will be changing around here. There'll be no more playing house. I can't believe this! Dykes! I've slept with a couple of dykes." He glanced angrily at Tiffany, deciding to vent his frustrations on her.

"Vaughn, sugar," she cried, running to his side and

clutching his arm possessively, "I didn't mean to hurt you. I didn't want to do it, but she made me." She pointed an accusatory finger at Cara. "She threatened me. She told me she would tell you I had been holding back when she was really the one." Tiffany clung to Vaughn, looking at him pityingly. His face remained impassive. She clung to him even harder. "Don't you believe me?"

Robyn couldn't believe what she was hearing. Tiffany was turning on Cara.

"That's a lie," Robyn shouted, jumping to her feet. "Cara didn't twist Tiffany's arm to make her sleep with her. It was her own decision. She's trying to save her own neck."

"Concentrate on saving your own," he replied. He turned to Tiffany and Cara. "Did you know I found her getting ready to slit her wrists? What do you say to that?"

Cara ignored Vaughn's question, still stunned by her lover's betrayal. She stared dumbly as Tiffany went to the closet, returning with a shoe box. Without a word Tiffany lifted the lid, showing the contents to Vaughn.

"How much?" he asked, running his fingers through the mass of bills.

"Ten thousand. I wanted to tell you, sweets, but she kept threatening me."

"Liar!" Robyn screamed. "Some of that money is yours. You said you planned on leaving one day."

Tiffany replaced the lid, handing the box over to Vaughn. "Pay no attention. She's hooked on pills and liquor. Cara's idea. She wanted Robyn under control. Don't blame her for the stunt she tried to pull tonight. Cara's been forcing her to sleep with her too."

Robyn ran to Cara's side, placing a protective arm around her, as though together they could beat the treachery before them. "Everything Tiffany has said is a lie. Cara's never done anything to hurt me."

Robyn's heart ached at the agony she was witnessing. Cara's face was etched with grief and doubt. Robyn knew how she felt. Vaughn's words of betrayal had cut deep into her soul, wiping away memories and killing all love.

"Tiffany, take Robyn out of here. Cara and I have a few personal matters to discuss."

"You can't," Robyn cried, lunging as Vaughn removed his belt, folding it in two. "She didn't do anything. It's all Tiffany's fault."

Robyn fought against Tiffany as she was dragged from the room. She broke free in the hall, but racing back to the bedroom, the door was slammed in her face. Using her fists, she pounded incessantly upon it. The noise did not prevent Vaughn's violence. Nor did it mask the sounds from within. Each time she heard the snap of the belt whipping across Cara's skin, she cringed, increasing her cries and begging Vaughn to let her in. Finally he stopped, and when he unlocked the door, Robyn raced to Cara, dreading what she would see.

Her body was a mass of bloody welts. She gaped in horror as her eyes traveled down Cara's once beautiful body, coming to rest on a bruised and battered face.

Robyn grabbed a sheet off the bed, ripping it into shreds. Rushing into the bathroom, she filled a basin with water, allowing the shredded pieces of cloth to soak. Gently she swabbed at Cara's welts, cleaning away the blood before applying a clean dressing and salve. Carrying a pillow and blanket, she made a bed on the floor for Cara, too afraid to move her.

Vaughn left the bedroom and Robyn waited, listening for the sound of his receding footsteps. She could hear soft murmurs of conversation with Tiffany, and then the apartment door slammed. Looking down at herself, she noticed that her nightgown was speckled with blood. Feeling nauseated, she decided to change and then return to Cara's side.

Entering her bedroom, she was shocked to find her closets and drawers open, with Tiffany packing.

"What the hell are you doing with my things?" she demanded, pulling a dress out of Tiffany's grasp. "Get the hell out!"

Tiffany went to the closet, returning with hangers. She deposited them unceremoniously on the bed. "I'm packing. Vaughn told me to have our things ready for tomorrow morning."

"Packing? Where are we going? Cara can't be moved in her condition."

"Our threesome has just become a twosome. Cara's been phased out. Vaughn's moving us in with him. Cara's remaining here until he decides what to do with her."

"I won't leave her," Robyn refused.

"Too bad. You'll be ready to leave at ten tomorrow or you'll be in worse condition than she is."

"I never thought I'd be capable of hating more than one person at a time," Robyn whispered fiercely, moving closer to Tiffany and pressing her face close. "I hope your soul rots in hell for what you did this evening."

She fled before Tiffany could respond, rushing to answer Cara's call.

"I'm here," she soothed, brushing away damp strands of hair.

"Robyn, you have to be careful," Cara warned, grasping for strength. "Tiffany is dangerous. She hates you and will stop at nothing to get what she wants. I won't be around to protect you."

"What am I going to do?" Robyn frantically asked.

"Don't trust anyone . . . only yourself. Survival," Cara emphasized. "Do whatever it takes to survive."

Cara's voice ebbed off as she lost consciousness. Robyn remained with her for the rest of the night. Through the walls she could hear Tiffany's movements. The night seemed endless, and Robyn counted each minute, wishing there was some way she could turn back the clock . . . not just for herself, but for Cara too. She dreaded the rising sun. What new horror would arrive?

Robyn resolved that she was going to stop drinking and stop taking pills. If she were going to escape from Vaughn, she needed a clear head. Determination coursed through her. She was going to belong to the real world again, regaining the life she had lost.

Never having gotten a chance to change her nightgown, Robyn felt sticky and grimy. She decided to take a shower.

She luxuriated in the shower for thirty minutes. The water not only relaxed her, but cleared her head. She no longer felt as though she was in a cloud.

Tiffany stuck her head in several times, and each time Robyn crossly snapped out a response. She wasn't going to try suicide again. There was too much to live for. She had lost sight of that. It would never happen again.

Vaughn arrived at ten while Robyn was helping Cara settle in bed. Plenty of liquids and painkillers were placed within reach.

Without so much as a look back or a final word, Tiffany went down to Vaughn's car. Robyn lingered for as long as she could until ordered to leave.

She kissed Cara's cheek. "I'm going to miss you."

Cara gave Robyn's hand a reassuring squeeze before wiping away both their tears. "Remember what I told you. Survival."

Vaughn broke their grip, taking a possessive hold of Robyn. "I'll be back tonight," he told Cara. "We've got things to discuss."

The ride down in the elevator was one of stony silence. Robyn stood as far away from Vaughn as possible. Once outside, firmly holding her arm, he steered her in the direction of his Mustang.

Never in her life had Robyn had an urge greater than the one she was experiencing. She could run from Vaughn's grasp and down the street. Never would she have a moment like this again. She was sure to be kept a prisoner once inside the walls of Vaughn's apartment.

They came to his car and the moment was lost. Tiffany was in the front seat, oblivious to Robyn and engrossed in a script. A considerable number of pages had already been read. Taking the back seat, Robyn wondered what had Tiffany so enthralled.

"Vaughn, this is so juicy," Tiffany cried with enthusiasm, sliding next to him as he got behind the wheel. "Can I have the lead? Please?" She started turning pages eagerly. "I can't believe we're going to be making a movie."

"Movie?" Robyn asked.

The Mustang pulled from the curb, drove a few feet and then stopped at a red light. Vaughn took his eyes from the streets, focusing them on Robyn with malicious delight.

"Baby, I told you I was into films. Guess who's going to be my new star?"

30

Things went from bad to worse. Robyn had been totally unprepared for life as a prostitute; now Vaughn expected her to make a movie.

"Take a look at this script," he announced back at his apartment. "We don't start for a few weeks. Familiarize yourself with the lines."

Robyn stared numbly at the script as Vaughn and Tiffany left her alone, locking the bedroom door behind them.

The title, *Head Nurse,* jumped off the page in huge block letters. Scanning the dialogue, reading key phrases, and visualizing key scenes made her sick. She threw the script across the room, where it crumpled to the floor. This was pornography, and she wanted no part of it. Touching the script had made her feel dirtier than she had in a long time. What she was forced to do with her johns was done within the privacy of four walls. This would be on display for the entire world to see.

Her head pounded incessantly and she reached for her pills. When was the last time she had taken one? Yesterday afternoon? Last evening? She couldn't remember. She only wanted to relieve the pounding.

Once her fingers wrapped around the smooth plastic bottle, she calmed down. She would take one pill to calm herself. She was going to cut down on her dosage, but it was going to take time. She knew she had made promises to Cara, and she intended to keep them. But how could she be expected to quit and go cold turkey? Impossible. At least not until her supply of pills ran out.

Robyn kept her promise to herself, cutting down her addiction as the weeks went by. It wasn't hard because she was no longer hooking for Vaughn. As she had suspected, she was a virtual prisoner in the apartment, never allowed outside. Whenever Vaughn or Tiffany left, she was locked in her bedroom. There was no phone in her room, and as Vaughn had the penthouse apartment, no one would hear her shouts if she cried out for help.

One day Robyn was in the kitchen with her pills when Tiffany noticed the bottle was almost empty.

"I can get you a refill on those," she generously offered with an outstretched hand, waiting for the bottle to be relinquished.

Robyn refused Tiffany's offer. "I don't need them as often as I used to."

After Robyn left the kitchen, Tiffany wasted no time running to Vaughn.

"If she doesn't stick with those pills, how are we going to get her to make the movie?" Tiffany worried. "Her willpower keeps getting stronger."

"Don't worry. There are other ways for us to control Robyn. We haven't put them into effect yet." Vaughn gave Tiffany a chilling smile. "But we will."

Robyn emerged from her bedroom, surprised to find Vaughn in the dining room. Usually he didn't return to the penthouse until midnight. His hours suited her fine. The less she saw of him, the better.

"What are you doing here?" she asked.

She was surprised by the way the dining room was set. The lights had been dimmed, there was candlelight, soft music, and an open bottle of champagne.

"You caught me off guard," Vaughn confessed. "I was hoping you'd stay out of sight until everything was ready." He gave her a ready smile, pouring out a glass of champagne. "Drink this. I'll propose a toast."

Robyn accepted the glass of champagne although she didn't really feel like drinking it. What was going on? Vaughn was behaving the way he used to, the way she remembered. She closed her mind to the memories. After all, they were worthless. There had never been any feelings behind any of Vaughn's actions.

"To Robyn, the most beautiful girl in the world." Vaughn

clinked his glass against hers. "Aren't you going to drink it?" he urged. "It's quite good."

Robyn brought the glass to her lips. She had no choice but to participate in Vaughn's game. She didn't want to invoke his anger. She took a small sip, making a face. "This is bitter."

Vaughn looked surprised. "It's the very best. Take another sip. I'm sure you'll appreciate the taste."

Robyn took another sip. Aware of Vaughn's eyes watching her, she emptied the glass in one gulp. Vaughn was immediately by her side, pouring more champagne. "Have some more," he urged. She was about to ask him why he wasn't drinking when a wave of dizziness overtook her and the entire room started turning in circles.

"Let me have the glass," Vaughn commanded, taking it from her hand. "I think you've had too much."

The words sounded far away, and when Robyn tried to respond, she found she couldn't. Her legs started to bend and, before she fell to the floor, Vaughn scooped her in his arms, carrying her to his bedroom. The satin sheets were already pulled back and Vaughn placed her upon them. He climbed onto the bed, boxing her between his legs. Towering over her, he lifted her hand to his chest, rubbing it slowly. Robyn tried to pull her hand away as she felt her insides turning as their flesh made contact, but she couldn't. She was too weak.

Vaughn brought his lips against Robyn's, kissing her slowly. "You've wanted me to come back to you for such a long time. Like the way it used to be. Admit it."

Robyn tried to say no but still couldn't speak. He lifted her up in his arms, untying the sash of her pink wraparound as it fell away. Her hair fell around her neck and the pillows, cushioning her as Vaughn gently placed her back down. He ran his tongue between her breasts, flicking from one to the other.

"This isn't enough, is it?" he asked.

Robyn wanted to open her mouth, to demand that Vaughn take his hands off her, but she couldn't. She didn't have the strength. She was powerless against Vaughn's manipulation.

"You want me to take you one step further, isn't that

right? You want it to be better than it was before." Vaughn brushed his lips against hers. Then he reached out to the nightstand, bringing a syringe to light. "This is something that will make tonight even more special."

Robyn's eyes widened with shock. She tried to break free of Vaughn as the syringe drew closer, but was unable to move. Her entire body was immobile. She hardly felt the pinch of the needle as it broke through her skin, watching in agony as the colorless liquid disappeared into her body.

"Did you give her the stuff?"

Vaughn, clad only in a short silk robe, was sprawled on a leather couch, a drink in one hand. He looked at Tiffany with contempt. "I told you I would handle everything. She took to heroin like a baby takes to milk. A few more shots and she'll be hooked. Then we hold back. When she needs a fix, we only give it to her once she promises to do the movie, and then we keep stringing her along." He raised his glass triumphantly. "Satisfied?"

Tiffany cackled wickedly, draping herself on Vaughn. "I can't wait to see her beg." She pulled off her skirt and blouse, taking him by the hand. "I'm getting horny. Let's fuck." She jumped off Vaughn's lap and hurried to the bedroom, then returned in outrage. "What's she doing in our bed?"

"I told you we had to do things my way."

"You slept with her!" Tiffany angrily accused.

"What if I did?" Vaughn's eyes glittered dangerously. "Did you expect me to hold her down and just jab the needle into her? Every move had to be carefully orchestrated."

Tiffany recoiled from his anger. "But what about me?"

"As long as we've got her in the palm of our hands, does it matter if I slept with her this one time?"

Tiffany grudgingly agreed. "But I'm jealous," she confessed in a baby tone. "Show me that Robyn means nothing to you."

"Tomorrow. I was in there all night and I'm exhausted. Take the bed in Robyn's room. I'd rather not move her, and if she sees me in bed when she wakes up, it'll help strengthen our hold." He dropped his empty glass in her hand. "Put this in the sink before turning out the lights. See you in the morning."

Tiffany gripped the glass in her hand so tightly that it broke, slicing open her palm. She was oblivious to the blood. "Damn Robyn Prescott to hell!" she shrieked. She knew a lie when she heard one. Vaughn had no intention of bedding her again now that he had Robyn back.

No one could say she hadn't made the rules straight from day one. Robyn would pay for this evening. She didn't care what Vaughn did or said. There was a score to settle. First Robyn had stolen Vaughn, then Cara, and now she had stolen Vaughn again. She'd teach Robyn a lesson she wouldn't easily forget.

"No, Vaughn," Robyn begged. "Don't give me another shot."

"Don't you want to feel good?" Vaughn persuaded, approaching with the glistening syringe. A shot of liquid was squirted in the air. "I want you to feel good. I want you to be happy. I don't share this with Tiffany. Only with you, Robyn." He caressed her cheek lovingly, reaching for her arm. "Only with you."

Vaughn gave Robyn a shot of heroin every morning, allowing her to spend the rest of the day in a misted bliss. At the end of two weeks he stopped. It was time to start things rolling. *Head Nurse* started filming the following week, and Robyn had to start getting prepared. One day without her fix and she'd be willing to do anything.

"Vaughn?" Robyn moaned upon awakening. "Where are you?"

Robyn hadn't seen Vaughn since the day before yesterday. That was the last time he'd given her a shot. Excrutiating pains were shooting through her stomach. It felt like knives were tearing her insides to shreds. She wanted to scream. She didn't know how long she'd be able to tolerate the pain.

She struggled from her bed, shuffling to the doorway. She wobbled uncertainly on legs that felt like rubber, clutching at the walls.

"Vaughn, where are you?"

"Pipe down," Tiffany shouted from behind her bedroom

door. "Vaughn went out. He'll be back soon." Tiffany emerged, zipping her leather skirt. "Aren't you dressed yet? Let's clean you up. You look awful."

Tiffany lead Robyn to the blue-tiled shower, throwing her in with her nightgown still on. "A nice cold shower will fix you up," she stated, turning the hot water on full blast. Within seconds steam was building up.

"Hey," Robyn croaked, holding onto the rail of the shower door. "It's hot!"

"Nonsense," Tiffany replied, pulling Robyn's grip free and flinging her back against the tiles. "You're imagining things."

"It *is* hot," Robyn cried, trying to claw her way out of the shower stall.

Tiffany pressed herself against the shower door as Robyn tried to push her way out. After a few minutes in there she would learn to keep her hands off Vaughn. Tiffany knew Robyn was still sleeping with Vaughn; he sure as hell wasn't sleeping with her. Robyn would learn to think twice in the future.

Robyn pounded against the frosted glass, trying to get out. She pressed herself as close to the glass as possible; as far away from the bursts of scalding water. She had tried turning the water off, but the knobs were too hot. How long was Tiffany going to keep her in here? She had to turn the water off. Maybe if she wrapped her hand around the hem of her nightgown, using it as a glove, she might be able to do it.

The water seared her arm as she reached out. Droplets splashed against her shoulders. Her hand slipped because the material of her nightgown was so wet, but she managed to turn the water off halfway. Quickly she reached for the cold water, turning it on full blast before collapsing at the bottom of the stall.

"How could you have been so stupid?" Vaughn shouted at Tiffany. "Did you see the burn on her arm? How about the blisters on her shoulders? We'll have to delay shooting. We're already behind schedule. I thought I could trust you to keep an eye on her. How could you allow her to take a shower in her condition?"

"So sue me," Tiffany snapped defensively. "I can't be

expected to guard her twenty-four hours a day. Who thought she would try killing herself again?"

Vaughn studied Tiffany intently. "You don't think it was an accident?"

"No way. She's ready to self-destruct. The sooner we make this film and get our money, the sooner we get her out of the way." Tiffany fastened her eyes on Vaughn. "Permanently."

Vaughn's eyes fell upon Robyn lying beneath the sheets. "Let's take things one step at a time. See if you can get Jason on the line. Fill him in on what's happened. Maybe we can work around her."

"Vaughn," Robyn cried out in her sleep, "where are you? Help me."

Vaughn knelt beside Robyn, taking her hand in his. "I'm here. Tell me what's wrong and I'll make it better."

Robyn's eyelids fluttered open and she gazed at Vaughn. He was back. He would take care of her and protect her from Tiffany. "She said the water was cold. It was hot. She wouldn't let me out. I pounded on the glass," she sobbed, "but she wouldn't let me out."

"Calm down, Robyn. I'm here to make everything all better. I've got what you like, but I'm only going to give it to you if you make me a promise."

"A promise?"

"If you promise to make the movie, I'll make sure that Tiffany never hurts you again."

Robyn's mind went back to the day when she had first read the script. She didn't want to make the movie. She didn't want to degrade herself any further.

"Do you promise to make the movie?"

Robyn could see anger glistening beneath his smile. What would happen if she said no? What would he do to her?

Robyn nodded her head. "Will you make the pain go away?"

"Of course," Vaughn promised. He placed a chaste kiss on the top of her forehead. "I knew you wouldn't disappoint me."

Robyn turned her face to the wall, ashamed to let Vaughn see her tears.

He closed the bedroom door behind him, making sure to

lock it. He was the only one with the key, and he intended on keeping it that way. From now on he would attend to Robyn's every need, never leaving her alone with Tiffany. For some reason he believed Robyn was telling the truth. He didn't trust Tiffany; she was one screwed-up chick. Jealousy made her react in the most violent ways. It was going to be a hassle keeping an eye on Robyn, but it would only be for the next few weeks. Once *Head Nurse* was completed, Tiffany and Robyn would be out of his life for good. They were both becoming nooses around his neck. It was time to cut them free.

31

Head Nurse told the story of Nurse Shana Divine, a dedicated and true nurse who believes "tender loving care" is the cure for all illnesses.

The movie was to be filmed in an abandoned warehouse along the Chicago harbor. The outside of the building was deceiving, with its grafitti splattered walls. The inside was another story, hosting a variety of film equipment and sets reminiscent of a Hollywood production. Vaughn, Tiffany, and Robyn arrived for the first day of shooting three weeks later than planned. Robyn's burns had healed and she had dutifully studied her lines, promising to do whatever she was told.

"Jason Bartlett," Vaughn introduced, propelling Robyn forward to a slick-looking blond man in his late thirties, "this is Robyn Prescott."

"Vaughn, you've picked a winner!" Jason praised, looking Robyn over from head to toe. "I can't wait to get her before the camera. Let's get them changed." He turned to Robyn and Tiffany. "The dressing room is two flights up. You'll find what you need."

Robyn followed after Tiffany as Jason and Vaughn watched them.

"She's hooked on something, isn't she?" Jason asked without turning around. Displeasure crept into his voice. "Coke?"

"Something stronger."

"Will it make her difficult to work with?"

"On the contrary," Vaughn smugly replied. "She'll do anything we want."

Robyn's costume was a half size too small and she could barely squeeze into it. She was supposed to be wearing a nurse's uniform, but it was unlike any Robyn had ever seen. The bit of white material plunged deeply down her chest, barely restraining her breasts. They pushed against the material, struggling to break free. Robyn was sure that was the look Jason wanted. The "uniform" barely reached her knees, revealing legs clad in white fish-net stockings and silver spiked heels. Robyn was afraid the moment she bent, the dress would tear in two.

"They're waiting for us," Tiffany ordered from the doorway, dressed in a similar outfit. "Let's go."

Robyn took a deep breath before following after Tiffany. The sooner she got this film over with, the sooner she could forget it.

There were three sets to be used. First there was the physical therapy room, where a jacuzzi took precedence. The second set was the nurses' station, consisting of a circular front desk and sofa. The last set was Nurse Shana Divine's office, consisting of one desk, one chair, and one brass bed.

"Robyn, before we get started," Jason said, "I'd like to introduce you to your costar, Dennis Lord."

Dennis Lord was a strapping young man standing well over six feet. He had wavy jet-black hair, a sardonic grin, and hard dark eyes that studied her intently. Muscles abounded everywhere, and Robyn could easily see where Dennis's true talents were. Her eyes fell upon a crotch clearly defined by the tight-fitting jeans he wore.

Tiffany stepped in front of Robyn, licking her lips

provocatively. "Tiffany Hunt. I hope we'll have a few scenes together. Maybe we can practice during our off hours." She giggled.

Dennis ignored Tiffany, moving closer to Robyn. "This is going to be great," he husked, running his fingers through her hair.

Robyn pulled away, trying not to feel like a trapped animal. There was no mistaking the look of hunger in Dennis's eyes, and he sounded like she was there to service him. She turned to the faces around her, searching for anyone who could help her, but no one could. When was this nightmare going to end?

"Cut," Jason cried two hours later. "We have to redo the scene. Dennis, you didn't give her enough time. Calm down, you'll get plenty of tit and ass. Don't be so greedy. Learn to enjoy it."

Vaughn pulled Robyn from the jacuzzi, wrapping her in a towel. "You seemed tense. Come with me. I have just the thing to relax you."

Robyn didn't want to go with Vaughn. She knew she was getting more and more addicted with each passing day. Soon there would be no turning back. She had to stop Vaughn from giving her injections.

"I'm all right. I was only nervous in front of the camera. I'll be better when we do it again."

"It was more than nervousness." Vaughn signaled to Tiffany, who came to stand on Robyn's other side. "I forgot to give Robyn her fix this morning and it's affecting her performance. Help me bring her to her dressing room."

"I don't need a fix," Robyn pleaded, steeling herself against the pains wracking her body.

The two of them led her up the stairs and into the dressing room. Tiffany tightly tied a rubber tube around Robyn's arm, prodding for a fresh vein. Vaughn approached with a syringe.

"We know what's best, don't we, Tiffany?"

"We certainly do," Tiffany affirmed with a nasty grin.

Filming continued and Robyn survived merely by blocking out each day. It was the only way.

After the film wrapped, Vaughn stopped giving Robyn heroin injections. His original plan had changed. He had intended on killing her with an overdose, but then decided to keep her around. It looked like *Head Nurse,* once released, would make money. Jason wanted to do another movie with Robyn right away. Vaughn had had no problem with that except he didn't want Robyn looking like a junkie. Her dependency, thanks to him, had already taken root, so it was time to uproot it. After the hell of withdrawal, Robyn would do whatever he wanted when threatened with becoming an addict again.

He loved the mind games he played with her. As long as Robyn kept making him money, she was a commodity he was going to keep very much alive.

Robyn's body reacted horribly to the withdrawal. She spent days retching, alternating between cold sweats, bouts of shivering, and burning fevers. Sleep was impossible. She spent days and nights twisting and turning, fighting against the demons of her dreams. She had little appetite and only picked at her food.

Vaughn kept her locked in her bedroom with only a stripped mattress. All sharp objects, as well as anything she could use to harm herself, were removed.

Vaughn's daily visits, which he used to witness her agony, were also used to discuss *Head Nurse.*

"Everything is on track with *Head Nurse.* We've decided to release it on video. There'll be more money that way." He took a closer look at Robyn, satisfied to see she was looking much better. The worst was definitely over. "Two distributors are fighting over the rights. I'm going to be showing them the master tape here tonight. It's our only copy, but after tonight I'm sure there'll be plenty. Maybe I'll have you do a little entertaining since you've gotten your strength back."

Vaughn brushed a palm across her forehead. "Why don't we just have you rest? You'll bounce back, and when you do we'll discuss the future. Jason and I have something new waiting. It's hot, Robyn. It's going to make you bigger than Traci Lords, baby. I promise." He kissed her cheek. "Have I ever broken a promise to you?" He laughed obscenely.

"Mark my words, you're going to be the new queen of porn. What do you think of that?"

Robyn wouldn't answer. She only curled herself into a tighter ball, clutching her pillow as she turned her back on Vaughn.

When he left, he didn't forget to lock the door behind him.

Tiffany waited until Vaughn left the penthouse before going to Robyn's bedroom. She had found his hiding place for Robyn's key and had made a duplicate.

Now she stood above Robyn's bed with a pillow in her hand. Looking down at Robyn's sleeping form, Tiffany gripped the pillow with excitement.

She couldn't wait to smother Robyn. Her urge to murder the bitch had intensified with Dennis Lord's rejection of her advances and the cutting of her scenes from *Head Nurse.*

The pillow slowly descended, inching closer to Robyn's face. She hoped the bitch woke up. She wanted to see her kick and thrash as she fought for oxygen. Killing Robyn was the first step in her revenge plan. The next step was Vaughn. The bastard was going to pay for everything he had done to her.

Tiffany leaned forward, ready to press, then stopped.

She had just gotten an idea . . . a brilliant idea. Tiffany tucked the pillow under her arm and left the bedroom. She had just figured a way to kill two birds with one stone.

Her mind busy plotting, Tiffany forgot to lock the door behind her as she left Robyn's bedroom.

Robyn opened her eyes. Her heart was beating furiously. She'd known Tiffany had intended to kill her and pretended to be asleep. What had stopped her?

Robyn didn't know and she didn't intend on finding out. After the two visits she had received, only one thing was clear. She had to escape.

Hurrying to the bedroom door, she opened it a crack, peeking out into the darkened hallway. She could see a faint light coming from the living room. There was no way she could get out of the penthouse that way. She headed in the opposite direction, for Vaughn's bedroom, careful not to make a sound.

In the darkness of Vaughn's bedroom, she reached for his bedside phone. The first time she dialed she got a wrong number. Again, the second time. She didn't dare turn on a light. The beating of her heart quickened with the fear of discovery. If Tiffany found her gone . . .

Robyn forced herself to concentrate. This was her only chance. Only one person could help her. She dialed again. The line rang and was soon picked up.

Robyn's heart soared with relief at the sound of the familiar voice. "Cara," she sobbed. "Help me. Please help me."

Tiffany was on the outdoor terrace, high above Chicago as the biting winds of Lake Michigan whipped at her.

In her hand she held a wrench. She was using it to loosen the bolts on the front railing. The railing was notoriously loose, and the building manager had been asked to tighten it a number of times. He never had. Tiffany jiggled the extra-loosened railing. There was hardly any support.

Her plan was to get Robyn out on the terrace, making sure she faced the loose railing. All it would take was a shove.

After Robyn fell to her death, Tiffany would leave the penthouse and call the police from a phone booth. She'd try to sound distraught as she told them the details of how Vaughn pushed Robyn off the terrace.

Vaughn would be charged with murder. His past, once exposed, would only make the noose tighter.

Tiffany couldn't wait to set things in motion.

Robyn looked up when the door opened. It was Tiffany. In her hands she held a pile of clothes.

"Put these on," she instructed.

Robyn slipped into the black seamed stockings and red leather miniskirt. Next came the leopard skin–fringed bra and spiked heels.

Tiffany tossed Robyn a hairbrush. "Use it."

Robyn brushed her hair with bold strokes. She didn't want to do anything that would agitate Tiffany. She needed to play for time until Cara arrived.

"Thanks for the clothes." She returned the hairbrush. "It feels good being dressed."

"Why don't we go out on the terrace?" Tiffany suggested. "Some fresh air would help. You've been cooped up too long."

Robyn walked ahead of Tiffany. When they neared the terrace, Tiffany gave her a small shove, pushing her through the open sliding doors.

"Sorry," Tiffany apologized. She took a look around. "I always like looking at the city at night, don't you?"

Being in such a close space with Tiffany made Robyn extremely nervous. She put some distance between them by sitting at a patio table. "The view is nice," she agreed.

"Don't sit down," Tiffany coaxed. She was leaning on the side railing. "The view is much better here. Come see."

Robyn remained sitting. "I'm fine here." She wasn't going any nearer. Something was wrong. She could feel it.

Tiffany's eyes narrowed. "What's the problem? Don't want to stand near me? Still think you're better than me? Take a look in the mirror, honey. You look like a whore."

Robyn gave Tiffany an even look. She no longer cared about placating her. Robyn's words slipped easily from her mouth. "What did you expect? The clothes came from your closet." She got to her feet. "I'm going inside. It's too breezy out here."

"You're not going anywhere." Tiffany blocked the sliding glass doors. She reached into a potted palm, grasping the wrench she had hidden. "I knew you wouldn't make this easy, but I don't care. I want to see you struggle."

Robyn started backing away as Tiffany neared with the wrench. Robyn wobbled in her heels, almost falling to the ground. "Tiffany, you don't want to do this."

"Don't I?" Her eyes gleamed with hatred. "I want you dead, Robyn. Dead." She lunged with the wrench, aiming for the side of Robyn's head. Robyn fell to the side, scrabbling to get inside. If she got inside, she could lock Tiffany out.

Tiffany threw herself behind Robyn's legs and pushed her to the ground. She crawled on top of Robyn, beating her with her fists. "You're not going anywhere, you little whore."

Robyn covered her face with her arms. Tiffany began battering Robyn's head against the concrete. Robyn reached with one hand to scratch Tiffany across the cheek. Tiffany screamed in agony as blood dripped from the deep gash. Robyn took advantage of the moment to knee Tiffany in the stomach. Doubling over in pain, Tiffany released Robyn, who crawled out from under her. She ran through the sliding glass doors and turned the lock with fumbling fingers.

Robyn collapsed in an exhausted heap while Tiffany howled with rage out on the terrace. Reaching for the wrench she had discarded, she started battering the glass doors. A multitude of cracks appeared until the glass shattered. Robyn scrambled to her feet as Tiffany stepped inside, brandishing the wrench from palm to palm.

"Where did we leave things off?" She held up the wrench, shaking it furiously. "Oh yes! I was about to bash your head in."

Robyn ran for the apartment door. She had to get out. Tiffany was clearly insane, determined to kill her.

When Robyn opened the door, she was startled to see Cara. She wrapped her arms around her, clinging for protection. "She wants to kill me!" Robyn sobbed.

Cara held Robyn tightly. "Don't worry, I'm here. No one will hurt you." She opened her purse and showed Robyn the gun hidden inside. "We've got protection if we need it."

Tiffany came barreling around the corner. "Cara?" She stopped in her tracks. "Is it really you?"

Robyn tensed, hovering behind Cara. Tiffany was no more than four feet away, still holding her wrench.

Cara gave Tiffany a freezing look. "Who else? Vaughn didn't do that bad a number on me, no thanks to you."

"I was wrong to do what I did," Tiffany whispered. "Every day I live with the memory of how I betrayed you."

"If you had a conscience, I'd believe you."

"Please forgive me," Tiffany begged, tears welling in her eyes.

Robyn blinked twice, unsure of what she was seeing.

"You hate me and I don't blame you," Tiffany wailed. "I don't deserve to live after what I did to you." She dropped the wrench to the floor with a heavy thud, running from Cara and Robyn.

Cara started to go after Tiffany, but Robyn put a restraining hand on her arm. "Let's leave, Cara," she pleaded. "Vaughn could be back at any minute."

"We can't just leave her."

"Why not?"

Cara pointed to the terrace. "That's why!" Robyn followed Cara's finger. Tiffany was preparing to climb over the side railing.

"You head downstairs." She gave Robyn her car keys. "I'll meet you. My car is an '87 Chevy."

"I'm not leaving you alone with her. She's dangerous, Cara. Let's just go."

Cara pushed Robyn in the direction of the elevators. "Go! I can't let her do this."

Cara ran onto the terrace, dropping her shoulder bag to the ground. "Tiffany! Stop!"

Tiffany paused, standing on the outside of the side railing. "Why? What have I got to live for? Look at what this life has done to me."

"You can come with us," Cara promised.

"I can?"

Cara nodded, holding out a hand. She'd say whatever was needed to get Tiffany off the railing. "All you have to do is climb back over."

Tiffany did as Cara asked. When she was back on the terrace, she went into Cara's arms, sobbing. Brushing away her tears, she looked into Cara's face. "Can I tell you something?"

"What?"

Tiffany's face contorted into an ugly mask of hatred. "You're a damn fool!" She tore herself free of Cara and shoved her into the front railing.

The loosened railing gave way the moment Cara hit it. She fell into open air, desperately trying to grab hold of anything that would save her. There was nothing. On her face was a look of surprise and shock. Tiffany watched Cara fall with rapt fascination, starting an insane litany of laughter.

Robyn screamed from the sliding doors. She hadn't gone downstairs as Cara had instructed. If only she had arrived sooner! Maybe she could have prevented this.

"You killed her!" Robyn shrieked.

Tiffany looked away from the torn railing. "That's right. You were supposed to have died that way, but I can't say I mind Cara taking your place," she gloated. "The stupid bitch got what she deserved." Tiffany reached for Cara's fallen bag, seizing the exposed gun. "Now it's your turn."

Robyn ran from the apartment. Behind her she could hear Tiffany in pursuit. When she got into the hallway she didn't bother with the elevator. She ran for the stairs, gripping the railing as she stumbled in her spiked heels.

When she reached the lobby she looked for help. No one was around. She burst out onto the sidewalk, but the streets were deserted. A row of cars were double-parked. In particular was a blue van blocking the view of oncoming traffic. Across the street she could see Cara's car.

Robyn ran from the apartment building and toward Cara's car, choking back sobs. She ran into the darkened street. The glare of oncoming headlights caused her to stop. Then scream. Before the driver could stop, he smashed into Robyn, flinging her body into the air. She screamed again before landing on the hood of the car, crumpling to the street in a silent, broken heap.

— BOOK FOUR —

New York
November 1989

32

Tiffany listened to Robyn's shocked gasp with satisfaction. Then, without another word, she hung up.

She went into the bathroom and proudly admired herself in the mirror, fluffing out her curls and touching up her makeup. A thrill of elation coursed through her and a devious laugh bubbled from her painted lips. With one phone call she had started unraveling Robyn's perfect new world.

And this was only the beginning.

With weakened legs Robyn managed to collapse on the sofa, ignoring the incessant buzzing of the dropped phone. Cradling her head in her hands, she tried to block out Tiffany's voice, but couldn't. Over and over she kept hearing the same question:

Remember me? Remember me? Remember me?

Her mind was overwhelmed by the images brought back to life. All were vying for attention. Robyn tried to shut them out but couldn't. The images were too dangerous . . . too deadly . . .

Her past could cost her Scott.

Tiffany had the power to destroy her. What would happen

if Scott learned of her past? Would her past make a difference in their relationship? Would she lose him?

Robyn stared at the phone on the floor. Her world was on the verge of collapse. She was at Tiffany's mercy, and could do nothing until Tiffany made the next move.

Back at her apartment Tiffany lounged in bed in a short silk kimono. In one hand was a glass of white wine. In the other a remote control. She aimed the remote at the VCR and television.

The machines clicked to life and Robyn's image filled the screen. The tape playing was *Head Nurse.* Draining her wineglass, Tiffany watched the movie with rapture. Snatching the tape had been the smartest thing she'd ever done.

After Robyn had fled from the apartment, Tiffany pursued her. If it was the last thing she did, she was going to kill Robyn. Killing Cara had given her some satisfaction, but she *had* to kill Robyn. She hated the bitch for so many things.

She was in the lobby when Robyn was hit by the car. Dashing outside where there were two possible corpses wouldn't be smart. Instead she returned to Vaughn's apartment and packed.

In Vaughn's bedroom she emptied his wall safe. He had foolishly given her the combination. There was a lump of cash, some gold jewelry, and a video cassette. It was all tossed in her suitcase. Tiffany only wanted to get away before the police arrived.

Only later, when she played the tape, did she realize what she had done. She had stolen Vaughn's only copy of *Head Nurse,* the copy he had planned on showing the distributors. Without the tape Vaughn had nothing, was nothing, except a pimp with no chance of getting himself out of the hole he was in. Tiffany knew Vaughn wanted his hands "clean"—that he wanted to make money in a "legitimate" way. His every last penny had gone into *Head Nurse,* and now she had the result of his gamble. He'd be furious.

The police were looking for Vaughn. They wanted to question him about Cara's death. His call-girl operation had been exposed and his ladies disbanded.

Tiffany relished the newspaper accounts she read. The police were really turning on the heat in their search for Vaughn. There had been mention of Robyn's accident, but no connection had been made between Robyn and Vaughn.

As the weeks passed and Vaughn's face disappeared from the newspapers, Tiffany started to worry. Vaughn could resurface. He could start looking for her. She didn't want to think what would happen then. She'd have to leave Chicago.

On the day she was to leave, a note was slipped under the hotel room door where she had been hiding out. The handwriting wasn't Vaughn's but she knew he had sent the message from wherever he was hiding. There were only three words: "I'll find you."

It was then that Tiffany started running.

Tiffany ejected the tape from the VCR. Thank God she hadn't thrown it out! The main reason she'd kept it was because she enjoyed watching Robyn doing something she so hated.

Tiffany began envisioning herself in silk . . . furs . . . jewels. She clutched the tape tightly, barely able to control her excitement. She had discovered the key to a golden kingdom.

Robyn needed to tell someone the story of her past. Although she wished that someone could first be Scott, she wasn't ready to take the risk yet. By telling Kristen, she would be relieving herself of a terrible burden.

"What's up?" Kristen asked, sitting cross-legged on the floor. "You look so glum."

"I have a story to tell. It's about me."

"Sure."

"There are a few things you should know. My story isn't very pleasant. Once I start, I don't think I'll be able to stop. Just let me finish, okay?"

Robyn started at the beginning and for the next two hours recounted her past. The emotions she had experienced at the time of each incident were relived for the first time. Surprisingly, she felt strengthened, and made a realization. Facing her past with courage, rather than shame and fear, would only be to her benefit. She could never change her past, but she shouldn't have to live in its shadow, especially not when there was a bright future awaiting with Scott.

When Robyn finished, Kristen reached for a box of tissues, dabbing her misty eyes. "You poor kid."

"Hey, it wasn't that bad." Robyn hadn't expected this reaction.

"The hell it wasn't," Kristen said. "You were abused and taken advantage of in the most horrible way."

"Do you think any less of me because of what I've told you?"

Kristen was shocked. "How can you ask that?"

"Scott doesn't know, and I'm afraid if I tell him, I'll lose him."

"You won't," Kristen stoutly affirmed. "Scott loves you. He's going to understand after you tell him."

"If I tell him." Robyn got to her feet, pacing from one end of the living room to the other. "I'll be taking such a risk."

"You took a risk in telling me. I'm still here."

"What am I going to do?"

Kristen joined Robyn. "I can't make that decision. I can only offer advice. Trust your heart. Scott loves you. If you honestly believe he loves you, then you're going to have to believe that the love you both share will get you through this. Otherwise, you never had anything special."

"Thanks, Kristen. You're a good friend."

"Hell, I'm your best friend." Kristen gave Robyn a hug. "Don't you ever forget it." She was silent for a moment. "What are you going to do about Tiffany?"

Robyn gave Kristen a firm look. "Blackmail is obviously going to be her game. I'm not going to give her a chance. I'm going to beat her to the punch." Robyn took a deep breath. She had reached a decision. "I'm going to tell Scott."

"When?"

"Tonight."

Anthony Calder reclined comfortably behind his desk. "I think you'll be pleased with this week's report." He waited for Beverly to remove the typed report from his desk, but she made no move to retrieve it.

"I'm waiting," she coldly instructed, "for an oral report."

Calder cleared his throat, sitting up straighter. "We've tracked down a few names."

"Specifically?"

"Tiffany Hunt."

"Enlighten me."

Calder formed a temple with his fingers, peering through them. "Flashing Ms. Prescott's photo around Chicago drew a blank until a former director of porn flicks said she looked familiar. He says she starred in a movie of his called *Head Nurse.*"

Beverly leaned forward eagerly. "I want a copy," she demanded.

"That's where we run into a problem. It seems the movie was never released and there aren't any copies."

"There has to be at least *one* copy."

"We're working on it."

"Is this man sure Robyn Prescott is the girl from his movie?"

"Positive."

"Where does Tiffany Hunt fit into all this?"

"She also starred in *Head Nurse.* According to Jason Bartlett, the director, there was bad blood between the two. I'd say she was our best bet."

"Where is she?"

"At the moment we're not sure. We think Las Vegas or L.A. We're checking both out." Calder settled back in his chair, confident that Beverly would have no qualms this week.

"What the hell do you think you're doing sitting on your ass?" she raged. "Do I have to spell everything out for you? Find Tiffany Hunt."

Although startled, Calder confronted Beverly's icy rage. "My men are working around the clock." Every week their meetings ended this way, with him cringing before her. How it galled him! Just once he'd like to put this rich bitch in her place. Maybe, just maybe, he would. He'd love to find out what kind of secrets she had.

"They'd better." Beverly paused at the door, slipping into a black mink cape. Lifting her head regally, she once again turned to Anthony Calder. Although she was a vision of elegance and beauty in her black mink cape, black silk Chanel dress, gold-encrusted earrings and black turban upon her head, her eyes glittered with stark savageness. "When you find her, bring her to New York."

At first Georgina didn't know which photos to send, but in the end decided to send them all. She carefully sealed the manila envelope containing the photos. A special messenger would soon be arriving. All she would have to do then was watch the fireworks. Considering the damaging evidence she held in her hands, it promised to be quite a show.

Georgina briefly considered the consequences of her actions. What would this do to Erica and Jeff? After all, they were living together and thinking of marriage. The photos would surely lead to a split.

Georgina clutched her wineglass fiercely, almost breaking the stem. Good. She wanted Erica to lose it all. For Erica her entire world was Jeff. Georgina laughed mirthlessly, draining her glass. Nothing could ever make up for the betrayal of a friendship. Beverly was her only true friend. She didn't know what she'd do without her. Beverly was always there when she needed her. It had been Beverly's idea to send the photos to Jeff after Georgina had told her about them. Beverly had told her the photos were a potent weapon against Erica. Why not use them?

Georgina had agreed.

Robyn called Scott at the office. He picked up after his secretary put her through.

"I was getting ready to call you," he said.

"Were you? Scott, would you be able to come over tonight?" Robyn cleared her throat. The words wouldn't come out! She was so afraid of losing him. "There's something we need to discuss."

"Nothing could keep me from your side, but I've got some bad news. It's the reason I was going to call. I've got to fly out to L.A. I'm catching a flight at six."

She had been given a reprieve. Robyn kept her voice steady. "Anything serious?"

"Some sort of crisis with our advertising firm out there."

"I'm sure you'll straighten things out."

"Just another inconvenience. What did you want to discuss?"

"It can wait till you come back."

"I can catch a later flight."

"Nonsense. The sooner you fly out, the sooner you'll be back."

"How are you feeling? Headaches still flaring?"

"No," she softly answered. "The headaches cleared up."

"Great. I'm going to miss you."

"Me too."

"Tell me you love me."

"I love you." Robyn closed her eyes, tightening her grip on the receiver. "Promise we'll talk when you get back?"

"Promise. I'll see you in a week. I love you, Robyn."

Robyn hung up the phone, pressing her head against her knees. "I love you. See you in a week."

The clock started ticking.

33

Beverly loved sleeping in the nude. There was nothing more exhilarating than the touch of cool satin against her bare flesh, unless it was the bare flesh of a man. Most mornings she awoke at nine, slipped into a peignoir and awaited the arrival of her breakfast.

This morning her usually uninterrupted pattern was disrupted at five A.M. by the incessant ringing of her door bell. Since the household staff was dismissed each evening at eleven, promptly returning at seven, there was no one to answer the door. Tossing aside her satin sheets, Beverly struggled into a silk robe, clumsily sashing it as she hurried from her bedroom. Passing a mirror, she saw she looked a sight. Whoever it was would pay dearly for this visit. Rarely did anyone see her in a less than perfect state. Flinging open the door, she was confronted by Anthony Calder as his finger rested on her bell for another ring.

"Morning, Ms. Maxwell," he greeted her solicitously.

Beverly's cheeks became flushed with anger. "What the hell is the meaning of this?"

"Mind if I come in?" He started to move forward, but Beverly barred his entrance. "Guess not." He leaned against the doorway. "Did I wake you?"

Beverly swiped at her sleep-mangled hair. "What do you think?"

"Sorry," he drawled, "but I'm sure you'll change your tune once you hear my news."

Beverly gave him a look of contempt. "I doubt it."

"We've made a breakthrough."

"Have *we?*" Her look of contempt didn't waver.

"My men have found Tiffany Hunt."

Beverly kept her face devoid of expression, fighting back her excitement over the news. Calder would love nothing more than to savor her impatience before revealing the rest of his news. "I'll believe you when I see her." She started closing the door in Calder's startled face. "If you'll excuse me, I'd like to get back to sleep."

"Didn't you hear what I said?"

"I heard you. I'm not deaf."

"Don't you want to examine what I've uncovered?"

"Let me be frank, Mr. Calder. I've had some dissatisfaction with your agency's performance. I think our business relationship should come to an end." That would certainly send a stab of fear through him. The discontinuation of her weekly checks would put a mean crimp in his budget.

"Why?" His look of perplexity had turned to one of desperation.

"You've made promises before," Beverly yawned, "and haven't delivered. You say you've found Tiffany Hunt. The only way I'll believe that, as I've already said, is if I see her."

His desperation disappeared, replaced by confidence. "No problem."

"No problem?" Beverly smirked.

Calder extended an arm to his left. "Let me introduce Tiffany Hunt."

Beverly followed Calder's arm as a woman approached from the opposite hallway.

"I hear you've been looking for me," she said.

Beverly sat at her kitchen table, watching as Tiffany ate.

"Would you like another muffin?" she offered. Beverly's culinary talents were few, but there had been a variety of frozen breakfast foods, as well as fruits, pastries, and muffins in her refrigerator. She had managed to whip something together.

When Calder presented Tiffany, the first thing Beverly had done was usher both of them into her duplex. Then she'd asked Tiffany if she cared to freshen up. Tiffany, gazing at the mass of luxury and wealth around her, hadn't heard until Beverly sharply repeated her question. Then, hearing the note of irritation, Tiffany had followed Beverly's directions. When she was gone, Beverly whirled on Calder.

"Are you crazy bringing her here? Suppose someone saw you?"

"At five A.M.?"

"I've got a household staff arriving in two hours," Beverly ranted. "How am I supposed to explain her?"

"Tell them she's a distant relative," Calder dryly replied.

Beverly gave him a freezing look before staring in the direction Tiffany had gone. "What possessed you to bring her here?"

"Have you forgotten? You paid me to find her."

"And extract a certain amount of information," she hotly amended.

Calder casually lit a cigarette. "Live with it. Would you prefer if I took her away?"

With Tiffany in her grasp, Beverly wasn't going to let her go until she had every last bit of damaging information on Robyn. "Your services shall continue until otherwise specified." She led Calder to the door. "We'll talk later."

"What about her?" he asked.

"I think a visit in New York will do her good, don't you?"

Tiffany had returned to the living room while Calder was leaving, and Beverly had directed her into the kitchen.

Now, before starting their talk, Beverly phoned her household staff, giving them the rest of the week off.

"Why did you do that?" Tiffany asked after the last phone call.

Beverly poured them both steaming cups of coffee. "To give us some privacy. Did you know we have a mutual acquaintance?"

"Do we?" Tiffany asked with disinterest, smearing a muffin with butter.

"Yes, we do," Beverly stated. "Her name is Robyn Prescott."

Tiffany nodded and took a bite of muffin, not at all surprised.

When Tiffany opened her door to Anthony Calder, she hadn't known what to make of him. All he would tell her was that someone in New York had asked him to find her. All her expenses to New York would be paid. Was she interested?

At first she had been a bit suspicious. Could Vaughn be behind this? Had he finally tracked her down and was he leading her into a trap?

"Who wants to see me?" she had demanded.

"A woman named Beverly Maxwell."

The name was unfamiliar. "What does she want from me?"

"Information."

"What kind of information?"

"Not much. Only a few select secrets that someone would like kept hidden."

His answer had intrigued her and she had an idea who he meant. "What's it worth to me?"

"Do you like money, Tiffany?"

She had nodded her head slowly.

"If you play your cards right, there could be money in this."

"How much money?"

"Big money." He had looked at her slyly. "More than you'll ever make whoring."

That was all it had taken.

* * *

"What can you tell me about Robyn?" Beverly began.

Tiffany looked at Beverly shrewdly. "Plenty. But what do you want to know and why should I tell you?"

Beverly was prepared for this. "I can make it worth your while. Here's the story. A friend of mine has a brother. He's in love with Robyn. My friend, Susan, is worried. No one knows anything about Robyn except what she's told them, and she hasn't told much. Susan asked if I would mind doing some snooping in Robyn's past, to be on the safe side. How could I refuse? Susan's my best friend. Looking into Robyn's past herself would put her relationship with her brother in jeopardy."

"So you hired Calder."

"Yes, and he came up with your name."

"What do you know about me?"

Beverly pressed her hand against her silk dressing gown, smoothing away the wrinkles, preening her neck and shaking her luxuriant chestnut mane. She was confident of her superior looks and loved flaunting them in this tart's face. "Dear, I'm not here to pass judgment. What you've done with your life is none of my concern. Let me assure you that you'll be well-compensated for your cooperation."

"Why would I want to betray Robyn?"

Beverly gave Tiffany a pointed look. "According to the grapevine, the two of you despised each other." Beverly took a sip of coffee. "I've also heard the two of you starred in a porn movie. Any truth to that?"

"Maybe we did," Tiffany alluded. "What's it worth to you?"

"I want tangible proof," Beverly demanded, her coffee cup tinkling against its saucer. "Something that can be shown to everyone, including Robyn, and not be denied. I want a copy of *Head Nurse.*"

Tiffany wasted no time getting to the point. She could smell money in the air and was going to grab a chunk. "How much?"

"How much do you think the tape is worth?"

Tiffany pondered before answering. She didn't want to seem too greedy, but who knew how high this rich bitch was willing to go? "Two hundred and fifty thousand dollars."

Beverly stared at her coldly. "Are you sure?"

"Positive."

"I'm doubling the amount to five hundred thousand."

Tiffany gaped at Beverly. "Five hundred thousand dollars?"

"Close your mouth," Beverly commanded. "This is just a precaution so you don't get greedy later." She whipped out her checkbook, writing out the amount. "I'll take this to the bank later this afternoon and have it certified. Then I'll rip the check in half. One piece will be given to you, and I'll retain the other piece. The other piece will only be given to you after I have received and viewed the movie. Simple enough?"

"When would you like to see it?"

"The sooner the better."

"I'd have to return to Las Vegas."

"I'll pay all your expenses."

"You're laying out a ton of money."

"Susan loves her brother very much. She'll do anything for him."

"I've got the movie on videotape. What's she going to do with it?"

"I'm sure it will be a useful bartering chip. I wouldn't be surprised if Robyn suddenly decided to leave New York."

"Temporarily?"

"Permanently."

Tiffany rose from the table. "I'd like to take a bath."

Beverly tried not to show her revulsion at the thought of this woman bathing in her tub. "Follow me. I have a fine selection of scented bath oils and powders," she said as pleasantly as she could.

Tiffany continued marveling at her surroundings as she followed after Beverly, a crafty grin on her face as wheels churned in her mind. "I'm sure I'll find something I like."

Tiffany was extremely content flying back to Las Vegas with half a check for five hundred thousand dollars in her possession. Keeping that copy of *Head Nurse* had paid off. She was going to be rich—richer than her wildest dreams. Visions of backgammon tables, slot machines, and roulette wheels danced in her mind. If she played her cards right, there could be even more money. Her fingers traced the jagged edges of the torn check. After all, she knew so many of Robyn's darkest secrets. Perhaps Beverly would be willing to pay some more. If not, Robyn could always buy her silence. She did owe her a phone call.

Tiffany was already formulating plans. This time she was going to be a winner.

What a loser! Beverly watched as Tiffany's plane headed for Las Vegas. Once Tiffany was able to cash her check, how long would it take before the entire five hundred thousand was gone?

Hailing a taxi outside the JFK terminal, Beverly wondered how much of the truth Tiffany suspected. Had she bought her story about "Susan"? Possibly. Talking money had instantly caused Tiffany's eyes to glaze over, dulling her street-sharp instincts. Still, if Tiffany so much as suspected there was a chance for more money, she wouldn't hesitate to make a demand.

Beverly knew she would have to keep her tracks well covered, treading very carefully with Tiffany once she returned.

Tiffany realized something was wrong after locking her apartment door. She froze. Had she heard something in the bedroom? She adjusted her eyes to the darkness, listening intently.

Was someone in the apartment or was she only being paranoid? She took a tentative step forward, keeping her hand on the apartment door.

She called out the name of her old roommate. "Kim?" No answer.

This was ridiculous! No one was here. She turned on a lamp, exposing the squalor of her apartment. She shrugged off her denim jacket, poured herself a scotch, then toasted the walls.

"So long! Tonight is the last night I spend in this dump." She once again examined her half of Beverly's check. Five hundred thousand dollars would soon be hers. All she had to do was get the tape and hop on the next plane out.

She went to the kitchen and opened the pantry. Rummaging through canned goods and boxes of cereal, she found what she wanted. She removed a sack of flour and dug through the fine white powder for an aluminum-wrapped rectangle. It was the tape.

At the sound of clapping, Tiffany whirled, spilling the flour to the floor. Vaughn stood in the kitchen entrance.

"Bravo! Aren't you a smart girl," he hissed, "taking care of everyone the way you did. You cost me plenty, bitch!" He took a step forward. "I did time for Cara's death. They said I pushed her to suicide. We know better, don't we?" He started rolling up his sleeves, revealing powerful forearms. "Your little murder cost me a year behind bars."

Tiffany reflexively took a step backward. She didn't like what she was seeing in Vaughn's eyes as he took another step toward her. There was a slow, burning fury growing with every word he spoke.

"You cost me my golden girl. You made me lose Robyn." His voice was a rasped whisper. "You took my tape." He held out a hand. "I want it back."

Tiffany clutched the tape tightly as she backed into a space between the refrigerator and butcher block. The wall pressed against her back as he approached. There was nowhere else to go.

"Seems like you've got something in the works," he noted. "Care to enlighten me?"

Tiffany nodded vigorously. "We can split the profits, Vaughn."

He stood before her. "Fill me in."

Tiffany told him about Beverly and showed him her half of the check.

"I like it," he affirmed. "I like the smell of this deal a lot."

"We can make lots of money," Tiffany stressed, eager to please.

"If anyone is going to get rich off this deal, it's me," Vaughn coldly informed her. He whipped out his switch-blade, closing the remaining few feet between them. "You're expendable, Tiff. You've told me all I need to know."

"You can't kill me!" Tiffany shrieked. "I told you about the deal!"

"So? It was only a bonus. I came here solely to kill you."

Tiffany couldn't believe she'd been foolish enough to

think Vaughn would let her live. Even so, she wasn't going to die without a fight. As Vaughn lunged for her with his switchblade, she grabbed for a square wooden mallet used for tenderizing meat off the butcher block and managed to pound the side of his head.

Vaughn fell to the floor in a crumpled heap. Tiffany stared at his fallen body in disbelief. Then, remembering all the times Vaughn had betrayed her, she fell upon his body and pounded away at his head with the mallet over and over and over.

Visualizing Robyn's head as the one making contact with the mallet made her task all the more enjoyable.

Anthony Calder couldn't believe what he was seeing. He loaded a fresh roll of film in his camera, adjusted the wide-angle lens, and started clicking away.

Across the street in a hotel room, Beverly Maxwell was having sex with a stranger. Dressed no better than a Times Square hooker, she had picked the man up in a bar. Witnessing the sight, Calder had almost swallowed his tongue. This was the aristocratic blueblood who gave him hell every week?

This was the second night he had seen Beverly in action. The woman had a voracious sexual appetite. Last night she had picked up three different men.

Calder finished his roll of film and started rewinding. He hadn't expected much when he'd started following her. Now he had three rolls of dynamite. Only time would tell how he used his newfound knowledge to his advantage.

In her duplex, three days after Beverly had made her deal with Tiffany, Beverly's state of mind was one of anticipation, similar to a child's on Christmas day. She couldn't wait to view the tape.

"You did bring it?"

Tiffany patted her shoulder bag. "Of course." Nothing would have prevented her from returning to New York with the tape. Vaughn had learned that. She wondered how long it would be before his body was found.

Trying to restrain her eagerness, Beverly led Tiffany into

the living room. The VCR and television were already assembled and waiting, but Beverly purposely avoided them. She'd let Tiffany make the first move.

"Would you like a drink?"

"Vodka." Tiffany settled on the couch, not releasing her shoulder bag. "Where's your friend Susan?"

"She's not coming."

"Why not? Doesn't she want to view the tape?"

Beverly handed Tiffany her drink. "Susan wants me to handle everything."

"Suppose she isn't satisfied with the tape?"

"She trusts me. I'm sure if the tape isn't adequate and Susan wants some more ammunition, she'll be willing to pay you more." A glimmer of greed returned to Tiffany's eyes, but Beverly extinguished it. "However, the tape is our sole interest for the moment."

"Are we going to watch the whole thing?"

"Naturally."

Tiffany drained her vodka, reaching into her shoulder bag. She tossed Beverly the tape. "What are we waiting for? Pop it in."

Ninety minutes later Beverly was ejecting the tape. "You've earned your five hundred thousand," she said, pressing the other half of the torn check into Tiffany's palm. Tiffany immediately formed a fist around the piece of paper.

"I'm not the only one who should be thanking you." Beverly picked up the phone, dialing a number. "It's me," she said into the receiver. "I've finished watching the tape. Your problems are over. Yes, she's still here. Would you like to speak to her?" Beverly held the phone out to Tiffany. "Susan would like to thank you personally."

Tiffany was flabbergasted. Until that moment she hadn't been sure if Susan really did exist.

The woman on the other end sounded as refined as Beverly. The details Beverly had given at their first meeting were repeated, with new ones added. Profuse thanks were also given. Tiffany returned the phone in a daze when Susan asked to speak with Beverly again.

"Yes, darling, I'll be right over. You're not going to believe what you see." Beverly hung up the phone, refastening the earring she had removed and returning her attention to Tiffany. "Looks like our business is finished."

"I suppose it is." Tiffany got to her feet. "I'd like to know how things turn out."

Beverly gave a malicious smile. "Keep an eye on the papers." She handed Tiffany an envelope. "Open it."

Tiffany counted out twenty-five thousand dollars and an airline ticket back to Las Vegas. "What's this?"

"A bonus. You've earned every cent." Beverly walked with Tiffany to the duplex door. "Enjoy your spending. Life's brass ring only comes around once."

Tiffany gave Beverly a shrewd look. "Not unless you grab it and don't let go," she countered.

Beverly couldn't believe how easy it had all been! Hiring an actress and providing her with a script as "Susan" had been a stroke of genius. Tiffany, dimwit that she was, hadn't suspected a thing, and was out of her life for good. Three hours ago she had checked her bank balance and called the airport. The check for five hundred thousand had been cashed and the ticket to Las Vegas used.

Beverly's fingers sensuously traced the smooth surface of the videotape. At any moment of her choosing she could destroy Robyn. How delicious! The first thing she had to do was make a few copies of the tape.

She decided she would wait and plan for the moment. Timing was of the essence. When Robyn was at her peak, with everything she had ever wanted, only then would she launch her attack. What else were scandals for? And in the aftermath of Robyn's shame, Scott would be left alone, ready to return to her.

"Soon, Scott," Beverly whispered aloud. "Soon we'll be together the way we were meant to be."

34

The bedroom was a shambles. Drawers were open, their contents messily spilling out over the edges. Closets were ajar, revealing a disarray of hangers within. A mirror was smashed, jagged pieces of glass mingling with the shattered remains of a vase. A jumble of photos were scattered on the carpet.

Although it was ten A.M., the bedroom was swathed in darkness. All lights were off and the drapes were closed to the morning sunlight. Amid the darkness was a huddle in a corner, her tearstained face etched with pain and loss. In her hands she clutched a man's shirt. It was all she had left of him.

The nude photos had been delivered to Jeff the week before at his law office. Storming back to their apartment, he had confronted Erica with them, along with a note implying an affair with Lance Richards. She had tried explaining things to Jeff, but his anger had been like a shield of armor. Nothing she had said or done had been able to penetrate.

Jeff had flung the photos in her face and then packed his suitcases, rummaging through drawers and closets like a madman. He had said a slew of ugly things to her, and despite her pleas and protests, wouldn't stop. As her own anger had escalated, she'd flung a vase, missing Jeff but smashing a mirror instead.

"Get out!" she screamed. "I won't let you say such things to me!"

"With pleasure," he replied, flinging his apartment keys at her.

With those final words he slammed out of the apartment and Erica collapsed into a flood of tears.

Now she wouldn't answer the door or pick up the phone,

choosing to leave on her answering machine. Why bother? Without Jeff, she was alone. Her life in New York was empty. She had blazed a career based on superficiality, in which nothing mattered more than one's looks.

Struggling to her feet, still maintaining her grip on Jeff's shirt, she headed into the kitchen to relieve her parched throat. She couldn't remember the last time she'd eaten or had something to drink. The last week was a blur. Days and nights meshed together as she tried to forget the outside world.

Constance was always calling. Dear Constance. The only thing the old bitch cared about was her commission.

She slammed the refrigerator door. She was out of orange juice. She was going to have to go out soon and stock up on groceries. Her entire refrigerator was bare. She would have to start living again, but how? She needed Jeff.

Slumped against the refrigerator, Erica buried her face in Jeff's shirt. How she missed him! She had tried calling his office, but she'd been coolly rebuffed by his secretary.

The phone started ringing, and Erica stared at it. Should she answer? She didn't have the strength to get up, let alone find the effort to make conversation. The phone stopped ringing, her answering machine clicked on, and then Constance's voice:

"Remember me? Your agent? This game of hide and seek has got to stop. I can't keep sending other girls out in your place. You've got commitments. Unless you want your ass sued off by a majority of advertisers, you better drag yourself out of this slump. Get your act together. The best way to start would be tonight. Since you've locked yourself off from the world, you've missed all the news. Scott Kendall is throwing together a party at Top of the Sixes to celebrate Wellington's recent success. Your invitation should have arrived in the mail. I hope to see you there."

Erica stood transfixed, listening to the message. Then and there she decided she would attend the Wellington party. She knew she couldn't blame Constance for Jeff walking out. Nor could she blame Georgina, although there wasn't a doubt in her mind that Georgina had sent the photographs. She had promised to get even. Erica's anger wasn't directed at either woman. It was aimed solely at Lance.

Returning to her bedroom, she rummaged through the drawers until she found what she was looking for.

Her gun.

She had been given the gun by her father when she'd first moved to New York. For protection.

Tonight she would use it for an entirely different reason.

Robyn wrapped herself in a towel, hurrying from the shower.

"I'm coming! I'm coming," she called. "Who is it?" she asked before unlocking the door.

"Just one guess."

"Scott!" Robyn cried joyously, twisting the array of locks to one side and throwing herself into his arms.

He laughed. "Guess my voice gave me away."

"I missed you so much," she said, kissing him without hesitation.

"And I missed you." He allowed his hands to slip beneath her towel.

His touch brought an instantaneous reaction. Her breathing increased, her cheeks flushed, and she wanted nothing more than to have him inside her.

"I got your suit all wet. We'll have to do something."

"Like?"

She led him by the tie into her bedroom. "Let's get you out of these wet clothes." Robyn slowly peeled Scott out of his garments. She started with his jacket, tossing it to one side. His dampened shirt clung to his muscled torso, and she pressed her lips to his chest as each button was undone. Next she loosened his belt, not wasting any time in unzipping his pants and pushing them to the floor. He wore no underwear.

"Planned on making a stop here?" she asked in amusement.

"Would you believe I ran out of clean underwear?"

Arms locked, they simply stared into one another's eyes, searching for a reflection of their feelings. Both found it. Then a wave of passion overcame them and they surrendered to its rush.

Falling into Robyn's bed, Scott's hands traveled from her cheeks to her breasts, then to her stomach and thighs, before retracing the route they had taken. He caressed her skin with the softest of touches and kisses, intending to convey how much he loved and desired her.

Robyn cherished the skillful maneuvering of Scott's fingers, relished the taste of his lips and tongue, anticipated his unhurried entry into her warm wetness until she reached a state of ecstasy overriding her present state of bliss.

She moved her fingers through the silkiness of his hair, burying her face into his neck.

"Hey, I want to see that beautiful face," he whispered. "You were all I thought about."

She didn't want to leave the warmth and comfort of his embrace. The safety of their lovemaking was a buffer against the harshness of the outside world. Of realities that had to be faced.

"Just hold me and make love to me," she told him fervently, wondering if this would be the last time.

Scott did as she asked, taking his time, trying to make their lovemaking even more special.

His entry was smooth and uninterrupted. Slipping into her hot moistness, he focused only on her pleasure, holding back his climax, riding her deeper and deeper until her heated frenzy infected him. No longer able to control himself, Scott joined in Robyn's passion, releasing himself into her, their lips joined together with an urging sweetness, sealing the climax of their love.

Unable to wait until she reached the gambling tables of Las Vegas, Tiffany had sold her plane ticket at a reduced price and then hopped on a bus to Atlantic City with her cashed check. She couldn't wait to hit the casinos!

At first the odds were in her favor. Then they turned. Now Tiffany watched with bated breath as the white ball of the roulette wheel traveled round and round, jumping from slot to slot before stopping.

"Red seven, red seven," she silently chanted.

"Black twelve," the croupier declared as the white ball settled.

Tiffany looked with dismay at the last of her departing chips. The entire five hundred thousand dollars was gone, including the bonus given to her by Beverly. Anger built as she watched the gambling around her continue. How could she have settled for such a low price for the tape? Opportunity was slipping through her fingers! She opened her purse, removing a slip of paper. On it was a phone number.

Time for her insurance.

Robyn stretched with a lazy yawn, reaching for the spot next to her. Instead of finding Scott, there was a note on his pillow.

Wasn't that fun? Wanted to stay for an encore, but I've got a million things to do before the party.

Love you.
Scott

Rolling against the sheets with Scott's note held tight, Robyn inhaled deeply of his scent, instantly visualizing him. The cleft in his chin. His mischievious grin and twinkling green eyes. That persistent lock of hair that kept falling over his forehead.

Deciding to finish her shower from earlier, she headed into the bathroom just as the phone started ringing. She chose to ignore it, too busy trying to decide how she would dress that evening. Whoever it was would call back. It probably wasn't even important.

Tiffany slammed the phone down in frustration. No answer! She'd have to try again later.

Looking into her empty purse, she saw she only had a handful of change. It was time to strut her stuff. Smoothing the front of her dress and unzipping her rabbit fur for a glimpse of ample cleavage, she headed for the boardwalk, figuring it would take no more than five blow jobs to get the money she needed. Then she'd have enough money for a bus ticket back to New York.

Beverly luxuriated in her bubble-filled tub, soaping her arms, then her legs, and finally her breasts.

With closed eyes she imagined it was Scott's hands caressing her breasts and massaging her erect nipples.

Scott's hands exploring between her legs until she thought she would scream.

After her indulgence in self-pleasure, Beverly returned her thoughts to the evening ahead. Tonight was the Wellington party. Naturally she was attending. Her invitation had arrived courtesy of Scott, no less. After all, they were friends.

Beverly smirked in anticipation. Whenever she wanted, she could destroy Robyn. The only question was when. She made it a point to always carry a copy of the tape. One never knew when opportunities would arise. She would wait and be patient. An inner sense would let her know when the moment was perfect to spring *Head Nurse* on an unsuspecting viewing audience.

"Why doesn't this stupid thing fit?"

Georgina tore the Karl Lagerfeld evening gown off in a huff, striding to the nearby scotch decanter. Today wasn't her day, she mused, filling her glass. First her appointment at Georgette Klinger had been pushed back, throwing her entire day off schedule. By the time she had gotten to Vidal Sassoon, her stylist had left for the day and she'd had to settle for some incompetent who hadn't known what the fuck she was doing.

Georgina took a sip of the scotch before picking up a hairbrush. What was with all these curls? She'd asked for a sleek look. Slamming down the hairbrush after getting no results, she decided she would shampoo her hair again, blow it dry, and then tie the whole thing back with a black velvet bow.

After her shower, she wrapped a towel around her head, padding nude into the bedroom.

"My, what a lovely piece of ass."

Georgina whirled around. "Lance, what are you doing here?"

"I live here, remember?"

"Could have fooled me, I see you so rarely," she stated sarcastically.

"Feeling neglected?" Lance moved closer. "Want me to make things up to you?"

Georgina looked into Lance's eyes. When was the last time they had made love? She couldn't remember. When it had last meant something went back even further. "I have to get ready for the party."

Lance placed a hand on her breast. "We'll be fashionably late."

Despite herself, Georgina's nipples were becoming erect. She took a step away from Lance, but he closed it.

"Come on," he urged, pressing his lips against hers, pushing his tongue into her mouth.

He moved her to the bed, pushing her down. The towel came free of her head and droplets of water splashed Lance's face. Georgina kissed them away.

She had an ache deep within her, an ache craving for love, attention, and passion. Each time she made love with Lance she silently prayed that what they had once shared would return. This time was no different.

While Georgina tried to make their union last as long as possible, hands and lips exploring languorously along Lance's face, arms, shoulders, legs, and chest, Lance pumped hard and furiously within her. He wasted no time with gentle touches, sweet words, or soft caresses. His tongue was hard and probing; kisses sharp and demanding.

Georgina's whispers to Lance went unanswered as they made love, and when their bodies drew apart, he left the bed and slipped into his jeans.

"Where are you going?" She sat up in bed, staring at him wistfully. She wanted him to stay. She wanted him to hold her in his arms.

"Back to my loft."

Instantly, Georgina's jealousy flared. "Meeting someone?"

"Like Erica?" Lance moved in on Georgina, seizing her face between his hands. "You've been quite a busy beaver. Spying on me. Snooping in my loft." He squeezed her face harder.

"You're hurting me," she squealed, trying to squirm free.

"Good," Lance cooed. "Maybe this will teach you a lesson. I don't like snoops. My loft is my private domain, so keep out of it."

Georgina pulled her face from Lance, massaging her cheeks. "As long as I keep paying the bills, since we know you're not as lucrative with your photography as you'd like others to think, I'll go to your loft whenever I please."

Lance ignored her, slipping into his shirt. "We've been married for seven years," he said, facing her as he buttoned his shirt, "and I still can't get used to it."

His eyes were flat and empty. His voice devoid of emotion. Georgina repeated his question. "Can't get used to what?"

"Making love to you."

"Then why have you?"

"Isn't an obligatory fuck expected when you're not saturated in booze?"

Georgina cupped her face in her palms, exhausted. Suddenly she was tired of the entire sham of their marriage. Why had she stayed with Lance all these years? She didn't love him anymore.

Then her words to Kyle Masters came back to haunt her. Without Lance she was alone. There would be no one to blame or point a finger of accusation at if she had to rely only on herself. Sooner or later she was going to have to reach a decision. Did she want to do something with the rest of her life or wallow in self-pity?

"Get out," she said, her voice tight and restrained. "Get out and don't come back."

"We're married, love. I'll come back whenever I feel like it. No way am I kissing away your five-million-dollar trust fund." He slipped into his leather jacket, pausing at the door and deciding to dig his knife a little deeper. "By the way, I was thinking of Erica the entire time we made love. Only way I could get it up," he explained expansively, tossing her a lewd wink. "See you tonight."

When Lance left, Georgina fumbled to the scotch decanter, pouring herself a hefty drink. She forgot her resolve of a few moments before. There would be time to change her life later. Right now she needed to assauge the stinging pain of Lance's words.

She drank in long greedy gulps. He had never loved her.

Why had she deluded herself for all these years? She emptied her glass, looking at the mess of jumbled sheets on the bed, remembering Lance's last words.

Pouring another drink, the scotch overflowed from her glass onto the white shag carpet. Looking down at the spreading amber stain, Georgina suddenly wished it was blood.

Lance's blood.

Erica's blood.

She emptied her glass, filling it again and grimly resolving that both would pay that night.

"You look fanfuckingtastic," Kristen raved.

"You have such a way with words."

"Turn around. Give me the full view."

Robyn, outfitted in a Christian LeCroix gown of shimmering blue, obliged Kristen's request, turning from left to right. "It's not too formal, is it?"

"Are you kidding? You look smashing."

"You don't look too bad yourself."

Kristen twirled around in a scarlet-beaded Valentino. "This old thing? I picked it up at a showroom sale. Think it'll knock some socks off?"

"How do you do it?" Robyn asked, amazed. "How are you always so confident?"

"Don't tell me you're nervous?"

"Petrified."

"There's no reason. This party is being given in your honor."

"I know, but I'm still not used to all the attention I'm getting."

"Nonsense. You've faced tougher crowds. Tonight is your night." Kristen scrutinized Robyn. "'Fess up. What's the real reason?"

"Nothing ever gets by you, does it?"

"Are you going to give me the scoop?"

"Tonight, after the party, I'm going to tell Scott about my past."

Kristen was unaffected by the words. "Anything else?"

"Didn't you hear me?"

"Is this why you're such a bundle of nerves? Robyn, listen

to me. Tonight belongs to you and Scott. Nothing is going to go wrong."

"I wish I could believe you."

"Believe me," she implored. "Scott is going to still love you after you tell him everything. The fact that you're telling him is what matters. Just be open, honest, and direct. Tell Scott how much you love him and how you almost didn't tell him because you were afraid of losing him. He'll understand."

"This is going to be one of the hardest things I've ever done."

"You'll do it." Kristen nodded sagely. "I know you will."

Honking could be heard from the street below. Robyn peeked out a window. "Scott's limo is here." She picked up her evening bag as she draped a white mink stole around her neck. "Ready to go?"

"I don't want to impose. I can catch a taxi."

A second honk came from the street as Robyn hooked her arm through Kristen's, leading her out of the apartment. "You won't be imposing. Scott's at Top of the Sixes taking care of a few last-minute details. I'd only be riding by myself."

"And if I took a taxi I'd be riding alone too."

Robyn held up a finger. "But if we ride together we arrive together. We can't deprive the paparazzi of such a dazzling duo."

"I agree wholeheartedly. Lead on," Kristen exclaimed. "Tonight is going to be a night neither one of us forgets."

35

Top of the Sixes had been transformed into a Wellington shrine. Bright red and white, the colors of the new packaging for Fresh and Lovely cosmetics, were everywhere. From the red and white balloons floating lazily against each other on the ceiling to the bouquets of red and white roses on tables alternately covered in red and white linen and the sprinkling of red and white confetti on the floor, one's eyes were dazzled by the bold splashes of color. If that wasn't enough, posters of Robyn as the Fresh and Lovely Girl in a variety of poses covered the walls while her Fresh and Lovely commercials played on television screens sequestered in upper corners of the walls.

The sight of Robyn at every turn was nauseating to Beverly, but she kept a smile on her face as she mingled from group to group, firmly clutching her evening bag under her arm, accepting compliments on the black silk polka dot Scaasi trimmed in white lace that she was wearing.

There was no way Beverly could describe the sense of power she felt. It was an indulgent emotion, more intoxicating than all the expensive wines and champagnes being poured. Now that she had the tape, she no longer needed Georgina.

She couldn't wait to get rid of her.

Wearing a silky sheath of jade green that plunged provocatively in the front and daringly down the back, Erica made her entrance. Arriving alone dressed this way sent out immediate signals to all unattached males. But the cold determination in Erica's eyes stopped them from making a move. She had eyes for only one man, and made a beeline for him.

Lance was talking to a bevy of females, and by the looks on their faces, he had them charmed. But as Erica drew closer, the women became aware of her destination and their smiles turned to frowns.

"What gives?" Lance asked, noticing the change in expressions.

"Competition," Erica announced.

Lance turned to the sound of her voice, nearly taking a step back. Was this Erica Shelton before him? He couldn't believe it!

The females surrounding Lance disappeared with haughty looks and mincing words. Erica ignored them, moving closer to Lance. She removed the empty glass in his hand, sucking on a melting ice cube.

"Scotch and soda. I'd like one of these."

There was no mistaking the order, but Lance chose to ignore it. "Aren't you going to wait for Jeff?"

"Haven't you heard? This girl has gone solo."

Lance looked at her skeptically. "Seriously?"

She locked eyes with him. "Would I lie?" She handed him back his empty glass. "This is the opportunity you've been waiting for, so you'd better grab it." She turned her back on him, eyeing the other males in the room. "Otherwise someone else will."

Lance didn't have to be told twice.

A pair of hands slid over Robyn's eyes as a voice whispered in her ear. "Having fun?"

Robyn caressed the hands while inching them toward her lips. "Do I have to answer right away?"

Scott pressed his lips to the nape of her neck, kissing softly. "You're the most beautiful woman here tonight."

Robyn snuggled against him, laughing as she enjoyed the touch of his lips, then turned around and admired his tuxedoed form. Basic black with a white shirt enlivened by a touch of red at the cummerbund, and a bow tie. A tiny white rosebud dabbed with traces of red was pinned to his lapel.

Gazing at him lovingly, adoringly, thinking of their past days of happiness and nights of passionate lovemaking, Kristen's words of advice remained fresh in her mind. She and Scott had shared so much, and there was still more to come. An entire lifetime of living and loving was waiting for them. And they could have it all—even after she told him of her past. A heart such as Scott's, so full of love and kindness, would not judge unknowingly. What was she afraid of?

"What are you thinking?" he asked.

"I'd give it all up if you asked me. None of it really matters." She waved at the glitter and glamour around them. "As long as you're in my life, I don't need anything else."

"I'd never ask that."

"But if you did, I'd do it without hesitation. There are more important things in life than material possessions."

"You're so right." Scott smiled mischieviously. "But who knows? You might have it all."

"Why the sudden change in attitude?"

Erica sipped at her drink. "Why not? Don't you like it?"

Lance nodded appreciatively. "Very much. But is it for real?"

She took another sip of her drink. "We can go somewhere to find out."

"Where?"

"Your loft."

"Are you serious?"

"Never more." Erica laughed condescendingly. "Surely you're not going to pass on the moment you've been waiting for?" She tossed her red curls saucily, knocking off the rest of her drink. "Don't tell me you're all talk and no action?"

"Give me the word and I'll be ready," he flared.

"Fine. Stay on standby." She handed him her empty glass. "I'm going to mingle. I'll let you know when I'm ready to exit."

Beverly checked the time again. Ninety minutes had gone by. The cocktail hour was drawing to a close as groups started moving to their tables. Dinner would soon be served, and still no sign of Georgina. Where was she?

Beverly's tongue was razor sharp, waiting to destroy Georgina's already waning self-esteem. Would her betrayal harvest a new crop of doubts? Would her words push Georgina over the edge? She certainly hoped so.

Thoughts such as these were the only thing helping her to maintain control. A deep, dark rage was simmering beneath her smiling face, dangerously threatening to overflow whenever she saw Robyn and Scott together. For this reason she was purposely keeping her distance from them. Yet she didn't know how much longer she could hold out. If she saw them embrace one more time . . .

If she saw their lips come together again . . .

She fiercely clutched her evening bag with the hidden tape.

Kristen glided across the dance floor in the arms of the man who had asked her to dance. Keeping a smile on her face while making polite small talk, her eyes weren't focused on the face before her. Rather, they were on Erica and Lance.

When the music ended, Kristen declined on another dance, moving through the shifting couples. Erica headed in the direction of the ladies' room—but not before kissing Lance, Kristen jealously noted. She went for a full frontal attack. "What gives?" she demanded. "You've been latched onto Erica the entire evening. You told me we couldn't be seen together because of Georgina, and she hasn't even bothered to show."

Great! Just what he didn't need. Another jealous woman. He glanced over his shoulder for sight of a returning Erica. None so far. He had to get rid of Kristen. He wasn't going to jeopardize his chance with Erica.

"Business, babe. Only business," he rushed to explain. "Erica's thinking of letting me represent her. She's still undecided, so I've got to give a little extra push. No more than wining and dining." He smiled winningly. "We'll get together later. Promise." He steered her in the direction of the bar. "Have a few drinks. Dance some more. I don't mind."

"How big of you." Kristen angrily shook him off. "I don't like what I'm seeing, Lance. I take second place to your wife. I'm not taking second place to anyone else."

He was flip and to the point. "You don't like the way things are? Fine. Move on. There are no strings attached."

Kristen was dumbfounded. "Don't I mean anything to you?"

Lance could see Erica was on her way back, and he didn't want to waste any more time with Kristen. Not when months of agonizing waiting would soon dissolve into a night of heavenly bliss. "I don't want to get into this discussion. I told you what the scene was with Erica. I thought you'd understand. Obviously I was wrong."

"Obviously, because I don't believe a word you've said." She glared at him as Erica drew nearer. "I'm not blind. I know you want to sleep with her." Lance didn't respond, which infuriated Kristen even more. "Haven't you got anything to say?"

Lance sighed. "What can I say? You're right."

"Fine," Kristen spat. "Sleep with her."

Riding up in the elevator, Georgina repaired her hair and makeup as best as she could. Although her champagne-embroidered gown had a few wrinkles, they would hardly be noticed upon her entrance. Her oversized silver fox fur would hide the wrinkles.

After the humiliating aftermath of her lovemaking with Lance, she had wanted to prove something to herself. She'd wanted to prove she was still desirable. So she'd gone on a hunt with herself as the bait. All she could remember was a string of bars. She'd gone from one to another, allowing drinks to be bought and compliments paid. She'd gloried in the attention given to her and had lost track of the time. She only hoped she hadn't missed too much.

Suzy and Liz Smith would be devoting columns to the party in tomorrow's papers, and a number of famous faces from the world of modeling and film would also be in attendance.

Scott's party was the only place to be tonight. She couldn't let the chance of a lifetime slip by.

Walking out of the elevator with her head held high, Georgina tried to remain steady on her high heels. She was still feeling the effects of the countless drinks she'd had, and found herself leaning toward the wall.

No one noticed her arrival. The party didn't stop.

Georgina hailed a passing waiter and snagged a fluted glass of champagne. Within seconds the glass was empty and another was in her hands.

Unknown to Georgina, someone had noticed her arrival —Beverly Maxwell.

Georgina scanned the party for a familiar face but couldn't find one. Then, from out of the crowd, Beverly appeared.

"Georgina, where have you been?" Beverly decided she would start sweet. "We've missed you. The party's been going on for hours."

Georgina's ears perked. "You have? Well, I dropped in on another party."

Beverly became as content as a cat purring over a bowl of cream. Her questions were rapid fire. "Really? Where? Who was there? Why didn't you bring anyone along?"

Georgina stammered for an answer. "They really aren't much to talk about. None of the really important people."

"Which is why you probably fit in so well with that crowd," Beverly laughed, deciding now was the time to begin her assault. "Seriously, who was there?"

Georgina laughed along with Beverly. After all, she *had* been kidding. "No one you'd know."

Beverly took a sip of her champagne. "In this town I know everyone and everything." She sniffed at Georgina's breath. "For instance, you've been bar hopping. Scotch, gin, vodka, and perhaps a touch of muscatel?"

"I have not!" Georgina vehemently denied.

"Darling, how much longer are you going to keep this up?" Beverly looked at Georgina sadly. "We all know you're a deplorable drunk."

"I am not!"

Beverly's voice overrode Georgina's protest. "And your husband sleeps with other women because he can't stand the sight of you."

"I'm not a drunk!"

"Of course you are," Beverly corrected. "Ask anyone in this room. They'll all agree with me. Ask Scott. Robyn.

Perhaps Lance? Yes, Lance would be a perfect authority. How about Erica? Don't all husbands share their wife's faults with their mistresses? Isn't that part of the reason they take mistresses? Let's face it, honey, Lance has been fucking around for as long as you've been drinking in bars. Ask any of his mistresses. They'll all agree to the same thing: Georgina Richards is a drunk.

"How you thought you could ever be the Fresh and Lovely Girl again is sheer madness." Beverly grudgingly acknowledged the posters of Robyn and her image on the television screens. "How did you think you could compete against her? Whatever you once had is gone."

Georgina blinked dazedly at Beverly. She had to be hearing things. Her mind was playing tricks on her. She'd had too much to drink. That was it. Georgina scrambled through her thoughts for the most coherent of reasons. Why was Beverly doing this? Why was she saying such things? Weren't they friends? She turned to her helplessly.

"I despise you," Beverly said. "You have no control over your life. You've lost your looks. You've lost your career." Beverly laughed maliciously. "And now you've lost your husband." She latched onto Georgina's arm, shoving her in the direction of Erica and Lance. "Take a good look. Flaunting their affair under your nose. They knew you'd be here, but did they exert any discretion? No. They decided to make you a laughingstock in front of everyone."

An evil thought crept into Beverly's mind and she seized it, deciding to make the most of it. After all, it would be at Georgina's expense. She softened her voice. "At one time I did like you, Georgina. But you've let me down. Let down our friendship. How can I respect you as a person when you're allowing Erica and Lance's affair to go on before your eyes? I'm sure if you did something about it, my attitude might change. We could even," she let the words dangle alluringly, "still be friends. You do understand that I only said those horrible things because you needed to hear them. I wanted to shake you up," she glibly explained, "and force you into action. You need to take control of your life. I promise I'll help you back to the top. Look," she prodded, "there's Suzy. While you handle Lance and Erica, I'll go talk with her. She's devoting two columns to the party, so I'm sure she'll have space for your name."

Off in a separate corner, Lance and Erica looked more than cozy. They looked intimate, and Georgina grew outraged. How dare Lance do this to her! The promise she had made earlier in the evening came back. Erica hadn't suffered enough. She was about to suffer some more.

Beverly watched in glee as Georgina tried not to drunkenly weave toward Lance and Erica. There was nothing more potent than a drunk's anger to wreak havoc. She couldn't wait for the excitement to begin.

"Kristen, what's wrong?" Robyn asked.

"Who said anything was wrong?"

"I can see it all in your face."

"It's Lance," she reluctantly admitted.

"What happened?"

"We got into a fight."

"Want to talk?"

Kristen shook her head. "Why don't I take you up on your offer tomorrow? You've got enough on your mind, and Scott looks like he's ready to make a speech."

The band stopped playing as Scott stood before the microphone. Conversation and dancing ceased as all attention focused on him.

"Ladies and gentlemen, I'd like to thank all of you for coming this evening. I hope you've been enjoying yourselves. Tonight is a celebration for all the good fortune that's come to Wellington. As you all know, I recently took over as head of Wellington Cosmetics. It's been a tough battle. A lot of hard work, long hours, and a bit of luck. But worth it. We're getting results. This afternoon I learned that sales for Fresh and Lovely cosmetics are up by fifteen percent."

There was a generous burst of applause for the man who had done the impossible. But Scott still had more to say, and the applause died down so he could continue to speak.

"Thank you for your applause, but it's misdirected. If there's one person to whom Wellington owes its success, it's none other than our Fresh and Lovely Girl, Robyn Prescott.

She generated the interest. She was able to get the women of America to take a look at our cosmetics and move them off the shelves."

The applause started again, thunderously this time as Robyn was led to the microphone and Scott. Almost everyone at the party knew of their romance.

"Not only has Robyn captured America's heart, she's also captured mine. If it's not already obvious, I'm in love with this woman. I want her to be my wife. Robyn," Scott said, turning to face her, "will you marry me?"

Robyn was stunned. Marriage! Scott wanted to marry her!

All at once she felt like laughing and crying. The love she had searched for so desperately had finally arrived. It would be hers to keep forever.

The only shadow on her happiness was the past. She still hadn't told Scott. If only she'd told him before tonight! No matter. Later, when they were alone after the party, she would tell him as she had originally intended. Then she would be free from her past.

"Yes," she whispered, tears glistening in her eyes, so overcome by the love she had for him. "I'll marry you."

There was an enthusiastic roar from the crowd followed by the popping of champagne corks. Glasses of Dom Pérignon were handed to Robyn and Scott.

"To the man who always makes my life complete," Robyn said.

"To the woman who finally has it all." Scott intertwined his arm around Robyn's as they sipped from each other's glasses. "Make sure you drink it all."

Robyn emptied half the glass before something heavy touched her lips. Looking into the glass held in Scott's hand, Robyn was shocked to see a diamond ring.

"Like it?" he asked.

They put down their glasses and Scott fished out the ring, slipping it on Robyn's finger. The seven carats glittered and glistened off the chandelier lights.

"It's gorgeous."

"I found it in a box of Cracker Jacks." Scott's eyes twinkled mischieviously. "Almost threw it away, but then thought you might wear it if I asked you to marry me."

Robyn laughed, waving the ring for all to see as she and Scott kissed and were toasted.

Lance decided it was time for Erica to put her cards on the table. "Why don't we shake this scene and head somewhere else?"

"Public or private?"

"Which would you prefer?"

"Private. Definitely private," she cooed, fingers moving up his chest. "Why don't we go back to your loft?"

"Sounds great."

"Doesn't it? You get my fur and I'll meet you downstairs."

Lance didn't like the last words he had just heard. Was Erica planning to pull another disappearing act on him? "Downstairs?" he skeptically asked.

"I'll be waiting," she promised. "No more games."

Once Lance went off, Erica sagged with relief. She only had an hour or two left of this revolting charade. Then she would be finished with Lance. Touching him the entire evening, having him touch her and pretending to be sexually interested in him, had turned her stomach. But soon it would all be over.

She opened her evening bag, gazing at her carefully hidden gun. As she was about to touch the cold steel, she heard a voice behind her.

"If it isn't New York's reigning slut."

Erica snapped shut her evening bag before slowly turning to face Georgina. She could see she was in a foul mood, and an inner voice told her to ignore the comment. Georgina needed her pity, not her anger. But the pain from her loss of Jeff was still fresh, so she lashed out just as scathingly.

"And if it isn't New York's reigning drunk. Ever think of rating bars, Georgina? You've been to so many, you could probably write a few books. Of course, you'd have to do some thinking, and that's not something you do too well."

"Don't talk to me that way!" Georgina's voice rose and was caught by receptive ears. Eyes turned to watch the two women.

"I'm here to warn you. Keep away from my husband."

"Shouldn't you be telling Lance to keep away from me?

After all, he's in hot pursuit, and I can't help it if I'm the one he prefers."

"Sluts like you are a dime a dozen." Georgina smiled smugly. "Jeff Porter will attest to that."

The mention of Jeff's name was like a slap in the face, enraging Erica even further.

"No thanks to you. Pull another stunt like the one you pulled with those photographs, and I'll make sure you regret it." With those final words, Erica left Georgina standing alone.

"Is that a threat?" Georgina screamed, no longer caring who heard her. "If it is, I've got one for you. Stay away from Lance or I'll kill you."

Erica didn't even turn around. She just kept walking to the elevators.

"Do you hear me? I swear I'll kill you!"

Beverly's knuckles were chalk white as she grasped her evening bag. Rage coursed through her blood, and a glare of searing hatred was directed solely at Robyn.

She wanted to scream at the top of her lungs in anguish. The unfairness of it all! Marriage! Scott was going to marry Robyn. He couldn't. She wouldn't let him. She wouldn't allow him to be deceived.

She had to save him from making a grave mistake. She had to open his eyes to the truth. The time to take action had arrived. She had to act before it was too late. Once Scott knew the truth about Robyn, there would be no wedding.

With that purpose in mind, Beverly glided in the direction of the VCR.

The exchange of tapes was pathetically easy. The VCR was hidden behind a curtained area. Robyn and Scott were surrounded by many well-wishers. Georgina and Erica had the rest of the party's attention. No one was looking at her or at the television screens which momentarily went blank. All she had to do was eject the first tape, insert her tape and then press the play button.

Easing from behind the curtain, Beverly rejoined the others, waiting for the show to begin.

* * *

First it was the changing expressions. Then the sound of the music. An audible gasp of shock replaced by the scent of scandal.

It was then that Robyn knew her past had caught up with her. But why tonight? Why tonight of all nights?

She turned her head to the giant television screen behind her and Scott. She nearly fell to her knees. One of the most sexually graphic scenes from *Head Nurse* was playing. The hot tub scene. Her face filled the screen as she knelt before Dennis Lord.

"Robyn, what's going on?"

No other words followed. With dread in her heart, Robyn looked away from the screen and into Scott's face.

Clearly he was shocked. The blood had drained from his face and he stood pale and trembling before her. She reached out a tentative hand to his, but it was angrily shoved away.

"What is this?" he whispered fiercely, suddenly aware of all the eyes watching the screen, watching them. "Some kind of a joke?"

"I meant to tell you."

His eyes were cold and passionless, devoid of their earlier love and warmth. "Convenient answer, wouldn't you say?"

"I *was* going to tell you," she implored. "You must believe me."

"When?" he demanded harshly. "When were you going to tell me? After the wedding?" He looked back up at the screen, and when he spoke again, his voice was broken. "My God, how could you not tell me? I thought you loved me."

"I do love you. I'll always love you," she cried. "You have to give me a chance to explain."

"What could you possibly say? How can you say you love me? How can I love you? I don't even know you."

The words stabbed achingly at her heart, and Robyn fought for the words that would fix everything between them. "Scott, don't do this to us!"

"I haven't done anything," he declared with finality. "You have. You've destroyed us."

Robyn struggled for an answer. Suddenly she became aware of the photographers and columnists swarming in. Cameras were flashing, pencils were scribbling and questions being thrown. Her past was on display for the entire world to see. Yet they had no right to witness what was private between herself and Scott. They had no right to judge her.

She brushed away her surging tears, plunging through the crowd as she tried to get away. She had only two words for Scott. "I'm sorry," she whispered, returning his ring as he stood alone before the microphone. "I'm sorry."

36

Beverly was so proud of herself! She almost couldn't contain her glee. The press had descended like vultures, Robyn had fled in shame, and now Scott remained a broken man in front of the microphone where only moments before he had proposed marriage to Robyn. Beverly managed to compose a look of comfort and sorrow as she made her way to the man she intended to regain.

Yet before she could even take two steps forward, she found her path blocked by Kristen Adams.

"Where do you think you're going?"

How tiresome. The devoted roomie protecting her best friend's interests.

"To Scott. He needs me."

"Scott doesn't need you. He hasn't needed you in a long time."

"Who does he need? Robyn?" Beverly scoffed harshly. "So she can spring a few more secrets on him? She's out of his life for good."

"Don't count on it. Scott and Robyn love each other. They're going to overcome this." Kristen sipped at her champagne, then unexpectedly splashed the front of Beverly's gown. "How clumsy of me." Kristen dropped her glass on a nearby table, waving her fingers at Beverly as she left. "Looks like you'll have to clean yourself up. You're all wet."

Fuming at Kristen, Beverly dabbed furiously at the champagne stain before giving up the task. A wet dress wasn't going to stop her. She raced toward Scott as he headed for the elevators, giving him her most sympathetic smile.

She reached for his arm through the crowd. "Scott, I don't know what to say."

He waved away her words. The pain was still evident on his face. "I can't talk about it. I can't."

She nodded understandingly. "I'm here if you need me. To talk or listen. Remember that."

"I will."

Beverly allowed her hold on Scott's arm to linger before the elevator arrived. While they waited, a photographer snapped away at the two of them.

For Scott the action was upsetting, the arriving elevator a sanctuary in which he made his escape, leaving Beverly behind. She didn't mind. Nor did she mind the photographer.

Erica took a deep breath. Having escaped into the loft's bathroom, she prepared the final steps of her plan while Lance, out in the bedroom, amorously awaited her return.

Once they had crossed the loft's threshold, he'd been on her. Hot. Insistent. Demanding. Ready to release his pent-up lust. Returning his kisses and caresses with equal fervor had only furthered his hunger, and he'd wasted no time steering her into his bedroom.

"I can't wait to have you," he had whispered in the darkness, his hands exploring her body possessively.

"Only a few seconds more," she'd responded, detaching herself from his arms and darting into the bathroom. "Let me take care of a few things."

Opening her evening bag, Erica removed the gun she had brought. It was an ugly, brutal-looking thing, weighing heavily in her hand. She hated the sight of it, the cold feel of it. But she reminded herself how much more she hated the man in the other room, and the gun slipped easily into her hands.

"Erica, I'm waiting," Lance called.

"Coming." She left her evening bag, positioning her arms behind her back.

Lance, still fully clothed, reclined on top of his bed. On his face was a look of anticipated content. His arms were open, waiting for her to drop into them. "I'm waiting," he repeated.

"Wait a little longer."

Thinking she was only teasing, he asked, "How much longer?"

"Forever."

Lance propped himself on a pillow, the answer confusing him. "What?"

"You must be insane if you think I'm going to let you make love to me."

"Cut the crap and get over here," he ordered, starting to rise from the bed.

Erica brought her arms into full view, revealing the hidden gun. She pointed it directly at him. "On your feet."

Lance laughed, clearly amused. "Know how to use that thing?"

"Would you like to find out?" She waved the gun threateningly between his legs. "Provoke me. I'd love the chance."

"What do you want?"

"The negatives."

"Negatives?"

"Don't play dumb with me. I know all about the nude photographs you took of me. I saw them. Jeff saw them. Georgina made sure of that."

Lance still wouldn't admit his guilt. "What are you talking about?"

"Don't deny it!" she screamed. "You drugged me the afternoon I was here. You stripped me and then took a whole series of nude photographs. You've destroyed my relationship with Jeff, and I'm not going to allow you to get away with it. You're going to fix things."

Lance reclined comfortably. "Am I?"

"You are," Erica pronounced with steely determination. "You're going to explain it all to Jeff."

"What's in it for me?"

"Nothing!" she shrieked. "You've got a gun pointed at you. It's going to stay pointed until you do whatever I tell you."

Lance gave a pompous laugh. "Wrong. Go ahead and shoot me. See how far it will get you. You need me to set things straight with lover boy. Jeff will still think you willingly posed for those photographs if I don't. If that happens, you haven't got a chance in hell of getting him back."

Erica stared at him coldly. "You're going to help me."

"Slip between the sheets with me and we'll discuss it."

Consumed with rage and her inability to force Lance to do her bidding, Erica stormed at him, brandishing her gun like a club. Springing from the bed, Lance seized her arms above her head and wrenched the gun free. It flew across the bedroom as Erica was thrown upon the bed. Without wasting a second, Lance jumped on top of her, pinning her down with his knees.

"This is the way it should be," he crooned.

"Let me go," she cried, struggling to break free.

"Such impatience." He meshed his lips to hers forcefully, pushing his tongue inside her mouth. He placed a hand on her neck. "So long and smooth. Soft. Like a swan's." He tightened his hold. "So easy to break."

"Please," she begged, an unwanted thought slipping into her mind. "Please."

His hand moved to the bodice of her gown, fingering the silk before ripping it away and exposing her breasts. "How lovely. Just as I remembered. I can't wait to see everything again."

Lance unbuttoned his shirt, tossing it to one side. Then his belt was undone and, at the sound of the dangling buckle joining with his opening zipper, Erica tried to renew her struggle. But the liquor she had consumed and the total exhaustion of her body defeated her. Try as she did, the determination of her soul against the violation about to take place wasn't enough to renew her strength.

"You don't want to do this," she reasoned, squeezing her eyes shut, as if by magic he would disappear. She opened her eyes and he was still there. She looked into Lance's eyes for mercy but found none. "You don't want to do this," she repeated.

"Don't I? I'm tired of waiting. Tired of playing games. You're going to get exactly what you've got coming to you." He seized her face between a hand, wedging her legs open with a knee. He allowed his eyes to linger between her legs. "And I'm going to get exactly what's coming to me."

There was a persistent knocking at the door, awakening a dozing Kristen. She jumped from the couch, scattering pillows and blankets as she hurried to answer the door.

"Robyn, I've been so worried. Where have you—"

The rest of the words died in Kristen's mouth as a sobbing Erica collapsed in her arms. Icy fear gripped Kristen at the bedraggled sight of Erica. Gone was the jealousy she had experienced earlier that evening. There were ugly bruises around Erica's wrists and neck, and the front of her gown had been torn open. Kristen led Erica to the couch before going into the kitchen for a bottle of brandy.

Kristen's hands fumbled with the glasses. She didn't want this to be what she was thinking. She would never wish such a thing on any woman.

She handed a glass of brandy to Erica, urging her to sip slowly. Some color returned to Erica's tearstained cheeks, although she was still trembling.

Unable to ask the question, Kristen placed a reassuring hand on Erica's. Erica looked up at her, nodding slowly.

"Raped," she whispered. "I was raped."

Kristen jumped to her feet, heading for the phone. "We have to call the police."

"You can't call the police. The police can't help me. Nobody can."

Kristen stared at Erica helplessly. "What do you mean? Of course the police can help you."

"You don't understand," Erica stated wearily, closing her eyes as she relived Lance's final words.

"Admit it. You loved it."

Covering herself with a sheet, Erica picked her torn gown off the floor, glaring darkly at Lance. "You'll pay for this."

"Will I?" he taunted. "I doubt it. Everyone at the party saw the way you were coming on to me. It was a foregone conclusion that we'd wind up in bed together. Half the party will attest to that."

He inspected himself before a mirror, noting the scratches she had inflicted on his arms and chest. "Cry rape if you like, but in the end whose story are they going to believe? Yours or mine? You'll only make things worse for yourself. Whatever hopes you had of getting Jeff back would be dashed. If he hears about this, you'd only be adding more fuel to his hatred. If you decide to press charges, I'll make sure he does. I'll definitely make sure he hears my version of the *truth* and not yours."

Lance picked up the gun he had thrown across the bedroom, emptying the bullets before dropping the gun at Erica's feet. "Next time you come, don't bring this."

"Next time?"

"Didn't I tell you?" He looked down at her. "We're going to be lovers."

"Never!" she raged.

"Never say never," Lance silkily explained. "Let me enlighten you. You signed a model's release for those nude photos. If you don't agree to sleep with me again, I'll make sure those pictures are printed in the sleaziest of magazines. You wouldn't want that. Think what it would do to your career."

"You can't get away with this!"

"But I can. Sleep with me one more time, in a more accommodating manner," he stressed, "and I'll be more than willing to hand over the negatives. Choose not to, and I'll ruin you."

"How can you expect me to trust you?"

"You can't," he flippantly replied. "I could be lying and force you to sleep with me again and again."

Numbed by Lance's words, words that held so much power, Erica did not respond.

"Face it, sugar. Your little plan backfired, and I now hold all the cards."

With those final words, he left. Erica didn't notice his departure. She just stared at the empty gun before her, wishing it had bullets, wishing she could use them on herself.

"Why can't you go to the police? Erica? Erica, are you listening?"

Erica looked into a concerned Kristen's face. "I'm sorry. I was remembering."

"Erica, you have to go to the police and tell them what happened."

"I've already told you. The police can't help me."

"Then why did you come here? What can I do that they can't?"

"Nothing. I didn't want to go to my apartment. No one is there. I'm all alone. I was afraid of what I would try to do to myself. It happened nearby and I had to tell someone. You were closest."

There were bars and nightclubs all over the Village. Erica must have been attacked after leaving one. But where had Lance been? "Where did it happen?"

"His loft."

The first alarm went off in Kristen's head. "Where was Lance?"

"I was so stupid," Erica raged, ignoring Kristen's question. "I thought I could handle him. I thought I could get him to do what I wanted. But I was wrong."

"Where was Lance?" Kristen asked again. "Did he leave you alone? Did someone break in? Was someone waiting when you got there?"

"He overpowered me and I tried to fight. I really did. It didn't do any good. He was just too strong."

Kristen seized Erica roughly by the shoulders. "Who did this to you, Erica? Who was it?" she demanded.

"Lance."

Kristen dropped her hands from Erica's shoulders, blinking uncomprehendingly. "No."

"Lance Richards raped me."

When Robyn walked into the apartment, she found Kristen still awake.

"You didn't have to wait up," she admonished.

"I wanted to see how you were doing."

Robyn gave a brave smile. "Hanging in there."

"Where've you been? It's two A.M."

"Walking . . . thinking . . . asking myself a lot of questions."

"Find any answers?"

"I don't know," she admitted. "My entire world has been torn apart. I've got to put it back together."

"Do you think Tiffany was behind the switched tapes?"

"I don't think so. With the tape out in the open, there's nothing left to use against me. She wouldn't be able to blackmail me. Tonight's stunt wasn't Tiffany's style. She likes to keep her tracks covered." Robyn gave Kristen a fierce look of determination. "I won't let myself be destroyed by whoever did this. I'm going to fight. I won't lose Scott. Not this way."

"You're not going to lose Scott. Give him some time. He'll come around."

"There's nothing else I can do," Robyn said resignedly.

"Think you can handle this? Erica Shelton is asleep in my bedroom. She came here looking a mess." Kristen took a deep breath before plunging into her next words. "She says Lance raped her."

"How horrible!" A fleeting image of Vaughn forcing himself on her flashed through Robyn's mind. She noticed Kristen's hesitancy to continue. "Don't you believe her?"

"I don't know." Kristen paced the floor furiously. "It's obvious she was attacked, but why would Lance do such a thing? I've been asking myself that question for hours."

"Isn't Erica going to the police?"

"She says she can't."

"Can't?" Robyn gave Kristen an incredulous look. "Why not?"

Kristen threw her arms up in the air. "She refuses to discuss it. She says nobody can help her."

"Sounds like there's more to this than meets the eye. I'd advise you to stay out of it."

"How can I? I'm already in the thick of it. I don't know what to do or who to believe." Kristen pointed in the direction of the bedroom. "For all I know, she could be making the whole thing up."

"Why would she?"

"Jealousy. Maybe she wants to break up Lance and me."

"You don't believe that," Robyn stated. "Have you spoken to Lance to get his side of things?"

"There's no answer at the loft. I thought I'd wait till you got back before going over. I didn't want to leave Erica alone."

"Why not wait until the morning?"

Kristen stubbornly shook her head, slipping into her leather aviator jacket. "This can't wait. Maybe Lance will be at the loft by the time I get there. If not, I'll wait outside his door. He has to explain this to me. He's the only one who can make sense out of it all." She grabbed her keys, giving Robyn a hug. "I'll see you in the morning. Try and get some rest."

"I will, but be careful."

"Don't worry. The night's almost over. What else could possibly happen?"

Robyn had just closed her weary eyes, drifting off to sleep, when the phone rang. Hurrying into the living room so she wouldn't disturb Erica, she quickly picked up.

"Hello? Kristen?"

"Wrong! Want to take another guess?"

Tiffany. Robyn grew cold at the sound of her voice. "What do you want?"

"I know you've been waiting for this call. How's tricks?"

Robyn gripped the phone tightly. "What do you want?" she repeated.

"Chill out," Tiffany cooed. "I thought we'd get together for a little face-to-face. Say in an hour at the Howard Johnson's in Times Square."

"Why?"

Tiffany's voice turned hard and dangerous. Gone was the sugar and sweetness overlaying her words. "Honey, I am living, breathing dynamite," she began in a carefully measured tone, "and if you don't get your ass down here, I'm going to blow the lid off your nice new world."

Robyn left a note for Kristen in case she returned before she got back. It was ambiguous, but she didn't want to go into details, nor did she want Kristen to worry.

She felt guilty about leaving Erica alone, but she was sure Erica wouldn't awaken. When she'd checked on her in Kristen's bedroom, Erica looked as though she were in a deep sleep.

As she was preparing to leave, the phone rang again. Was it Tiffany checking to see if she was on her way?

"Hello?"

No one answered on the other end.

"Hello?" Robyn could hear the sound of deep breathing. "Is anyone there?" Still no answer. But someone was listening. The deep breathing was making Robyn nervous, although she didn't know why. She hung up and quickly hurried out of the apartment.

At first Erica had no recollection of where she was. But then, as sleep slipped away, she remembered. Two hours had elapsed since she had closed her eyes. It was three-fifteen.

She knocked on the bedroom door across the hall, and when no one answered, peeked in. The bed looked like it had been recently slept in. Heading into the living room in search of Kristen, she found Robyn's note.

Suddenly aware that she was alone in the apartment, Erica wrapped her arms around herself. In doing so, she touched the tattered remains of her evening gown. The jade-green silk she had purposely worn to entice Lance, to show off her body in a sexy, provocative way, was a reminder of the battle she'd lost.

Stripping off the gown, Erica jammed it into the garbage, then decided to take a shower. All she wanted to do was cleanse herself. She had to rid herself of Lance's touch.

Luxuriating under the warm cascading water, she relished the relief it brought. It loosened her muscles and lessened her soreness as she looked forward to returning to bed. All she wanted to do was sleep. Then she could forget the nightmare of this evening.

Wrapping her wet hair in a towel, she searched in Robyn's bedroom for something to wear. Her fingers touched the silk monogrammed negligee and covering sheath from the fashion show. She removed it from the closet so she could admire its loveliness closer.

As she was getting ready to return the negligee, she heard

a knock at the front door. Without thinking, Erica threw the negligee and sheath over herself.

Could Kristen or Robyn have forgotten their keys? Pressing her eye to the peephole, she was surprised at what she saw.

It was the back of a blond head, descending into the high collar of a silver-fox fur. There was no mistaking either.

Georgina. But what was she doing here, and how had Georgina known she was here?

Erica wasn't in the mood for another confrontation, and didn't have the strength for it. All she wanted was to sleep . . . sleep forever.

Opening the door only a fraction, she pressed her face into the crack. "What do you want, Georgina?"

The door, flung suddenly back, smashed into Erica's face, sending her reeling into the wall and onto the floor. Blood spurted from her nose, and before she could get back on her feet, she was struck and felt a sharp prick between the shoulders.

She sprawled back on the floor, landing hard on her stomach. At first she cared only about the blood spurting from her nose. Then she saw that there was too much blood.

Flowing down her arms.

Snaking down her legs.

Sprinkling her neck and breasts.

So much blood. It couldn't all be coming from her nose.

Then, twisting around, she saw the flash of a long silver blade stained with blood before it sank into her back. And then she felt the pain. Hot and searing. The blade was removed and droplets of her blood splashed through the air, landing on the wall and floor.

Erica fought to retain consciousness. Tried to fight back. But couldn't.

Blood began pooling on the floor.

The knife kept entering and leaving her back.

Her arms.

Her neck.

Again.

And again.

* * *

The cup of coffee was placed before Robyn. Forty-five minutes later the cup of coffee remained untouched. There was still no sign of Tiffany. Except for Robyn and two waitresses, the restaurant was empty. Robyn decided she would give Tiffany fifteen minutes more before leaving.

Obviously blackmail was on Tiffany's agenda. What other reason could there be for this meeting? Had Tiffany been the one to show *Head Nurse* at the party? Had that been meant as a warning? If so, Robyn was prepared to deal with her. Once Tiffany started listing her demands, she was going to be speechless at Robyn's response.

"Waiting long?"

Robyn threw her head back at the sound of Tiffany's voice.

"My, aren't we antsy!" Tiffany slid into the booth. "Not used to keeping such late hours? You used to, remember?"

"I remember a lot of things," Robyn stated coldly.

"Still carrying a grudge about Cara? She's dead and buried. Forget about her. You should remember other things. Things you'd like to forget."

"Let's get down to business."

"What? No small talk?" Tiffany pretended to look affronted. "Aren't you the least bit curious as to what I've been up to?"

"Not particularly. What do you want?"

"You don't have to sound so suspicious. I haven't asked for anything." Tiffany gave a cunning smile. "Yet. But since you've brought up the topic, I'm ready to go into details. You have an excess of cash and I have a lack. I want five hundred thousand dollars by tomorrow evening."

"What am I paying for?"

"Silence. You won't have to worry about Scott Kendall finding out all your nasty secrets. They'll remain confidential. Only between us."

"Until the next time you demand payment."

Tiffany shrugged her shoulders. "Probably. I can't predict the future. However, it would be nice to know there was someone I could depend on to lend a *helping hand* should I ever need it."

"If I decide not to pay?"

"Then I'll let the cat out of the bag," Tiffany declared without hesitation. "I'll make sure your past is exposed, and you'll lose it all. Money. Career. Lover." She glared hatefully at Robyn. "Don't think I won't. You don't know how much of a temptation it's been. But if I'd squealed, I would have come up empty-handed, and I intended on collecting from you." She waved to the waitress, ordering a cup of coffee and a doughnut, then turned back to Robyn. "What's it going to be?"

Robyn didn't hesitate. "I'm not paying you a dime."

"Don't mess with me, Robyn, otherwise you'll learn the same lesson as Cara and Vaughn." Tiffany saw the look of shock on Robyn's face. "That's right. Vaughn is dead. He tried crossing me, and I killed him. He had it coming. Don't you think you at least owe me for that?"

"I don't owe you anything! Vaughn got exactly what he deserved. Don't expect me to start shedding tears, and don't expect me to give in to your blackmail."

"You'll pay," Tiffany ordered, "or you'll find your past splattered on every tabloid from coast to coast."

"It's happening as we speak."

"What are you talking about?"

"The morning papers should be hitting the stands soon. Pick one up. Someone's beaten you to the punch. My past is already news."

A look of disbelief washed over Tiffany's face as she stubbornly shook her head. All the money she had dreamed of getting was gone. "It can't be."

The waitress arrived with Tiffany's coffee and doughnut but she pushed them away, looking at Robyn beseechingly. "Couldn't you help me? I wouldn't have blown the whistle on you. Those were only empty threats."

"Hah! What a lie! You would have milked me dry and then gone to the press."

"A few thousand dollars," Tiffany begged. "You'll never see me again."

"You're right about never seeing you again." Robyn got to her feet. "Try calling or coming near me, and I'll have you arrested for harassment. Everything I have today I've earned through hard work. I've built a new life for myself. You were too lazy to even try, and now you think I'm going to let you sponge off me? Guess again." Robyn threw a five-dollar bill on the table for her coffee. "I should feel sorry for you, but I don't. Your life is a mess and you have no one to blame but yourself.

"My past has nothing to do with my life today. You and Vaughn caused me to suffer. I did what I had to do in order to survive. I have nothing to be ashamed of. Neither you or anyone else is going to take away my self-respect."

Without so much as a look back at Tiffany, Robyn left the restaurant, vowing she was no longer going to hide from her past. Her encounter with Tiffany left her feeling victorious. She was going to confront the scandal and gossip over *Head Nurse.* She was going to stand up for herself, and she was going to win!

37

At first Robyn thought the bright red splotches were paint. Splattered on the walls. Pooling on the floor. Sprinkling the furniture. Puzzled, she brought her finger to a shiny droplet. It was blood.

Moving deeper into the apartment on legs ready to collapse, Robyn tried to remain calm. Then her eyes fell upon Erica's bloody corpse.

Deep gouges had been inflicted on her arms and legs. Her back was crisscrossed with bloody slashes, and her face had been savagely sliced to ribbons. She was splayed out on the floor, and through the bloody pulp which had once been her face, her eyes stared out sightlessly in terror. Her mouth was frozen open in a final agonized scream.

Closing her eyes in the hopes of blotting out the carnage before her, Robyn could still visualize the scene. It smothered her senses, and for a moment she thought she would faint. Reeling into the kitchen, she picked up the phone and dialed 911. As soon as a voice answered, Robyn released a hysterical sob before trying to describe the scene in the next room. Words failed her. The sight was just too brutal and horrifying. Who could have done such a thing?

Georgina groggily opened her eyes to darkness. She was in her bedroom but couldn't remember how she had gotten there. The last thing she remembered was being at the Wellington party, confronting Erica.

She was still wearing her gown from the previous evening, and there was a constant throbbing in her head. Cupping her face in her palms while massaging her temples, she grimly noted that her palms were sticky.

Georgina suddenly felt like sobbing. Once again she had spent a night in drunken oblivion. When was it going to end? When was she going to put a stop to it all? This time she was scared, and a premonition of doom washed over her. Maybe it was too late. Maybe she had waited too long to help herself.

Deciding she might feel better after a shower and a fresh change of clothes, she went into the bathroom. Only after turning on the fluorescent lights did she see that her hands were covered with blood. She froze at the sight, instinctively knowing the blood was not hers.

She didn't even stop to think. Instead, she raced for the shower, tearing off her clothes and plunging herself under the water, immediately scrubbing herself with soap and not looking at the draining water, thinking if she washed away the blood, she could pretend it had never existed.

But when she returned to the bedroom, opening up the drapes and turning on the lights, wracking her brains to recall the elusive bits of the previous evening, she found herself facing another piece of evidence. Draped across the bottom of her bed was her silver fox fur, its sleeves covered with blood. Shocked, Georgina slumped to the floor.

What had she done? Where had she gone? She forced herself to concentrate, but came up with nothing. Looking around the bedroom, she saw empty liquor bottles. Clearly she had gone on a binge, but what results had it brought?

With trembling fingers she dialed the only person who could help her, the only one who might have a clue as to what she had done last night. Desperately clutching the phone to her ear, she prayed for Beverly to pick up.

"Hello?"

Georgina tried to keep her voice calm. "Beverly, it's Georgina."

"Georgina?" A sound of relief entered Beverly's voice. "I've been going frantic."

Georgina felt her stomach tighten. "Why?"

"Don't you remember?"

Pinpoints of fear traveled through Georgina's body. "Remember? Remember what?"

"Last night. You were in such a state! You wouldn't listen to a word I said, and after you left my duplex I was worried to death."

"What are you talking about?" Georgina asked sharply, trying to get her wits together. She didn't remember going to Beverly's duplex, but was reluctant to admit her mind was a total blank. "I had too much to drink last night and just woke up. My memory is a little fuzzy. Try to fill me in."

"You arrived at my duplex around one-thirty—"

"How was I?" Georgina broke in.

Beverly's voice became concerned. "There's no other way to say this except that you were extremely drunk and you were in a violent, ugly mood, ranting and raving about Erica Shelton."

"What did I say?"

"You called her a whore and said she didn't deserve to live after coming between you and Lance. You said you wished she were dead. I tried to calm you down. I made a pot of coffee and insisted you spend the night, but you wouldn't listen. All you wanted was more liquor. When I wouldn't give you any, you pulled out a knife. It was then that I got scared."

Georgina tried to recall the scene Beverly was replaying but came up with nothing. "Then what happened?" she whispered harshly.

"You left. You wouldn't let me come near you. You kept waving a ten-inch knife in my face, and I certainly wasn't going to try and take it away. You told me you were going to track down Erica and put a scare into her. You didn't do anything you'll regret, did you Georgina?"

Georgina's eyes locked on the bloodstains on her silver fox fur. Was it Erica's blood? Had she done something to her? She stared numbly at her washed palms as her body sagged at the news just given to her. "I don't know what I did last night," she admitted. Her voice started rising hysterically. "I can't remember a thing."

"Calm down. I'm on my way over."

Georgina pulled frantically at her hair after disconnecting Beverly, not knowing what to do. Then she dialed Erica's number. The line kept ringing and ringing but no one answered. She refused to hang up.

Erica, where are you? she fearfully wondered, her eyes falling back to the bloodstained sleeves of her silver fox fur.

In her hotel room Tiffany stared at the array of newspapers she had bought. Robyn hadn't been lying. Last night the elite of New York had had a sneak preview of *Head Nurse.* The shit had really hit the fan. Obviously Robyn wasn't going to cough up any cash. But there was another source. No matter what the situation, Tiffany always managed to find an angle. This time was no exception.

She stared at the photograph of Beverly and Scott, savoring the information in the sidebar. How enlightening. The two had once been lovers and talk of marriage had been in the air. With Robyn out of the way it looked like Beverly had a clear path back to Scott.

Suddenly it all became crystal clear. No wonder Beverly had been so anxious for any damaging information on Robyn. Like a fool, she'd fallen for Beverly's story, given her the tape and then been brushed aside. Beverly had been after Scott the entire time. Robyn had been an obstacle needing elimination.

There was money to be made. Lots of it. More than she had even imagined getting from Robyn. If she revealed to Scott Kendall Beverly's part in the unveiling of Robyn's past, Beverly wouldn't stand a chance of getting him back. He had dropped Robyn faster than a hot potato. He'd do the same with Beverly. Scott Kendall didn't seem to approve of deception and lies. Learning of Beverly's underhandedness would not only ruin the chances of a reconciliation, but might also send Scott back to Robyn.

Yes, Tiffany mused, she certainly had that rich bitch over a barrel. There was no way Beverly would want her handiwork revealed. Helping Beverly keep her little secret was going to cost her plenty.

"Gentlemen, I've called this meeting because we must discuss a strategy." Scott locked eyes with each member of the board. Notwithstanding his own personal feelings, as president of Wellington Cosmetics he could not ignore what had happened the previous evening. Despite the pain he was in, the company still came first. "I'm sure you're all aware of the fiasco that took place yesterday evening."

"What are your suggestions to alleviate the situation?" Richard Templeton asked sharply.

"Do tell us," Arthur Landers quipped sarcastically. "I'm sure you've got another dynamic plan."

With exhausted eyes, Scott looked from Templeton to Landers. Apparently they weren't ready to support him as they had at the first meeting. They were out for blood.

Today promised to be a major headache. He had gone without a wink of sleep and was still in a state of confusion, shuffling through a kaleidoscope of feelings as he tried to accept, or at least acknowledge, what he had learned about Robyn. Despite the evidence, it was impossible.

He needed some time alone, yet everyone was fighting for his attention. Phones were ringing off the hook, and reporters and photographers were camping out in front of the building and at his apartment. Now he had to contend with an angry board of directors.

"I don't have a plan," he admitted wearily.

"Then we will present one before taking a vote," Richard Templeton decreed as Arthur Landers nodded his approval, indicating Templeton should continue. "Robyn Prescott has a morals clause in her contract. We will invoke the clause and force her to resign as the Fresh and Lovely Girl."

"Isn't that rash?" Kyle said. At Scott's insistence, Kyle had appeared at the meeting. In his current state of mind, Scott believed it would be better if Kyle were present. "Robyn Prescott has given one hundred percent to this company. She's done a fantastic job for us, and we shouldn't drop her so fast. During her entire time as the Fresh and

Lovely Girl she hasn't done anything we should be ashamed of."

"Mr. Kendall didn't waste any time dropping her," one board member pointed out.

"My private life is my own affair," Scott declared stiffly, attempting to smother his growing anger.

"Wrong," Arthur Landers stated forcefully. "Where's our credibility if we keep Robyn as the Fresh and Lovely Girl after you've dropped her from your life? She goes."

"Has anyone spoken with Robyn to get her side of the story?" Kyle asked in general, although his words were aimed directly at Scott. "I think it would be wise before taking a vote. I'm sure there's more to this than meets the eye. Don't you agree, Scott?"

"I suppose," he grudgingly admitted.

"I don't see the point," Templeton stated. His next words were interrupted when Scott's secretary stepped into the boardroom. Scott tried not to be annoyed with the woman, even though he had left strict instructions that he was not to be disturbed.

"Yes, Janet?"

"Excuse me, but there's a call on your private line. Samantha D'Urban. She insists on speaking with you."

In his office Scott angrily seized his private line. "Look, Samantha, we're still trying to wade through this mess. Get off my back. As soon as we've reached a decision, you'll be the first to know."

"This doesn't have anything to do with business," Samantha replied. "Just get yourself down to St. Vincent's Hospital."

"Are you insane? I'm in the middle of a board meeting."

"Scott, there's been a murder at Robyn's apartment."

He didn't hear anything else. Dropping the phone, he raced from his office to the elevators.

"Mr. Kendall, what's wrong?" Janet asked, alarmed at his agitated state.

"Get Kyle Masters. Have him speak with Samantha."

"Where are you going?"

Scott didn't even bother to answer, rushing into the arriving elevator.

* * *

"You're looking much better than last evening," Beverly greeted, brushing cheeks with Georgina. Beverly headed into the living room, tossing her mink to one side and settling on the couch as she removed her black leather gloves in one fluid motion. "Start from the beginning."

Georgina shivered, trying to block out the bloody images she kept forming in her head. "I'm afraid I might have harmed Erica," she whispered hoarsely.

"What gave you that idea?" Beverly picked up on Georgina's hesitancy. "I want to help. Don't you trust me? Anything you say will stay between us."

Georgina wiped away the tears streaming down her cheeks. "I woke up with blood on my hands."

"Is that all?" Beverly was hardly shocked. "I'm sure there's a perfectly logical explanation."

"There's more," Georgina continued. "My silver fox fur has blood on it, and I haven't been able to get in touch with Erica. I've been calling all morning."

"Did you try Lance?"

"There's no answer."

"You're jumping to conclusions. Where's the fur? I'd like to have a look at it."

"Upstairs in my bedroom closet."

Beverly went to the bar, pouring a stiff drink. She handed it to Georgina. "Lord knows you don't need any more liquor, but you're a bundle of nerves. Stay down here and sip at this. I'll take a look at the fur myself."

Ten minutes later Beverly was back in the living room. Georgina jumped to her feet.

"It's blood, all right," Beverly confirmed, "but how do we know it's human blood? Could you have had an accident with your car? Maybe you ran over a dog or a cat and then got out of the car to take a look."

"There's nothing I'd like to believe more, but there isn't a dent or scratch on my car."

"Suppose it is human blood. Why are you so sure it's Erica's? You could have been involved in a barroom brawl."

"It's a possibility I hadn't thought of," Georgina conceded.

"Listen, I'll take the fur back to my duplex and have it cleaned. Would that make you feel better?"

"Yes. I'd like it out of the house. All I do is stare at it."

"What about the knife you brought to my duplex?"

"What about it?"

"Where is it?"

"I don't know." Georgina started getting agitated. "I don't remember bringing a knife to your duplex. I don't even remember going there."

"Calm down. We're going to straighten this out. I promise. Let's go look in the kitchen," Beverly suggested.

Arranged over the stove were a selection of carving knives. All were clean and gleaming. Beverly removed the largest, holding it before her eyes. She twisted it from left to right, the sharp blade catching the light. "This is the one you had last night," she confirmed.

Georgina's stomach lurched at the idea that she might have used the knife on Erica. "You don't really think I went after her, do you?"

"Of course not." Beverly replaced the knife, leading Georgina back to the living room. "I think you're making too much out of this. You went on a binge and blacked out. My advice is to forget the whole thing and let this be a lesson. You've got to get help for your drinking problem. I'm sure Erica is fine, but next time you might not be as lucky." Beverly wrapped an arm around Georgina's shoulders. "Why don't we have Bettina fix us lunch?"

"Bettina's on vacation."

"Oh yes, you told me last week," Beverly remarked. "How could I have forgotten? Well, since Bettina's not here, let's go out for lunch. My treat. I've got an interesting stack of newspapers in my limousine. I'm sure you'll enjoy them."

"Really?"

"They'll definitely perk you up. Robyn Prescott is in all the columns. She's probably no longer going to be the Fresh and Lovely Girl. Isn't that marvelous?"

"I suppose." Although she was trying to concentrate on Beverly's words, she couldn't stop thinking of Erica.

"What's wrong?" Beverly asked as her chauffeur pulled the limousine to the curb.

"I can't shake the feeling that something's happened to Erica. I can't help feeling I'm somehow responsible."

"Nonsense." Beverly waved a dismissive hand. "Forget Erica Shelton."

Scott arrived at St. Vincent's in record time, immediately searching for Samantha. The words from her phone call kept reverberating in his mind. Murder. His fears only increased as he went from nurse to nurse. No one named Robyn Prescott had been admitted into the hospital. With relieved eyes he caught sight of Kristen coming off the elevators and rushed to her side.

He demanded answers. "Kristen, what's going on? Where's Robyn? Has anything happened to her?"

"Scott, calm down. I've had a hell of a night and need some coffee. Come with me to the cafeteria."

Scott grabbed Kristen roughly by the arm. "The last twelve hours haven't exactly been a picnic for me. I want answers! Samantha said there had been a murder at the apartment. Robyn isn't listed as a patient, and you're standing before me. What's going on?"

"Robyn was admitted under a different name. We thought it would be best, considering the press and all."

Scott released his hold on Kristen's arm. "She's all right?"

"Only in a state of shock."

"When Samantha told me there had been a murder at the apartment, I assumed the worst. Robyn was all I could think about. I didn't bother listening to the rest of the conversation. I raced over here. What happened?"

"Erica Shelton was murdered."

Scott rubbed a hand over his face. "I don't believe it. She was such a sweet kid. But what was she doing at the apartment, and where were you and Robyn?"

Deciding it would be best not to say much until after she had spoken to the police, Kristen sketched in only the barest details. "Erica had a rough time with her date last night. She was in the area and asked if she could spend the night. Not wanting to leave her alone, since she was pretty upset, I waited until Robyn came in before going over to Lance's."

"Why were you going to Lance's?" Scott asked, puzzled.

"Lance and I are having an affair." Kristen gave Scott a deliberately closed look, indicating she wasn't going to discuss Lance any further. "After I left, Robyn also went out, leaving Erica alone. Robyn was the one who found the body."

"How was she killed?"

Kristen shuddered at the memory of the sight that had greeted her when she'd arrived back at the apartment. "She was stabbed repeatedly."

"Do the police have any leads?"

"They're questioning the neighbors to see if anyone heard anything. They think she was killed around three-thirty or four. I'll be seeing someone in a few minutes. Robyn will be questioned when she feels up to it."

Scott ran a hand through his tawny hair. "Thank God Robyn wasn't there when it happened. Or you," he quickly added. "Do the police think it was a bungled burglary attempt or maybe a drug addict looking for some cash?"

"I don't know. I can't imagine anyone deliberately doing what was done to Erica."

"What floor is Robyn on?"

"Six. She's been sedated. She won't be awake for at least a few hours. Scott, I don't think you should see her."

"Why not?" he demanded. "I want to make sure she's all right."

"Is that all?"

"What are you getting at?"

"Robyn's my best friend. You hurt her terribly last night. I don't want to see her getting hurt again. If the only reason you've shown up is out of concern, nothing more, then just send some flowers and take my word that she'll be fine."

"I'll admit I'm still sorting through my feelings. Seeing that tape gave me a jolt. But I'm not the only one at fault. Robyn is too. She lied to me."

"Not deliberately," Kristen voiced loudly. "She wanted to tell you about her past but didn't know how. She was afraid of losing you. You reacted exactly the way she feared you would. Robyn's the only one who can explain her past. Not me. But I want you to know that it was hard for her to fall in love with you. It was hard for her to learn how to trust again."

"You knew about her past?"

"You sound disappointed." Kristen gave him a sour smile. "Robyn wasn't trying to deceive you. She was going to tell you everything after the party. Only someone beat her to it. Have you given any thought to the tape, Scott? How it showed up on the most important night of Robyn's life? Someone wanted to hurt her. Scott, Robyn loves you. The question remaining is, do you still love her?"

"I'm hurt, angry, and confused. I need some time. How can I trust her again?"

"How can you *not* after all you've shared? Don't throw it away, Scott. Think long and hard about your decision, or one day you'll regret losing her."

Scott pressed for the elevator. "I'll only stay five minutes, and then I'll give serious thought to what you've said."

After Scott left, Kristen went to a pay phone, dialing Lance. She waited for him to pick up, but there was still no answer. It was the fifth time she had called.

She had spent eight hours camped in front of Lance's apartment door, waiting for him to show up. He never did. Finally giving up at ten, she had returned home, instantly becoming plunged in an unfolding nightmare.

Could Lance have murdered Erica? Had her story of rape been true, and had Lance feared she would go to the police? Had he wanted to stop her?

Kristen dialed his number again. She had to speak to him before speaking with the police. If she told them what she knew, Lance would become their number-one suspect.

"I'm surprised to find you here. Aren't you usually holed up in a bar at this time of day?"

"What are you doing here?" Georgina stood in the bedroom doorway, staring at Lance, trying to conjure a look of malice. Maybe he could settle the question of Erica's whereabouts.

Lance displayed a pile of clean shirts. "Just picking up a change of clothes."

"Bettina's been complaining about doing your washing and ironing, considering how you hardly live here." She would pick a fight and then drag in Erica's name.

"Tough. Bettina gets paid to do the laundry."

"Why don't you get Erica to do your laundry? Doesn't she do everything so well?"

"Next time I see her, I'll ask her."

"Aren't you two usually shacked up at this time of day?" Georgina walked over to Lance, scattering his shirts to the floor. "Ask her to iron them when you get back to the loft."

Lance gathered his shirts with a foul look. "I'm not seeing Erica today."

"Is she old news already?" Georgina eyed the collar of the shirt he was wearing. "The least she could have done for a night of passion was iron your shirt this morning."

Lance zipped up his leather shoulder bag, brushing Georgina aside. "I haven't seen Erica since last night."

After Lance left, Georgina's fears doubled. He hadn't seen Erica since the previous evening. Where the hell was she?

Georgina relentlessly paced her bedroom, trying to block out the images forming in her mind. It was impossible. She reached for a bottle of sleeping pills, shaking four into her palm and swallowing them with a glass of water. All she wanted was oblivion.

She turned on the TV, settled down on her bed and closed her eyes.

Outside the town house Lance sat in his black Maserati, revving the engine and wondering about Georgina. She had been fishing for answers. Had she spoken to Erica this morning? Had Erica told her about the rape?

Lance pulled his car into traffic. Erica could talk all she wanted. She couldn't prove a thing.

By three o'clock that afternoon the murder of Erica Shelton was front-page news. Although few facts had been released, the brutality of the murder, combined with Erica's glamorous lifestyle, was all the press needed. The New York *Post* came up with an eye-grabbing headline in its usual tactless style, FINAL ASSIGNMENT IS MURDER, and the hit of tabloid TV, "A Current Affair," was rushing to put together a segment on Erica's life.

But when the first afternoon newsbreak came on, reporting Erica's murder, Georgina was deeply asleep.

38

Kristen was arranging a bouquet of flowers when Robyn opened her eyes.

"How are you feeling?" She held up the flowers for inspection. "Thought these might brighten the place."

"They're very nice," Robyn whispered dryly.

"They looked so perfect in the gift shop window that I couldn't resist. But I can't keep my hands off them." She shifted a few more leaves and stems. "My mom has always had a knack with flowers. So have my sisters." She accidentally snapped off an unopened rosebud. "But I've always been the klutz." Kristen closed her eyes, pushing away the flowers. "I'm babbling, but I can't help it. I'm just so nervous. I saw what the apartment looked like."

"What time is it?"

"Seven-thirty."

"Have the police been by?"

Kristen nodded. "I spoke to them this afternoon. They'll be coming by later. They're going to want to know where you were at the time of the murder. Robyn, you never told me you were planning to go out."

"I got an unexpected phone call. I had to meet with someone."

"At three A.M.? Robyn, was it Tiffany?"

"I handled it. She won't be back."

"Where did you meet?"

"A coffee shop in Times Square. What about you? Is Lance your alibi?"

"I didn't get a chance to see Lance last night."

"What do you mean?"

"Lance wasn't at his loft. I waited for hours. He never showed."

"Where did you wait?"

"In front of his door. There was a party in the building. Plenty of people coming and going. I can be placed at the time of Erica's murder."

"What about Lance?"

"What about him?"

"Did you mention him to the police? Did you tell them Erica claimed Lance had raped her?"

"If Lance did rape Erica, I think it's highly unlikely that he murdered her after allowing her to leave his loft. If he had wanted to kill her to protect himself, he would have done it when he had the chance."

"So you didn't say anything?"

"No," Kristen admitted, "I did. I felt I owed Erica that much." Kristen pointed a finger at Robyn. "But I also told them about the way Erica and Lance were all over each other at the party, and how I wasn't a hundred percent sure of Erica's rape story."

"You did the right thing."

Kristen shrugged her shoulders. "I suppose. Only I can't stop thinking about her. What sort of animal would do such a thing?"

"One with a twisted mind."

"The police are starting to believe it was someone Erica knew. There was no sign of forced entry."

"How would someone know she was at our place? Could she have been followed?"

Kristen shuddered. "Too creepy. Let's change the subject."

Robyn shifted the sheets around her. "When can I leave? I hate hospitals."

"Tomorrow morning. I'm going to spend the night with a friend."

"Is Lance the friend you're staying with?"

"I haven't been able to reach Lance all day," Kristen stated quietly.

"That doesn't look too good, does it?"

"Lance may be a lot of things, but he's not a rapist," Kristen emphasized, "or a murderer. I'm sure he'll have an explanation once he surfaces."

Two men then entered the room. "Excuse us for interrupting," the taller of the two explained. He was sandy-haired and muscular, with gray eyes and a mustache. His partner was short, stocky, and dark-haired. "I'm Detective Daniels and this is my partner, Detective Reynolds. If you're up to it, we'd like to ask you a few questions, Ms. Prescott."

Kristen gathered up her things, edging around the detectives. "I'll be out in the hall. Call me when they're done. Do you want me to bring you back anything? A shake? Coffee?"

Robyn shook her head, turning to the detectives. "Shall we begin?"

Thirty minutes later Detectives Daniels and Reynolds were finished.

"I'll be right in," Kristen promised before following the detectives to the elevators. "Was she any help?" she said to them.

"We really can't discuss the case, Ms. Adams," Detective Daniels said. "You understand."

"Are you any closer to catching the maniac who murdered Erica?"

"We have a list of suspects."

"Suspects?" Kristen swiftly picked up on the plural. "Does this mean Lance Richards isn't the only one under suspicion?"

"Lance Richards was cleared hours ago. Didn't you know?"

"No one told me."

Detective Daniels whipped out his note pad, flipping through the pages. "After Ms. Shelton left Mr. Richards's loft last evening, he spent the remainder of the evening, as well as most of this morning, with Yvette Moore. She's a model who lives on the Upper West Side in an extremely posh and secure apartment building. All the entrances have video cameras, and they also record the time. We've got Lance's arrival and departure on tape. He couldn't have murdered Erica Shelton."

Kristen smiled weakly. "That's a relief. Thank you, officers. I'll be getting back to Robyn." She left the detectives.

"She looked a bit pale," Detective Reynolds commented to his partner.

"Why shouldn't she?" Detective Daniels bit into a cigar. "Her married lover has been screwing around behind her back."

"In the mood for a visitor?"

Robyn looked up from the magazine she'd been trying to read. "Quinn!" She threw down the magazine. "What are you doing here?"

"I came as soon as I could." He gave her a fierce hug. "Thank God you weren't hurt."

Robyn hugged Quinn just as fiercely. "Do you know about my past?"

"Yes." He pulled back and looked into her eyes. "Why didn't you tell me once you had remembered?"

"I couldn't. I was too ashamed."

Quinn looked at Robyn sternly. "Don't you know you can tell me anything? We're friends."

Robyn gave Quinn a quiet smile. "We are, aren't we?" Robyn indicated a chair. "Ready to listen?"

When Robyn finished, Quinn wrapped a reassuring arm around her. "It's over, Robyn. You don't ever have to be afraid again. You can go on with your life."

Robyn shook her head. "I can't."

"Scott?" Quinn tentatively broached.

"I love him so much, but he's shut me out of his life. I can't lose him, Quinn."

"There isn't much you can do, Robyn. Scott has to make his own decision." Quinn tilted Robyn's face to his, giving her a soft kiss. "He's a damn fool if he lets you go."

"Service with a smile. You haven't already eaten dinner, have you?"

Scott closed the door of his apartment, staring with surprise at Beverly. "No, I haven't."

"Good." She tossed off her mink and silk scarf, unloading the packages she had brought. "I've got spinach quiche, mushroom salad, and white wine."

"Beverly, you shouldn't have gone to so much trouble."

"Don't be silly. I'm sure I caught you off guard," Beverly called from the kitchen as she gathered plates, silverware, and glasses, "but I thought you might like some company. If I had called, you probably would have told me not to come and said you were fine, but I wouldn't have believed you until I saw for myself."

Beverly began setting the dining room table as Scott spread out the food.

"What's the verdict?" he asked.

"Looks like you're holding up pretty well."

"What's with the suitcase?" Scott pointed out. "More goodies?"

"I'm going to be spending the night in a hotel. My duplex is being painted, and the fumes are making it impossible to breathe." Beverly sat down, fixing a plate for Scott. "I must admit I'm not too keen on staying alone in a hotel. After what happened to Erica Shelton, I don't think I'll be getting any sleep tonight."

Scott opened the bottle of wine, filling his glass and Beverly's. "You're more than welcome to use my guest room."

Beverly sipped her wine. "Are you sure? I wouldn't be imposing?"

"Of course not."

"Then I accept. Even the idea of being alone at the duplex scares me."

"I hope the police catch the maniac who murdered her."

"I'd only met Erica once or twice, through Georgina, and she seemed like a lovely girl."

"She was. Very sweet. I always liked her."

"Will you be going to the funeral?"

"Yes, I will."

"Do you mind if I accompany you? If I went alone, I would feel awkward. Like I said, I really didn't know her, but I would like to express my condolences."

"As soon as I know the details, I'll give you a call. Unless you're still here."

"I promise not to overstay my welcome." Beverly handed Scott his plate. "How are things going with Robyn? Do you mind my asking? Let me know if I'm prying."

Scott tasted his quiche. "This is delicious." He then took a sip of his wine. "You're not prying. I think it would help if

I spoke with someone. I love Robyn, but a part of me can't forgive her for the secret she's kept."

"You feel betrayed," Beverly stated. "You trusted her with your love. There's no reason for you to feel guilty."

"Is that how I sound?"

"Scott, you're not the one at fault. As much as I like Robyn, and knowing how deeply you feel about her, there's still no excusing what she's done. I can't help but become angry. She hurt you. She never gave any thought to the consequences of her actions. She only thought about herself." Beverly nibbled at her mushroom salad. "I know how much she means to you, and I want to see you happy, but maybe she isn't the one. Maybe you were meant for someone else."

"Maybe you're right," Scott conceded, "but what we had was special. Shouldn't I try to recapture it?" He twirled his fork. "I spoke with Kristen today. She told me Robyn meant to tell me the truth."

"Nothing personal against Kristen, but she isn't exactly impartial." Beverly smiled at Scott. "Scott, there isn't a doubt in my mind that Robyn loves you and will take you back with open arms, but are you ready to take her back into your heart? Will you ever be able to trust her again? Think about it long and hard before making a decision. Promise me you'll do whatever makes you happy."

"Promise. I've got some brie in the fridge. Want a taste?"

"You sit," Beverly ordered. "I'll get it."

In the kitchen Beverly found the cheese along with some crackers. Before returning to Scott, she took the kitchen phone off its hook. The last thing a romantic evening needed was a ringing phone.

"Found it." Beverly sliced a piece of the cheese, placing it on a cracker and feeding it to Scott. "Open wide."

"Delicious." Scott prepared one for Beverly but didn't feed it to her. "Thanks for being here. Thanks for being a friend. You've really helped."

Beverly's fingers entwined between Scott's before brushing them against his cheek. "I'll always be a part of your life. I'm the one person you can depend on."

* * *

"Who else have we got on our list of suspects?" Detective Daniels asked his partner.

"We've got Jeff Porter, who's down in interrogation, and Georgina Kendall Richards."

Daniels propped his feet up on his desk, rubbing a hand over his stubble-covered chin. "What's the background?"

"Porter is a lawyer who was Erica's live-in lover. They'd been planning to marry, although nothing was official. They broke up around a week ago, after Porter received some nude photographs of Erica. He also claims she was having an affair with Lance Richards. The pictures and the alleged affair led to a breakup. He moved out and found his own place."

"Has he got an alibi?"

"Airtight. He's also genuinely upset over Erica's death. Keeps saying he should have listened to her. She denied the affair with Lance Richards. Porter still had strong feelings for Erica but didn't try for a reconciliation. He wanted her to come back to him."

"It's too late for that now. What's the story on Georgina Kendall Richards?"

Detective Reynolds sat up with excitement. "I think you're going to like this. Last night Georgina publicly threatened to kill Erica unless she stayed away from Lance. We've got a dozen witnesses who heard the threat." Reynolds took a sip from a container of coffee. "The story gets better. Around a month ago, before Jeff Porter received the nude photos, Georgina and Erica had a public confrontation."

"Where did this take place?"

"Midtown bar."

"Witnesses?"

"Plenty."

"Anything else?"

"Jeff Porter says the pictures he received came to him anonymously. Among them were some shots of Erica and Lance in bed. A witness in the bar remembers Georgina flashing some pictures at Erica."

"You think she was the one who sent them?"

"Why not? I don't know what else could enrage a wife

more than nude photographs of her husband and his mistress. She probably sent the photos to Porter for revenge. But was it enough? Or did Georgina's anger go beyond revenge?"

"When do you want to bring her in for questioning?"

"The sooner the better. She's our only solid suspect. I also think we should ask for a search warrant."

"Think it's necessary?"

"Somehow Georgina Richards found nude photographs of her husband and Erica Shelton, indicating an affair. It's a possible incentive for murder. If she's still got any of the photographs, it could help build a case."

"If there is one," Daniels reminded. "Georgina Richards has a drinking problem. She was plastered both times she made her threats. Drunks usually don't resort to violence."

"Sometimes they do."

"Go for the warrant. See if we can have it for the morning. Then we'll pay a visit to Mrs. Richards."

39

When Georgina awoke it was eight A.M. Opening her eyes, she decided she would go over to Erica's apartment. Perhaps one of her neighbors knew where she was. She could have gone on a trip for a few days. If her neighbors knew nothing, she would try Constance Carter. It could be that Erica was out of town on assignment. Whatever the answer, Georgina vowed to find it.

After dressing, she went down to the kitchen and brewed a pot of coffee. She was sipping her first cup when the door bell rang.

"Who is it?" she asked before opening the door.

"Police. We'd like to ask you a few questions."

Georgina tried to remain calm. The police had to have a

logical reason for wanting to question her. "What's this in reference to?"

"If you're not aware, Mrs. Richards, Erica Shelton was savagely stabbed to death the night before last."

The coffee cup fell from Georgina's hand, crashing to the floor. Suddenly she couldn't breathe. Erica was dead! The police had to suspect her, otherwise why would they be here? But she couldn't have killed her. She didn't remember a thing. Yet . . . there was her fur, with bloodstains on it. There was the blood she had found on her palms. Erica's blood. Her stomach turned and she gripped her forehead, wanting to tear at her skin and rip at her brain. Whatever had happened had to be buried in her mind. Why couldn't she remember?

"Mrs. Richards, we must ask you to let us in."

Georgina fumbled with the locks, opening the front door. She gave a sheepish smile. "I'm still half asleep. Watch the spill. I'll get some paper towels and clean it up."

Detective Daniels held Georgina in place, instructing a uniformed officer. "Ben, go in the kitchen and find some paper towels." Daniels steered Georgina into the living room. "Mrs. Richards, we're here on a serious matter. Erica Shelton is dead. On two separate occasions you publicly threatened her."

"Those were just threats! I never meant them! I only wanted to scare her."

"I'm sorry," Detective Daniels said, "but a woman is dead and you're our prime suspect. We'd like you to come down to the station. You may call an attorney and have him present during questioning." The detective reached into his trench coat, handing Georgina a folded piece of paper. "This is a search warrant." He nodded to Detective Reynolds. "Start upstairs. Ben and I'll look down here."

There was a strained silence as Georgina watched the search. When she heard Detective Reynolds call from upstairs, her heart plunged.

"Matt, you better come up here."

"I'm coming with you," Georgina told Daniels.

"What did you find?" he asked when they got to Georgina's bedroom.

Reynolds pointed to an open dresser drawer, the clothing

removed and on the floor. Inside the empty drawer were a variety of photographs taken from magazines and newspapers. All were of Erica and each photograph had a red X slashed across her face.

"I've never seen those before," Georgina declared. "Never."

"There's more." Detective Reynolds led them into the bathroom, pointing to the clothes hamper. Daniels opened the lid. Resting on top of the clothes was a knife with dried blood.

"Our murder weapon," he pronounced.

Before Georgina even realized what was happening, Detective Daniels was handcuffing her and began reading her her rights.

"I didn't do it," she sobbed. "I didn't do it!"

Breakfast in bed. The one bit of pampering Beverly never did without, even if it wasn't her own bed.

She inspected the tray she had fixed for Scott from things she'd found in his well-stocked kitchen. Piping hot blueberry muffins cut in two and smothered with melting butter. A fresh fruit cup of blueberries, strawberries, and raspberries. Two poached eggs, orange juice, and freshly brewed coffee tinged with a trace of mint.

Had she forgotten anything? She stared at the headline of the morning paper she'd picked up in the hallway, wondering if Georgina had seen it yet.

Beverly decided Scott didn't need such unpleasantries this morning. The phone was still off the hook and she was wearing her most alluring negligee. She dumped the paper in the trash and headed for Scott's bedroom, discreetly knocking on the door before entering.

He was still asleep. There was a look of peacefulness on his face. She was tempted to slip between the sheets next to him and press herself against his warmth, wrapping her arms around him and proclaiming her love, but she didn't. That time would soon come.

"Wake up sleepyhead," she exclaimed.

Scott opened his eyes, smiling at Beverly. "What's this?"

"A small token of my appreciation for letting me stay the night."

"You shouldn't have gone to the trouble." Scott sniffed the muffins. "Why don't we take this into the kitchen?"

"You stay in bed and relax." She placed the tray on his lap as he sat up in bed. "Enjoy your breakfast. I've already eaten. I'm going to take a shower before heading back to the duplex. I have to straighten out my painter. I spoke to him this morning, and he told me he doesn't think he'll be finished for another two days."

"My invitation to stay is still open."

Beverly gave Scott a grateful smile. "I'll see what I can work out."

"Call me at the office. We can even go out for dinner. Pick a place and let me know what you decide."

"I'll call you later," Beverly gushed.

Robyn dejectedly hung up the phone.

"Still busy?" Kristen asked.

"Still busy," Robyn replied. "It was even busy last night."

"He probably took the phone off the hook."

"I have to talk to him."

"You will, honey," Kristen soothed. "You will. Let me go find a nurse and see what we have to do to get you out of here."

After Kristen left, Robyn unfolded the page she had torn out of yesterday's paper. Last night, after visiting hours had ended, a hospital volunteer had come around with magazines and newspapers. On the society page she found the photograph of Beverly and Scott.

There was a distraught look on Scott's face, and it was obvious that Beverly was trying to comfort him. A capsulated version of the unveiling of the videotape, followed by speculation of a reconciliation between Beverly and Scott, accompanied the photo.

After reading the column, Robyn had decided to call Scott. Kristen had told her about his brief visit and the call would be a way of thanking him for his concern. If Scott wanted, Robyn thought, the conversation could continue in any direction he chose. She'd listen to anything he had to say. She didn't want to be shut out of his life.

"Ready to check out?" Kristen announced, following an orderly with a wheelchair.

Robyn refolded the clipping before Kristen could see it. "Absolutely."

Beverly stepped from the shower, wrapping a towel around herself and her hair before hurrying to answer the door.

"Did you forget your keys—"

She tried not to appear startled by the sight of Robyn. In turn, Robyn tried the same. She hadn't expected to see Beverly Maxwell at Scott's.

"Sorry to pull you from your shower," Robyn apologized. "Is Scott in?"

"He went to the store to get me some conditioner." She held the door open. "You're more than welcome to wait till he comes back."

"If you'd just tell him I stopped by," Robyn said stiffly.

Beverly tightened the towel around her. "I hope you're not upset at seeing me. My duplex is being painted and Scott invited me to spend a few nights."

"This is Scott's apartment. He can invite anyone he likes."

"Yes, he can," Beverly agreed. "I'm not going to apologize for being here."

"I didn't ask for an apology or an explanation," Robyn pointed out. "You seem to be providing both without my asking. Guilty conscience?"

"Are you sure you don't want to wait?"

"I really must be going."

"How are you doing? Your life must be totally upside down. Seeing that videotape at your party, losing Scott, and then discovering Erica's body."

"I haven't lost Scott," Robyn flared.

"Really? I wouldn't be so sure," Beverly purred.

"Why? Think you have a chance of getting him back?"

"Getting him back?" Beverly laughed. "Robyn, Scott and I are good friends. Nothing more. You're making too much out of this."

"Am I?" Robyn demanded.

Beverly nodded, preparing to close the door. "Yes, you are. Scott and I share a history and a friendship. Whether you like it or not, I'm a part of his life. I always will be," she emphasized. Beverly gave Robyn a quiet look of triumph. "Will you? I'd be more concerned with that question than with my relationship with Scott. You never struck me as the type to waste your time with petty jealousies. Don't start now." She took a step back into the apartment, starting to shut the door. "Excuse me, but I'd like to return to my shower. If I remember, I'll be sure to tell Scott you stopped by."

Robyn stared at the closed door in indignation, tempted to pound her fist on it. The nerve of Beverly talking down to her and thinking she was jealous. But she was jealous! The threat of competition, dangerous competition—even though Beverly claimed she wasn't interested in Scott—unnerved her. Robyn didn't think Beverly would allow anything to stand in the way of what she wanted. In this case, Scott.

Back at her duplex later that afternoon, Beverly went from room to room, debating if she should actually repaint.

Scott was so easy to manipulate. He had accepted her story without question and was pouring out his heart. With Robyn no longer in the picture, he would soon be hers again. Their "friendship" had gone from casual to warm and trusting. She'd have to step things up a bit. Scott was at his most vulnerable. She had lost him when his father died. She wasn't going to waste this second chance.

All she had to do was make him forget Robyn. She surveyed her wardrobe, going through the hangers. No problem. Her taste and class would obliterate any memories of that cheap gutter whore.

For dinner tonight with Scott she would wear a clinging Halston jersey of deep gold with padded shoulders. For Erica's funeral, a simple black suit with cloche hat. This morning's negligee had done justice to her figure, but if she were going to seduce Scott, she'd have to do better.

After packing the items she was going to take back to Scott's, she went downstairs for her car keys, preparing to load the suitcases into the trunk of her Corvette. When she opened the door of her duplex, she nearly slammed it shut. The last person she had ever expected to see again was standing before her.

"Isn't this nice? You're home." Tiffany strutted into the duplex, taking off her rabbit fur. "I've been calling and calling but no one answered. I'm so glad I caught you. We have things to discuss."

"We have nothing to discuss," Beverly stated coldly.

"But we do," Tiffany corrected, inspecting herself in a mirror. "The money you gave me is all gone. I need another advance."

Beverly's body went rigid and she kept the door open. "Get out. You're not getting another cent from me. Get out before I call the police."

Tiffany settled herself on the couch. "Close the door, will ya? I'm gettin' a draft." She pointed to the bar. "While you're up, fix me a drink. Bourbon on the rocks. Wild Turkey. None of that cheap mash you served me last time I was here."

Beverly slammed shut the door of the duplex, storming to the phone. "I'm calling the police."

"Make it short." She pulled out a compact and lipstick, repairing her makeup. "After you finish, I want to call Scott Kendall." She recited his number at the apartment and at Wellington Cosmetics.

Beverly clenched her jaw, forgetting about calling the police. She planted herself in front of Tiffany. "How much?"

"Two million dollars."

"Are you insane?"

"Too high? Fine. If you're willing to lose Scott Kendall after all you've done to get Robyn out of his life, then I won't hesitate to call him." Tiffany shook her head. "Come on, Bev! I thought you were smarter than that."

"You can't prove a thing," Beverly crowed.

"Can't I?" Tiffany reached into her purse, handing Beverly a piece of paper. "This is a Xerox copy of the check you gave me. Scott's going to wonder why you paid a hooker from Las Vegas five hundred thousand dollars."

"He'll never believe you," Beverly ranted.

"No?" Tiffany pondered the thought for a moment. "You could come up with an acceptable excuse for the check," she agreed. "Admitting you're into the lesbo scene would work wonders for your relationship. But let's get real. It's highly unlikely Scott would buy your story after hearing mine."

"I'll take my chances." Beverly didn't know what she was saying. All she was concerned with was getting rid of Tiffany. She had to bluff her. Deceive her. Trick her into believing she didn't pose a threat. Otherwise . . . no! She couldn't lose Scott. Not again.

Tiffany sighed. "You've disappointed me, Beverly. I really thought we could handle this between ourselves." She went to the phone, dialing a number. "I've no choice but to bring my partner into this."

"Partner?" The danger of the situation doubled.

"It's me," Tiffany said into the receiver. "I'm at her place. Yeah, you were right. She won't give in."

"Give me that phone," Beverly demanded, ripping it from Tiffany's ear. "Whoever the hell this is, you're not going to get away with this. Do you hear me?"

"Loud and clear," Anthony Calder answered, "but I'm afraid I'm going to have to disagree. You see, I've got photos of your nighttime activities, Beverly. You wouldn't want those photos made public. Think of the scandal!"

"What do you want?" Beverly asked in a tight voice.

"Terms have changed. Our price has doubled. We want four million."

"Anything else?"

"How could I have forgotten!" Calder brightly exclaimed. "There *is* one other thing. You have to sleep with me."

"You're despicable," Beverly spat out.

"Let's not be a hypocrite, Bev. I've been watching you. Obviously you believe in free love." Calder laughed and then hung up.

Beverly replaced the receiver numbly. She was boxed in. Trapped. Turning, she found Tiffany at the bar, pouring a drink.

"I wanted to come after you myself, but I wasn't sure if you'd give in. Calder struck me as the type who wouldn't pass up a good deal. Imagine my surprise when he told me he was cooking up a deal of his own. He showed me the goods he had on you. Naughty, naughty, Bev! You even put me to shame in those photos."

"Get out!" Beverly ordered, voice rising and teeth gnashing. *"Get out!"*

Tiffany sipped her drink nonchalantly. "I'm the one calling the shots. All along you thought you were better than me because of your looks and your money, but I've got something you haven't got." Tiffany pointed to her head. "Instincts," she exclaimed. "From the moment I met you I knew money could be made. Your money doesn't hide the type of person you are. You're just as bad as me. We don't give a shit about anyone but ourselves, and we'll do whatever it takes to get what we want. The only difference is that you're on a pedestal and I'm in the gutter." Tiffany finished her drink. "But not much longer. Think about what Calder and I can do." She got ready to leave the duplex. "You've got seventy-two hours to make a decision."

After Tiffany left, Beverly flew into a rage. She tore at the drapes, ripped open couches and armchairs and threw anything she could at the walls.

How could she have been so stupid? How could she have allowed herself to be cornered? Unless she met Tiffany and Calder's demands, she would lose Scott. Forever. She wasn't going to allow that to happen. *She wasn't!*

She threw a vase of roses at a mirrored wall, watching as the wall broke into shards. She would find a way to beat them. Both would regret crossing her.

No one crossed Beverly Maxwell.

No one.

"I can't get through to my brother. Can I try calling my husband?" Georgina tried not to sound pleading. She felt like dying. She had never felt so humiliated in all her life. Her fingers were still smudged with ink from fingerprinting, she'd been photographed, and everyone in the police station was staring at her with malice.

The matron nodded, and Georgina dialed Lance at the loft, holding her breath as the line rang.

"Lance Richards speaking."

"Lance?" Georgina wept with relief. "I need you."

"What is it now?" he asked in annoyance.

"I'm in jail. I need you to call an attorney."

"Drunk driving again?"

"I've been arrested for Erica's murder."

"Georgina, are you drunk?"

"Lance, *please,*" she pleaded. "They think I murdered Erica."

"You're telling the truth," he uttered in amazement. "I don't believe it."

"I want to go home. Call someone and get me out of here."

"Hang tight. I'm on my way," Lance promised.

"My husband is on his way," Georgina informed the matron. "He's on his way."

"Are you leaving?" the woman next to Lance asked when he got out of bed.

"Are you kidding?" He left the bedroom and returned shaking a bottle of champagne. He released the cork, spraying a burst of foam on himself and the naked woman. "I'm celebrating!"

It was six o'clock when Scott called Beverly at his apartment.

"We're going to have to cancel dinner."

As soon as she heard the words, Beverly's anger started bubbling. Somehow Robyn had gotten to Scott. She'd begun plotting her next move when Scott's voice interrupted her thoughts.

"Georgina's been arrested for Erica's murder. I'm down at the police station. I haven't seen her yet."

"I'm on my way," Beverly instantly offered. "Georgina needs to know there are people who believe she's innocent."

"The evidence is piling up," Scott confessed. "Beverly, I'm worried. Not only do they have the murder weapon with her fingerprints, but a witness who saw her leaving the building."

"She must have been drunk. Can she plead insanity? You don't believe she plotted to kill Erica, do you?"

"I'm not going to make any sort of judgment until after

I've talked with her. I've gotten an attorney, and he's seeing what can be done to arrange bail."

"Stay calm, Scott. I'll be there soon. I want to do whatever I can to help Georgina."

"Thank you, Beverly. I don't know what I'd do without you."

"We're going to get through this," Beverly promised. "Together."

40

It was inevitable. The flashing cameras. The shouted questions. Departing from the limousine that had delivered her and Kristen to St. Patrick's for Erica's funeral, Robyn hurried up the steps of the church, hiding behind a pair of dark sunglasses and averting her face from the hordes of waiting reporters and photographers.

She held onto Kristen's arm for support, and once inside the church, slipped into a pew, removing the sunglasses and closing her eyes, comforted by the peace and serenity offered.

No matter where she went these days, she never managed to go undetected. Someone always recognized her. When she had accompanied Quinn to Kennedy Airport for his flight back to Chicago, the press had been relentless, swarming all over the two of them. She just wanted it to end. She was tired of the notoriety and gossip, the open stares and speculating tongues. She wanted her life back.

"I know how you feel," Kristen whispered sympathetically, watching as the pews filled. "Let's hope this all ends soon. Maybe then we can get our lives back on track."

Robyn opened her eyes, smiling at Kristen. If anyone knew how she felt, it was Kristen. After Georgina's arrest,

Kristen's affair with Lance had somehow become public knowledge. Nobody knew how the affair had been revealed. Journalists and newsmen didn't care. Story after story, theory after theory, was formulated and printed. The public gobbled it up, demanding more for their unquenched appetite.

Kristen shunned all interviews and denied comment. Georgina maintained her own silence, and Lance kept a low profile.

"Don't look now," Kristen whispered, "but the queen has arrived."

Beverly swooped into the church, keeping an iron grip on Scott's arm as they also avoided the press. Catching sight of Kristen and Robyn, Beverly steered Scott in the direction of the farthest pews.

Kristen nudged Robyn. "How much longer are you going to put up with this? She's after Scott."

"Both she and I know that," Robyn confirmed, "no matter what she says."

"What are you going to do?"

"What can I do? Scott will have to make his own choice," Robyn declared. "Does he want me or Beverly?"

For the first time in two days Beverly allowed herself a moment to relax. Despite her calm outward appearance, her world was close to crumbling.

Bail for Georgina had been set at $750,000. After Georgina had been released, Scott had asked if his sister could stay at the duplex.

"I know it's a lot to ask," he had begun awkwardly, "but I don't have anyone else to turn to. Neither does Georgina. You're her closest friend. If I weren't having so many problems at Wellington, I could be there for her."

Beverly had hushed him. "Don't say another word. Didn't I promise to do whatever I could?"

With those final words the matter was settled and Georgina was sequestered in Beverly's duplex. Having her around was nerve wracking. She spent her days crying, or denying Erica's murder, whenever she could grab Beverly's ear.

The other problem was Tiffany. The woman was constantly calling. Beverly had turned off her answering machine and given strict instructions to Georgina never to answer. Whenever Tiffany did call, Beverly told her she was in the process of getting the money together.

Beverly fidgeted in the pew, listening to the droning words of the priest officiating the service. She moved closer to Scott, and from the corner of her eye she could see Robyn trying not to glare. Beverly smirked. Let the little bitch eat her heart out. Scott was *hers*.

Faces around Beverly were etched with sorrow and grief. Even Scott had a pained look on his face. How boring. She stifled a yawn. Thirty minutes were still left to the service. What could she think of to amuse herself? She stole a look at Scott, a smile coming to her lips.

Seduction. She would think of a seduction.

After all the waiting and planning, she was ready to make her move. Confidence surged through her. She was ready to claim her stake in the most pleasurable way.

Today was the day she would seduce Scott.

When the service neared completion, Erica's coffin was wheeled back up the center aisle. A waiting hearse was outside the church, ready to take the coffin to the cemetery. Before anyone knew what was happening, a male figure suddenly jumped from one of the pews and threw himself on the coffin, clawing through the arrangement of flowers to the smooth bronze lid. The man was Jeff Porter.

From his throat came anguished sobs. "I'm sorry, Erica. I'm so sorry. I loved you so much. Why didn't I forgive you? Why didn't I take you back? You were the best thing that ever happened to me. Erica, can you hear me? I'm sorry. I'm so sorry."

Jeff was gently removed from the coffin. He continued sobbing brokenly. The rest of the church watched as he followed after the coffin with the help of two friends. Quiet murmurings began as the pews emptied.

"Aren't you coming?" Beverly asked.

Scott, pale-faced and shaken, remained in the pew. Jeff's outburst had stabbed at his heart. His words had been so full of regret. Jeff had been too late in forgiving Erica—too stubborn to give her a second chance. Now Jeff would always be haunted by memories and regrets.

Would the same thing happen to him? Would he one day regret not having given Robyn a second chance? Did their love still have a chance?

"I'm coming," he told Beverly as she hooked her arm through his.

There was only one way to find out.

"I've got an appointment to see Samantha in an hour," Robyn told Kristen as they climbed into their limousine. She dabbed at her tears. "Want to tag along?"

"I've got a personal matter that can't wait." She sniffed, dabbing at her own tears.

"Lance?"

Kristen stared out the window as the limousine moved along. "So much of that sorrow is his fault." She gave Robyn a determined look. "We're going to clear the air and then we're going to split."

Georgina restlessly paced her bedroom. She had come back to the town house that morning while Beverly and Scott went to Erica's funeral. Georgina felt she had been imposing on Beverly for too long.

Yet being alone was getting to her. All she did was think about Erica. She had to get out and be among people.

With her hair wrapped in a scarf, no makeup, and dark sunglasses, she knew she was unrecognizable, easily blending into the city streets. Taking deep breaths, she cleared her lungs and tried to unload the fears that smothered her day and night.

The trial would be starting in a month. The assistant D.A. wanted her charged with murder in the first degree. The thought of a trial was terrifying; the possibility of prison was paralyzing.

She hadn't murdered Erica. No matter what the evidence, she hadn't done it. She had been shown pictures of Erica's corpse and had cringed. There was no way she would forget committing such a brutal act.

All she remembered was the party. She'd confronted Erica and then gone to the bar. Beverly had been there, and Georgina had asked her if she had watched her exchange with Erica. Then Beverly had gotten a fresh drink and brought one back for her. After that everything went black.

When she reached a newsstand, she decided to buy a paper. She hadn't read one in days. Scott and Beverly hadn't wanted her to read what was being printed. It seemed most New Yorkers had already formed an opinion: guilty.

About to purchase a copy of the *Times,* her eyes fell upon the *Post.* A small photo of Lance was on the front page, and Georgina flipped to the related story.

The top of the page read, A MAN AND HIS MISTRESSES. There was a large photo of Lance surrounded by a number of smaller photos. Among the women was Kristen Adams.

Reading the story, Georgina became angry. Lance depicted her as an alcoholic who had singlehandedly destroyed their marriage. He had turned to other women "only to find the love and warmth Georgina denied him." Claiming Georgina was a woman with "deep psychological problems, in need of professional help," Lance could no longer help her and a divorce was "imminent."

Georgina stared at the page after finishing the story. Then she hailed a taxi, giving the driver the address to Lance's loft.

He wasn't going to get away with this. She was in enough trouble. She didn't need him to paint an uglier picture. Was he purposely trying to destroy her? He hadn't come to post her bail when she had called for his help. She had neither seen nor heard from him since her release.

She wasn't going to allow him to condemn her in the public's eye. She had to put a stop to it.

"Would you like to stay for lunch?" Beverly asked.

"I haven't the time. I've got a board meeting rescheduled for this afternoon. I just want to check on Georgina before I go."

Beverly watched as Scott headed for the guest room. Something had happened at the church. She didn't know what, but she didn't like what she was sensing. Their limousine ride had been one of pensive silence. Of course,

Scott's mind could be preoccupied by his upcoming board meeting, but she didn't think so.

It was time she made her move. If she waited any longer, she might lose him.

Scott returned from the guest room with a note. "Georgina's returned to her town house."

"Don't sound so worried. She'll be fine."

"I'm not sure I like the idea of her being alone."

"If she can't handle it, I'm sure she'll come back."

"I'm going to give her a call."

While Scott dialed Georgina's number, Beverly retreated to her bedroom. From her closet she removed a box she had kept hidden for weeks. Opening the box, she pushed away mounds of tissue paper, revealing a white silk and lace negligee. Breathlessly, Beverly lifted the negligee from its box and gently placed it on her bed.

Shedding the black dress she had worn to the funeral, she slipped into the negligee, admiring herself in a full-length mirror. She thrilled at her image.

Loosening her chignon, she shook free her long chestnut hair. Using a silver hairbrush, she arranged her hair around her neck and shoulders, luxuriating in its silky smoothness. Soon Scott's fingers would be weaving through the strands.

She dabbed Christian Dior's Poison behind her ears and between her breasts. Again she looked at her image. She was so beautiful. Scott would be unable to resist.

She heard him call her name. "Beverly? Where are you?"

"Upstairs. In my bedroom."

"She's not answering." When Scott reached the doorway he stopped, startled by the sight of her.

"Cat got your tongue?" she teased. She went to him, taking him by the hand and leading him to her bed. "I dressed this way especially for you."

She sat at the edge of the mattress, looking at him with soulful eyes. "I want you to make love to me." She rubbed his hand sensuously against her cheek. "I want you so badly."

"Beverly . . ." he croaked, trying to find the words.

She pulled him down beside her, pressing her lips against his. "No words," she shushed. "No words."

She kissed him urgently as her hands explored his body

with abandon. How long it had been since she had felt him so intimately! She began trying to undress him—tearing at his clothes.

Pressing herself against him, she brought Scott on top of her as she sank into her pillows. "I want you," she moaned. "I've waited so long to have you again."

He broke their kiss. "Beverly, listen to me," he pleaded, trying to explain and straining to break free.

She wouldn't let go. She ripped at his belt, fumbling to unzipper his pants, until Scott angrily pushed her away, jumping to his feet.

"Enough!" he exclaimed. His face was flushed and he attempted to straighten his appearance.

"Scott?" Beverly looked at him from the bed, hurt and puzzled. "Don't you want me?"

He looked at her helplessly. "Beverly, you're a desirable woman."

"Then what's wrong?"

"I can't make love to you."

"Why not? Scott, I love you," she implored.

"Don't say that."

"Why not? It's true. Don't you love me?"

With a pained look, he shook his head. "I'm sorry, Beverly. I never meant to hurt you. Not again."

"Scott?" Her voice trembled.

"I don't love you," he admitted.

"You can't mean that."

"I do. I'm sorry."

"But why can't you love me? Why?" she begged. "Tell me."

"I'm still in love with Robyn. I'm going to try to get back with her."

"You can't be in love with her. Not after what she did to you. The way she lied!"

"I still love her," Scott quietly affirmed, "despite everything."

"No," Beverly denied. "No!"

"I never meant to mislead you. All I wanted was your friendship. I'm sorry if I gave you any indication of wanting anything more. You're trying to recapture what we once had. As lovers, it's over between us."

"What about me?" she whimpered, burying her head in her pillow. "What about me?"

He touched her shoulder but she jerked away. "Please leave," she pleaded. "I want to be alone."

Taking his jacket, Scott left the bedroom. Only after Beverly heard him leave the duplex did she scream in agony. *"Damn you to hell, Robyn Prescott!"*

Looking across the bedroom at her tearstained image, Beverly picked up her hairbrush and flung it at the mirror. As it shattered to pieces, the phone rang. Thinking it was Scott calling with an apology or change of mind, she snatched it up. "Hello?"

"It's me," Tiffany greeted. "Got the cash? Today is payday." She gave an obscene giggle. "Calder left me with instructions for his part of the deal. You're to meet him at a hotel off Forty-sixth and Sixth Avenue. A real seedy joint chosen especially for you. Ask for his name at the desk and you'll be given a key. Wait for him in the room. When you finish, head over to my hotel. Got it?"

Beverly wiped away her tears. "Yes, I've got it," she replied. After hanging up she added, "You and Anthony Calder are both going to get exactly what you deserve."

"Georgina, what are you doing here?"

She barreled past Lance. "I'm out on bail. If you'd had your way I'd still be rotting in a jail cell."

"Let me explain."

"Save it," she cut him off, waving her folded newspaper in his face. "I came to discuss our divorce."

Lance held the door open. "I think you should leave. My lawyer will be in touch with yours."

"Not so fast, darling." She placed a finger to his lips. "I'm laying down the rules. If anyone is entitled to this divorce, it's me. I'm not totally blameless, but the bulk of failure of our marriage falls on your shoulders. I know you're not accustomed to living a simple life, but you better start. You're not getting a cent from me."

"Really? I beg to differ. Give me any trouble and I'll make our divorce a long and dirty battle."

"Let your lawyer pull out his fancy terms like 'emotional distress' or 'mental cruelty,'" Georgina scoffed. "Not only will my lawyers use those same terms, but we'll also parade your mistresses on the stand."

Lance laughed gleefully. "I don't have a thing to worry about. You'll never find anyone credible."

"Watch me," Georgina promised.

"I intend to. After all, you mistakenly thought I was having an affair with Erica."

Georgina stared at him in shock. "What?"

Lance abandoned the door, walking deeper into the loft. "I've always depended on your incompetence, and you've never failed me. Erica and I were never having an affair, although I kept trying to force her into one."

"I saw the two of you together so many times." Georgina refused to believe Lance was telling the truth. "What about those nude photos of the two of you in bed together?"

Lance grinned at Georgina. "The infamous nude photos. Those opened such a nasty can of worms. I really wanted to sleep with Erica," he stressed, "but she rebuffed all my advances. No matter what, I decided I would have her. One afternoon she was here and I drugged her. While she was unconscious I took the photos, intending to blackmail her. But you ruined my little plan. When you showed her the photos, she wanted revenge for what I'd done." He laughed aloud. "She enticed me at the party, and when we came back here, she pulled a gun, demanding the negatives. It was so amusing. I overpowered her and then gave her what she had been wanting all along. She loved it. Too bad you murdered her. I'm sure she would have been back for more."

Georgina stared at Lance in disgust. "You raped her. You made that poor girl's life a living hell and then you raped her."

Lance bowed gallantly before his wife. "Let's not be so modest, my love," he corrected. "You were constantly tormenting her as well."

"Because of you," she whispered. "For some stupid reason, I still wanted you."

"Did I forget to thank you?" he asked. "You did me a favor by killing her."

"You're sick," Georgina stated, her voice dripping with revulsion. "The sooner I divorce you, the better."

"File for divorce. I'm still getting half of everything."

"Not if I have anything to say about it," a voice pronounced.

Kristen stood at the loft's open door. "I heard it all." She walked to Lance, staring at him from head to toe. "To think I had doubts about Erica's story because of my feelings for you. What did I ever see in you to begin with?"

Lance grabbed Kristen around the waist, pressing her body against his. "You wanted a good fuck," he leered.

She slapped him across the face. "Bastard. I hope you burn in hell."

Lance massaged his stinging cheek. "Nothing like the fury of a woman scorned."

"Don't flatter yourself. I'm thrilled to be out of your self-centered life. I don't know why it took me so long to wise up."

Georgina absorbed the exchange with confusion. What was going on?

"Allow me to clarify," Lance told Georgina, "since your brain cells are so few. Kristen was my mistress."

Kristen's photo from the *Post* flashed through her mind. Lance wasn't lying. It was true. Did that mean he *wasn't* lying about Erica?"

"Out of curiosity," he innocently asked, "was Kristen the one you originally intended to butcher that night?"

"I didn't murder Erica!" she vehemently exclaimed. "I'm innocent."

"Sure, babe. Tell it to the jury," he taunted. "It won't do much good. You've already been tried and convicted. Too bad New York still doesn't have the death penalty. I'd love to see you sizzle in the electric chair." He dabbed a finger at Georgina. "Zzzzttt!"

Georgina fought back the tears. She wasn't going to let Lance do this to her. Kristen shoved Lance away. "Leave her alone," she ordered. "Haven't you hurt her enough?"

"This is only a taste of what she'll get if she gives me any trouble with the divorce."

Kristen looked at Lance smugly. "You don't stand much of a chance if I testify for Georgina."

"Go ahead." He gave a confident wave of his hand. "My case is still strong."

"You might have a point," Kristen agreed, "but what's

going to happen if I tell Jeff Porter what I overheard? He'll come after you with murder in his eyes, ready to avenge Erica."

Lance paled, knowing Jeff would believe Kristen, if no one else did. Jeff would also do anything. His life could be in danger. "You wouldn't . . ."

"Try me," she dared.

Lance turned to Georgina. "Perhaps I was a bit hasty. I'm sure our lawyers can work on a reasonable settlement."

"Wrong," Kristen proclaimed. "Georgina is divorcing you without a settlement. Like she said, you're not getting a cent." She left with those final words.

"You can't do this to me," he shouted. Without Georgina he'd be penniless. The good life would cease to exist.

"She just did." Georgina paused at the door, smiling brightly. "I'll have my lawyers draw up the papers. After seven years of marriage it feels *sooo* good to finally be screwing you."

"Despite speculation and rumor, your career is still in excellent shape," Samantha proudly announced, "although I think we can say good-bye to Wellington Cosmetics." She swiveled from her view of West Fifty-seventh Street, refocusing her attention on Robyn. "No big loss. Wellington was a springboard that will lead to bigger and better things. I'm not promising the road ahead will be totally smooth, but you'll weather it. Look at Vanessa Williams. She survived those nude photos. You'll survive too. But I still want to take some precautions."

"Precautions?"

Samantha tossed back her cap of jet-black hair. "For the record, I want to hold a press conference so you can explain your side of things."

"I've already issued a statement. What more do you want?"

"Robyn, we want a more personal touch. We don't want the press to think you're hiding," she emphasized. "How do you feel about doing one or two talk shows?"

Robyn started to protest, but Samantha cut her off.

"Think about it. Carson would love to have you. Meanwhile you can start doing some charity work."

"Such as?"

"I'm not sure," Samantha mused. "Something to let the public know you haven't forgotten where you came from. How does working with runaways sound? We'll have you do that for a few months and then cut back on the number of hours you donate."

"I'm not a hypocrite," Robyn flared. "If I start working for a cause, I'm going to do it because I want to. I'm not going to do it for my image, and I'm not going to drop it because the hours no longer fit my schedule."

"Relax," Samantha soothed. "We'll cross that bridge when we come to it. The next thing I want to discuss is your social life. You've got to start getting out more. You can't hide as if you were ashamed. We're going to have to take the press head on. I've arranged for you to be seen around New York with a number of escorts. All are handsome, eligible bachelors. We'll plant an odd rumor or two in the gossip columns about a possible romance, and that should smooth over the damage of your breakup with Scott."

Robyn shook her head in amazement, not believing what she was hearing. "You can't be serious about everything you've just said?"

Samantha looked at Robyn point-blank. "I am. Why not? Don't you want to salvage your career? Aren't you paying me to look out for your best interests?"

"My life isn't going to come to an end if I lose my modeling career." Robyn stood. "I appreciate your efforts, Samantha, really. I know you're looking out for my best interests, but I'm not going to cater to others because I'm afraid of what they'll say. This is my life. I'm going to live it my way.

"If any assignments come in for me, call. I'll gladly take the work. If not, don't worry." Robyn gave Samantha a bold look. "I'll survive. I've done it before and I'll do it again."

41

"Georgina, what a surprise." A perfectly composed Beverly held open the door of her duplex. "I was getting ready to call you."

"Have I caught you at a bad time?"

"Of course not." Beverly ushered Georgina in, taking her coat. "Sit down," she urged. "You look like you have some news. Good, I hope?"

Georgina tried to suppress a smile, but couldn't. "I'm doing something I should have done ages ago. I'm divorcing Lance."

"How wonderful! This calls for a drink. Nonalcoholic," Beverly hurriedly corrected. "Come into the kitchen. I just finished making a pitcher of iced tea."

In the kitchen Beverly poured Georgina a glass of iced tea while she sipped at her customary Perrier. She patted Georgina's arm reassuringly. "This is only the beginning. I'm sure more good things will come."

Georgina took a sip of her iced tea. "My fingers are crossed." She made a face. "This is bitter."

"Add some more sugar." Beverly passed the sugar bowl. "Don't worry. This nightmare will soon be over. Let's go to my bedroom. I want to show you something."

Sipping her tea, Georgina followed after Beverly.

Like herself, Beverly's bedroom had been restored to perfection. The broken pieces of mirror had been swept away and the empty frame hidden from sight. Beverly went to her closet, removing Georgina's freshly cleaned silver fox fur. "What do you think?" She rubbed the bloodstain-free sleeves between her fingers. "Good as new. Come take a look."

Georgina refused, stepping back from the offered fur. "Take it away. I don't ever want to see it again."

Beverly slipped into the fur, snuggling her cheeks against the collar. "How can you say that? It feels divine."

Georgina continued sipping her iced tea, the glass half full. "Keep it. Throw it out. I don't care."

Beverly brushed her fingers along the fur. "I always disliked this fur of yours, but now I don't know why. I suppose I could wear it if I went skiing in Aspen. Are you sure you don't want it?"

Turning to Georgina, she was shocked to see how pale she was. "What's wrong?" Beverly cried in alarm, rushing to Georgina's side.

"I feel dizzy," Georgina mumbled, dropping her empty glass.

Beverly wrapped her arm around Georgina's shoulders, leading her to the bed. "Lie down. You've been under such a strain."

Georgina gratefully sank upon Beverly's bed, closing her eyes as soon as her head hit the pillow.

"That's right, Georgina. Sleep," Beverly whispered, placing a palm on her forehead before checking her pulse. "Take a nice long sleep."

"We're sorry, Scott," Richard Templeton somberly stated. "Our decision is unanimous."

Scott looked around the boardroom before rising from his seat. Thirty-five minutes was all it had taken. In that time Robyn had lost her position as the Fresh and Lovely Girl and the board had decided to accept a takeover bid. In their eyes, Wellington was once again a sinking ship, and they wanted out.

"Gentlemen," he began, maintaining a tone of respect he didn't feel, "I don't care what your decision is. Do whatever you want with Wellington. I won't offer any resistance. I will say, though, that you're making a mistake. The only reason the Fresh and Lovely line succeeded was because of Robyn Prescott. Watch what happens when she's replaced with a new model. The results won't be the same.

"I'm not going to stay and watch your failure. I hereby

resign as president of Wellington Cosmetics. Turning the company around was a challenge, and I'm sure there are plenty of other challenges for the taking. Thanks for the chance you've given me."

"What will you do?" Arthur Landers harumphed out of curiosity.

Scott looked at the members of the board. "I'm going to find Robyn and make her a part of my life again. I love her. It took me too long to find her. I'm not going to lose her again."

"I didn't think you would show," Anthony Calder said triumphantly.

Beverly was fully dressed, lounging on the bed. Beneath her was a stained bedspread. Paint was peeling off the walls and the rug was bare in patches. The air was thick with the smell of smoke and whiskey. The squalor of the room repulsed her, but not as much as the sight of Anthony Calder. "I had no choice, remember?"

He closed the hotel room door, removing his jacket as he loosened his tie. He sat on the bed, running a hand over Beverly's stockinged leg.

She tried not to jerk back, keeping her leg immobile. He looked at her with steady eyes moving up the length of her body. "I'm disappointed." He fingered her open blouse before sticking in his hand and seizing a breast. "Don't I rate one of your sexy outfits?"

She tried not to squirm. He tore her blouse open, pulling out her breast and bringing it to his lips. "What does it matter what I'm wearing?" she reasoned, moving a hand through his hair. "In the end you still get me."

He moved closer, bringing his lips from her breast to her neck. She tried not to cringe. His lips became more urgent as he pushed her against the headboard, kissing her with growing desire. While wrapping her legs around his waist, Beverly locked his head in place with her right hand.

She kissed him with an open mouth, allowing his tongue to explore and probe. Soft moans of satisfaction began escaping from his throat.

"Is this the way you thought it would be?" she cooed.

"Yes," he murmured, "oh yes." He reached for his belt, struggling to unzip his pants.

"Not yet," she stressed, removing his hand. "Slow down. Let's have some fun first. We have plenty of time."

With her legs wrapped around his waist, Beverly pulled him even closer. Returning his kisses with equal fervor, she kept his head in place with her right hand. His attention was focused solely on her as she reached with her left hand for the letter opener she had hidden earlier.

Removing the letter opener from beneath the pillow she was leaning upon, she gripped it tightly before ramming it with all her might into Anthony Calder's heart.

At the impact of entry he jerked in her arms, but she ignored the motion, savagely twisting the pointed blade of steel as far as it would go.

He gave a small gurgle as his eyes stared at her in comprehension. Then they glazed over and his body went limp in her arms.

Beverly looked down at Calder's corpse with satisfaction before throwing it down on the floor.

There wasn't time to savor her victory. She still had work to do.

"Who is it?" Robyn cautiously asked before opening her hotel room door. She was at the Plaza, and only a few people knew where she was staying.

"It's Scott. May I come in?"

Robyn was stunned by the sound of his voice. She opened the door. "How did you know I was here?"

"I called Samantha."

"Then you're here on business?" she inquired somewhat softly.

"The board had its meeting."

"Did they reach a decision?"

Scott slowly nodded. What was wrong with him? He didn't know how to apologize. Robyn's voice was so cold and detached. It was driving him crazy.

"And?" she prodded when he wouldn't provide any further information.

"They've decided to drop you."

"I see. Well, thank you for coming to tell me in person."

"If it counts for anything, I think they're making a mistake," he stated in a rush of words.

Robyn didn't disguise the sparks of anger in her eyes. Or in her voice. "It doesn't!" she snapped. "If I'm not good enough for you, then I'm certainly not good enough for your company."

"Robyn—"

"Save it! Just go." She turned her back to him, trying to hide her pain. She thought Scott had come to give her a second chance. Perhaps to try and work things out. She was wrong. "You said what you came to say."

"No, I didn't. I'm not finished."

Robyn looked at Scott brazenly. "Is this the part where you tell me off? Tell me how deeply I've hurt and betrayed you? Am I supposed to stand here and take it, begging for your forgiveness?

"I never meant to hurt you," she cried, the barriers to her pain crumbling. "I never meant to keep those secrets. I wanted to tell you the truth. I wanted to tell you about my past, but I was afraid. Don't you see? I was afraid I'd lose you." She stormed over to Scott, pounding his chest with her fists. Tears flowed freely down her cheeks. "Why wouldn't you give me a chance? Why wouldn't you let me explain? I was going to tell you the truth. I love you, Scott. I do."

Scott tried to take Robyn in his arms, but she fought off his embrace. "Easy," he softly whispered. "Let out the pain. Let it all out. I'm sorry for all the pain I caused you. I've missed you so much. I didn't realize how important you are to me until I saw Jeff Porter at Erica's funeral. Only then did I realize what a fool I'd been. I can't let you go, Robyn. You mean too much to me. Nothing else matters except us."

Robyn looked at Scott in disbelief, unsure of his spoken words; words she had so wanted to hear. "What did you say?"

"Robyn, I love you. I want you back," he implored, "if you'll take me back."

Robyn wiped away her tears. "Yes, I want you back. Only I have to tell you everything."

"You don't have to."

"I do," she insisted. "Let's do this right. We'll put the past behind us and then get on with the rest of our lives. Okay?"

Scott placed a finger under Robyn's chin, tipping her face to his. Bringing down his lips, he kissed her as though it were the first time. His kiss was one of hesitancy, expectation, and love.

"I'm ready whenever you are," he responded.

When Robyn finished, Scott continued to hold her in his arms. Then, starting from her lips and moving down to her neck and breasts, he lavished with deliberate slowness the softest of kisses.

At the joining of flesh, renewed passion combined with burning desire, flaming their hunger, heightening their demand for satisfaction.

Robyn's body instantly responded to the return of Scott's touch. Molding herself against him as she fully embraced him, she grinded her hips to his, wanting nothing more than to have him inside her again. Her center was already moist and ready with anticipation. All she wanted was for them to be one again.

She probed his muscles and feathered his tawny hair. She caressed his face and fondled his chest, reacquainting herself with the body of the man she loved.

Scott tore at the clothes restraining them. To his fingers Robyn's skin was like hot satin. Yet under the touch of his tongue it sizzled to cool silk. Her lips were lush and moist. The taste and smell of her inflamed him. Releasing his erection, he allowed it to traverse down the inside of her thigh. The touch was sheer ecstasy and torture. He had to rush to slip his erection between her legs.

Robyn thrilled at having him back inside her. She had thought such pleasure would never again be experienced. She rode Scott in a fevered pitch, grasping his buttocks as her legs scissored around him. She closed her eyes dreamily as her climax approached, tensing her body in sensuous welcome. Scott was so loving. She couldn't imagine living without him. No one could possibly know how she felt when she was with Scott.

* * *

"Nice fur," Tiffany commented, fingering the silver fox. "What's with the blond wig?"

Beverly put down the briefcase she was carrying. "Think I'd want anyone recognizing me?"

Tiffany leaned against the closed door of the hotel room, arms crossed over her chest. A lewd smile twitched her lips. "How'd your session with Calder go?"

Beverly took off the fur, draping it over a corner chair. "Successfully." Refusing to comment any further, she pointed to the briefcase on the bed. "Let's get this over with."

Tiffany opened the briefcase with glee. Her fingers brushed over the neat stacks of bills. "Is my share all here?"

Beverly was inspecting her image in a mirror, fiddling with the silk scarf around her neck. She waved a dismissive hand. "Don't trust me? Count it."

Tiffany removed a stack of bills, rubbing the money across her cheek. "I'm in heaven. I think I'm going to fill the tub with all this cash and then jump in."

"I don't know what's wrong with this outfit," Beverly fretted, completely ignoring everything Tiffany said. "Do you think it's the scarf?"

Tiffany, absorbed only in herself and the image of casinos, grunted with disinterest.

Beverly removed the scarf, draping it around Tiffany's shoulders. "This looks much better on you." She stepped back to admire the look. "Would you like to have it? It's a Hermés."

Tiffany, her attention still on the money before her, briefly fingered the scarf. "Sure. Why not?"

Taking the scarf from Tiffany's shoulders, Beverly folded it into a narrow strip. "Tiffany, you should be more fashion conscious," she scolded. "A silk scarf is a must in any wardrobe. It adds a dash of color and can be worn with anything."

Tiffany closed the briefcase. "Yeah, well, I don't read *Women's Wear Daily.*"

"I'll bet this would look lovely around your neck."

Beverly gripped the scarf between her two hands as she crept behind Tiffany. With lightning speed she wrapped the scarf around Tiffany's neck and pushed the startled woman down to the floor.

She twisted the scarf with all her strength as Tiffany desperately clawed at her throat, struggling for air. Tiffany's face turned red and her eyes bulged as she fought for her life.

"No one is going to take Scott away from me!" Beverly screamed, uttering the same words she had used on the night she had murdered Erica Shelton.

Erica Shelton hadn't been Beverly's intended victim. Robyn Prescott had. For weeks she had toyed with the idea of murdering Robyn. With the arrival of the videotape her plans of murder had been temporarily abandoned. Yet it had been Kristen's words at the party that had spurred her into action. Despite the scandal of Robyn's past, Beverly would never have a chance with Scott as long as Robyn was around. There was still a chance the two could get back together. Beverly was not one to take chances. She had to eliminate that chance.

All along she had planned on framing Georgina. Call it her revenge for having to put up with the drunken simp. She had been useless in helping her get back with Scott. Besides, Georgina did have a motive. Robyn had replaced her as the Fresh and Lovely Girl.

A spiked drink was all it had taken. She'd had a prescription for secobarbitol filled weeks in advance and carried it at all times. After Georgina collapsed, she would leave her in her duplex and then disguise herself. Practically everyone in New York who knew Georgina knew she owned a silver fox fur. With a blond wig and sunglasses, she'd be mistaken for Georgina.

With Georgina drunk at the party, Beverly knew she had an opportunity she couldn't pass up. Offering to fetch Georgina a fresh drink after her confrontation with Erica, she had easily added the secobarbitol. After Georgina finished her drink, Beverly offered to drive her home. Georgina collapsed once they reached Beverly's car.

Arriving at Georgina's town house, she left Georgina in the bedroom as she donned her disguise. With Georgina's housekeeper on vacation, it had been easier to bring her there. From the trunk of her car she carried the blond wig she had purchased. After securely fixing the wig in place, she slipped into Georgina's silver fox fur.

Beverly had known there was a possibility that Kristen would be at the apartment. If so, she would be murdered as well. Remembering the drink Kristen had splashed on her, Beverly smiled in anticipation. She'd love to see the little bitch's face etched in terror before she carved it.

Figuring Robyn wouldn't return straight home after losing Scott, Beverly waited before driving over. She drove around the block of the apartment, parking out of sight and making a call from a corner phone booth. When Robyn answered, Beverly knew she was ready to act.

With the butcher knife she had specifically purchased for the murder hidden in a cavernous pocket of the fur, she entered the building and went straight to the apartment. She knocked on the door before turning her back. As expected, when the door opened she heard Georgina's name called.

Whirling around, she had shoved the door inward. When her eyes fell to the stunned body facedown on the floor, she had only seen the negligee . . . the negligee bought at the auction by Scott.

Immediately she had seen red. Slamming the door shut she had thrown herself on the body, stabbing once between the shoulders and then attacking with vigor and glee.

Only after the towel covering Erica's hair fell away, revealing her red hair, did Beverly see her mistake. She had killed the wrong woman.

Remaining calm, she escaped back to Georgina's town house, carrying out the rest of her plan. She left the bloodstained fur on the bed and wiped the flat, bloody sides of the knife on Georgina's palms. Then she had Georgina grip the knife's handle before hiding the knife in the clothes hamper.

Returning to her duplex, Beverly started planning. She'd have to fine-tune the situation. Fate had presented her with such a lovely twist. She couldn't have done better herself.

Rummaging through old newspapers and magazines, she found a number of photos of Erica. After each was cut out, a red X was slashed across Erica's face. Tomorrow morning she would be the first person Georgina called, asking about the night she couldn't remember. Beverly would have to provide the "truth." Then, when she went over to Georgina's, she would plant her remaining pieces of incriminating "evidence."

The animosity that had existed between Georgina and Erica had been well-known, and Georgina had publicly threatened to kill Erica that evening. Combined with the "evidence" she had planted, an ugly case had been built. All she would have to do was wait and watch.

Yet although she had committed the perfect crime, her intended victim still lived. But not for long. Robyn Prescott was still going to die.

Beverly released her grip on the scarf, watching as Tiffany's body slumped. Slipping into Georgina's silver fox fur, Beverly refastened the scarf around her neck. Looking in the mirror, she checked to see that her wig was still in place.

She shook her head pitifully. Poor Georgina. Hardly out on bail and committing murder. Tsk. Tsk. When would she learn? Beverly laughed aloud. She had purposely made sure she had been seen by a number of witnesses both here and at Anthony Calder's hotel.

Reaching into her purse, she removed an extra copy of *Head Nurse,* dropping it next to Tiffany. Scott was going to be so shocked. How would he be able to accept his sister's betrayal? After the police questioned Georgina, who would undoubtedly deny everything, Beverly would have no choice but to step forward, painfully revealing how "Georgina" had hired Tiffany and then succumbed to blackmail.

After a thorough inspection of the room, Beverly found no evidence to incriminate her. All fingerprints were wiped away. Everything pointed to Georgina.

The worst was still to come. Would Scott be able to forgive "Georgina" for the murder of his beloved Robyn?

"Can you forgive me?"

Robyn shifted in the darkness, nestling closer to Scott. "You have to ask? Didn't I show you?"

He grinned. "I guess you did."

"I was so afraid I was going to lose you to Beverly," she confessed. "She wants you back."

"I know."

Robyn was startled. "You do?"

"At her duplex this morning she told me how she felt."

"She *only* told you?"

"She tried to seduce me. I didn't handle her very well."

"You're not the one at fault."

"I know, but we've got each other. Beverly doesn't have anyone. I think she's very lonely."

"Did you want to go see her? Apologize?"

"I'll drop by later." He kissed Robyn deeply. "Let's only talk about us." He slipped the ring he had given her on the night of the party back on her finger. "I asked this before but I'll ask again. Robyn, will you marry me?"

She didn't hesitate, throwing her arms around him. "Yes," she joyously exclaimed. "Yes, I will."

42

Scott rang the bell of the duplex again.

Before leaving Robyn, Scott had tried calling Beverly, but her line had been busy. He suspected the phone was off the hook. Repeatedly ringing the duplex's bell gave him no answer. Either Beverly wasn't at home or was refusing to answer.

Wanting only to make amends, as well as soothing his troubled conscience, Scott entered with the key Beverly had once given him. Knowing how sensitive Beverly was when it came to her privacy, he decided he would only take a brief look around. If she was in, he'd try to talk with her. If not, he'd leave a note along with his key.

The first floor of the duplex proved empty, and calling

Beverly's name got no response. Although confident Beverly hadn't done anything drastic, Scott still wanted to make sure. He went to the second floor.

Through the half-open bedroom door he could see a pair of legs on the bed. Relief flooded his body. She was asleep. But when he entered the bedroom and saw Georgina on the bed, his relief turned to temporary confusion.

What was Georgina doing here? Hadn't she decided to return to her town house? Granted, she had spent a few nights and Beverly had said Georgina would be welcome to return, but what was she doing in here and not in the guest room she'd been using?

"Georgina," he called softly, not wanting to frighten her. Perhaps she knew where Beverly was. Yet why hadn't Georgina heard him call Beverly's name? He gave his sister a gentle nudge. "Georgina," he voiced louder. Still no response. Edges of panic pricked him. Why wouldn't she answer?

He spied the empty iced tea glass on the floor, a few spots clinging to the sides. Dabbing a finger at the bottom of the glass, he brought a drop to his lips and tasted. Bitter. A wave of apprehension engulfed him. Could Georgina have tried suicide?

Rushing to his sister, he shook her forcefully.

"Georgina, wake up! Wake up!"

In the bathroom he soaked a washcloth in cold water. Rubbing it in Georgina's face caused her to wriggle and squirm. She was responding! Maybe she hadn't taken a strong enough overdose.

Wrapping an arm around her shoulders, he pulled Georgina to her feet, walking her around the bedroom. "Georgina, can you hear me?"

She mumbled incoherently, resting her head on his shoulder. Panicked that she was slipping away, Scott rubbed her face in the washcloth again.

"Stop," she protested, averting her face from the cold contact.

"What did you take?" Scott asked. "What kind of pills?"

"Pills?" Uncomprehending eyes tried to focus on him. "D-d-didn't take any pills . . ."

She didn't take any pills? Then why was she in such a drugged state?

"Can you tell me what happened? What did you drink?"

"Iced tea," she mumbled. "Beverly gave me a glass of iced tea. Then the room started to spin."

Scott couldn't make sense out of what she was saying. Had her mind become so muddled that she'd forgotten what she had done? Although Georgina seemed to be coming around, he didn't want to leave anything to chance. He went to the phone on Beverly's vanity table, dialing 911 for an ambulance.

As he talked into the phone his eyes fell upon the rubble before him. Hairbrushes. Perfumes. Lipsticks. A stack of newspapers and magazines. Such a mess. Beverly had always been fastidiously neat. Glancing at the newspapers, he saw they went back months. Each had an article or column circled in red. Taking a closer look, Robyn's name appeared in them all. How strange. What possible reason could Beverly have for circling all those items?

Turning to check on Georgina, he accidentally knocked over the newspapers. Falling to the floor, they revealed a videotape buried beneath them. At first Scott stared at it in confusion. Then the confusion cleared.

No. It couldn't be. Beverly wouldn't do such a thing.

After he was reassured that an ambulance was on the way, he dropped the phone. Checking again on Georgina, who didn't appear to be in such a deep sleep as earlier, Scott decided to head for the living room and Beverly's VCR. It was the only way he would get an answer.

Preparing to leave the bedroom, he caught sight of Beverly's open closet. The videotape fell to the floor, forgotten. What he saw inside the closet froze his blood.

All of Beverly's clothes had been slashed to shreds. The bottom of the closet was sprinkled with broken pieces of mirror, amidst which were the shredded remains of the white silk and lace negligee she had worn that morning.

Entering the spacious walk-in closet, Scott looked to the far wall and saw a poster of Robyn as the Fresh and Lovely Girl. There was a jagged red slash through Robyn's face. Beneath the poster, bunched into a ball, was the Scaasi gown

Beverly had worn the night of the Wellington party—the night of Erica's murder.

The gown was speckled with splashes of dried blood.

Looking from the clothes to the poster and the blood-stained gown, Scott knew Beverly was more than enraged. She was insane. The woman he loved was in danger because another woman refused to let him go.

He had to find Robyn. He had to protect her.

Before it was too late.

Not wanting to be separated from Scott any longer than she had to, Robyn decided to go over to his apartment and wait for him to return from Beverly's.

Belting her trench coat, she admired the night sky. It was misted yet starry. Only one more month till Christmas. Robyn couldn't wait for the holidays. She was going to spoil Scott rotten. Looking around, she saw the streets were nearly deserted, but there were still some people out. She decided to walk leisurely, thinking only of Scott and their future.

Robyn was oblivious to the footsteps echoing behind her. As they drew nearer, becoming heavier and more hurried, Robyn snapped back to attention. Ahead she could see the glowing lights of Scott's lobby. Only a short distance to go. But it was too late. As she was getting ready to walk at a brisker pace, a furred arm wrapped around her neck as a gun was pointed at her back.

"Don't turn around! Keep walking."

The voice was female and guttural. Tiffany?

"Move it!" The gun was jabbed sharply into Robyn's back as she was steered in the direction of Scott's building.

"This isn't going to get you anywhere, Tiffany." Robyn spoke over her fear. "I'm still not going to give you the money you want."

"You think I'm Tiffany?" A harsh laugh. "If Tiffany had been smarter, she would have done what I'm going to do to you tonight."

Robyn swallowed over the lump in her throat. "What are you going to do?"

"Kill you."

Reaching the delivery entrance, they entered the building. Instructed to keep her back to her unknown assailant, they rode the service elevator in silence.

Robyn was petrified. She didn't know what to do. But she had to do something. Anything! If she didn't, she would die.

Who was this woman? How did she know about Tiffany?

When they reached Scott's floor the woman checked the hallway before they backed out of the elevator.

After Robyn opened the apartment door she was shoved into the darkness. The door slammed shut as she sprawled to the floor. The lights were turned on as she twisted to her side, struggling to get back on her feet. It was then that she saw her attacker. She almost fell back to the floor.

Their eyes met. "You," Robyn uttered in astonishment, her stomach lurching at the sight of Beverly in a blond wig. "Why?"

The hatred in Beverly's eyes was proudly displayed. "I gave you a chance to leave New York, but you wouldn't take it. You should have left after you disgraced Scott. He would have been better off without you."

"You're the one," Robyn gasped. "You're the one who switched the tapes."

Beverly looked at Robyn knowingly. "Of course I was the one. I'll do whatever it takes to get Scott back. Even commit murder." She raised a hand flippantly. "I've already killed three people."

"Who?" Robyn dared to ask.

"Erica Shelton, Tiffany, and a sleazy investigator I had hired. I'm quite proud of my handiwork. I've made it look like Georgina was the killer."

Robyn looked at the blond wig and silver fox fur with new awareness. "You can't be serious. No one will believe Georgina's a murderer."

"They already do. Everyone believes she murdered Erica Shelton, and I've made very sure she gets framed for the other murders, including *yours.* She came over to my duplex this afternoon. I drugged her and donned my disguise. All the evidence has been planted. Plenty of people saw me . . . I mean"—Beverly corrected herself with a smirk—"her. When she awakens, I'll fill her head with a story like I did last time. She won't know what to believe, and after she's arrested again, I'll regretfully have to tell the police what I know. Here's the story:

"Georgina never got over you becoming the Fresh and Lovely Girl. She hired an investigator to look into your past, and he found Tiffany. Tiffany provided a copy of *Head Nurse,* but then tried to blackmail Georgina into giving her more money, otherwise she'd go to Scott. The investigator did the same thing. After killing them both, Georgina knew she had nothing left to lose, and decided to come after you. What's the difference if it's one murder or four? She's still going to be locked away for life." Beverly gave Robyn a proud smile. "Like it?"

Beverly's confession and plans to frame Georgina were staggering. The woman was demented, completely deranged. Robyn's mind raced for a means of escape.

"I'll leave New York. I promise. I'll never come back. I'll never get in touch with Scott."

Beverly viciously struck Robyn across the face with her gun. "Do you take me for a fool? I can't let you live! Scott would come after you. He'd search for you no matter where you went, and wouldn't give up until he found you. You see, my dear, Scott has to have proof that you're never coming back. Only then will he surrender to me. What more proof does he need except your corpse?

"Don't worry, I'll allow Scott to grieve for you. I'll even let him keep your photograph for a few months before shoving it in a drawer and ultimately tossing it out in the trash. When his period of grief is over, I'll start planning our wedding."

Beverly's eyes gleamed insanely as she became enraptured with her twisted dreams. "It's going to be a June wedding. Did I tell you my gown is being made in Paris? The engraved invitations will be hand-delivered on a silver platter by an English butler. Right now I'm working on the guest list. Only the finest names in New York will be attending. It's going to be a wonderful, lavish affair. We'll probably have it at the Met.

"I'll always cherish the memory of my wedding day," Beverly confessed, "but murdering you will be a memory I'll treasure forever."

Robyn became petrified. Beverly meant to do it. She

meant to kill her. Where was Scott? She had left him a note, telling him where she had gone. He should have gotten back to the Plaza by now. Hurry, Scott, please hurry.

Scott burst into Robyn's hotel room, anxiously calling her name.

"Robyn, where are you? Answer me."

"Scott, what's wrong?" Kristen came out of the bedroom. "Robyn's not here."

"Where is she?"

"Over at your place. She left a note. What's going on?"

"She's in danger. I'm afraid Beverly is going to try and kill her."

"Beverly Maxwell?!" Kristen exclaimed dubiously. "Are you sure?"

"She's the one who murdered Erica. She framed Georgina. I went over to Beverly's duplex and used my old key. I wanted to apologize to her over a misunderstanding. Instead I found Georgina drugged and evidence that Beverly has gone over the edge."

"Dear God!" Kristen covered her mouth in horror. "Let's go. I'm coming with you."

"Let me call the police and have them meet us at my apartment. We have to get to Robyn before Beverly. We have to. There's no telling what Beverly will try to do. I lost Robyn once. I'm not going to lose her again."

Beverly pointed the gun at Robyn. "Turn around."

The last thing Robyn wanted to do was turn her back on Beverly. Once she did, searing bits of hot metal would tear into her skin, digging deep into her flesh. Again she wondered where Scott was before calming herself. All she had to do was bide her time. Keep Beverly talking. Scott would be here. He would.

"I don't want to die," Robyn said.

"Too bad. Think you're too beautiful to die at such a young age? You could have had any man, but you chose my Scott. I tried to bring Quinn Marler to New York, but you discouraged his attentions. You had to have *my* Scott. You *stole* him from me!"

"I didn't steal Scott from you! When I came to New York it had already been over between the two of you."

"Liar! You knew he was mine, yet you seduced him with your whoring ways. Turn around," she ordered, releasing the safety on the gun. "If you don't, I won't hesitate to shoot."

"Please don't," Robyn begged.

"Turn around," Beverly screamed. "Now!"

Robyn turned her back resignedly, closing her eyes. This couldn't be. Her life couldn't be ending this way.

"Don't worry," Beverly lied, loosening the scarf around her neck, "I'll make sure your death is as painless as possible. Five bullets in the back. It'll be over in seconds." She put down her gun, silently creeping up on Robyn while tightly wrapping her scarf between her hands. "You'll hardly feel a thing. When Scott finds your body and looks at your face, he'll think you're sleeping." She moved closer with the scarf.

Beverly couldn't wait to twist the silk material around Robyn's neck. She would twist and twist, bruising Robyn's long, slim neck, damaging her silky smooth skin and causing blood vessels to burst until Robyn's once beautiful face was red, ugly, and bloated.

This was her revenge against Scott. When he found Robyn's body, he'd cringe in horror. His final image of Robyn would be one of agony and death. He'd never be able to think of her without pain.

"You can kill me, but I'll always live in Scott's heart," Robyn declared. "You'll never, *ever,* erase my memory."

The words incensed Beverly beyond control. She lunged at Robyn, twisting the scarf around her neck. Elation ripped through her as she felt Robyn's resistance, and she gloried in Robyn's struggle. This was the moment she had waited for.

In minutes Robyn would be dead.

Scott and Kristen rushed into his lobby, expecting to find the police waiting. They weren't.

"You stay down here," Scott instructed. "I'm going up."

"Be careful."

Scott took the stairs over the elevator, unable to wait.

"Please be safe," he fervently prayed. "Please be safe."

* * *

Blackness started descending. Robyn tugged at the scarf around her throat, desperate for air. The more she moved forward, the worse it became.

Throwing her head back, she smashed it into Beverly's while jamming her elbow into her stomach. Both actions caused Beverly to writhe in pain, falling back and loosening her hold on the scarf.

It was all Robyn needed. Slipping her fingers into the sudden space between her neck and the pink material, Robyn tore the scarf free. Collapsing to her knees, she gasped for air between sporadic coughs, inhaling deep breaths and massaging her bruised throat.

Beverly wasted no time in getting back to her feet. She had only one goal, and she wasn't going to fail. Retrieving the gun she had put down earlier, she lifted it and aimed directly at Robyn.

When Scott burst into his apartment he was unable to believe the scene he was witnessing. Without wasting a second, he lunged at Beverly from behind, knocking the gun from her hand and pinning her to the floor.

She fought like a tigress. "Let me go!" she screeched. "Let me go!" Twisting her head, she saw it was Scott on top of her. Her fighting ceased. "Scott, why are you doing this? Help me up." He didn't answer, not knowing what to say, concerned more for the safety and well-being of the woman he loved.

He looked to Robyn, who was watching the scene with horrid fascination. He could see she still feared Beverly despite his presence.

"Scott? Darling?" Beverly asked. She followed his gaze, instantly metamorphosing. "No!" she howled from the depths of her twisted soul. "Not that bitch!" She fought ferociously to free herself from beneath Scott, who was using all his strength to keep her down. She thrashed from side to side, knocking off the blond wig. "I love you! She'll never love you the way I love you! Never! I did it all for you, Scott. I did it all for you!"

She fixed wide, bulging eyes—the eyes of a madwoman—on Robyn. "I'll never let you have Scott! Never! If it's the last thing I ever do, I'll kill you! I promise I'll kill you one day!"

Robyn pressed her hands to her ears, not wanting to hear any more. Shuddering with sobs, she watched as Kristen and the police arrived. Kristen hurried to Robyn's side, shielding her from the rest of the sight as Beverly's crazed howls of anger and hatred continued.

Robyn buried herself in Kristen's arms, openly sobbing.

"It's over," Kristen whispered. "It's all over."

— BOOK FIVE —

The Wedding
February 1990

43

Scott hugged Robyn fiercely. "Two more days. Think you can hang on?"

"Unless something better comes along," she teased, "I think I can."

"Mr. and Mrs. Scott Kendall. I like the sound of that. Don't you?"

"Very much," Robyn agreed.

It had been three months, and Robyn and Scott had managed to put the horror of Beverly behind them, continuing with their lives. Thanksgiving, Christmas, and New Year's had been wonderful holidays. Now, in two days, on Valentine's Day, they would be married.

When the full story had hit the press, Robyn and Scott found a special place in a number of hearts. It was as if their slate had been wiped clean and a new beginning was theirs for the taking. Robyn's career became hotter than ever. She was in high demand but purposely kept a light schedule. As she had told Samantha, her career wasn't her life. Only Scott mattered.

Wellington tried to woo both Scott and Robyn back. Both turned the company down. Joining forces with Kyle, Scott planned on opening his own advertising agency.

"I wish the newspapers hadn't made such a big deal out of our wedding," Robyn commented, showing Scott the column she had been reading in the *Times*. They were in bed together in their new apartment on West Eighty-first and Central Park West.

Scott nuzzled Robyn's neck, inhaling her perfume. "We're only getting married once," he reminded. "Let's go out with a bang."

"Are you sure you don't want me to come with you?" Kyle asked.

Georgina smiled at his handsome face. "You've been with me every step of the way. Now it's time I took a step by myself. I've got to do this alone."

Kyle kissed her. "I'll pick you up later."

Georgina watched him drive away. In three months she had turned her life around. At Kyle's suggestion, she had pursued her earlier interest in acting, enjoying herself immensely. Who knew? Perhaps one day she would be a professional actress.

Lance was out of her life for good. Their divorce had become final last week and she had thrown a party to celebrate. Although she and Kyle seemed headed for a relationship, she was taking things slowly. After regaining her freedom, she wasn't in a rush to give it up. She liked the way she was living her life and wanted to savor it for a while.

She and Robyn had formed a friendship. Some days they went shopping; other days they had lunch. When Robyn had asked her to be in her bridal party, she had been touched, eagerly accepting the invitation.

Beverly was never thought of. After Georgina had been cleared of Erica's murder, and Scott told her everything Beverly had done—all to implicate her—Georgina had been stunned. At first she wouldn't believe him. She didn't want to believe something so horrid. But then she remembered all the times Beverly had given her harsh words and haughty looks. Those had been Beverly's true feelings, despite her explanations. Georgina had refused to acknowledge those feelings not only because she had been desperate for a friend, but because she had been blinded by her drinking.

Her days of drinking were over now. At first it had been hard. It still was, but with each passing day it became easier. There were still times when she wanted a drink. When that happened she raced to the phone or refrigerator, whichever was closer, doing whatever she could to take her mind off her craving.

The meeting had already started. She slipped into a chair at the back, smiling at a few familiar faces. When the speaker called for a volunteer, she raised her hand. Acknowledged, she stood up and faced the group. She spoke clearly and concisely, wanting all to hear.

"My name is Georgina and I'm an alcoholic."

Kristen breezed into Maxim's, handing her packages to the head waiter. "Sorry I'm late," she apologized.

"I hope my maid of honor is going to be on time this Saturday."

"I bought out the stores," Kristen confessed glumly. "I'm depressed. Larry's relocating to California. He landed a film." She rolled her eyes over her menu. "Actors. You can't depend on them."

"Did the two of you break things off?"

"He promised to keep in touch, but I'm not holding my breath."

"So you didn't break things off."

"No."

"Don't write him off so fast," Robyn admonished. "I liked Larry. He was really interested in you."

"I'll let you know what happens." She sipped from the glass of white wine Robyn had ordered for her. "You'll never guess who called me the other night."

"Who?"

"Lance! Can you believe it? The little worm wanted to let me know he was available, and if I wanted, we could pick up where we left off."

"What did you tell him?"

"I laughed in his ear, told him to take a hike and then hung up. He probably read about the modeling contract I landed with Revlon." She took another sip of her wine. "I hope the weasel gets exactly what he deserves."

* * *

From the day Georgina had started divorce proceedings, Lance's life had descended in a spiral. Specially made shirts, suits, and jackets were no more. Expense accounts at restaurants, bars, and hotels ceased to exist. He'd had to give up his spacious loft and move into a smaller, less fashionable apartment. The only photography jobs he seemed to land these days were for pornographic magazines.

Lance pumped hard and furiously at the woman beneath him. She was hideous, but rich. Very rich. She'd been charging up a storm at Bonwit's when their eyes had met. Now they were in her posh Upper West Side apartment. They didn't even know each other's names. Lance intended to make sure she knew his once he was finished.

"You're a marvelous lover," she told him between gasps.

He forced himself to kiss her lips. "I couldn't resist you."

"My husband never satisfies me," she sighed.

"Husband?" Lance stopped in mid-thrust, jerking up. There hadn't been a wedding band on her finger and he had *specifically* asked if she was married. "You didn't tell me you were married."

She ran a finger down his back. "I didn't want to lose you," she purred. "Don't worry." She licked at his ear. "Boris never comes home at this time of the day."

Lance shed the sheets, gathering his clothes. "Jealous husbands aren't my scene." Only last month he'd barely escaped when an older husband had caught him making love to his rich, younger wife.

"Anna!" a voice roared. "Where are you?"

She paled, clutching the sheet. "It's Boris! He's home."

There was nowhere to hide in the bedroom. Lance rushed to hide in one of the rooms outside the bedroom when the door swung open, crashing against the wall.

Boris was a hulking brute who blocked the doorway. Lance gulped in fear. He was doomed.

"Anna, you've brought another man into our bed," he said, looking at Lance coldly.

"I'm sorry," she whimpered. "I'll never do it again."

"You promised last time. When will you learn?" He seized Lance by the arm, his grip like an iron manacle. "You remember what I did last time?"

"Yes."

"This time I'm breaking *both* arms," he roared.

Lance passed out after the first sickening crack.

Beverly had been declared mentally insane, committed to an asylum in northern New York. She didn't respond to the treatment provided. Instead she reacted with bursts of violence so severe, she was kept locked in a padded cell. Some days, when she attacked herself, tearing at her hair and clawing at her face, she was additionally restrained in a straitjacket.

Lately, however, she had been subdued. The staff took it as a sign of improvement. As a reward, they allowed her to mingle with the other patients.

In the recreation room Beverly stared at the other patients, all wearing the same gray smock as she. They were slobbering fools, and she was locked in with them, thought to be one of *them.* Everyone said she was crazy, but she wasn't. *No,* she wasn't. She didn't belong here, but no one would listen to her. No one. Not even Scott.

She had decided she would have to escape.

A nurse seated her at the window where she always sat, placing a newspaper in her hands. Beverly accepted it but didn't bother reading. She was looking outside.

The asylum was surrounded by an iron link fence topped with barbed wire. Impossible to climb. At the front gate there was a guard who only checked incoming cars. Beverly always saw him stop those cars, peering at the identification offered. Outgoing cars belonging to those who worked at the asylum were always passed through and never stopped.

Not wanting to arouse any suspicion, she pretended to read the paper she had been given. She looked at the date. It was at least a week old. How typical.

When she came to the column she fought to control herself. They would be watching. Yes, this was a test. They had purposely given her this paper mentioning Scott and Robyn's upcoming wedding just to watch her reaction.

She looked at the calendar posted on the recreation room wall, checking the day and date. Today was Thursday, the twelfth. She referred back to the column. On Saturday the fourteenth Robyn and Scott would be married.

She neatly folded the paper in half, turning her gaze back out the window. She'd have to move up her plan.

She had a wedding to stop.

The following morning Beverly huddled in the corner of her padded cell when a nurse came to get her. She was a young, inexperienced girl who had only recently started.

"It's a new day, Beverly. Why don't we join the others?"

"I don't want to." She hugged herself closer to the wall, keeping her hands hidden in her lap between the folds of her smock.

"You joined the others yesterday." The nurse approached Beverly without hesitation, bending over to take Beverly's arm. She wasn't afraid. Beverly was such a docile thing. She didn't know what the other nurses were always so worried about. Ever since she had started, Beverly had been a lamb.

When the nurse bent over, Beverly made her move.

The night before, she had torn at the bottom of her smock. The result was a thin, yet strong, strip of material. It was the same strip wrapped around the young nurse's neck.

After the nurse was dead, Beverly stripped her, changing into her uniform and shoving her unkempt hair into the nurse's cap. Grabbing the nurse's keys, she locked her in the room and headed for the stairs.

She was outside in seconds, heading for the parking lot and the nurse's car. From her window she had watched the nurses come and go, learning who drove which car.

There was a pair of sunglasses on the dashboard. Putting them on, Beverly started the car and headed for the main gate.

There was no problem driving out.

After driving a short distance from the asylum, she pressed her foot on the gas and headed for the highway.

44

"Time to wake up," Kristen announced, carrying a breakfast tray. "Today's the day."

Robyn gave a sleepy smile, rubbing her eyes. "Is it morning already?"

Kristen handed Robyn a cup of coffee, plopping down on the bed. "Bet you can't believe it's really going to happen."

"I can't. In seven hours I'll be married to Scott."

"And then you'll be on a jet headed for Europe for your honeymoon. Tell me again where you're going."

"Paris, Athens, Rome, London, Zurich . . ." Robyn paused to catch her breath. "I can't remember where else, but we'll be gone for six months."

"Scott is *so* romantic. Imagine! Getting married on Valentine's Day and then making love in almost every major city in Europe. Heaven!"

The phone rang and Kristen answered. "For you," she said, handing it over. "Your groom."

Robyn took the phone. "Hi. Calling to change your mind or can I expect to see you at the church?"

"I'll be there," Scott promised. "You know, I missed you last night. I was lonely, and this bed is so big."

"I missed you too, sweetie, but you know why I had to stay at Kristen's. It's bad luck to see the bride before the wedding."

"Why don't we chuck it all and elope?"

"No way! After all the weeks of planning? You wanted a big wedding, buster."

"Okay, okay," Scott surrendered, "no elopement. Besides, I can't wait to see you walk down the aisle. I'll be counting the hours."

"Me too. I love you, Scott."

"I love you, Robyn, more than I'll ever be able to let you know."

The hours flew by, and before Robyn knew it she was being whisked to St. Patrick's along with Kristen. When they arrived at the church, they were sequestered in a back room where hair and makeup people put the finishing touches on Robyn. After they left it was only Kristen and Robyn.

Kristen looked awkwardly at her bouquet. "I'm supposed to give you some words of advice but I don't know what to say. Be happy, Robyn. Love Scott with all your heart. I know that's how he loves you. Nothing else matters."

"You've always been there for me, Kristen. You've never let me down."

"Same here. Guess that's why we're best friends. Larry called this morning." Kristen crossed her fingers. "I think you may be right. He may be the one. Keep your calendar open six months from now." She looked at the clock on the wall. "Ready?"

"You go ahead." Robyn turned back to her reflection, fussing with her veil. "I want to take one last look."

Kristen's eyes twinkled. "See you outside."

Beneath her dark veil Beverly watched Kristen leave. Robyn was all alone. It was the perfect time to make her move.

Returning to Manhattan yesterday, she had gone to one of the banks where she had kept a deposit box under an assumed name. The box had been loaded with cash, but she had taken only what she needed to purchase a black dress and a wide-brimmed hat with dark veil. Then she had purchased the gun and bullets.

Now she would triumph.

Slowly she opened the door. Robyn turned from the mirror. Beverly could see the confusion on her face. She couldn't wait till the confusion turned to comprehension.

She closed the door, approaching Robyn and answering her questions until recognition suddenly flashed across Robyn's face. Robyn *knew* who was standing before her.

Beverly smiled beneath her veil, reaching into her purse for her gun.

It was time to reveal the gift she had brought.

Epilogue

"Robyn, can you hear me?"

Robyn groggily opened her eyes. Surrounding her were the concerned faces of Scott, Kristen, Georgina, and Kyle. Kristen and Georgina were still in their lavender bridal gowns, and Scott and Kyle were still in their tuxedoes. Also in the room was Quinn, Ruby, and Samantha. All of them looked haggard and disheveled. The worry and concern in all their eyes was apparent.

She was in a hospital bed and struggled into a sitting position. At first she couldn't remember what had happened. Then it all came back in a suffocating rush. Beverly . . . Scott . . . the gun . . . the struggle . . . the shots.

Scott saw the fear return to Robyn's eyes. Gently, he wrapped his arms around her. "Beverly will never hurt you again. She's dead. I had no choice."

Scott would never forget the shock he had experienced after knocking away Beverly's veil. It hadn't been so much seeing Beverly, but the look in her eyes. Her eyes had glowed with insane hatred, burning into him.

"I hate you!" she had screamed, aiming her gun at him. "I hate you for choosing her over me!"

They struggled for the gun, and when Robyn came

between them she was hit in the shoulder. Watching Robyn's gown turn crimson as she crumpled to the floor consumed Scott with pain. Using all his strength, he threw Beverly off him. She crashed into a wall as her gun skittered across the floor.

"Robyn!" Scott cried in anguish, rushing to her side. Tearing off his cummerbund, he used it as a tourniquet, trying to staunch the flow of blood. All thoughts of Beverly were forgotten.

Rising to her feet, Beverly desperately searched for her gun, but couldn't find it. Spying a heavy brass candelabra, she picked it up, hefting it between her two hands before closing in on Scott, preparing to bash his head in.

Looking into the mirror before him, Scott saw Beverly charging. Grabbing the gun by his side, he twisted around, getting ready to stand.

"Stop!" he ordered, half crouched, with the gun in full view.

Beverly refused, continuing to lunge at him, swinging the candelabra against his head. Stunned, he fell back to the floor. As Beverly closed in, prepared to strike again, Scott had no choice but to squeeze the trigger.

"She's out of our life forever," Scott finished.

"Does it hurt?" Robyn asked, looking at the ugly bruise on Scott's forehead.

"I'm fine. How do you feel?"

She touched her bandaged shoulder, giving a smile. "I'm okay. Looks like we should have eloped."

"We can if you want. Or we can still have a wedding."

Robyn gave a rueful smile. "I'm in no shape to walk down the aisle."

Kristen's face became animated. "Why don't we have the wedding here? Now!" she enthused, looking from Robyn to Scott. "What do you say?"

Scott patted his breast pocket. "I've still got the rings."

"I'm ready whenever you are," Robyn excitedly agreed.

"I'll get some flowers in the gift shop," Georgina offered.

"I'll find a priest," Kyle said.

"And I'll help the bride make herself beautiful for her groom." Kristen scooted everyone out of the room, then turned to Scott. "You too. You're not supposed to see the bride until the ceremony."

"Are you serious?" he joked.

"What? Oh, yeah!" Kristen exclaimed, remembering that afternoon. "Let's toss tradition out the window! Just find us some champagne for a wonderful toast."

"I'll be back," Scott promised, brushing his lips against Robyn's. "Don't go away."

Robyn gave Scott a radiant smile. "Don't worry. I'll be waiting for my groom."

An hour later the priest arrived and the ceremony began.